About t

Pamela Yaye has a bac... Education and her love fo... ...merican fiction prompted her to pursue a career in writing romance. When she's not working on her latest novel, this busy wife, mother and teacher is watching basketball, cooking or planning her next holiday. Pamela lives in Alberta, Canada with her gorgeous husband and adorable, but mischievous son and daughter.

USA Today bestselling author **Kat Cantrell** read her first Mills & Boon novel in third grade and has been scribbling in notebooks since she learned to spell. She's a So You Think You Can Write winner and a Romance Writers of America Golden Heart® Award finalist. Kat, her husband and their two boys live in north Texas.

Yahrah St. John is the author of forty-four published books and won the 2013 Best Kimani Romance from *RT Book Reviews* for *A Chance with You*. She earned a Bachelor of Arts degree in English from Northwestern University. A member of Romance Writers of America, St. John is an avid reader, enjoys cooking, travelling and adventure sports, but her true passion is writing. Visit yahrahstjohn.com

Sugar & Spice

Sugar & Spice:
Baked with Love

PAMELA YAYE

KAT CANTRELL

YAHRAH ST. JOHN

MILLS & BOON

First Published in Great Britain 2024
by Mills & Boon, an imprint of HarperCollins*Publishers* Ltd,
1 London Bridge Street, London, SE1 9GF

www.harpercollins.co.uk

HarperCollins*Publishers*
Macken House, 39/40 Mayor Street Upper,
Dublin 1, D01 C9W8, Ireland

Sugar & Spice: Baked with Love © 2024 Harlequin Enterprises ULC.

Mocha Pleasures © 2016 Pamela Sadadi
Best Friend Bride © 2017 Kat Cantrell
Cappuccino Kisses © 2016 Harlequin Enterprises ULC

Special thanks and acknowledgement are given to Yahrah Yisrael for her contribution to *The Draysons: Sprinkled with Love* series.

ISBN: 978-0-263-31980-4

MOCHA PLEASURES

PAMELA YAYE

I want to thank my husband, Jean-Claude,
for his love, support and guidance. I couldn't have
written twenty-three Mills & Boon novels without
you, Papito, and I appreciate everything you do for
me and the kids. You mean the world to me,
and I'm grateful to have you in my life.
Thank you for allowing me to live my dream.

Chapter 1

Jackson "Jack" Drayson stood behind the counter of his family's bakery, Lillian's of Seattle, spotted the mother of two struggling to get her deluxe stroller inside the crowded, bustling shop and felt a rush of compassion. Reaching the family in three strides, he pulled open the front door and stepped aside to let them enter. "Welcome to Lillian's of Seattle."

"Thank you so much," the mother said, her tone filled with gratitude.

"It's my pleasure." Jackson wore a boyish smile. "I've always had a thing for redheads with freckles."

Her eyes brightened, and she giggled like a kid at the circus. "You do?"

"Yes, so if you need anything just ask. I love helping beautiful women."

Another high-pitched laugh. "You just made my day!"

Jackson knew the compliment had guaranteed the

bakery a sale. It always did. At twenty-eight, he'd perfected the art of flirting, and knew Chase would be proud of him for charming another customer. A savvy accountant with a thirst for success, his thirty-one-year-old brother was the perfect person to oversee the financial operations at the bakery. To ensure the bakery's success, Chase had taken a leave of absence from his high-powered corporate job, and when he wasn't wooing his fiancée—talented jewelry designer Amber Bernard—he was working hard to boost sales. Chase and Amber were on a pre-honeymoon trip at a luxury hotel overlooking Snoqualmie Falls. Jackson hadn't heard from his brother since he'd left town yesterday and didn't expect to. Chase was with Amber, and when his lady love was around, nothing else mattered to his big brother.

Glancing around the bakery, Jackson remembered the first time Chase approached him about an exciting new business venture.

They were at Samson's Gym, talking smack, lifting weights and eyeing the ladies. Chase suggested going to work for the Draysons, and Jackson had laughed out loud. Hell, no. He'd always resented the Chicago branch of the family. Why were they so high and mighty? Why had they shut out their Seattle relatives for so long? More persuasive than a politician, Chase had convinced him that a bakery would be an excellent business opportunity, and posed it as a challenge. What if they could make Lillian's of Seattle more profitable than the Chicago store? What if they became the number-one bakery in town? Jack had never been able to walk away from a challenge or a dare, and when Chase suggested he was afraid they weren't good enough to "keep up with the Draysons," Jack was in. Though, initially, he didn't think he could work with his perfectionist brother. Where Chase had always been a methodical rule-follower, Jackson's favorite motto was By Any Means Necessary. He often wondered if he could have been adopted, because he was so different from his siblings. He'd attended three different colleges, and had quickly gotten bored by the classes, the course work and the dreary study groups. His faculty mentor told him he was smart, with a great mind for business, but his dislike of convention had often gotten in his way. He'd finally graduated from Seattle University with a business degree but he could have just as easily obtained a degree in science, math or history.

"Wow, I heard this place was nice, but that's an understatement." Wearing an awestruck expression on her chubby face, the mother of two slowly took in her surroundings. "It looks more like a high-end boutique than a bakery."

Her words filled Jackson with pride. Everything about the shop reeked of class and sophistication—the large gold script bearing Lillian's name on the front door, the gold chandeliers, the glass cases holding bite-sized pastries, and the attractive tables and chairs inside the adjoining café, Myers Coffee Roasters. Located in Denny Triangle, a residential and professional community teeming with restaurants, bars, specialty shops and parks, the bakery had opened to rave reviews two months earlier and was now a Seattle favorite.

"I don't know what to order. Everything looks amazing."

"That's because it is," Jackson said confidently. "At Lillian's of Seattle, we believe in using only natural ingredients, so whether you choose a double-fudge brownie or a slice of pecan pie, you can be sure that it's one hundred percent fresh and one hundred percent delicious. Our mission is to make Seattle happier and tastier, and we will. One decadent dessert at a time."

Thanking him again, the mother wandered off in search of a sweet treat.

Customers streamed through the open door and Jackson greeted everyone with a nod and a smile. The aromas of baked apples, cinnamon and freshly brewed coffee wafted out of the kitchen, reminding Jackson of all the summers he'd visited his great-aunt Lillian in Chicago and worked at her bakery. There he'd gained a love of cooking and developed a keen interest in the family business. His parents, Graham and Nadia, thought he was wasting his time at Lillian's. A savvy real estate agent and self-made man, his father had built a successful life for himself in Seattle and wanted the same for his children. Last week at Sunday dinner his mother had admonished him to quit baking and find a "real" job. A *man's* job. Jackson didn't let her comments get to him. Instead he let them roll off his back. He wasn't going to bail on Chase and Mariah—or disappoint his great-aunt—and he wanted to make Lillian's a success.

The mood inside the bakery was festive and Jackson noted customers were talking, laughing and stuffing their faces with pastries. Thanks to his twenty-six-year-old sister, Mariah, the bakery had quickly become a popular hangout spot for stay-at-home moms, chic twenty-somethings and college students. A former advertising assistant at a billion-dollar food company, she put her knowledge and training to good use. She ensured everything ran smoothly at Lillian's and had proved to be a skilled baker, as well. Everyone had an important role at the bakery. Chase was the brains, Mariah was the talent and Jackson not only made specialty cakes, but he was also the face of the company, the unofficial spokesperson. He loved people—especially women—and since most of their customers were females, he manned the register, chatted them up and encouraged them to return. They always did. Chase believed Jackson was Lillian's secret weapon and Jackson appreciated his brother's faith in him.

Jackson checked the time on his platinum wristwatch. Where was Mariah? She used to be the first one at the bakery, but these days she spent more time with her millionaire boyfriend, Everett Myers, than she did at the shop. Jackson teased her for falling head-over-heels for the widowed coffee importer and his eight-year-old son, EJ, but he was secretly thrilled for her. Chase, too. His siblings had found love, and even though Jackson had zero desire to settle down or have a family of his own, he was happy for them. Love would never be in the cards for him. He easily got bored, craved spontaneity and excitement, and couldn't imagine wanting to be with the same person for the rest of his life.

"Good morning," a blonde cooed, sailing through the open door.

"Welcome to Lillian's," he greeted. "If you need anything just let me know."

"I will." Winking lasciviously, she licked her lips. "You can bet on it."

Glancing outside, Jackson was surprised to see the weather had changed from a warm and sunny June morning to windy and overcast. He'd been too busy baking to notice. He had to make a baseball-themed cake for a fiftieth birthday party, and since he didn't want to disappoint the owner of the Seattle Mariners, he'd started working on it bright and early that morning.

A wistful smile found his lips. Two months at Lillian's and it still blew Jackson's mind that he was a baker. After watching seven seasons of *Cake Boss*, and several online tutorials, he'd tried his hand at making a three-tier fondant cake for Chase and Amber's engagement party. Not only did Mariah love the elaborate design, she'd also said it tasted delicious and commissioned him to make samples for the bakery. Within a week, he had so many orders to fill he'd had to hire another baker to keep up with the demand. His specialty cakes were a hit, and Jackson was confident his one-of-a-kind chocolate creation would wow guests at the party on Friday night.

"Good morning. Welcome to…"

His eyes fell across the tall, willowy woman standing outside at the crosswalk at Denny Way, and Jackson lost his train of thought. Couldn't speak. Feeling his knees buckle, he leaned against the door to support his weight. Everything screeched to a halt as he gazed at the attractive female in the sleeveless blue dress. Her pixie cut drew attention to her big doe eyes, her lush pink lips and blinding white teeth. There was something sad and pensive about her, a vulnerability he found oddly appealing. She wore a don't-mess-with-me expression on her face and her arms were crossed, but there was no disputing her beauty.

Jackson openly admired her, told himself to quit staring but he couldn't look away. She was a stunner. Beautiful cleavage, slim hips, curves that made his mouth water. He was a leg man, had been since the first time he'd seen Tyra Banks on the cover of *Black Men* magazine back in the day, and the woman had a long, sleek pair. *The model doesn't have a damn thing on her*, he thought, his gaze gliding down her thighs, his hands itching to follow suit.

Intrigued, he continued watching her. The older gentleman standing to her left in the charcoal-grey suit tapped her on the shoulder, but Luscious Lips was having none of it. Giving him her back, she stared intently at the traffic light and the moment it changed she left the stranger in her dust. She moved with poise, carried herself with inherent grace, and Jackson knew she came from money. His gaze zeroed in on her left hand. No ring. That meant she was fair game. Women who looked like her—young, supple and hot—always had several boyfriends, and if by some stroke of good luck she was single, it was by choice.

Jackson was so busy staring at her, admiring her sexy, mesmerizing strut and every swish of her hips, he didn't realize she'd breezed into the bakery until the scent of her perfume tickled his nostrils.

Snapping to attention, he straightened to his full height and checked his black T-shirt and khaki pants for any traces of flour. Like everyone in the room, he immediately took notice of her. Drawn to her, he trailed her around the store at a distance as she moved from one display to the next, carefully perusing the baked goods inside. Her big brown eyes missed nothing, read the handwritten note cards above each case as if she was about to be quizzed on the content. Minutes passed, but Luscious Lips still didn't place an order.

Catching himself gawking at her, Jackson warned

himself to get a grip. Luscious Lips marched toward the register and he slid behind the counter, curious about the woman with the model good-looks. She smelled of peaches and jasmine, an intoxicating scent that wreaked havoc on his body. He couldn't get his thoughts in order, couldn't get his mouth to work, and felt an erection stab the zipper of his jeans. Heat singed his cheeks, drenching his skin with perspiration. Jackson couldn't think of anything but kissing her, ravishing her with his mouth. He was dying to touch her, wanted to caress her from her shoulders to her hips, and between her thighs.

"Are you going to help me, or stand there staring off into space?"

Her tone was clipped, full of annoyance, but she had a lovely voice. The gap between her two front teeth enhanced her one-of-a-kind look. The more Jackson stared at her the more he wanted her, desired her, imagined himself stealing a kiss from her plump, moist lips. "I'm Jackson Drayson, one of the owners of this fine establishment."

Her eyebrows drew together in a questioning slant, but she didn't speak.

"Lillian's is Seattle's favorite bakery, and I'm confident you'll love our pastries, especially our baguettes and croissants. They're better than the ones they make in France!"

"You're not the only bakery in town."

"That's true," he conceded, "but I've tried the others and they're not even in our league. Our baked goods are the best in town, and we'll prove it next month at Bite of Seattle."

A scowl bruised her delicate features. "For a newcomer, you're awfully sure of yourself."

"Draysons always are, and for good reason. Our sister company, Lillian's of Chicago, has been in business for over forty years, but its humble beginnings won't stop us from expanding our beloved pastry empire and winning the hearts of Americans."

"Thanks for the history lesson."

To let her know he was interested, he wore a broad grin and leaned over the counter. "What's your name, beautiful, and when can I take you out? Is tomorrow soon enough?"

"I don't mean to be rude, but I came here to eat, not to make a love connection."

An awkward silence fell between them, but Jackson wanted to make her smile. Down but not out, he spoke in a casual, relaxed tone, refusing to show that her words had rattled his confidence. "You must be a foodie," he joked, determined to brighten her mood, "because I've never seen anyone take twenty minutes to decide what to order."

"Is that a crime?" she quipped. "I didn't realize I was being timed."

His gaze strayed from her eyes to her lips. He liked watching them move, imagined how they'd feel around his— Jackson slammed the brakes on the explicit thought. Luscious Lips was stunning, no doubt, one of the sexiest women he'd ever seen in the flesh, but he could do without her brusque tone and frosty attitude.

"I'll have a pistachio cupcake."

Jackson punched in her order, and took the ten-dollar bill from her outstretched hand. Their fingers touched, brushed against each other, causing an electric current to shoot through his body. He stood, frozen in place, his leather Kenneth Cole shoes rooted to the floor, unable to move. Their attraction, the chemistry crackling between them, was so potent it consumed the air, made it impossible for Jackson to do anything but stare at her. Embarrassed by his physical response to her touch, he broke the spell by giving his head a shake and expelling a deep breath. He had to get ahold of himself, or he'd be the laughingstock of the bakery. His employees were watching him, all wearing the same puzzled expressions on their faces, and Jackson wanted to kick himself for acting like a horny teen.

Man, snap out of it! yelled his inner voice. *You're a player, not a scrub, so get your head in the game, or she'll never,* ever *give you the time of day.*

"Can I get my change? I'm pressed for time, and I don't want to be late for work."

Snapping out of his thoughts, he nodded, and gave Luscious Lips her money. Seconds later, he handed over her purchase. He expected her to turn and march off—giving him another view of her perfectly round backside—but she opened the dainty white take-out box, immediately took out the cupcake and tasted it. Surprise flashed in her eyes, and Jackson didn't know if that was good or bad. Once again, he was captivated, unable to look away.

She chewed slowly, thoughtfully, and then said to herself, "The vanilla extract is excessive. Half a teaspoon would have been more than enough."

Jackson raised an eyebrow. *What? Where does she get off criticizing my baking?* He'd followed the recipe to a T and customers had been raving about his cupcakes all morning. Oddly enough, he was insulted by her critique *and* turned on. Luscious Lips obviously knew something about baking, and how to leave a man breathless. As she marched out the door, swishing her shapely hips, Jackson felt his pulse throb in his ears.

Curious, he opened the case, grabbed a pistachio cupcake from the top shelf and took a bite. The cupcake was moist and flavorful, but the vanilla extract *was* excessive. Dang it if she wasn't right! His desire for Luscious Lips cooled, evaporating like smoke. Jackson loved women, and in all his twenty-eight years he'd never met a female he didn't like—until now. Why did she have to be so cold? Why did she have to dog his baking? Didn't she know how hard it was to wake up at 5:00 a.m. and bake hundreds of pastries after a night of clubbing?

Hearing his cell phone buzz, he took it out of his back pocket and punched in his password. He had two new text messages. As usual, Diego was checking up on him. He'd call his buddy during his lunch break to touch base with him. Jackson considered Diego Maldonado—his friend since the fifth grade—and his large, loving, Portuguese brood to be his second family. Reading the second text, he couldn't believe his good luck. His ex-girlfriend wanted to know if he was free tomorrow night. She had two front-row tickets for the T.I. concert, and VIP passes for the after party at Trinity Nightclub. Did he want to go?

Hell, yeah, Jackson thought, immediately responding to her message. He'd dated the paralegal for three months, but called it quits when she started dropping not-so-subtle hints about moving into his Beacon Hill bachelor pad. They weren't soul mates, but they'd always be great friends. Jackson hung out with all of his exes—except Mimi. They hadn't spoken since he'd called off their engagement last year, and he had no intention of ever speaking to Mimi Tanaka again. As far as Jackson was concerned, she was dead to him.

Remembering the night they broke up, he realized he'd dodged a bullet by ending their relationship. Marriage wasn't for everyone, and Jackson was smart enough to realize it wasn't for him. He had decades of bachelorhood ahead of him, years of skirt chasing to enjoy, and he wasn't going to screw that up by getting hitched. His brother and sister were over-the-moon in love, walking around the bakery all day long with permanent smiles on their faces, but Jackson had zero desire to find love. That didn't mean he didn't value and respect women. He did. Thought they were exciting, fascinating creatures, and for that reason just one would never do.

"We're running low on éclairs and we're out of lemon scones, as well…"

Jackson blinked, returning to the present. Kelsey Andrews, an intern from the Seattle Culinary Academy, sidled up beside him, eyes bright, smile in place, curls tumbling around her face. Yesterday after work she'd invited him to Zani Bar for drinks, but he'd turned her down, lied and said he had plans with his dad. Kelsey was ten years his junior, and he didn't want to give her the wrong idea or encourage her advances. Workplace romances never worked, and if he hooked up with the fresh-faced barista, Mariah would kick his ass.

"If you don't mind manning the till, I'll head to the kitchen and make another batch."

"No problem," she purred, her gaze full of longing. "Anything for you, Jackson."

Put off by her seductive tone, Jackson stalked out of the bakery and into the bright, spacious kitchen. He grabbed an oversized mixing bowl and the ingredients he needed from the cupboard. Getting down to work, he put all thoughts of Luscious Lips out of his mind. She wasn't the only beautiful woman in town, and if she didn't want to go out with him it was her loss, not his. He had things to do, had to finish the pastries before the insane lunch rush, but this time when he made pistachio cupcakes he'd go easy on the vanilla extract.

Despite himself, he wore a rueful smile. What a morning. *What a woman*, he thought, remembering their terse exchange. Jackson was mad at himself for not getting her name. He wished he knew more about her besides her penchant for pistachio cupcakes. He had a feeling Luscious Lips would return to Lillian's one day soon, felt it in his gut, and when she did he was going to get her name *and* her phone number—even if it meant using every trick in his arsenal.

Chapter 2

"You did what?" Doug Nicholas roared.

He cursed, yelling so loud it caused the window inside his elegantly decorated office at Sweetness Bakery to shake. The room was filled with vibrant area rugs, cozy chairs and potted plants, but Grace would rather be at the dentist than stuck in her father's office, listening to him rant and rave about how irresponsible she was. She was a twenty-six-year-old woman with a strong head on her shoulders, but he made her feel like a screwup.

"What were you thinking? Have you lost your mind?"

Of average height, with thinning grey hair and eyeglasses perched on his nose, he had a grumpy disposition and spoke in a low, clipped tone. He was rough around the edges, gruff at times, but Grace loved him with all her heart. "Dad, calm down—"

"What possessed you to go to Lillian's?" he said, speaking through clenched teeth. "What if a reporter was on hand and snapped a picture of you stuffing your face at our competitor's shop? Do you know how embarrassing that would be?"

Grace bit her tongue, didn't dare answer because it wasn't a rhetorical question, and she didn't want to make the situation worse. Swallowing a yawn, she snuck a glance at her wristwatch. It was eight o'clock and the bakery was closed for the day, but her father was making such a fuss she feared the cleaning crew would come running. Grace managed Sweetness, had since her mother's untimely death, but her father was always on hand to help. It had been a banner year for the bakery, but Doug wasn't satisfied, never was. They had an exceptional team that loved Sweetness Bakery, just as Rosemary had, and she knew her mother was smiling down on them. Thinking about her mom made her heart ache. Grace would do anything to see her again, to hug her, to hear her voice just one more time. "Dad, relax, it wasn't that serious."

"Don't tell me to relax," he snapped. "You could have humiliated the shop, and caused irreversible damage! Your behavior was dumb and reckless."

His words stung, bruised her feelings, but Grace straightened in her chair and projected confidence, not fear. She'd made the right decision. She'd had no choice but to march into the splashy new bakery after reading the food blogs during her commute to work. According to bloggers, Lillian's was the best thing to ever happen to Seattle. Their cupcakes were divine, the ambiance darling, the staff personable and attentive, the location a winner. Unfortunately, Grace had to agree. She couldn't deny the truth. Her visit had been memorable—and not just because she'd met the hunky owner, Jackson Drayson—and she was curious if all of their pastries were to-die-for, or just the pistachio cupcakes. "Dad, I was merely checking out the competition and I'm glad I did. Now that we know what we're up against we can formulate a plan."

A pensive expression on his face, he stroked his pointy jaw. "What did you find out?"

That the picture in the *Seattle Times* of Jackson Drayson at Lillian's grand opening in April didn't do the baker justice! Grace felt a nervous flutter inside her belly. *He's even sexier in person, and his voice is so seductive I shivered when he spoke to me. Add to that, his cologne, like his smile, was intoxicating.*

"Don't keep me in suspense," Doug admonished. "Spill it."

Grace chose her words carefully, didn't reveal everything at once. She told her dad about her visit that morning, but didn't mention her run-in with Jackson. It wasn't important. *He* wasn't important, and she didn't want to waste time talking about him. She'd sized him up in five seconds flat. He was a lady-killer, a man who took great pleasure in seducing women—not her type in the least. Jackson Drayson was the personification of the term *deadly sexy*, and when she'd entered the bakery she noticed every female in the room was staring at the dreamy baker with lust in her eyes. The man was an attention seeker who wasn't happy unless women were fawning all over him, and Grace planned to stay far away from Mr. Smug.

"Tell me more." Doug leaned forward in his leather

chair. "Was the bakery packed? What is the mood and feel of the shop? Did you enjoy the cupcake?"

Grace answered her dad's questions the best she could. The more she spoke the more stress lines wrinkled her father's forehead. She'd never seen him like this—fidgeting with his hands, shifting around on his chair, grumbling under his breath—and feared he was having a nervous breakdown.

"I owe you an apology. You were right. Checking out Lillian's was a smart move."

"Thanks, Dad, and now I think it's the perfect time to implement some of the changes we spoke about last month," she said, feeling a rush of excitement. "Seattle has the best indie artists in the country, and I think we should showcase their talents at Sweetness. We can extend our weekend hours and offer two-for-one specials, as well. Poetry Fridays and Talent Night Saturdays will definitely attract new customers."

"This is a bakery, Grace. Not *America's Got Talent*."

"Dad, at least consider it—"

"There's nothing to consider. It's a stupid idea and we're not doing it. Case closed."

Flinching, as if slapped across the face, she dropped her gaze to her lap and blinked back the tears in her eyes. It was moments like this Grace wished she had siblings. Someone else she could vent to about the bakery, her promotional ideas, her dreams of moving to New York. After graduating from the Seattle Culinary Academy, she'd planned to relocate to the Big Apple to take the culinary world by storm. But it wasn't to be. Her mother's death had changed everything. She'd put her plans on ice and devoted her time and energy to growing the family business. To better aid her dad, she'd enrolled in graduate school and acquired a master's degree in accounting and financial management. It was tough, working at the bakery during the day and attending school at night, but she'd pulled through and graduated at the top of her class.

Her gaze fell across the framed photographs hanging on the ivory walls. Images of her mother—cutting the ribbon at the bakery's opening in the early eighties, rolling cookie dough, laughing with customers, manning the till—brought a sad smile to her lips. Her dad could be stubborn and narrow-minded at times, but he was the only family she had left. Since she'd never do anything to disrespect him, she held her tongue.

"Now is not the time to shake things up. We could alienate customers." Grunting, he scooped up the papers on his desk and shook his hands in the air. "Lillian's of Seattle opened a couple months ago, but they're already cutting into our profits. Sales are down nine percent since April, and those jerks are the reason why. We have to stop them before it's too late."

"Dad, what are you saying?"

A devilish gleam darkened his face. Her father had a reputation for playing dirty, for outwitting his business rivals with skillful maneuvers, but Grace wanted no part of his schemes. It wasn't her. Wasn't in her DNA to be sneaky and underhanded, and she didn't want to do anything she'd live to regret. Her mother's words came back to her, playing in her ears loud and clear. *Be a woman of integrity*, she'd admonished one afternoon while they were baking pastries for a two-hundred-guest baby shower. *And don't let anyone change who you are.*

"Your mother built Sweetness through blood, sweat

and tears, and it's more than just a bakery. It's her legacy, and I'd never forgive myself if I lost this place."

"Dad, you won't. Sweetness has been the leading bakery in Seattle for decades and that will never change. Our customers are loyal and they won't desert us."

"I won't lose to a bunch of rich kids who've had everything in life handed to them, who've never had to work for anything. It's not going to happen because I won't let it."

Grace wanted to correct him, to tell her dad that based on what she'd read and seen about Jackson Drayson his assumption couldn't be further from the truth. But she knew it was a bad idea to defend the enemy. Her mind returned to their conversation that morning. She vividly remembered his scent, the sound of his voice, how his eyes twinkled with mischief when he'd asked her out. Reflecting on their exchange, Grace wished she hadn't been so mean to him. She heard the talk around the bakery, and in her upscale Bellevue neighborhood. She knew what men said about her. They called her the Ice Queen, a man hater, and complained she was more difficult than a pop star.

Painful memories flooded her heart, piercing her soul like a dagger. Before Phillip Davies, she'd always thought the best of people, but after their bitter breakup she'd lost faith in not only men, but also her ability to choose the right one. Love was overrated. For women who believed in fairy tales. A waste of time, and she'd vowed never to put herself out there again. Why bother? Love didn't last, didn't work, and Grace wanted no part of it.

Seeing Jackson's image in her mind's eye, despite

her futile attempts to block it out, Grace wondered if he had a girlfriend. She snorted, snickering inwardly. *Of course* he had a girlfriend. Probably several. One for every day of the week, and in every state, no doubt. Not that she cared. Everything about the overconfident baker screamed *player*—his swagger, his bad-boy grin, the tattoo on his left bicep that said "Live each day as if it's your last." And since he wasn't her type, Grace shook off her thoughts and stood. It had been another ten-hour day and she was beat. She wanted nothing more than to crawl into bed and fall asleep. "Dad, I'm tired. If it's okay with you, I'll prepare the profit-and-loss statements in the morning."

"On your way in tomorrow, stop in at Lillian's and sample something else." Doug snapped his fingers. "I know. Buy one of those dragnet things they're advertising all over the place. I want to see what all the fuss is about. The food critic for the *Seattle Times* said 'It's heaven in your mouth' but I think she's exaggerating. You know how women are."

"Dad, I don't think returning to Lillian's is a good idea."

His eyes dimmed, and a frown pinched his thin lips. "Why not?"

Because I'm attracted to Jackson Drayson's light brown eyes, full lips shaped by a trimmed goatee and muscled biceps. I'm liable to trip and fall flat on my face the next time he smiles at me!

Knowing she couldn't tell the truth, she said the first thing that came to mind. "If I go back it might raise suspicions."

"Nonsense. They have no idea who you are." Doug waved off her concerns with a flick of his hands. "It's crucial you find out more about Lillian's. If we're going to crush them—and we will—we need to gather more intel, so return to the bakery and uncover their secrets."

Her shoulders sagged and panic ballooned inside her chest. It was official. Her dad had lost it. Gone off the deep end. And now, more than ever, she missed her mom. Rosemary had died fourteen months ago and not a day went by that Grace didn't think about her. Losing her mom had been a devastating blow, and if not for her father she never would have survived Rosemary's death. He'd been her anchor, her rock, and although she couldn't shake the feeling that she was making a mistake, she asked, "Dad, what do you want me to do?"

For the first time since she'd entered his office an hour earlier, her dad's face brightened and he grinned like a five-year-old who'd been given a new bike. "Maybe you can fake food poisoning or a nasty spill as you leave the shop. Bad publicity will drive customers away from Lillian's and straight through our doors."

Too shocked to speak, Grace dropped back down in her chair, her mind reeling. Her dad mistook her silence as acquiescence and offered one nefarious idea after another. Grace struggled to make sense of what he was saying and couldn't believe this was the same man who'd raised her to be an honest, trustworthy person. He loved money, would do anything to make more, and hated that Lillian's was cutting into his profits. For that reason he was willing to break the rules. Speaking in an animated voice, he encouraged her to return to the bakery, admonished her to befriend the baristas, and even the owners.

"Grace, are you in?"

Feeling trapped, her lips too numb to move, she slowly nodded.

"That's my girl!"

Chuckling, he rose from his chair and came around the desk.

Standing on wobbly legs, Grace dug her sandals into the carpet to steady herself.

"We got so caught up talking about Lillian's, I forgot why I asked you to come to my office in the first place," he said, shaking his head as if annoyed with himself. "I'm having Mr. and Mrs. Ventura over for brunch next Sunday, and I want you there."

Grace thought hard, but couldn't recall ever meeting the couple. "Who?"

"Mr. Ventura is an anesthesiologist, his wife is a pharmacist, and they own a slew of pharmacies on the west coast. They're a wealthy, well-connected couple with friends in high places, and I'm dying to join their social circle. Hence, the dinner party."

"Dad, I can't. I have roller derby practice at noon. "

He snorted. "I wish you'd quit that stupid team."

"And I wish you wouldn't work 24/7."

"If I host a dinner party on the twentieth, will you come?"

Grace had a game that afternoon, but she didn't tell her dad. Didn't want to upset him. "Sure, Dad," she said with a forced smile. "I'll bring the wine."

"Wear something nice," he advised. "They're bringing their son and he's single."

"That's nice, but I'm not interested."

"You should be. Ainsworth Ventura owns a profit-able management company and was recently named entrepreneur of the year. Do you know what dating him could do for us?"

Grace didn't know, didn't care and had zero desire to meet the Seattle businessman.

"Like you, he's ready to settle down and start a family."

"Settling down is the furthest thing from my mind—"

"You'll change your mind once you meet Ainsworth. He's a ridiculously wealthy young man with everything going for him. Google him. You'll see that I'm right."

Yawning, she reached into her pocket for her cell phone, curious if her girlfriend Bronwyn Johansson had answered the text she'd sent that morning. They hadn't seen each other in a week, and Grace was looking forward to catching up with her bestie.

"Think you can make some of your apple beignets and toffee cookie bars for dessert?"

Grace shifted her weight from one foot to the next, fidgeting with her fingers. She hadn't set foot in the kitchen since her mother's death and didn't plan to. She used to love baking, would spend hours experimenting in the kitchen, but without Rosemary at her side, cooking held no appeal. These days she worked in the back office, managing the bakery the best she could. "No. I can't," she said, unable to shake her melancholy feelings.

"The regulars keep asking when you'll be back in the kitchen and I want to know, too."

"I don't know. I just don't feel up to it right now."

"Grace, it's been fourteen months. You have to move on."

Her stomach churned and pain stabbed her heart. Was there a time limit on grief? A predetermined mourning period her therapist had failed to mention to her? Grace wanted to turn the tables on her dad, wanted to ask him when *he* was going to quit hiding out in his office and start living again, but knew better than to question him. "Dad, I'm beat. I'm going home."

"All right. Good night, pumpkin. Text me when you get home."

Living at home wasn't ideal, especially when Grace wanted to entertain, but whenever she broached the subject of finding her own place, her dad got upset, said he couldn't stand to live in the house alone, and she'd bury the idea. He still missed her mom, continued to grieve her death over a year later, and balked whenever Grace encouraged him to join a social club, or try online dating. "Don't worry, Dad. I will. I always do."

"I know. You're such a good girl. The best daughter a father could ever ask for."

He wasn't one to show affection; Grace was shocked when her dad hugged her and kissed her cheek. She couldn't remember the last time he'd held her, and she was comforted by his touch. Hearing her cell phone, she took it out of the pocket of her blazer and glanced discreetly at the screen. Grace groaned inwardly. What did Phillip want now? He was as annoying as a pesky mosquito, buzzing around in the dead of night, and she was sick of him blowing up her phone. Why was he calling her? Couldn't he take a hint? It was the third time he'd phoned her that afternoon, but since Grace had nothing to say to him she let the call go to voice mail.

"We need to work together to save your mother's shop," her father said quietly, sorrow flickering across his strong facial features. "I'm counting on you to come through for me."

"Dad, I will. I'll do whatever it takes to keep Sweetness on top. I promise." But as the impassioned declaration left her mouth, Grace knew it was a lie.

Chapter 3

This is so *wrong. I shouldn't be here*, Grace thought, her conscience plagued with guilt. *I should be at Sweetness getting caught up on paperwork, not sitting here like a groupie hoping to catch a glimpse of Jackson "player extraordinaire" Drayson.*

Seated at a corner table inside Myers Coffee Roasters café, sipping an espresso topped with oodles of whipped cream, Grace watched the comings and goings inside Lillian's with keen interest, wondering where the man of the hour was.

For the second time in minutes Grace glanced at her watch, then around the room. She didn't see Jackson anywhere and she'd been looking out for him since arriving at the bakery an hour earlier. Grace was filled with mixed emotions. Relief, because she turned into a jittery fool whenever Jackson was around, and disappointment, because she enjoyed their playful banter. On Monday he'd teased her for ignoring him, on Wednesday he'd complimented her BCBG keyhole dress—claimed he couldn't keep his eyes off of her—then suggested *she* take *him* out for a romantic dinner. He'd slipped a handwritten note into her purse when she wasn't looking, and finding it hours later made her heart smile. It was a cute gesture, one that made her crack up every time she reread his message, but Grace couldn't call him, not without looking desperate, so she hid the note in her top drawer and deleted all thoughts of Jackson from her mind.

Ha! barked her inner voice. *If you were trying to forget him you wouldn't be in* his *bakery.*

Grace lowered her coffee mug from her lips and cranked her head to the right. Every time the door chimed her heart raced. *Where is he?* Did Jackson have the day off? Was he out with one of his girlfriends? Wining, dining and seducing his flavor of the week? Of course he was, Grace decided. The baker was an affable, laid-back guy who obviously loved women, and it would be wise to keep her distance.

Reflecting on their heated exchange the day they'd met, Grace wished she hadn't let Jackson get under her skin. It was clear from then on that she was going to have her hands full with the hottie baker, and yesterday he'd been in fine form. Every time she entered Lillian's he was charming his female customers, and when Grace pointed it out to him, he'd teased her for being jealous and insisted she wanted him all to herself.

Snorting in disgust, she shook her head at the memory. Grace couldn't believe his nerve, how smug he was. To keep her anger in check she'd had to bite her tongue. Despite her misgivings about her "assignment" she'd stopped in at Lillian's every day to sample something new. Peanut-butter-sandwich cookies on Monday, orange-marmalade coffee cake two days later, a walnut muffin on Thursday and today a Draynut. The pastry was a combination of croissant and donut, and customers were lined up around the block to get their hands on the pricey dessert that her father had mistakenly referred to as a "dragnet."

Grace stared at her gold-rimmed plate, wondering if the pastry was as delicious as the food bloggers said it was. So far, she'd been impressed by the quality of the baked goods at Lillian's. She'd assumed the bakery wouldn't live up to the hype or her implausibly high standards. Trends came and went, and a little bit of buzz could go a long way when a business first opened. Grace was pleasantly—or rather unpleasantly—surprised to learn that yes, Lillian's was that good. She'd made the mistake of mentioning that to her father last night at dinner, and once again he'd urged her to return to the bakery to sample the rest of the items on the menu. Her father wanted to know exactly what the Draysons were producing, and expected her to report back about the inner workings of the family-operated bakery.

Reflecting on her mission, Grace considered what her dad wanted her to do. One week of spying and she was still uncomfortable about it. Sure, she wasn't doing anything illegal, but she felt like a snake for spying on the competition and wanted to stop. The biggest problem? Each day she returned to Lillian's brought her into close contact with Jackson—a man with soulful eyes, juicy lips she wanted to kiss and muscles she was dying to stroke. He was intelligent and perceptive, and Grace feared he'd catch on to what she was doing and expose her. Deep down, she was afraid of how attracted she was to Jackson and decided in her mind to ignore him—*if* he ever showed up at the bakery.

Grace glanced at her wristwatch again. She knew she should get going, but she didn't want to leave. Looking out the window, hoping to catch a glimpse of everyone's favorite baker, Grace couldn't believe how dark and gloomy it was. She couldn't remember the last time she'd seen the sun, and hoped the thick storm clouds held back the rain until she reached work.

"Rodolfo and I are abstaining from sex until our wedding night. Isn't that romantic?"

Grace swallowed the quip on the tip of her tongue. She'd asked her bestie, Bronwyn, to meet her at Lillian's for breakfast, but regretted it the moment their orders had arrived. When the speech pathologist wasn't cooing about her nectarine honey tart, she was gushing about her decades-older fiancé and their fall wedding. Slim, with hazel eyes and blond curls, Bronwyn exuded such warmth and confidence she made friends everywhere she went. "Yes," she drawled sarcastically. "It's the most romantic thing I've ever heard."

"You're just jealous. You *wish* you had a man as sweet and as loving as Rodolfo."

No, I wish *my vibrator wasn't on the blink, because it didn't get the job done this morning and I need an orgasm in the* worst *way!* Grace finished her coffee and set aside her mug. Anxious to sink her teeth into her dessert, she picked up her fork and cut into the Draynut. "Doesn't it bother you that Rodolfo isn't working?"

"No. I make enough money for the both of us and I love taking care of my Pooh Bear."

The fork slipped from Grace's hand and fell on the plate. Speechless, she stared at her friend in shock. Bronwyn liked to boast about all the nice things her fiancé did for her, but he was buying her expensive gifts with *her* charge card. Who did that? A real man would never take money from his woman, let alone demand a weekly allowance, and Grace didn't understand why her bestie was cool with supporting a grown-ass man.

"The economy's in the tank. People aren't buying luxury cars like they used to—"

"Then he should get a job at another dealership instead of mooching off you."

"No one's mooching off anybody. Rodolfo's a great catch, and I don't mind helping him out financially from time to time. We've had our ups and downs and even split up for a while, but I'd rather be with Rodolfo than anyone else. He's the only one for me..."

Listening to Bronwyn wax poetic about her fiancé, Grace realized she'd never loved anyone with unwavering devotion. Truth be told, she didn't understand men, couldn't figure them out, and doubted she ever would.

"Relationships are hard," she quipped, with a knowing look, a smirk sitting pretty on her lips. "*You* of all people should know that."

Grace ignored the dig, refusing to think about the night she'd dumped Phillip. To this day, Grace didn't know what had possessed her to date the loudmouth physical trainer. Her father had always warned her that men would be after her for her money, but she didn't believe him. Unfortunately, her dad was right. At the memory of the slap heard around the world—or rather inside Bronwyn's elegant Capitol Hill home—Grace groaned as if she was being physically tortured. "I don't want to talk about it. It wasn't my finest moment, and every time I think about it I want to hide. It's so embarrassing."

Bronwyn pushed a hand through her long, curly locks and Grace peered at her engagement ring. The diamond was so small she'd need a magnifying glass to see it, and the thick band looked cheap and old-fashioned. Grace was convinced Rodolfo had bought it at a pawn shop, or stole it from his great-great-grandmother, but she kept her thoughts to herself.

"Don't sweat it, slugger. Philip's face healed just fine."

Grace stuck out her tongue, then laughed when Bronwyn did the same.

"Hey, don't get mad at me. I'm not the one with the mean right hook."

"You're the worst, you know that?"

Bronwyn sobered. "If Philip apologized would you give him another chance?"

"No. Never. We have nothing in common, and we had no business dating."

"Rodolfo and I ran into him yesterday while shopping at Bellevue Square, and he said you're just taking a break, and you'll be an item again in no time."

"Ha!" Grace barked a laugh. "Girl, please, I'd rather join a convent!"

Bronwyn's shrill, high-pitched giggles drew the attention of the patrons seated nearby.

Hungry, Grace picked up her fork and put it in her mouth. Her eyelids fluttered closed as she savored the rich, sweet pastry. Tasting cinnamon and hints of nutmeg on her tongue, she moaned in appreciation. The dessert did not disappoint. Grace sampled another bite of the Draynut and decided she didn't like the dessert; she loved it.

"Tell me again why you wanted to meet here, and not at the bakery?"

"My dad asked me to check out the competition so here I am—"

"Sweet mother of God! Who is *that* and where has he been all my life?"

Grace didn't have to turn around to know who Bronwyn was referring to, knew there was only one man inside Lillian's of Seattle who could elicit such an emphatic response, but she did turn. Casting a glance over her right shoulder, she caught sight of Jackson stalking through the door, looking all kinds of sexy in a black sports jacket, crisp slacks and leather shoes.

Grace couldn't take her eyes off of him. The man was a force of nature, so freakin' hot her body tingled in places that made her blush. He must have sensed her watching him, felt the heat of her stare, because he met her gaze. She wore an aloof expression on her face and didn't react when he winked at her, but her heart was doing backflips inside her chest. His grin revealed a set of matching dimples, straight white teeth and a twinkle in his eyes. Jackson moved with confidence, as if he could have anything in the world—including her—and that drew Grace to him.

"Do you know him?" Bronwyn asked. "Have you seen him here before?"

"That's Jackson Drayson. He's one of the three owners."

"No," she quipped, her gaze dark with lust. "That's my second husband!"

Grace cupped a hand over her mouth to smother her girlish laughter.

"You tricked me." Wearing an amused expression on her face, Bronwyn leaned across the table and leveled a finger at Grace. "You didn't ask me to meet you here so we could catch up. You came down here to drool over that tall, beautiful specimen of a man."

"As if. He's not my type—"

"Says the girl who's drooling all over her expensive designer dress!"

Grace noticed she wasn't the only person in Lillian's eyeing the dreamy baker. He'd captured the attention of everyone in the room and connected with patrons in meaningful ways. He shook hands, kissed babies, chatted with the group of senior citizens drinking coffee and saluted a female soldier waiting in line for her order. Jackson was a man's man, a woman's man, too, and it was obvious his customers loved him.

Watching Jackson charm everyone in the bakery made Grace realize her own inadequacies as an employee at Sweetness. She spent most of her days in her office, chained to her desk, and on the rare occasion she treated herself to lunch she sat outside in the park, not in the kitchen. Too many memories of her mother in there. Too many unfulfilled hopes and dreams, so she avoided the room at all costs. Customers, too. Everyone had a story to share about Rosemary, and hearing them broke her heart, overwhelmed her with pain and grief. For that reason, she kept her distance from the regulars.

"What's his story?"

Grace told Bronwyn what she knew about Jackson, which wasn't much, and noticed the expression on her friend's face morph from excited to skeptical.

"Single, fine and successful?" she drawled. "There *must* be something wrong with him."

"You mean besides that fact that he has a monster-sized ego?"

Bronwyn's giggles skidded to a stop and her eyes widened with interest as Jackson stopped at their table. "Well, hello."

"Good morning, ladies. Care to sample one of my Peppermint cheesecake bites?"

"Absolutely," Bronwyn cooed, helping herself to one of the round minicakes.

Stuffed, so full she couldn't move, Grace shook her head. "Nothing for me, thanks."

Bronwyn popped the dessert into her mouth, declared it was the most delicious thing she had ever tasted and stuck out her right hand. "I'm Bronwyn Johansson, and you're Jackson Drayson. I've heard a lot about you."

"Everything Grace told you is true."

Laughing together, Bronwyn and Jackson shook hands.

"It's true what they say. Beautiful women *do* travel in packs."

Bronwyn smiled so brightly she lit up the entire bakery. Grace tried not to gag. Surely, her friend wasn't impressed with his pickup lines. But, sadly, she was. Silent and wide-eyed, she couldn't believe her friend was flirting shamelessly with the bad-boy baker. Amused, Grace sank back in her chair and enjoyed the "Bronwyn and Jackson" show.

"You're a great baker," Bronwyn announced, her tone full of awe., "Your wife is one very lucky woman."

"I'm not married." His gaze slid across the table and landed on Grace. "But that could change any day now."

Heat singed the tips of her ears and flowed through her body. Jackson made her hyperventilate, caused her thoughts to scatter in a million directions, and there was nothing Grace could do to stop it.

"I haven't found Mrs. Right yet, but things are definitely starting to look up."

"Describe your ideal woman."

Grace kicked Bronwyn under the table, but her friend continued chatting a mile a minute.

"Don't be shy," she said, reaching out and patting his forearm good-naturedly, as if they were lifelong friends. "I love playing matchmaker, so let me help you find your soul mate."

Jackson rested the wooden tray on the table. "That's easy. I know exactly what I want."

"Do tell. Inquiring minds want to know."

"Bronwyn, don't encourage him," Grace implored, speaking through dry, pursed lips.

"I want to hear this. Go ahead, Jackson. I'm listening."

His stare was bold and raked over her body with deliberate intent. "She's five-ten, give or take a few inches, with mocha-brown skin, hourglass curves and legs like a Vegas showgirl."

Oh, my goodness, he's talking about me! Grace resisted the urge to cheer. Pride surged through her veins as she sat up taller in her chair. Fire and desire gleamed in his eyes, radiating from his chiseled six-foot body. Grace didn't speak, kept the leave-me-the-hell-alone expression on her face, but when Jackson flashed his trademark grin her heart smiled. It must have appeared on her face because he looked pleased with himself, as if he'd developed an antidote for an incurable disease.

He sat down in the empty chair beside her, and it took every ounce of her self-control not to kiss him.

"I know *just* the girl," Bronwyn said, vigorously nodding her head. "Want her number? It's 206-621—" Pop music played from inside her gold Michael Kors purse and she broke off speaking. Singing along with Taylor Swift, she retrieved her BlackBerry and checked the screen. "It's my Pooh Bear! Jackson, keep Grace company until I get back. I won't be long."

"My pleasure," he said, pouring on the charm. "Take your time."

Her breakfast forgotten, Bronwyn surged to her feet and strode off.

"You look amazing. Do you model for Gucci, or are you just a huge fan of their clothes?"

"Surely, there's someone else in here you can hit on," she said with a nod toward the cash register. "How about that cute young barista with the curly hair? She's always staring at you, and I'm sure she'd be flattered by your pickup lines."

"I don't spit lines. Just the truth."

Seeing her cell phone light up, she glanced down at the screen and read her latest text message. Of course. It was from her dad. He wanted to know how things were going, but Grace decided not to respond. Not with the enemy sitting so close.

"When are you going to let me take you out? You know you want to."

"I grew up here," she said, "so there's nowhere you can take me that I haven't been to a million times before."

"Try me. When we go out on Saturday night, I'll knock you off your feet. *Literally.*"

"Are you always this cocky?"

"Yes, as a matter of fact I am. I have reason to be. I'm a pretty cool dude!"

His facial expression tickled her funny bone. Grace didn't want to laugh, tried to swallow it, but it burst out of her mouth. Damn him! Why did he have to be funny and ridiculously hot?

"I love your laugh. It's as captivating as your smile."

"You wouldn't be flirting with me if you knew who I was."

"Ya think?" he said, leaning forward in his chair, his gaze full of interest. "Try me."

"I'm your worst enemy."

"Is that so, Ms. Nicholas? I prefer to think of us as colleagues, not rivals."

Grace choked on her tongue. Oh, hell no!

The fact that Jackson already knew who she was and had been flirting with her anyway made her mad, but more than anything she was disappointed. All this time, she'd thought she was pulling one over on him, but he'd been pulling one over on her! Swallowing hard, Grace reclaimed her voice and asked the question racing through her mind. "You know who I am? But I never told you my last name. How did you figure it out?"

"Google. Twitter. Facebook. There are no secrets in this day and age. A few clicks of my mouse and I knew everything I wanted to know about you..."

Jackson spoke in a tone so seductive her nipples hardened under her fitted teal dress, and her thighs quivered. It took everything in her not to crush her lips to his mouth and steal a kiss. The man was long, lean and ripped, and Grace imagined all of the delicious things they could do together. Dirty dancing. Skinny-dipping. Tantric sex. Stunned by her lascivious thoughts, she tore her gaze away from his face and took a moment to gather herself.

"I like the quote you posted on your Facebook page this morning and couldn't help wondering if it was about me. 'Don't be afraid of change. You may lose something good, but you may gain something infinitely better.'"

Everything in the bakery ceased to exist, faded to the background. Mesmerized, Grace listened to Jackson with growing interest, realized she'd been too quick to judge him. He was wise and insightful, and to her surprise she agreed with everything he said.

"There is no reason for us to be enemies. In fact, we could probably help each other. There is plenty of room for more than one bakery in town, and to prove it I'd be more than happy to give you a behind-the-scenes look at how things work at Lillian's."

His friendliness confused her. Why was he so willing to reveal company secrets?

"Come back after closing and I'll give you a tour of our state-of-the art kitchen."

Grace considered his offer. She suspected his invitation was the modern-day equivalent of inviting her upstairs to see his etchings, and wondered what *else* the hunky baker wanted to show her. The thought aroused her body, infected it with lust. *What's the matter with me? Why am I undressing him with my eyes? Why am I fantasizing about a man who has the power to break my heart* and *ruin my mother's business?*

"I better get back to the kitchen, or my sister will skin my hide." Standing, tray in hand and grin on display, he winked good-naturedly. "See you at seven o'clock, beautiful. Stay sweet."

Then, without waiting for her answer, he turned and strode off, as if the matter was decided. And that was when Grace knew she'd bitten off more than she could chew.

Chapter 4

Jackson kept one eye on the clock hanging above the kitchen door and the other on Mariah. His sister was flittering around the room, wiping counters, cleaning cupboards, rearranging spices and supplies—all in all ruining his plans. He couldn't cook a romantic dinner with Mariah lurking around, not without her asking a million questions, and if he didn't get rid of her ASAP the appetizers wouldn't be ready when his date arrived.

Jackson caught himself, striking the word from his mind. It wasn't a date. It was a business meeting, an opportunity to learn more about the enemy and her shop, Sweetness Bakery. It was Lillian's biggest competitor, the only thing standing in the way of greater profits and success. Jackson knew what he had to do. He had to get rid of the city's oldest bakery—and its titillating master baker with the gap-toothed smile and decadent, Lord-have-mercy curves.

Past conversations with his dad while golfing at Rainier Country Club played in Jackson's mind as he scrubbed the metal muffin tins soaking in the sink. Graham had always admonished him to keep his friends close, and his enemies closer—within striking distance—and he intended to take his dad's advice. There was no way in hell he was going to let Grace and her father outshine Lillian's of Seattle. He thought of telling Mariah about his numerous conversations with the master baker, but sensed it was a bad idea. He'd tell her tomorrow, after he'd successfully seduced Grace, and would call Chase to bring him up to speed, as well.

"Things were so busy this afternoon I didn't get a chance to tell you the good news," Mariah said, her tone infused with excitement. "Belinda called at lunch to tell me the Chicago clan is coming down for Bite of Seattle."

Jackson twirled a finger in the air. "Lucky us."

"Jack, give them a break. They're trying to make amends for the past and build relationships with us. What more do you want them to do?"

"They think they're better than us because Lillian's of Chicago blew up but we're every bit as good as they are, if not better."

"I agree with you, but that doesn't mean we can't be one big happy family."

Jackson was confused. He couldn't figure out why his siblings, namely Mariah, wanted to be besties with their snobby Chicago relatives. Over the years he'd reached out to them numerous times—invited them to his parents' anniversary bash, to come celebrate the Christmas holidays and even offered to fly them to Seattle for a weekend—and even though they attended family events Jackson still didn't feel close to them. And after the success of their "Brothers Who Bake" blog and bestselling cookbook, Carter, Belinda and Shari were busier—and snobbier—than ever. "What are you doing with yourself tonight?" he asked, wisely changing the subject. He didn't want to argue with Mariah, and talking about their relatives always put him in a bad mood. "Where is Prince Charming taking you?"

A girlish smile covered Mariah's face. "I don't know. Everett said it's a surprise, but I think he's treating me to a home-cooked meal, and I can't wait. He's an incredible cook."

"I'll finish up here. Go ahead and get your grub on," Jackson joked.

Instead of leaving, Mariah opened the closet and grabbed the wooden broom. "You've been here early every day this week, so if anyone should leave it's you, so go ahead."

"But it's almost six thirty. Aren't you going to go home and freshen up for your date?"

"There's no time. I'll just go straight to Everett's place from here."

"Dressed like that?" he asked, knowing full well his comment would get a rise out of her. "Okay, suit yourself, but don't say I didn't warn you."

Now he had Mariah's attention. She stopped sweeping, hitched a hand to her hip and fixed him with a dark, steady gaze. "Warn me about what?"

To buy himself some time, he turned the water on full blast and rinsed the dishes. Jackson didn't know what Everett had planned for his sister, but faked like he did. Mariah had to leave before Grace arrived, and if he had to fib to make it happen then so be it. "Maybe

Everett's taking you *out*." Jackson shut off the tap and dried his hands on his green apron. "Maybe he's taking you to Le Gourmand for a romantic dinner, then to the Usher concert."

Her eyes brightened, lit up like fireworks.

"Everett loves seeing you all dolled up, so go home, change out of those dirty clothes and put on your fanciest designer dress," he instructed. "Trust me. You'll thank me tomorrow."

Mariah squealed and Jackson chuckled. He'd never seen his sister so excited. Glad the pain of his sister's divorce was finally behind her, buried in the past where it belonged, Jackson made a mental note to thank Everett for taking good care of his sister when they played basketball on Wednesday.

"Does Everett have something big planned?"

"I don't know," he said shrugging his shoulders. "But what if he does? You don't want to be covered in flour when your man romances you, do you?"

Mariah untied her apron and tossed it down on the counter. "Good point."

"Have fun, sis, and tell Everett and EJ I said 'What's up.'"

The moment Mariah left the kitchen Jackson sprung into action. He had thirty minutes to cook and no time to waste. He was going to seduce Grace Nicholas, then persuade her to spill bakery secrets. The thought heartened him and a grin claimed his mouth. When he was through with the gorgeous master baker, she wouldn't know what hit her. Whistling along with the hip-hop song playing on the satellite radio, Jackson grabbed the bottle of bourbon he'd hidden under the sink and got down to work.

* * *

Grace sat inside her silver Jaguar XF, berating herself for driving to Lillian's after work instead of going home. Eight hours after leaving the bakery, with Bronwyn in tow, Grace was back, and for the life of her she didn't know why. Common sense told her to drive off, implored her to stay far away from Jackson Drayson, but she couldn't shake the feeling that tonight could be a game changer. Maybe Jackson was right. Maybe they could be friends...allies.

Raindrops beat against the windshield and a cold chill flooded the car. The forecast called for heavy rain, which should have been reason enough for Grace to leave, but she didn't. Couldn't. Wanted to see what Jackson had up his sleeve. Why he'd invited her back to the bakery after closing. And if he was serious about them working together, or just playing mind games, like her ex. It was probably the latter, but Grace wanted to know for sure.

He invited you back here to put the moves on you. Isn't it obvious?

The thought should have scared her, should have sent Grace running for the hills, but it didn't. Deep down, she was attracted to him and flattered by his attention. Who wouldn't be? Jackson knew what to say to make her smile, plied her with compliments, and Grace looked forward to seeing the sexy baker every morning. Truth be told, their flirtatious banter was the highlight of her day, a welcome reprieve from her troubled thoughts.

Go home before it's too late, warned her inner voice.

Grace couldn't leave even if she wanted to. She'd made the mistake of telling her dad about Jackson's offer and he'd practically shoved her out Sweetness's doors at six thirty. He'd insisted she return to Lillian's, and although he was having dinner with friends tonight, he expected a full report tomorrow morning. Hell, he'd probably be sitting in her bedroom when she got home, champing at the bit for salacious gossip about their biggest competitor.

Thunder boomed and the wind howled, whipping leaves and tree branches around. The street was so dark Grace couldn't see where the bakery was. Was Jackson even inside? Had he changed his mind about meeting her, and left at closing? There was only one way to find out.

Twisting around, she searched the backseat for her belted trench jacket, but didn't find it among her things. *If I'd gone inside ten minutes ago instead of hiding out in my car, I wouldn't be stuck in the rainstorm now*, she thought, annoyed with herself for acting like a scaredy-cat.

Grace dug around in her Fendi purse for something to shield her from the rain. Picking up her cell phone, she noticed she had two messages from Phillip and snorted in disgust. She wasn't returning his call. What for? They were over and she had nothing to say to him.

Hearing a knock on the driver's side window, Grace glanced to her right. Standing in the street, holding an oversized umbrella, Jackson looked more like a knight in shining armor than her business rival. Drawn to him, Grace feared she'd be putty in his hands when they were alone, but willed herself to resist his seductive charms. She saw his lips move, heard his voice, but the rain was so loud she couldn't understand what he was saying.

"Let's go inside. Everything's ready…"

He gestured for her to come out of the car and stepped back to make room for her to exit the vehicle. Throwing open the door, Grace hopped out of her seat and took the hand Jackson offered. It was firm, felt nice around hers, and her heart smiled when he pulled her close to his side. Cold water covered her ankle-tie sandals and rain beat against her lace dress. The fabric stuck to her body like paint as they sprinted down the sidewalk and into the bakery.

Her eyes wide in surprise, a gasp fell from her lips. Grace was struck by how intimate the space looked, how sensual and romantic it was. The air held a savory aroma, potted candles filled the space with light and Bruno Mars was playing, singing earnestly about the woman he treasured. The table at the rear of the shop— the one they'd sat at that morning—was dressed in fine linen. Roses sat in a glass vase and a wine bottle was chilling in a bucket of ice.

"This isn't a date, is it?"

Radiating positive energy, his expression warm and welcoming, he spoke in an animated tone. "Of course not. I do this for all my customers, especially the ones who insult me!"

Jackson chuckled and the sound of his hearty laugh ticked her off. Grace couldn't think of a witty comeback and decided this would be her first and last visit to the bakery after dark. In a moment of weakness, she'd let her dad pressure her to return to Lillian's, but clearly, accepting Jackson's offer had been a mistake. *Why did I come here? What was I thinking?*

You weren't *thinking. You were lusting!* quipped her inner voice.

"I'm glad you're here." His husky voice broke into

her thoughts, instantly seized her attention. "I wasn't sure if you were going to show up."

"You didn't give me much choice," she teased, flashing a cheeky, good-girl smile. "I was afraid if I didn't come you'd hijack my Facebook page!"

Jackson stared at her, and Grace feared she had something on her face. Her heart raced, thumped so loudly she could barely hear the Luther Vandross classic now playing.

"I love when you do that."

His words confused her, caused a frown to crimp her dry lips. "Do what?"

"Smile," he said in a seductive whisper. "It dazzles me every time."

Grace tore her eyes away from his mouth. Determined not to cross the proverbial line, the one that could destroy her mother's legacy and dash her father's hopes and dreams, she inched back, out of reach. Jackson moved closer, boldly pursuing her. Her worries grew, intensifying like the storm raging outside. Aggressive, take-charge men were her weakness, and Grace feared if Jackson kissed her she'd fall into his arms and succumb to the needs of her flesh. Isn't that what she wanted? What she desired more than anything? To be ravished by this suave, debonair man who smelled of herbs and spices?

"I hope you're hungry, because I made all of your favorites."

"How do you know what I like? We've never gone out to eat."

His grin was sly. "Twitter, baby!"

"Of course. I should've known. Up to your old stalking ways, I see."

"A quick scroll through your posts revealed you love seafood almost as much as I do, so I made crab cakes, smoked salmon pinwheels, ginger-baked shrimp in pear sauce and some delicious desserts, as well. You're going to love it."

Grace felt her mouth drop open. Slamming it shut, she wondered if this was all a wonderful, amazing dream. Was this guy for real? Her ex had never cooked for her, but expected elaborate meals every weekend. Worse still, he was a homebody who'd rather watch CNN than wine and dine her. Jackson, with his outgoing, down-to-earth personality, appealed to her, especially after the likes of Phillip "Bore Me to Death" Davies. Grace craved excitement, spontaneity, and her ex didn't cut it. She wanted to be with someone who spoiled her, who treated her as if she mattered more than anything in the world—a Renaissance man who cherished and adored her. Was that too much to ask? Apparently it was, because after countless blind dates she'd yet to find the man of her dreams.

"I'm glad you're here, Grace."

Jackson squeezed her hand, stroked her wrist with his fingertips, turned her on with each tender caress. Why did the gesture make her feel special? Desirable? Relationship advice her mother had given her years earlier echoed in her thoughts. *Do what feels right and you'll never go wrong.* Consumed with emotions—lust, hunger, desire and need—Grace decided to do just that, what she'd been fantasizing about doing to Jackson all week. Before she could stop herself she kissed him hard on the mouth. Crushed her body to his. Draped her arms around his neck, pulling him close. Licked his lips as if they were covered in chocolate. Touching his face, she inclined her head to the right and deepened the kiss. Encouraged by his groans, Grace slid her tongue into his mouth, boldly mated with his. And what a sweet, decadent treat it was.

Jackson pinned her to the wall, moving his hands down her shoulders, over her breasts, along her hips and thighs. It was too much. Had to be a dream. Couldn't be happening. Five minutes after arriving at the bakery they were French-kissing. How was that possible? Between kisses, Jackson told her she was sexy, how much he desired her, that he'd been thinking about her all day. His confession fueled her passion, made her want him, need him, even more. The magic and euphoria of his kiss was her undoing, causing her senses to spin and her body to tremble. His urgent caress made her nipples erect, her clit tingle and her panties wet.

An acrid odor polluted the air. Breaking off the kiss, her eyes flew open and her nose twitched. "Do you smell that?" she asked, peering over his shoulder.

Panic flickered across his face. "Shit! The appetizers!"

Whipping around, Jackson tore out of the room.

Grace followed him through the bakery, hoping and praying the kitchen wasn't on fire. Mad at herself for losing control, she inwardly berated herself for making the first move. *This is all my fault. I should have kept my hands to myself, and off of Jackson!*

Sprinting into the kitchen, Jackson swiped cooking mitts off the counter and slid them on without breaking his stride. In his haste to reach the stove, he knocked over the orange bottle beside the blender and it crashed to the floor. Glass flew in every direction, and the dark liquid pooled under the workstation. A strong, piquant

scent that made Grace think of cherries and warm caramel filled the air, and she knew it was bourbon. Springing to action, she grabbed the mouth of the bottle, tossed
it in the garbage can and searched the closet for a mop
and a broom.

Clouds of smoke billowed out of the oven. Waving
a hand in front of her face, Grace felt her eyes tear, but
she focused on the task at hand, on doing what she could
to help Jackson. Within seconds, the floor was swept,
mopped and gleaming.

One by one, Jackson retrieved the blackened baking trays and dropped them on the counter. The appetizers were so badly burned Grace couldn't decipher
what they were. A gray haze, thicker than LA smog,
engulfed the kitchen.

"Sorry about this. I feel like such an ass."

"No worries," she said with a small smile. "It can
happen to anyone."

"You must think I'm a total screwup."

His words—and his harsh tone—surprised her.
In that moment, Grace realized she'd pegged him all
wrong. Jackson was arrogant, sure, but he was also
kind, terribly sweet and sincere. Feeling guilty for causing the fire, and hoping to make amends, she leaned
over and gave him a peck on the cheek. "No way. Not
at all. You're a perfect gentleman."

His eyes smiled. "Why, thank you, Ms. Nicholas."

"It's the thought that counts, and you get an A for
effort."

And *for that amazing first kiss!*

"Really? An A for effort *and* another kiss?" Grinning, he wiggled his eyebrows and glanced frantically

around the kitchen. "It's like that? Hold on. Let me burn something else!"

Grace burst out laughing. She couldn't believe Jackson was making light of the situation. Her ex would have thrown a fit, blamed her for ruining his dinner and sulked for the rest of the evening. Giving it more thought, Grace realized the fire never would've happened because kissing wasn't Phillip's thing—spending her money on frivolous crap was, but after she'd discovered the truth about him she'd dumped him and cut him out of her life. It hurt that he didn't love her, but Grace chose to focus on the present instead of the demise of their relationship.

"That was some kiss," he said. "Next time I'll make sure I turn off the oven before you arrive—"

"There won't be a next time." She fervently nodded her head. "It was a crazy, spur-of-the-moment thing that caught me off guard, but it won't happen again. It can't."

His face fell, but Grace didn't let his wounded expression stop her from speaking her mind. The kiss was a mistake and she wanted Jackson to know exactly where she stood, so there were no hard feelings later. "I'll admit it. I'm attracted to you," she confessed. His gaze was distracting, but Grace spoke with confidence, refusing to be sidetracked by his dreamy eyes. "We can't be friends, and we'll never be lovers—"

"Never say never. I've been told I can be quite persuasive." His grin was back in full force, weakening her resolve. "Let's start with dessert," he proposed, gesturing to the glass case at the rear of the room. "I made mint truffles, bourbon bread pudding and chocolate *stracciatella* cupcakes."

Her mouth watered and her stomach groaned. Grace

didn't know what *stracciatella* was, but she liked the way the word rolled off his tongue and wondered what else his tongue could do. Washing the thought from her mind, she fingered the hair at the nape of her neck, weighing the pros and cons of breaking bread with a man she found irresistible.

"Care to join me?"

Without hesitation, Grace said, "I'd love to." And she meant it. Hanging out with Jackson beat going home to an empty house, and she wanted to learn more about him and his successful family business. After all, that was the reason why she was here. To dig up dirt on the Draysons. To unearth their secrets. Back on her game, she fixed him with a seductive gaze and flashed her brightest smile. "Lead the way, Jackson. I'm right behind you."

Chapter 5

"**W**hy aren't you married?"

Surprised by the question as they sat at the table eating their dessert/dinner, Grace picked up her glass and drank her tangerine cocktail to buy herself time. The drink was ice-cold, sweet and delicious, and she finished it within seconds. "Wow, talk about wasting no time getting into my business," she quipped, pointing her spoon at him. "If I wasn't starving and this bourbon bread pudding didn't taste like heaven, I'd be out of here."

"You can't blame me. Beautiful women usually have several boyfriends, and I don't want some muscle-bound jock busting in here, ready to beat me to a pulp for romancing his bae."

A giggle tickled her throat. "How many times do I have to tell you that I'm single?"

Jackson picked up the pitcher, filled her glass to the brim and Grace nodded her thanks.

"You didn't answer my question."

"No one's ever asked."

"Bullshit!" he argued. "You have 'wifey' written all over you and I find it hard to believe men aren't beating down your door to get to you."

"My focus is on the bakery, not finding Mr. Right. Not that I believe he exists. I don't."

He looked doubtful, as if he didn't believe her, and slowly stroked his jaw.

"This is crazy. We've only just met and here I am spilling my guts to you."

"No worries, bae. I'll send you my bill."

This time Grace couldn't stop it and a laugh fell from her lips.

"Most women your age are champing at the bit for an engagement ring."

"Not me," she quipped, dead serious. "Relationships are a pain in the ass."

"Care to elaborate?"

Tasting her cupcake, she decided it was divine and savored every delicious morsel. "Men are weird, complicated creatures and I don't have the time or the energy to figure them out. There are only so many hours in the day, and I'm a busy girl with a million things to do."

"It sounds like you've been dating the wrong men."

"Honestly, I don't get you guys," she complained, voicing her frustrations about the opposite sex, namely her ex-boyfriend. "You act like committed relationships are a death sentence, but you want all the perks and benefits of being my man. What's up with that?"

"You're overthinking things."

"Care to elaborate?" she said, posing the question he'd asked her seconds earlier.

"Men are simple. We only need three things to make us happy. That's it. Give us what we need and you'll have our heart forever."

"Is that so?" Skeptical but intrigued, she leaned forward in her chair, desperate to get the inside scoop on the opposite sex. *This is better than reading* Maxim *and* GQ, Grace decided, unable to control her excitement. She didn't have any guy friends, and since she didn't feel comfortable talking to her dad about her dating life she kept her questions to herself. Hearing Jackson's take on relationships was a treat. "Don't keep me in suspense. What are they?"

"ESPN, steak and mind-blowing sex."

Cracking up, Grace picked up her napkin and threw it at his face. "Now I see why you're still single. You're a handful and too slick for your own good!"

Thunder roared and lightning lit up the sky, but Grace was having such a good time with Jackson she didn't care about the havoc Mother Nature was unleashing on the city. Grace hoped her dad was home from dinner, and planned to text him before she headed home. Although she wasn't ready to leave the bakery just yet. Ready to talk for hours more she asked Jackson about his professional background. "Don't take this the wrong way, but you don't look like a baker."

"I get that all the time, but there's more to me than meets the eye."

"What were you doing before you opened Lillian's with your siblings?"

His deep, hearty chuckle filled the candlelit room.

"What *haven't* I done? I've been a bank manager, a business consultant, worked in real estate—buying and flipping commercial and residential properties—and I was even a professional poker player."

"Were you any good?"

"Google me."

Jackson winked and for the second time in minutes Grace laughed out loud. They'd been talking nonstop since they sat down at the table an hour earlier, and the more she learned about Jackson, the more she liked him. He was a character—loads of fun and sexy as hell, too.

"My winnings were enough to buy my dream car and a gorgeous home in Beacon Hill."

"Then why quit? Surely it was more glamorous than whipping up scones and éclairs."

Jackson parted his lips but didn't speak, then swallowed hard. He popped a truffle into his mouth, then washed it down with tangerine juice. "I got tired of the fast-and-furious lifestyle," he explained. "Every day was one big party, and soon I was spiraling out of control."

"When did you know it was time to walk away?"

"Last winter when I woke up in Amsterdam, hungover, disorientated and sick as a dog. Thanks to my family I got out of the game before it destroyed me."

Riveted, her ears perked up. Grace straightened in her chair, eager to hear more.

"Initially when Chase approached me about opening a bakery I laughed in his face, but once I spoke to my great-aunt Lillian and realized she had faith in us, I had a change of heart. I liked the idea of working with my siblings, and after Chase crunched the numbers and showed them to me, I jumped on board."

"Any regrets?"

"None whatsoever. I love this community, the shop and our customers, and most days I can't wait to get here and experiment in the kitchen." Jackson sighed, a wistful expression on his face as he glanced around the shop. "Life is a trip sometimes. After I quit poker and my engagement ended, I'd planned to go backpacking through Europe, but look at me now. I'm running a successful business with my siblings and, most shocking of all, I can actually bake."

Engagement? Speechless, the word rattled around in her brain. Grace wanted to know details, but Jackson changed the subject. Making a mental note to ask him about his former fiancée later, she answered his question about her favorite hobbies and interests. Nothing was off-limits—past relationships, stresses at work and sex—and his jokes put her in a playful state of mind. Jackson's eyes lit up when the conversation turned to travel. He spoke about the trip he'd taken to Barcelona with his father and brother last summer, vividly recounting the highlights of their two-week excursion.

"Do you have any vacation plans this year?" he asked.

Grace made her eyes wide, faking a bewildered look. "Vacation? What's that? It's been so long since I had one I can't remember what that is!"

"That's a shame. We'll have to remedy that, and the sooner the better."

His words, though spoken in jest, made her feel warm and giddy inside.

"Have you ever been to Fiji?"

"No, why?" she asked. "Trying to sell me your timeshare?"

Jackson chuckled and the sound of his hearty laugh brought a smile to her lips.

"I'm going there in October for a few days. You should come and keep me company."

"Do you invite everyone you meet at Lillian's on vacation?"

"No, just smart, captivating beauties named Grace."

"You'd make a great politician," she joked, wagging an index finger at him. "You always know just what to say, and you're not only charming, but persuasive, as well."

"Does that mean you'll come?"

"No, it means I'll think about it. A lot can happen in four months."

Jackson nodded, then spoke in such a smooth voice her heart swooned. "You're right. We could end up eloping to Las Vegas and celebrating there."

"Or," she said with a laugh, "I'll go with my dad to London to check out an NBA pre-season game as planned. No offense, Jackson, but no one gets in the way of me and my favorite sport."

Happiness covered his face. "You like basketball? No way! Who's your team?"

"New York. They're going all the way this season."

"You wish. Me and four of my friends have a better chance of winning the NBA championship than your sorry, punk-ass team."

"Wanna bet?"

"Name your terms, Ms. Nicholas."

Grace wore a triumphant smirk. She knew Jackson would never agree to the wager, but she enjoyed teasing him. Hearing her cell phone buzz, she glanced down at the table. She had three new text messages from Bronwyn, but she decided to read them later. "A thousand-dollar donation to the winner's favorite charity."

"A thousand dollars? That's a lot of money."

"Put up or shut up," she quipped, an amused expression on her face.

"I'm in, but I also want a home-cooked meal as a part of the wager." Jackson wore a wry smile, took her hand in his and squeezed it. "It's been a long time since I had steak."

"Then I suggest you eat at your mother's house, because I don't cook. I bake."

No, you don't, whispered her inner voice. *You haven't stepped foot in the kitchen since your mom died, remember?*

He licked his lips. "No sweat. I'll teach you."

Thoughts of kissing him, of having her way with him, bombarded her mind, giving her goose bumps and heart palpitations. Earlier, she'd allowed herself to get caught up in the moment, and kissing him was the sexiest, most liberating thing she'd ever done.

"Did you go to culinary school?" Jackson asked.

"Yes, of course. You?"

"No. Seattle University."

"I graduated from the Seattle Culinary Academy, but everything I know about baking I learned from my mom—" Feeling her cheeks flush with heat and her throat close up, Grace broke off speaking and willed herself not to cry.

Jackson was mad at himself for upsetting her. Through his research, he'd read numerous articles about Rosemary Nicholas, the quiet, soft-spoken founder and proprietor of Sweetness Bakery who'd died last year.

Jackson couldn't take his eyes off Grace. He could see her inner turmoil, how the pain of her mother's unexpected death affected her, and admired her strength. Jackson didn't know what he'd do if something ever happened to his parents. Graham and Nadia Drayson were the heart and soul of his family and he couldn't imagine his life without them.

Gently caressing her hand, which was cradled in his, he spoke quietly, hoped his words would make her smile. "Your mom opened Sweetness Bakery when you were just a toddler. Did she immediately put you to work, or wait until you were out of diapers?"

Grace had the prettiest eyes and they twinkled as she spoke about her mother. Listening to her, Jackson was struck by two things—how much she loved her family and how knowledgeable she was about the bakery business. Grace knew her stuff, and became animated discussing the widely successful ads and promotions she'd done over the years with her mother's blessing.

"You've been baking your entire life," he pointed out. "Do you ever get sick of it?"

"I don't bake anymore. After my mom passed, I decided to take a break from the kitchen and help my dad manage the shop instead."

"Do you like crunching numbers?"

She nodded, but Jackson saw sadness flicker in her eyes and knew she was lying.

"How did I do? Did you enjoy your dessert/dinner?"

Her smile returned, blinding him with its warmth. "You knocked it out of the park!"

"I was hoping you'd say that."

"Everything was delicious, Jackson."

"I'm glad you approve."

"You're an amazing baker," she said, her tone filled with awe. "I'm sure your girlfriends love your culinary skills, but I bet your boys give you a lot of grief for working here."

"Not just my boys. My parents, too. My mom hates that my siblings and I opened a bakery, and thinks we should close up shop. According to Nadia, we're squandering the education she helped pay for, and embarrassing her and my father in the process."

"Does it bother you that your parents aren't supportive?"

Jackson shrugged. He couldn't bring himself to admit the truth out loud—not without sounding like a wuss—but it hurt that his parents thought he was a joke. Pushing his problems to the farthest corner of his mind, he returned to the conversation, giving Grace his full attention. He didn't want her to think he was bored. He wasn't. Far from it. He was enjoying himself immensely and couldn't remember the last time a woman had held his interest for this long. "Why did your last relationship end?" he asked, studying her over the rim of his glass.

"Holy moly! What's with all the personal questions?"

He met her gaze, heard her girlish laugh and felt ten feet tall. Making her smile gave him great satisfaction. Her sultry stare made his pulse soar and his heart raced faster than a Ferrari zipping down the freeway. "You're like a piece of baklava. Hard on the outside, but soft and fluffy in the middle, and I'm completely intrigued by you."

A smirk lit her lips. "Did you just compare me to a Turkish dessert?"

"I want to get to know you better—"

"Me, too," she said, cutting him off. "So, tell me more about your broken engagement."

Jackson coughed into his fist and shifted around on his chair. Mimi had betrayed him in the worst possible way and he had to forget her. He couldn't get his lips to work and struggled with his words for several seconds. "Mimi wasn't the woman I thought she was."

"I *told* you relationships were a pain in the ass!"

They laughed and nodded their heads in agreement.

"To friendship," Grace proposed, raising her drink in the air. "And decadent desserts!"

They clinked glasses and Jackson decided he was definitely seeing her again.

The niggling voice in the back of his head reminded him that Grace was the enemy, not an ally, but he ignored the warning. Tonight, she was sexy eye candy, the only woman he wanted to be with. Beneath her frosty facade was a fiery, spirited woman who'd been blessed with beauty and smarts, and he wanted to take her out on a formal date.

It was a wonder they hadn't met before last Friday. They ate at the same restaurants, enjoyed the same local bands and knew a lot of the same people. Their personalities definitely complemented each other, and they had so much in common the time quickly slipped by. Jackson liked her authenticity. Her honesty was refreshing and her girly, high-pitched laugh made him crack up every time.

"Gosh, this is good," she said. "I might have to steal the recipe when you're not looking."

Watching her devour her third mint truffle brought a grin to Jackson's mouth. He'd never seen a woman eat like Grace. She nibbled on each pastry and seemed to savor every bite, oohing and ahhing with more zeal than a game show audience.

A Lenny Kravitz song came on the radio and Grace danced around in her seat. Singing "American Woman" in perfect pitch she rocked her shoulders from side to side and snapped her fingers to the pulsing, infectious beat.

"Have you tried the Draynut yet?" he asked. "There's some in the fridge if you're interested."

"I got my hands on one this morning and it was amazing. I bet it's your best seller."

"No, actually our specialty cakes are and you'll never guess who makes them."

"What do you know about designing cakes?"

"Initially, nothing, so I watched online videos, got tips from my great-aunt Lillian and baked for hours every day. Fast forward two months and I'm busier than ever! On Sunday, I made a Lightning McQueen cake for a nine-year-old's birthday, on Tuesday I made a replica of the Holy Bible for a church appreciation luncheon and this morning I finished an elaborate cake for a Bollywood-themed wedding at the Four Seasons tomorrow."

"No way! Are you serious? What does it look like? How many tiers does it have?"

"I'd rather show you than tell you."

Jackson stood and came around the table. A month ago he'd been hired to make the wedding cake, and his goal was not only to impress the fortysomething couple tying the knot on Saturday, but also their four hundred guests. Excited to show Grace his latest design, he helped her up to her feet and pulled her to his side.

"Where are we going?"

"To see my newest creation, of course."

Taking her hand, he led her through the store, past the offices, kitchen and pantry, and into the cake storage room at the rear of the building. Jackson strode through the door and flipped on the lights. They flickered, cut in and out, and he made a mental note to change the weak bulb in the morning.

Spotting the covered wedding cake on the back table of the temperature-controlled room, Jackson felt a rush of pride. If someone had told him a year ago he'd quit playing poker and start designing specialty cakes, he would have accused them of being crazy. But here he was, doing just that, and making the bakery oodles of cash.

The door slammed shut and Grace yelped.

"Don't worry. It's not locked."

"So where's this one-of-a-kind, Jackson Drayson creation you've been bragging about?"

Whipping off the plastic cover with a flourish, he stepped aside and gestured to the gold-and-white cake with a nod of his head. "There it is. The Taj Mahal—"

Eyes wide, Grace gasped. Cupping a hand over her mouth, she glanced from Jackson to the wedding cake and back again. "Oh, my goodness! It's stunning!" she said, gushing, her excitement evident in her jubilant tone. "How did you make it? It must have taken you forever."

Grace had a million questions and he answered them all, taking the time to explain why he'd created the edible masterpiece. "The couple asked me to wow their guests, and since they grew up in Agra, India, I thought a Taj Mahal–shaped cake was the perfect choice."

"I'm blown away…"

Her words, like her lush red lips, were a turn-on.

"You weren't kidding," she continued. "There *is* more to you than meets the eye."

"Likewise, Ms. Nicholas. You're some kind of woman."

Jackson hooked an arm around her waist and pulled her right up to his chest.

"What are you doing?"

"Isn't it obvious?" His gaze zeroed in on her mouth. "I'm going to kiss you and it's going to be hot. Just like the first time."

Inhaling a sharp breath, she slanted her head to the right and stared deep into his eyes.

Jackson brushed his lips against her cheeks and over her delicate button nose, then slid his hands down her hips to grab her big, beautiful ass. Grace whimpered and clutched desperately at his T-shirt—it was all the encouragement he needed. He kissed her so hard on the mouth, with such hunger and passion, it stole *his* breath. He tasted bourbon on her tongue as it flicked eagerly against his own, and hints of nutmeg and cinnamon, too. His body ached for her, throbbed with uncontrollable need, and an erection rose inside his boxer briefs.

Overtaken by lust, his mind was bombarded with thoughts of sexing her, right then and there in the storage room, and Jackson fought the urge to do just that. To bend Grace over his work station, rip off her panties and take her from behind. If it wasn't their first time nothing would have stopped him from sexing her. Grace wanted him. That, he knew for sure. He felt it in her kiss, heard it in her moans and her urgent caress. Her hands were everywhere—buried in his hair, stroking his face, touching him through his shirt. Jackson nibbled on her bottom lip, licked the corners of her sweet, intoxicating mouth. "I've never wanted anyone as much as I want you right now," he whispered, shocked by his admission. "I have to get you out of this dress."

Her head fell back and Jackson placed soft kisses up her long, slender neck.

"Let's go to your place. It's closer."

Grace froze, her body tensed. "We can't."

"Why? Do you have roommates? Are they home right now?"

"No roommates, just an overprotective father who still treats me like a little girl."

Jackson disguised his disappointment by wearing a blank expression on his face. Second thoughts about hooking up with Grace flooded his mind. He didn't want trouble with her father and feared he was barking up the wrong tree. Then she gave him a shy smile, one that lit up her amazing brown eyes, and an electric shock zapped his body. He had to have her. Tonight. By any means necessary. Even if it meant breaking his rules and taking her back to his place.

"I live at home," she said, "and even though I have the basement all to myself my father would kill me if he came home and saw you inside my suite."

"Baby, no problem. I understand. We'll go to my crib instead."

"We just met. Furthermore, I'm not that kind of girl."

"Yes you are. You're a fun, gregarious woman who likes living on the wild side."

Grace laughed. "Hardly. I cover my eyes during thunderstorms and scary movies!"

"We won't do anything you don't want to do."

Dropping her gaze to her hands, she checked her gold watch.

Fearful she was going to turn him down, he said,

"I'm having a great time with you and I don't want it to end. We'll talk, listen to music and share a few more kisses. No pressure. I promise."

Unable to keep his hands off of her, he grazed his lips against her neck, nibbled on her earlobe. She made his heart rev, his mind spin, and one kiss wasn't enough. Would never be enough. Jackson was so busy devouring her mouth and stroking her supple flesh he didn't notice the light had gone out in the storage room until he opened his eyes and saw pitch-black darkness.

"Can we get out of here? This place is cold and dark and it's giving me the creeps."

Jackson couldn't see Grace's face, but he heard the apprehension in her voice, the fear. To reassure her everything was all right, he patted her hips and dropped a kiss on her cheek. Taking his cell phone out of his back pocket, Jackson pressed the power button and used the illuminated screen to find the door. He grabbed the handle and turned it. It didn't open. Puzzled, he scratched his head. "What the hell? This room is never locked."

"Let me try."

While Grace fiddled with the lock, Jackson moved around the small room, hoping to find a phone signal. "My cell doesn't get reception in here. Try yours."

"I—I don't have it," she stammered. "I left it on the table."

"Damn, I was hoping to call Mariah to come get us—"

"Are you telling me we're stuck in here? Trapped like damn mice?"

Grace lost it. Banged on the door. Screamed for help. Stomped her feet, then kicked off her sandals and threw them in frustration. "Don't just stand there!" she snapped. "If we're loud enough, someone walking by the bakery will hear us and call for help."

It wasn't going to happen, not with a violent thunderstorm raging outside, but Jackson knew better than to argue with her. To appease her, he banged on the door until his arms ached and his hands throbbed in pain. Reality set in, hitting him like a fist to the gut. They were stuck in the walk-in fridge and he had no one to blame but himself.

Chapter 6

The refrigerated storage room was a narrow space, smaller than a prison cell, and freezing cold now that they'd been there for four hours. Feeling a bitter chill stab her flesh, Grace rubbed her hands together and rocked back and forth on her sandals, which she'd put back on to warm her body. Her limbs were numb and her teeth were chattering so loud in her ears she couldn't think straight. She didn't have the mental fortitude to create an escape plan.

The display light on Jackson's iPhone illuminated the space, but the butterflies fluttering in her stomach intensified. Grace searched for a way out, staring in every nook and cranny for freedom. Metal shelves, as high as the ceiling, were stocked with bagged fruits, frozen pastry shells and an assortment of baked goods. The sweet, intoxicating scent in the air made Grace think of her mother. Rosemary grew fruits in their backyard, and as a child Grace used to pick raspberries and eat them straight off the bush.

"Grace, are you okay?"

Snorting, her lips pursed together in suppressed rage, she shot him a dirty look. "What do you think? I'm stuck in a cold, dark fridge, and no one knows I'm even here."

"Sit down. Let's talk. You can tell me more about Sweetness." Jackson put his cell phone on one of the shelves, sat down on the tile floor and crossed his legs at the ankles. "You might as well get comfortable. We're going to be here for a while."

"I—I can't stay in here," she stammered, willing herself not to cry, her voice trembling with fear and emotion. "I'll freeze to death, or die of asphyxiation!"

"Grace, calm down. You're yelling—"

"Don't tell me what to do."

"We're not going to die. It's a fridge, not a freezer..."

Her eyes narrowed, focusing on his face. Was he laughing at her? Making light of the situation? To regain her composure, she inhaled the fruity aroma in the room. It didn't help. The more she thought about her predicament, the more hopeless she felt, the more afraid.

"There's plenty of air in here and tons of food," he continued in a soft, quiet tone.

Pacing the length of the room, she racked her brain for the solution to her problem, because there was no way in hell she was spending the night in the storage-room fridge with Jackson. "I can't stay in here. I have things to do."

"Did you have another date lined up tonight?"

"This isn't a date. It's a business meeting."

"Do you kiss all of your business associates, or just me?"

Stumped, unable to think of a fitting response, Grace slanted her head to the left and hitched a hand to her hip. The next time Jackson said something smart to her, or flashed that stupid I'm-the-man grin, it was on. She'd had enough of his fresh mouth for one night.

"You don't strike me as the booty-call type."

"It's your fault we're even in this stupid mess," she grumbled.

"How was I supposed to know the door was locked? It's never locked."

"This wouldn't have happened if you weren't showing off."

Jackson pointed a finger at his chest. "You're blaming me for trying to impress you?" he asked, shock evident in his voice. "Have you looked in the mirror lately?"

Grace pretended his words didn't faze her, but inwardly her heart was dancing.

"You're stunning, in every sense of the word, and I'll do anything to make you smile, including showing off my one-of-a-kind specialty cakes."

And just like that, her anger abated, her expression softened and heat flooded her body. Jackson had a hold on her she couldn't explain, and it boggled her mind.

"Grace, hang in there. It will be five a.m. in no time and we'll be out of here."

"Ever the optimist," she said sourly, shaking her head. "I wasn't kidding when I said you'd make a great politician. You always know just what to say to smooth things over."

"I know," he teased, his face alive with mischief. "But I only use my powers for good."

"You think you're so cute—"

"I'm not? But my grandmother says I am!"

"God, you think everything's a joke, but it's not. This is serious. We're trapped!"

His gaze darkened and his jaw clenched, but Jackson didn't argue, didn't fight back.

Silence descended on the room, engulfed the space like smoke. They stood in silence for what felt like hours, but Grace didn't mind the quiet. She was glad to be alone with her thoughts, relieved to finally have some peace.

Tired of pacing, her feet sore, she sat down on the floor. Jackson was an arm's length away, and his spicy, woodsy cologne tickled her nostrils. Sleep pulled at her eyes, making her feel tired and weak. Grace thought about her dad, the mounds of paperwork on her office desk and her roller derby match on Sunday afternoon. Thinking about her teammates—her eleven sisters— made her smile. They'd been there when she needed them most, in her darkest hour, and Grace felt fortunate to have them in her life.

"Grace, I'm sorry. I know it stinks being in here, but it could be a lot worse…"

Really? Because I can't think of anything worse than being stuck in this fridge!

"I'll make it up to you," he continued. "Courtside seats to New York's season opener should do it, don't you think? I hate your team, but I love NYC, and since I know all the best places to eat, shop and play we'll party like it's 1999!"

"You'd fly across the country just to watch a basketball game?"

"Of course." Jackson nodded his head, wore a serious face. "Life is meant for living and I won't squander it, because tomorrow isn't promised to anyone."

"I guess that's one way of looking at it."

"Trust me, Grace, that's the *only* way of looking at it."

"Have you always had a laissez-faire attitude about life?"

His gaze dimmed and the smile slid off his mouth.

What was wrong? Grace wondered, scanning his face for clues. Why did he suddenly look so sad? So heartbroken? To lighten the mood and his spirits, she joked, "What do you do when you're not charming customers and whipping up Jackson Drayson specialty cakes?"

Jackson took such a long time to answer the question Grace was sure he'd missed it.

"I work out, play golf with my old man, hang out with my boys and coach basketball."

"No way!" she said, pleased to learn they had something else in common. "I played point guard for my high school and college teams."

"Were you any good?"

Grace winked. "Google me."

His dreamy grin knocked her for six, hitting her like an arrow to the heart.

"What grade do you coach?"

"I coach a wheelchair basketball team and we won the championship last year."

"Wow, Jackson, that's amazing! Congratulations," she said. "How did you get involved with the team?"

"In college, my roommate was struck by a distracted driver while walking to class," he explained in a solemn tone. "Diego was paralyzed from the waist down, but he never lost his zest for life or his love of sports.

Once I saw how much fun he was having in the league I wanted to get involved, so I offered to coach and the rest is history."

"How is your friend doing now?"

"Better than me!" Jackson chuckled good-naturedly. "He has a lovely wife, three great kids and a successful software business. Diego's living the American dream and I couldn't be happier for him. He deserves every success…"

Grace admired how open and honest Jackson was about his life. He spoke about his sheltered upbringing, his past mistakes and his disastrous dating history. His charity work and his dedication to his wheelchair basketball team impressed her the most. Jackson was a great conversationalist, by far the most interesting person she'd ever met, and although Grace was shivering like a nudist caught in a snowstorm, she was enjoying his company. "Wow, you have more layers than a *chocotorta*!" she joked, giving him a taste of his own medicine. "You strut around Lillian's like some badass baker, but you're actually a softie with a huge heart."

Their eyes met, zeroing in on each other, and desire singed her flesh.

"Did you just compare me to an Argentine chocolate cake?"

"Yes," she quipped, full of attitude. "You're welcome."

"You're a ballsy spitfire, and beautiful too…"

His voice tickled her earlobes, and south of the border. His piercing gaze made her mouth dry and scattered her thoughts. Memories of their first kiss filled her mind, causing her skin to tingle with desire, and

Grace wondered if he was thinking about their steamy lip-lock, too.

"Do you still play basketball?" he asked. "My rec team could use another point guard."

"Not anymore. I used to be on a coed team, but I quit once I joined the Seattle roller derby. I didn't have enough time to play both and once I started skating, I was hooked."

"No way. I don't believe you."

Grace rolled her eyes; she couldn't help it. Most people—namely her father's snotty society friends at the country club—were shocked and appalled to learn Grace played such a rough, physical sport, so Jackson's reaction didn't surprise her. "Looks can be deceiving," she reminded him, recalling their conversation during dinner. "You of all people should know that. After all, you are a former poker player turned baker who coaches wheelchair basketball."

"You're a roller derby girl? Get out of here. Seriously?"

Oozing with confidence, Grace nodded and pointed her thumbs at her chest. "My nickname's Lady MacDeath and I'm the lead jammer for the Curvy Crashers. We compete all over the country and finished third in our division last season. This year, we have a shot of winning it all, and we will. You just wait and see."

"Damn, I never would have guessed it. You're so soft and delicate."

"There's nothing *soft* or *delicate* about me."

Jackson raised his hands in the air. His expression was contrite and his tone was remorseful. "Grace, I didn't mean to offend you—"

"Just because I grew up in the suburbs doesn't mean I'm a wallflower. I'm not. I'm strong and tough and I have a mean right hook, so don't mess with me."

He chuckled and told her he'd never dream of it. "When's your next match? I want to come."

"Why? So you can make fun of me?"

"No, so I can cheer you on. In case you haven't noticed I have a sweet spot for smart, captivating beauties who aren't afraid to speak their minds." He added, "And that's you."

Sitting motionless, transfixed by the intensity of his gaze, Grace imagined herself kissing him and ripping his clothes off his body. Shivers spread from the tips of her ears to her toes. His smile stirred her senses, made her brain short-circuit and her limbs shake uncontrollably. To conquer her explicit thoughts, Grace pressed her eyes shut and rested her head against the wall.

"You're cold." Jackson moved beside her, slid his arms around her shoulders and held her tight. "I'm not putting the moves on you. I just can't stand to see you shiver…"

Too tired to argue, Grace snuggled against him, relishing the feel of being in his arms. His touch was needed, welcome, and his clean, refreshing cologne helped soothe her mind. Dozing off, Grace couldn't help thinking, *I wish you* were *making a move!*

Jackson glanced down at his cell phone, checked the time and sighed in relief. Mariah would be at the bakery within the hour and this bizarre ordeal would finally be over. So much for keeping his plan under wraps. Mariah would have a million questions about

Grace, and if Jackson wanted to keep his life—and his job—he'd have to tell his sister the truth.

Grace stirred beside him, murmuring softly in her sleep, and Jackson tightened his hold around her. Pulling her close to his chest, he shut his eyes and inhaled her soothing lavender scent. He liked feeling her body against his, imagined them naked, moving together as one, and desire scorched his flesh. Jackson touched her hair, tenderly caressed her neck and the enticing curves of her hips. He wanted Grace, could almost taste her kiss, but he feared she'd spurn his advances. And for good reason. He'd blown it last night, messed up. Everything that could go wrong had, and he blamed himself for their current predicament. Hell, he'd screwed up the moment Grace had arrived. He'd burned the appetizers, knocked over an expensive bottle of bourbon that splashed onto her designer clothes and, if that wasn't bad enough, they'd been forced to spend the night in the storage-room fridge. After their wild, crazy night Jackson wouldn't be surprised if Grace never wanted to see him again. He'd messed up royally, but was determined to make it up to her.

He considered their night together. Yeah, they'd yelled and bickered, even insulted each other, but as far as Jackson was concerned it was water under the bridge. Grace had captured his attention the moment they'd sat down to dinner. She was so energetic and fascinating that he'd committed everything about her to memory. She loved jazz music, had dreams of relocating to New York, was addicted to raisin bagels and coffee and spoke Spanish fluently. Added to that, she had a blinding white smile and the best pair of legs in the city.

Jackson lowered his mouth to hers. He couldn't help

it. He cautioned himself to pull away, before he lost control, but her eyes fluttered open and she returned his kiss. It was filled with passion and hunger. Grace didn't speak, didn't need to. She communicated what she wanted with her lips, tongue and hands.

The light from his cell phone illuminated the sparkle in her eyes, the smirk on her lips and her come-hither expression. Sliding onto his lap, Grace grabbed his shirt collar, yanked him forward and mated desperately with his tongue. *Hot damn!* His body hardened and an erection grew inside his pants. Grace was ballsy and aggressive and Jackson loved it, loved not knowing what to expect next. She stroked his neck, slid her delicate hands down his shoulders, turned him out with each flick of her tongue against his ear. Did it ever feel good. Her moans consumed the air, exciting him, making him want her even more.

Jackson undid the buttons on her dress. Surprised to see a butterfly tattoo painted above her right breast, visible through her white push-up bra, he kissed it, then drew his tongue along the intricate design. He couldn't stop kissing her, licking her, stroking her warm, sweet flesh.

Arching her back, she swayed her body to an inaudible beat. Grace told him how good it felt, how much she desired him, and begged for more. He couldn't believe this was the same woman who'd given him the cold shoulder days earlier, who'd adamantly refused to give him her phone number. "Damn," he breathed, nibbling on the corners of her lips. "I want you, Grace, God knows I do, but not like this. Not in the fridge inside my family's bakery."

"Slow your roll, Jackson." Her eyes were bright, alive

with warmth and humor. "We've only known each other for a week. What kind of girl do you think I am?"

"The spontaneous type who enjoys breaking the rules and living in the moment."

Desire was etched on her face, seeped into her sultry tone. "Only time will tell."

"Your beauty boggles my mind, you know that?" Nuzzling his nose against hers, then along her bare shoulder, he playfully cupped her ass in the palms of his hands, rubbing and squeezing it. Desperate for her, it took everything in him not to free his erection from his pants and plunge it deep inside her sex. "I'm glad you don't have an Instagram account."

"Why? Afraid of a little healthy competition?

"No, because your smile's so beautiful it would break the internet!"

Grace laughed and Jackson decided it was the loveliest sound he'd ever heard.

Chapter 7

"I wish we were at my place." Jackson brushed his mouth against her ear. "I'd carry you into my master suite, give you a champagne bath, then make love to you…"

Grace sucked in a deep breath. *Oh, my. Yes! Take. Me. Now!* Delicious shudders racked her body, prickling her skin with goose bumps. Jackson spoke in a low, seductive tone that made her skin tingle and her panties wet. His gaze slid down her curves, boldly assessing her, turning her on like only he could. It had never been like this. No one had ever made her feel this way before—desperate, ravenous—and Grace didn't know how to regain control.

His mouth, on hers, put her in an amorous mood, and nothing else mattered but pleasing him. The magic and euphoria of Jackson's kiss weakened her resolve, stole every rational thought from her mind, and Grace knew they were going to have sex on the storage-room floor. At the thought, every nerve in her body quivered.

Grace inhaled his scent, drank in his cologne, fighting the urge to rip the clothes off his body. Her hands had a mind of their own. She touched and caressed his face, his shoulders, and stroked his six-pack underneath his T-shirt.

Overcome with desire, Grace did what she'd fantasized about doing all week—she kissed Jackson passionately, fervently, and it felt amazing. Feeling his hands on her breasts, cupping them, kneading them, teasing her erect nipples with his thumbs, she hoped they'd dive between her thighs to play there, too.

Light flooded the room and high heels slapped violently against the floor.

"Jack, is that you? What the hell is going on in here?"

Grace froze. Startled, her eyes flew open and she jumped to her feet. Squinting to see who'd barged inside the storage room, she dropped her hands to her side and studied the new arrival in the handkerchief-hem blouse and skinny jeans. Grace wondered who the petite beauty was, and why she was yelling at Jackson. Her stomach clenched, then dropped to her feet. Was the woman his girlfriend? Grace gulped. Were they serious? Did he love her?

"Thank God you're here," Jackson said. "Are we ever glad to see you."

Confused, she gave Jackson a sideways glance. *We are?* Staring down at her clothes, she was shocked to see her push-up bra on full display. She did up the buttons, straightened her dress and stuffed her feet back into her sandals. Grace didn't have to look in the mirror to know her appearance was frightening. Day-old makeup, wrinkled clothes, wild, messy hair. It was a wonder the woman didn't spin around and run screaming from the room.

"What's going on? Why are you in here playing tonsil hockey with this skank?"

"Excuse me?" Grace cocked her head, glaring back at the stranger. *Who was she calling a skank?*

"Mariah, relax. It's not what you think. This is my friend Grace." Nodding, Jackson clasped her hand and wore a broad, reassuring smile, one that caused her anger to dissolve. "Grace, this is my sister."

Sighing inwardly, Grace felt the tension leave her body. *Thank God.* She liked Jackson and wanted to get to know him better, but not if he was dating every woman in Seattle. Grace was annoyed his sister had insulted her earlier, but she decided to take the high road, and smiled politely. "It's wonderful to meet you, Mariah. I've heard a lot about you."

"I can't say the same."

"I brought Grace in here to show her the fondant cake I made for the Chakpram wedding and we got locked inside," Jackson explained. "Needless to say, it's been one hell of a night."

Mariah adamantly shook her head. "That's impossible. The door's never locked."

"Crazy, I know, but we've been stuck in here for the past six hours."

"I'm *sure* you made good use of your time."

Mariah gave her a disgusted look, and Grace wished the ground would open and swallow her up. How much had Mariah seen? Had she seen them pawing each other? Heard them groaning? Grunting?

"I tried to call for help, but my cell doesn't get reception in here."

"Jack, you shouldn't have been back here to begin with. The storage room is for supplies, not late-night booty calls."

"Mariah, you're way out of line. It wasn't like that."

"Yes, it was. With you it *always* is."

"It won't happen again."

"Sure it won't," she grumbled, giving him her back.

Jackson walked up behind his sister, shifted her around and gave her a loud, wet, kiss on the cheek. Mariah giggled and swatted his shoulder. "Cut it out." Her voice was stern, but her eyes were smiling. "You're going to ruin my makeup and Everett's coming by later for lunch."

"I'm going home to shower and change. I'll be back in a few."

"Please hurry. Kelsey called in sick again and Nita doesn't start until ten o'clock."

"No worries, sis. I'll be back before you know it."

The siblings embraced and Grace decided it was the perfect time to make her getaway.

"It was nice meeting you, Mariah. All the best with the bakery."

"Grace," she said tightly, her tone colder than the storage-room fridge.

Anxious to leave, Grace marched out of the room, past the offices and down the hallway. The music was still playing in the bakery and if not for her sour mood she would've laughed at the irony of the situation. Pharrell was chirping about how happy he was, his vocals suffused with joy and cheer, but Grace was pissed, so wound up her body was shaking for all the wrong reasons. Mad at herself for getting caught in the act with Jackson, she swiped her things off the table and dropped her cell phone in her purse. Desperate to make a hasty getaway, she sped through the bakery and burst through the front door. The sooner she got away from Mariah and her ugly attitude, the better.

Hazy and covered with clouds, the morning sky looked somber and bleak, but Grace had never been so relieved to be outside. Putting on her sunglasses, she inhaled the crisp, warm air.

"Grace, wait! Hold up! I'll walk you to your car."

Hearing Jackson's voice, Grace stopped and glanced over her shoulder. At the sight of him, her mouth dried and her heart stopped. God, he was dreamy. She couldn't look at Jackson without thinking about sex, and wanted him now. Could almost taste his kiss, and his gentle caress. Even though she'd insulted him, he'd taken great care of her last night and she'd never forget how special he made her feel. And what an amazing kisser he was. If not for Mariah busting into the storage room, they probably would have made love on the floor. The thought made her girly parts tingle and goose bumps flood her skin.

"Sorry about that."

Jackson slid a hand around her waist and hugged her possessively to his side, as if they were a couple in a loving, committed relationship. The gesture made her feel cherished, cared for, and though she tried she couldn't wipe the lopsided smile off her face.

"Mariah didn't mean any harm—"

"Is that why she called me a skank?"

"Don't take it personal. She didn't mean anything by it."

Grace couldn't stop from rolling her eyes.

"Mariah came in this morning, found the bakery a mess, couldn't reach me on my cell and was shocked to find us kissing in the storage room."

His explanation made sense, as did his sister's behavior, but her run-in with Mariah had left a bitter taste in her mouth and Grace didn't care if she ever saw his sister again. Troubled, she asked the question at the forefront of her mind. "Are you seeing anyone?"

"You mean besides you? Why date around, when I can have the sexiest woman alive?"

He drew her into his arms, held her tight.

"You'll be in later, right? What time?"

"No, my days of spying on you are over."

"They are?" He sounded disappointed and surprise colored his cheeks. "Really?"

"Jackson, I'm sorry," she said, overcome with guilt and shame. "I never should have done it in the first place. I don't know what I was thinking."

"Apology accepted. I probably would have done the same thing if I were you." He shrugged, wore an impish smile. "Actually, I have. Poker is a cutthroat game and sometimes to win you have to play dirty."

Grace wanted to know more about his past, but before she could ask the question running through her mind, Jackson spoke. Mesmerized by his husky tone, she couldn't concentrate on what he was saying. The man was a perfect ten. Boyish grin, hot body, smart, confident and romantic, he was everything a woman could want.

"I'm taking you out tonight," Jackson announced.

Remembering the last time she'd heard those words, her body tensed.

"We can go anywhere you want. Canlis. Metropolitan Grill. El Gaucho." Jackson winked and affectionately patted her hips. "New York City."

A smile tugged at her lips, threatened to explode across her mouth, but Grace kept a straight face. She couldn't risk losing her heart to a man who'd never commit to her, so it was imperative she keep her distance. "I don't think we should make seeing each other a habit."

"Why not?"

"Ask your sister."

"We'll talk tonight. What time's good for you?"

"I have plans with my dad." It was a lie. She had nothing to do besides wash her hair, but Grace didn't want to hurt his feelings. They'd had a great night together, filled with tons of laughs, interesting conversation and scorching French kisses, but they could never be more than friends, so why bother? Why risk her heart for a man incapable of love and commitment?

"Tomorrow then," Jackson said, as determined as ever to get his way. "We'll have Sunday brunch, then spend the rest of the day exploring this great city."

"I can't. I have a game at five o'clock."

"Even better, we'll have a victory dinner at Palisade fit for a roller derby queen." Jackson touched her face, drew a finger against her cheek. "Please don't shoot me down again. I don't think my ego could take it. I'm enthralled by you, Grace, and I don't care how long it takes. I'll make you mine."

Stunned—and aroused—by his declaration, all Grace could do was stare at him. She couldn't catch her breath and struggled to find the right words. Didn't have any. Couldn't think of anything to say. Grace wanted to see Jackson again, loved the idea of having a romantic dinner with him, but she didn't want to go to the most expensive restaurants in the city. If they did, word could get back to her father, and he'd kill her for publicly breaking bread with the enemy. "I'll have dinner with you next weekend," she said quietly, loving how his hands felt on her skin, how her body responded enthusiastically to his touch.

"I don't think I can wait that long."

Grace laughed. "You'll survive."

"Seven days sounds like an eternity."

You're right. It does. But I have to be smart about this. I don't want to get hurt again.

"Can we go somewhere less popular?" Grace asked. "If we go to Palisade there's a good chance I'll run into someone I know and that would be a disaster."

Jackson nodded his head, gave her a sympathetic smile. "I understand."

"You do?"

"Honestly, I don't care where we go as long as we're together." He cupped her chin in his hands, gave her a pensive look. "I'll pick you up next Saturday at seven o'clock sharp—"

"No!" Her voice was loud, filled with panic. "Let's meet here. It's safer that way."

"You don't want me to meet your pops? Why? Are you ashamed of me?"

"No, of course not, but no one can find out about us. My father would kill me if he knew about last night, and with everything going on at the bakery I don't want to add to his stress."

To smooth things over, she reached up on her tiptoes and gave him a peck on the lips.

"I won't tell a soul. It will be our little secret."

"And Mariah's," she quipped.

"I'll talk to her. Don't worry."

"Thanks, Jackson. That means a lot to me."

"Wear a short red dress for our date," he instructed, brushing an errant strand of hair away from her face. "I love the color on you, and your long legs, as well."

"I'll see what I can do."

"You better, or you'll never have my bourbon pudding again."

Grace widened her eyes and clapped her hands to her face. "Oh, no!" she wailed in an anguished voice. "Not the bourbon pudding! Whatever will I do?"

Jackson cracked up and Grace laughed, too.

The sun crept over the horizon, lined the sky with brilliant shades of yellow, orange and pink, and Grace knew if she didn't hurry she wouldn't have time to change before work, and if she showed up at Sweetness in the same outfit she wore yesterday, her dad would put two and two together and there'd be hell to pay. "We'll talk later." She unlocked her vehicle with the keyless remote, and as the headlights flashed and beeped she hurried toward it. "See ya!"

"You drive a Jaguar XF?" Jackson asked, gesturing to her car with a nod of his head.

"It was my mother's car. I'm more of an SUV girl, but it's growing on me. Why? Do you have a problem with the brand?"

"Not at all. In fact I have the exact same car, except mine has tinted windows…"

Following his gaze, Grace spotted a black Jaguar XF parked across the street under a lamppost and laughed to herself. *Wonders never cease*, she thought, reading his personalized license plate. "'Bigshot,' huh?" she teased, wiggling her eyebrows. "How fitting."

"I think so. Why be mediocre when I can be the best?"

Jackson opened her car door and Grace slid inside. Taking her cell phone out of her purse, she noticed it was dead and plugged it into the charger.

"Speaking of the best, I need your phone number. How am I supposed to sweep you off your feet if we don't talk every night for hours on end about how perfect you are?"

Amused, Grace rattled off her cell number while putting on her seat belt.

"Drive safely, beautiful. I'll call you later."

"I will. Thanks for everything, especially dessert. It was delicious."

"Are you talking about me, or my pudding?"

Grace laughed, told him he was crazy and put the key in the ignition. As she turned to wave goodbye, Jackson captured her lips in a kiss. Warmth spread through her body, scorching her skin with fire as his tongue boldly claimed her mouth. Fighting the urge to pull him into the car and pick up where they'd left off in the storage room, Grace braced her hands against his chest and broke off the kiss. "Bye, Jackson."

Reluctantly, Jackson stepped onto the sidewalk. He watched the Jaguar cruise down the street, turn left at the intersection and disappear out of sight. Damn, what a night. He'd spent it with an angel and wanted to reunite with her tonight. There was no way in hell he was waiting until next Saturday. Screw that. He'd make an impromptu visit to Sweetness if he had to, because seven days without seeing Grace would be torture.

Turning toward the bakery, he spotted Mariah in the front window and released a deep sigh. He contemplated jumping in his car and driving off, but decided better of it. No sense making a bad situation worse. Besides, he wouldn't get far. His sister was pissed, no doubt about it.

Her arms were folded across her chest, her eyes were dark with anger and if looks could kill he'd be six feet under the ground.

Chapter 8

"**W**hich team is Grace on?" Diego asked. "What position does she play? Is she any good, or just eye candy?"

Grace Nicholas isn't just eye candy, Jackson thought, his chest puffed up with pride, his smile bright enough to power the entire Seattle roller-skating rink with light. She was infinitely more. *Grace is, hands down, the smartest, most appealing woman I've ever met, and I want her bad.*

"How long has Grace been a roller derby girl?"

"Beats me." Jackson sat down in the seat beside Diego's wheelchair, and handed him an ice-cold beer. The arena was filled with fans, reeked of sweat, cheese nachos and cotton candy, and the drunken women seated behind him giggled as they sang off-key. It wasn't Jackson's scene, but since Grace was in the building and he wanted to surprise her, he'd stick it out until her match was over. "If we didn't hear about this game on the radio, I would have missed it. I spoke to Grace last night, and twice today, but she didn't mention her big match."

"You know why, right?"

"No, but I'm sure you're going to tell me."

"It's obvious," he said smugly, his raised eyebrows crawling up his forehead. "Grace didn't invite you to her game because she didn't want to risk you running into her *real* boyfriend. I don't blame her. You're not exactly a catch…"

Jackson didn't speak, but the murderous expression on his face must have terrified his buddy because Diego bumped elbows with him in an attempt to smooth things over.

"Relax, man. I'm just playing. Everyone knows roller derby chicks love bakers!"

Diego chuckled, guffawed as if he was watching an HBO comedy special.

"No offense, bro, but your career sucks." He snorted and shook his head as if he was scolding his five-year-old son. "Quit playing Martha Stewart and get a real job. A *man's* job."

His best friend had been teasing him ever since they'd left the house, but Jackson knew what to say to shut him up. "Diss me one more time and you're uninvited to Chase's bachelor party next month. Now, *that's* funny!"

Panic flashed in his eyes. "We always joke around," he argued, raking a hand through his short brown hair. "We're boys. That's what we do. When did you get so touchy?"

When the woman of my dreams walked into my fam-

ily bakery and turned my life upside down. Startled by the realization, Jackson deleted the thought from his mind and picked up his beer. It had been a week since Freezergate—what Grace jokingly called the incident in the storage room fridge—but it felt like months had passed since the ordeal. They'd seen each other every night, and their secret affair was not just thrilling, but hot. Some nights Grace came to his place for dinner, one night they went dancing and out for drinks and yesterday they'd both played hooky from work and drove the eighty miles to nearby Ashford, Washington.

His thoughts returned to yesterday and a grin claimed his mouth. To impress her, he'd planned several fun-filled activities and romantic surprises. They'd kicked off the day with a two-hour food tour that took them from one delicious restaurant to the next, then enjoyed a massage at the best spa in the city, but the highlight of the day was boating along Mineral Lake. The sky was clear, the weather perfect, and Grace was warm and personable. They'd talked and laughed, kissed under a curtain of stars, and by the time they returned home Jackson was so hot for Grace he couldn't think about anything but making love to her.

"Don't do anything stupid like fall for her," Diego warned. "Grace works for the competition, and Mariah and Chase will kill you if you hook up with her. Don't do it, man."

Jackson tuned him out and kept his eyes open for Grace, searching the arena hoping to catch a glimpse of the brown-eyed beauty. At home, watching TV earlier, he'd texted Grace so many times Diego had accused him of being sprung. Jackson didn't mind his buddy poking fun at him—he didn't give a rat's ass what he thought.

Grace was special to him, more important than any other woman in his life, and he wanted her to know he was thinking about her when they were apart. Add to that, they had incredible chemistry. Jackson had needs, insatiable sexual desires, and something told him the roller derby beauty with the luscious lips and banging body could make his fantasies come true.

"Introducing the Curvy Crashers!" the female announcer shouted, her voice slicing through the noise in the packed stadium. "Make some noise for Lady MacDeath!"

Jackson surged to his feet and pumped his fists in the air. Cheering louder than anyone, he watched as the Curvy Crashers took to the rink, smiling, waving and blowing kisses to their fans. Grace looked tough but sexy in her purple starred helmet, fitted tank top and itty-bitty black shorts. The number 49 was written on her cheeks, her makeup was eye-catching and her fishnet stockings drew his gaze down her thighs and legs. He followed her around the rink, tracked her every move, thoughts of making love to her dominating his thoughts.

"Who's Grace?"

"Number forty-nine."

Diego whistled. "Jack, you were right. She *is* stunning."

"She's also fun, sophisticated and ridiculously smart," he said, his heart filled with pride.

"Start an I-Love-Grace fan club," he joked. "You're damn near blushing!"

The teams found their place at the start line, the referee blew the whistle and they were off. Roller derby was high-energy, loud and physical, and Jackson loved everything about it. The noise, the hits, how tough and competitive the players were. The crowd was wild, the air was charged with electricity and the excitement was palpable. Flying around the track, Grace showed off her incredible agility, strength and speed. Hectic and fast-paced, there was a lot happening on the track—players fighting, pushing and falling on top of each other—but Jackson kept his eyes on Grace, blocked out everything else in the vicinity, and focused his gaze on her pretty face.

"Man, this game is intense."

"You're telling me," Jackson agreed, blowing out a deep breath. "They've only played fifteen minutes, but I'm sitting here sweating bullets and we still have another period to go."

"How do they score points?"

"Hell if I know! I'm a roller derby virgin just like you."

Diego took his iPhone out of his jacket pocket and accessed the internet. "Thank God for Google."

The men chuckled and bumped beer bottles.

"I remember Grace mentioning that she was the lead jammer for her team, whatever that means, but I have no clue how the ref is calling the game, or how the teams earn points."

"'Each team puts five players out on the track. One jammer, one pivot and three blockers,'" Diego said as he slid his index finger across the screen. "'The lead jammer is the only person who can score, and does so by passing the skaters on the opposing team.'"

Listening to Diego read the rules of the game, he realized Grace was the only person on her team who could score, and cheered when she crashed into an opposing player, and the buxom blonde fell to the ground.

Decked out in elbow, wrist and knee pads, Grace looked ready for combat, and watching her fight to the lead of the pack made him wonder what kind of lover she was. Was she expressive in bed? Passionate? Erotic? Down for whatever? They hadn't made love yet, but remembering their X-rated make-out session in his car last night as they were parked on a secluded area on Highland Drive gave Jackson an instant erection. He desired her more than anything, but he sensed she wasn't ready to take their relationship to the next level, and Jackson didn't want to pressure her to have sex. Grace was worth waiting for, and he knew when they finally made love it was going to be incredible. Just like her kisses.

Jackson heard his cell phone chime, read his newest text message and smiled. Chase was checking up on him, and wanted to know how he was doing. Jackson missed his brother and wished he was back from his trip with Amber. If Chase was around he'd have someone to vent to, because talking to Diego was out of the question. His friend was in a sour mood, upset because he was at odds with his wife, and his negativity was depressing. Mariah was ten times worse. Jackson sent Chase a text, then put his cell in his pocket.

His thoughts returned to Freezergate and the heated argument he'd had with his sister that morning. He'd made the mistake of telling Mariah he was romantically interested in Grace, and she'd erupted like Mount St. Helens. She'd threatened to disown him if he hooked up with the competition again, and insisted they summon Chase home for an emergency family meeting.

A week later, Mariah was still giving him the cold shoulder, and the tension inside Lillian's was stifling his creativity. He had a week to make three speciality cakes, but hadn't started them yet. Jackson couldn't get Mariah's accusations out of his mind, and when he wasn't reliving their argument he was fantasizing about Grace. Daydreaming about her mouth, her fine feminine shape, squeezing her plump, juicy ass. Tomorrow, after basketball practice, he was going to Lillian's and he wasn't leaving until he finished the wedding cakes he'd been commissioned to make.

"Are you inviting Grace to the Heritage Arts and Awards dinner?"

"So Mariah can kill me with her bare hands? No way. I'm flying solo that night." To please Diego's wife, Ana Sofia, he'd bought two tickets to the black-tie event, but he didn't know which of his female friends to invite. *Damn, I wish I could take Grace*, he thought. He enjoyed her company, knew she'd look great on his arm, but if they went to the awards dinner together the whole world would know they were an item, and Mariah would be pissed if she found out he was romancing the enemy.

Jackson remembered the conversation he'd had with his sister two days earlier in the bakery storage room and felt guilty, knew he'd done wrong. While doing inventory Mariah had asked him point-blank if he was sleeping with Grace, and he'd told her there was nothing gone on. Sweating profusely, he'd swiftly changed the subject, got his sister talking about the new recipes she was working on for the Bite of Seattle festival and fled the room the moment Kelsey walked in, looking for a rolling pin.

"Give it up to the Ballet Misfits for their 220-170 win! Better luck next time, Curvy Crashers," the announcer said. "And a special thank-you to all the fans who braved the rain to come out and cheer on the home team."

While the crowd filed out of the stadium, Jackson and Diego finished their beers.

"I'll be right back. I want to see Grace before she leaves."

Diego glanced at his watch. "If you're not back in ten minutes, I'm out of here."

"What's the rush? It's only five o'clock and the boxing match won't start for hours."

"Yeah, but if we turn up late the food will be gone and I'm starving."

Jackson left the stands and walked through the tunnel, searching for Grace. He stood in the hallway, waiting patiently as players streamed out of the locker rooms, but he didn't see number forty-nine. An Asian woman with dyed red hair and heavy makeup flashed him a salacious smile and he nodded in greeting. "Do you know Grace Nicholas?" he asked, taking his cell out of his pocket to check for missed calls. "Is she still in the changing room?"

"Yeah, the trainer's looking at her knee. She banged it up pretty bad in the second period, but Shannon's taking good care of her."

Jackson took off down the hall, pushed open the door marked Home Team and strode inside. He smelled soap and perfume, noticed the Nike posters on the walls featuring famous female athletes and heard the distant sound of voices.

Entering the showers, he saw Grace and stopped dead in his tracks. She was sitting on a wooden bench, wearing nothing but a black sports bra and boy shorts, clutching her right knee.

"Grace, baby, are you okay?"

Surprise colored her cheeks. "Jackson, what are you doing here?"

"I came to cheer on the home team, of course. You were amazing out there."

"But the game wasn't even close. We lost by fifty points," she argued.

"So? I think you were spectacular tonight, and that's all that matters."

"Sir, you have to leave. Fans aren't allowed in the changing rooms."

"I'm Grace's boyfriend. Who are you?"

"The trainer for the Curvy Crashers," he replied, standing to his full height.

Jackson blinked, regarded the heavyset man in the weathered Reebok sweatsuit that had his name stitched on the top left and swallowed a laugh. He couldn't believe this big, burly giant with the piercings and tattoos had a female name. "Bro, I got it from here. I'll take care of my girl."

The trainer's face fell and he glanced at Grace with a pleading look. "I'll take you home."

"Shannon, I'm fine. Really. It's a small bruise. No biggie."

"Are you sure?" he questioned, a frown wedged between his thick, fuzzy unibrow. "The last time you told me you were fine you ended up in the emergency room in excruciating pain."

"That's not going to happen on my watch." Jackson stalked over to the bench, sat down and inspected Grace's knee. It was bruised, but she stood without difficulty and gave the sour-faced trainer a hug. "I'll see you at practice next week."

Shannon shuffled out of the room with his head down and his shoulders bent.

"I wasn't expecting to see you tonight."

Jackson was trying to concentrate, but it was hard to focus when Grace was standing in front of him practically naked. God had blessed her in many ways and he admired them all. The large breasts, the flat stomach, thick thighs and long, toned legs. His eyes zeroed in on her silver belly ring and Jackson smiled to himself. What else was she hiding? Did she have another piercing down south? Swallowing hard, he pictured them at his house, doing wicked and salacious things in his bedroom, things that would make a rock star blush—

"Earth to Jackson."

At the sound of her voice, he blinked and shook the thought from his mind, giving Grace his full attention. "Why didn't you remind me about your game tonight?"

"Because you think roller derby is a joke and I didn't want you making fun of me."

"I'd never do that. You're strong and powerful and I don't want you to kick my ass!"

"Damn right, and don't you forget it."

Jackson grabbed her around the waist and pulled her down onto his lap. To make her laugh, he screwed his eyes shut and waved a hand in front of his nose. "You stink!"

"Thanks a lot." Grace stuck out her tongue and gave him a shot on the arm. "You sure know how to make a girl feel good after a heartbreaking loss."

"Just doing my part, bae."

Grace linked her hands around his neck and snuggled against him, and Jackson decided there was nothing better than holding her in his arms. "Is forty-nine your favorite number?"

She dropped her gaze to her lap, blew out a deep breath and shook her head.

"What is it?"

"My mom was forty-nine years old when she died." Tears filled her voice, swam in her eyes, and she swallowed hard. "I wear the number in remembrance of her."

They sat in silence, didn't speak, just held each other tight.

"Your mom is gone, but she's in your heart forever so don't run from your memories of her, embrace them," Jackson said in a soothing tone. "I was incredibly close to my grandfather, Oscar, and when he died it felt like my heart had been ripped out of my chest..."

Jackson trailed off, taking a moment to gather his thoughts. He hadn't planned to tell Grace about his grandfather's death, but he felt compelled to, hoped his words gave her strength.

"You know what helped me heal?"

Grace sniffed, shook her head. "No. What?"

"Doing all the things we loved doing together."

"Was your grandfather an avid sportsman, too?"

"Yes. I learned everything I know about golf—*and* women—from him."

"That explains why you have so many female admirers."

"Does that bother you?" he asked, studying her face for clues. Grace wasn't the jealous type, didn't give off that vibe, but Jackson wanted to know for sure. He didn't want to upset her and wanted to be upfront about everything. "Would you prefer if I didn't hang out with my exes?"

"No, of course not. You can do what you want. I have no claims to you."

Ouch. Her words were a slap in the face and moments passed before he recovered.

"It doesn't matter what I think. You told Shannon I'm your girlfriend so he wouldn't kick you out of here, but I'm not."

"Do you want to be?"

"So you can break my heart?" she quipped, shaking her head. "No, thanks. I'll pass."

"Grace, you act like you're the only one who's been hurt. I've been lied to, cheated on and betrayed."

"You have? No way. Someone actually cheated on you?"

"Why does that surprise you?"

"Because you're attractive and successful and smart," she said. "You can have any woman you want, and you probably have!"

"Not any woman. I don't have you."

A seductive grin curled her lips. "Do you want me?"

"Baby, you have no idea."

"Then what are you waiting for?" she teased, cocking her head. "Let's do this."

Her words excited him, caused his erection to harden and strain against his boxer shorts. Jackson kissed her with a savage intensity, mated hungrily with her tongue as it danced around his mouth. He'd never done anything like this before, never had sex in a women's locker room, but everything about it turned him on. The spontaneity. The excitement. The thrill of getting caught in the act—again.

Grace unbuttoned his shirt, shrugged it down his shoulders then tossed it to the floor as if it was a filthy rag rather than a Kenneth Cole design. Rocking her hips against his crotch, she kissed from his earlobe to his neck and along his shoulders. Grace turned him out with her tongue, licked and sucked his nipples as if she was starving and he was the main course.

Kicking off his shoes, he tightened his hold on her hips and stood to his feet.

"Jackson, what are you doing?" Grace tossed her head back and shrieked with laughter. "If you throw out your back and end up on bed rest, don't blame me."

"As long as you're my sexy nurse, it's all good."

"Where are we going?" she asked, her words a breathless pant.

"To get you clean, of course. You're dirty, remember?"

Realization dawned and her face lit up. "You're a *very* bad boy, Jackson Drayson."

"I know, and you love it."

"You're right, baby, I do." Grace clamped her thighs around his waist and placed kisses along his ear and neck. "Being with you makes me high, gives me a rush…"

Jackson entered the shower stall farthest from the locker room, stripped off the rest of his clothes and turned the water on full blast. Steam rose, filling the air, but there was no mistaking her excitement. It shone in her eyes, covered her face, tickled her lips. "Take off your panties, or I'll rip them off," he commanded, setting her down on the ground.

"I like how you think."

"And I like that ass, so turn around, bend over and touch those pretty pink toes."

Chapter 9

Instantly wet, her body throbbing with need, Grace licked her lips as her eyes slid down Jackson's naked body. Lean and toned, he had the physique of a man who spent hours lifting weights at the gym, and staring at his erection made her mouth dry. Thinking about making love to him, of finally doing all the wicked things she'd fantasized about in her dreams, left her breathless and panting for the main event.

"I need you," he declared, his tone a husky growl. "Right here, right now..."

Hypnotized by his touch and his assertive, take-charge tone, Grace did as she was told, assuming the position he'd demanded. His mouth, tongue and hands paid homage to her curves, and her body trembled as he placed kisses down her spine.

"I'm desperate for you, Grace. Have been since the first time you entered Lillian's."

"Then what took you so long to make your move?"

"I don't want a girlfriend, just sex, and I didn't want to give you the wrong impression."

"I don't want anything long-term, either."

"I'm glad we're on the same page."

Jackson kissed her and she laughed inside his mouth. He brushed his nose against hers, told her she was sexy, captivating, said she belonged to him and no one else. Taking her bottom lip between his teeth, he ran his hands up her thighs to her sex. He swirled his fingers in her dark, tight curls, played with them, tugged on them.

Massaging her outer lips with slow, sensual strokes made her thighs quiver. Jackson mashed her breasts together and sucked her erect nipples into his mouth, sucking so vigorously that pleasure and pain exploded inside her body in equal measures.

"Grace, is this what you want? Is this how you like it?"

"Oh, yes," she moaned. "Deeper, Jackson, harder, faster..."

His fingers worked their magic between her legs, stirring and probing her wet clit. Her breathing grew thicker, louder, and when Jackson rubbed his erection against her ass Grace cried out. The move triggered an orgasm so powerful her knees gave out and she collapsed against him. Skin-to-skin, her back pressed flat against his chest, water raining down on them from the showerhead, Grace decided it was the sexiest, most erotic moment of her life. And she wanted more. Jackson must have read her thoughts, sensed what she was thinking, because he slid his hand from between her legs, stalked over to their clothes scattered around the room and took a condom out of his jeans. He ripped open the gold packet and rolled the condom down his shaft.

Excitement fluttered inside Grace's belly. The water was warm and nice, felt good against her skin. Approaching her with a broad grin, his body glistening with water, Jackson looked more like an underwear model than a baker, but when Grace shared her thoughts he laughed. "Tonight, I'll be anything you want me to be."

"I bet you say that to *all* of your customers," she joked with a teasing smile.

"No, just you. You're one in a million, Grace, and I'm going to prove it right now."

Spreading her legs wide, she braced her hands against the wall and arched her back. Slowly, he eased the tip of his erection inside her sex, taking his time filling her with his impressive length. Savoring the moment and how amazing Jackson felt inside her, she pressed her eyes shut and threw her head back. His erection was the best thing that had ever happened to her. It was an instrument of pleasure, and her body responded eagerly to his slow, penetrating stroke.

Taking his hands in hers, Grace used them to roughly cup her breasts. He tweaked her nipples, plucked them, rolled them between his fingers, sending her body into an erotic tailspin. Jackson pumped his hips, thrust powerfully inside her, used his erection to turn her out. Her ears tingled, her knees buckled and her toes curled.

Grabbing a fistful of her hair, he pulled her face toward his and kissed her hard on the mouth. The heat from his tongue spread through her body, setting it on fire. Grace was losing it, didn't know how much more she could take. Jackson moved faster, thrusting, pumping, pounding into her with all his might. Their lovemaking was savage and intense, everything Grace wanted and more.

"Baby, come," he urged, reverently massaging her backside. "Come for me again, and this time don't hold back. Explode for me, baby. Do it now."

Arching her back, she opened her eyes and shot him a sultry smile. "You first."

Jackson spanked her, slapping her bottom once, twice, three spine-tingling times. Grace moaned, then begged him to do it again.

"Keep talking like that and I'll keep you in this shower for the rest of the night," he vowed, slowly licking his lips. "Is that what you want?"

Yes! Yes! Yes! she thought, poking out her butt and rocking against his groin.

"You're a hellcat, and I love it."

Grace raised an eyebrow, feigned an innocent look. "Is that all you love?"

"No. I love your intelligence, and wit, and how you walk into a room and command everyone's attention, and this, of course..." Jackson slid his hands between her legs. "I think I love this the most. It's mine now. Understood?"

His words and his powerful thrusts caused dynamite to explode inside her body. His erection swelled, filling her, consuming her sex. Cursing, he gripped her shoulders, increased his pace, moving faster, thrusting deeper still. The water drowned out his guttural groans as he climaxed, and Grace's frenzied, out-of-control screams. Savoring the feel of him, the sound of his voice, his slow, passionate kisses, she collapsed against the shower wall, trying to catch her breath.

"The next time I come in here I'll have to remember to lock the door."

"Don't bother," he said with an impish grin. "I'll break it down to get to you."

Grace stepped past him. Her legs were wobbly, but she had to get dressed. She searched the floor for her panties. "We better get out of here before the cleaning crew arrives."

"Where do you think you're going?" Jackson captured her around the waist, pulled her back into the shower stall and drew the curtain. "Not so fast, Ms. Nicholas. We're not done yet."

Her eyes widened. "We're not?"

"No. Not until you come inside my mouth." Without warning, Jackson dropped to his knees, hiked her leg up in the air and dipped his tongue inside her, swirling it around in slow, sensual circles, using it as a weapon. He did things with his lips and teeth she'd never experienced, but she enjoyed every second. His mouth hit her pleasure zone over and over again, holding her in place as she unraveled, coming undone.

Hot and tingly all over, she pumped her hips, increasing her pace, desperately chasing her third orgasm. Then it hit, and once the tremors in her sex started she couldn't stop them.

Grace turned into the cul-de-sac, noticed all the lights were on in the house and slammed on her brakes. Through the living room curtains, she spotted someone pacing swiftly back and forth, with their hands propped on their hips, and she frowned. What the hell? The figure could only be one person: her dad. Why wasn't he in bed? Had he had another nightmare? Is that why he was up? He'd called her numerous times that evening, but since he didn't leave a message she didn't phone back and figured she'd talk to him tomorrow instead.

Besides, she'd been tied up—literally—and Jackson wouldn't let her leave his house until she'd had something to eat. After their tryst in the woman's locker room, Jackson had insisted they have a romantic dinner at a trendy, downtown restaurant followed by a nightcap at his place. Promising her an orgasm she'd never forget, he'd bound her hands together with a Burberry scarf, then proceeded to lick her from head to toe, as if she was a Popsicle. An orgasm had rocked her body, leaving her spent and weak, and by the time Jackson slid his erection inside her she was a trembling, quivering mess. They'd enjoyed an explosive night of sex, had made love so many times, Grace was sore all over, but she'd hook up with Jackson again in a heartbeat. The man had a way with words—and had scrumptious lips—and she was counting down until their next date. He was taking her to the symphony tomorrow, then for Creole food, and Grace was so anxious to see him again he was all she could think about.

Sensing what was about to happen next, Grace parked under a lamppost, took her cell phone out of the cup holder and punched in Bronwyn's number. No answer. Determined to speak to her friend, Grace hung up and hit Redial. On the third try, a female voice grunted, "Hello?" and she sighed in relief.

"Bronwyn, I need a favor."

"Grace? Is everything okay?"

"Of course. Everything's great."

"Are you sure? It's…" Bronwyn trailed off speaking,

then gasped. "It's three o'clock in the morning. Where are you? What's going on? "

"Sorry for waking you up, but I need a favor," Grace repeated, her eyes glued to her childhood home. Her father was still pacing, but now he was clutching the cordless phone in his hands, and Grace feared he was calling their friends and family to find out where she was.

"Sure, girl, anything for you. What's up?"

"If my dad calls and asks where I've been, tell him I was with you."

"What's going on? Why are you lying to your old man? Who are you with?"

"I'll explain tomorrow. Just cover for me, okay?"

Bronwyn squealed and Grace feared she'd go deaf in her right ear.

"It's that hottie baker from Lillian's, isn't it? I knew you liked him!"

"Bronwyn, focus—"

"Of course, I'll cover for you. We're girls and, since I love gossip almost as much as I love your macaroon bites, you can tell me about your date with the dreamy baker when I return from my business trip next week. You're making brunch on Wednesday. Don't forget!"

Grace laughed, unable to believe her best friend was hitting her up for a home-cooked meal during her time of need. Desperate, she agreed, but groaned inwardly when Bronwyn squealed again.

"I'm off, so we can spend the whole day together." She added, in a cheeky voice, "That's unless you're not *doing*, I mean, seeing the hottie baker. *Ciao, mamacita!*"

Ending the call, she opened the garage with a click of a button and drove inside. Like a ghost, her dad appeared in the doorway. Annoyed, Grace expelled a deep breath and stepped out of the car. Forcing a smile, she tried to be as casual as possible. "Hey, Dad. You're up late—"

"You missed dinner."

Guilt troubled her conscience, but Grace pushed aside the feeling, telling herself she'd done nothing wrong. She'd spent the night with an exciting, exhilarating man who loved her like she'd never been loved before, and just the thought of him—and his dynamic moves between the sheets—made her body yearn for more. "I had other plans." Grace strode inside and felt a pang of sadness, an overwhelming sense of loss. Her mom would never welcome her home with a hug and kiss again, and the bitter realization brought tears to her eyes. "Dad, it's been a long day. I'm going to bed. We'll talk in the morning, okay?"

"No, we'll talk now." He stood in front of the staircase, cutting off her escape route. "Ainsworth and his parents wanted to meet you, but you were a no-show."

Grace winced. Feeling guilty for letting him down, she couldn't look him in the eye for fear he'd know the truth. "Dad, I'm sorry. It completely slipped my mind."

"I figured as much, so I called to remind you. Why didn't you answer your phone?"

Because I was with Jackson, and nothing else mattered.

"Ainsworth was very disappointed, so I suggested he come by the shop on Friday." His face brightened and his tone softened. "You'll be in, right, pumpkin?"

"Yes, of course, but I have tons of work to do."

"Please? For me? If sales continue to decline at the bakery we're going to need more investors, and if you and Ainsworth become a couple, his parents will definitely back the shop."

"Fine, I'll have a drink with him." Grace raised an index finger. "One coffee. That's it."

"One last thing. We're having dinner at the Ventura estate next Sunday so don't make any other plans. This is important."

"Good night, Dad. I'll see you in the morning."

He leaned in and kissed her forehead. "Have you been drinking?"

Grace swallowed hard, racking her brain for a suitable explanation.

Sniffing the air, he scrutinized her face. "Yes, you definitely smell of alcohol. What's going on? You don't drink and drive. Your mother and I raised you better than that."

"I haven't been drinking, per se. I had a whiskey pear tart for dessert."

Nodding in understanding, he patted her forearm good-naturedly. "Was it good?"

"The best I've ever had."

Grace kissed her dad on the cheek and headed downstairs. Thoughts of Jackson on her mind, she strode into her bedroom suite with a smile on her face and a song in her heart, and the hottie baker was the reason why.

Chapter 10

Grace slipped on her Prada sunglasses, threw open the French doors and strode along the stone walkway, feeling like a million bucks. Clad in a polka-dot bikini, her arms filled with magazines, she set off for the pool, wanting to take advantage of the hot July weather.

Plopping down onto an orange lounge chair, Grace closed her eyes and soaked in the world around her. She heard birds chirping, felt the sun on her face and decided it was going to be a great day. Better than yesterday.

Her body tensed. Yesterday had been a disaster at the shop. Two baristas had called in sick, another had burned her arm on the stove, which resulted in a trip to the emergency room, and a cashier had accidently knocked over a German chocolate cake. Grace shuddered at the memory of the exchange she'd had with the

customer who'd arrived to pick up the ruined gradua-
tion cake and hoped she never saw the foul-mouthed
attorney again.

All week, she'd been working around the clock—
manning the till because the bakery was short-staffed,
interviewing potential candidates for the head baker
position, cleaning the shop after closing—so when her
dad suggested she take today off, she'd accepted his
offer without hesitation. Rashad J was playing on her
cell phone, singing about lost love, and the sound of his
soothing, soulful voice put Grace in a tranquil mood.

Grace heard her cell buzz, knew she had a new text
message and grabbed her phone off the side table. She
hoped it wasn't Ainsworth. They'd met at the shop last
week and he'd been blowing up her phone ever since.
He'd invited her to the Seattle Art Walk, and although
Grace had no plans for Sunday she'd politely declined
his offer. Ainsworth was a conservative man, with old-
fashioned family values, a catch according to her father.
He was nice, sure, chivalrous, too, but Grace wasn't
attracted to him. The Ventura family had money like
Oprah, but Ainsworth didn't do it for her. Didn't ex-
cite her. Not the way Jackson did. Jackson showered
her with affection, knew how to make her laugh and,
most important, treated her like his equal, not a weak,
docile woman who needed his protection. Ainsworth
wanted a puppet, a Stepford wife, and if not for her father she'd have nothing to do with him.

Noting the time, she realized she'd forgotten to have
lunch and decided to order in. Surprised, but pleased to
see the message was from Jackson, Grace bolted upright
in her chair. They'd been texting each other all morning, and every time his name popped up in her inbox

her heart soared. Smiling from ear to ear, she slowly and carefully read his latest message.

Do you want some company? I'll bring you lunch and a kiss.

At the thought of seeing Jackson again, desire warmed her skin and images of last night flashed in her mind. Salsa dancing at the Corbu Lounge. Feeding each other appetizers in their cozy booth. The French kiss that led to a quickie in the darkened coatroom. Locking them inside, he'd yanked down her panties, slipped on a condom and taken her from behind. His behavior had been shocking and unexpected, but Grace didn't stop him. She'd been aroused, turned on by his raunchy sex talk, and encouraged his advances. Minutes later, she'd experienced an orgasm so explosive she'd cursed in Spanish. The memory of their lovemaking made Grace yearn for more. Her gaze strayed to the pool, zeroed in on the cobalt-blue water, and suddenly, sexing Jackson was all she could think about.

Grace considered her response, weighing the pros and cons of inviting Jackson over. Her dad was at work, the housekeeper would be finished and leaving within the hour and Grace would have the entire house to herself. She wanted to see Jackson, but knew if he came over they'd end up in bed, and if her dad found out, he'd never forgive her for disrespecting his home.

Absorbed in composing her message, she didn't notice Edwina was standing in front of her lounge chair until the housekeeper cleared her throat.

"I brought you a snack," she said, resting a tray filled

with fruits and vegetables on the side table. "Can I get you anything else before I leave?"

"No, thank you, Edwina. That will be all. Have fun with your grandkids this afternoon."

"I will, Ms. Grace. See you on Monday."

Settling back in her seat, she crossed her legs at the ankles. Grace enjoyed texting Jackson and cracked up at his jokes. She ate up his compliments like Rocky Road ice cream and couldn't get enough of his wit and humor. Add to that, he was an exquisite lover. It was no surprise she was hot for him. Jackson was a great guy, exactly what she needed in her life, and Grace considered herself lucky to be dating one of the sexiest bachelors in the city. It could all be over tomorrow, and she was going to have fun while it lasted.

"Honey, I'm home!"

Hearing her best friend's voice, Grace tore her gaze away from her cell and glanced at the wooden gate. Looking fresh and vibrant in her sleeveless pink romper, Bronwyn breezed through the backyard, smiling and waving frantically, as if they hadn't seen each other in months rather than a few days.

"Hey, girl, how are you doing?"

Bronwyn groaned and clutched her stomach. "I'm starving, so please feed me!"

"Help yourself." Grace gestured to the table. "Eat as much as you'd like."

Dropping onto a lounge chair, she wrinkled her nose and puckered her lips. "I can't eat this. I need *real* food. Like one of your amazing sriracha burgers with sweet potato fries, and pecan pie for dessert."

"Not today. I don't feel like cooking. Maybe another time."

"Grace, you've been saying that for over a year. When are you going to return to the kitchen and start cooking again? Your customers are dying to know, and so am I."

"I don't want to argue, Bronwyn, so drop it."

"I can't. This pity party has lasted long enough."

Pity party? Pain stabbed her heart. *I lost my mom, not my favorite pair of earrings.*

"I know the last year has been rough on you, but you're a fighter..."

Too choked up to speak, water filling her eyes, Grace dropped her gaze to her lap.

"You *can* overcome this, so dust your apron off and get back in the kitchen."

Her nose itched and her vision blurred but she didn't break down. Was Bronwyn right? Should she quit working in the office and resume baking? Was that the answer to her problems?

"My bridal shower is three weeks away and I need you to whip up some of your scrumptious pastries for the party," she said with a pleading expression on her face. "I want Rodolfo's bitchy mother to like me and your confections are my secret weapon. One bite of your mango cheesecake and the old biddy will be eating out of the palm of my hand, *literally*!"

A giggle fell from Grace's mouth. Leave it to Bronwyn to make her laugh.

"I want to hear what happened with you and baker boy while I was away, so dish the dirt."

"What dirt?" she asked, playing coy. "We've hooked up a few times. No biggie."

Bronwyn tucked her feet under her bottom. "I want

to know everything. Where was your first time? Is Jackson a good lover? Does he go down south?"

Does. He. Ever. Grace couldn't put her thoughts into words, didn't even try. Her friend wouldn't understand, and she didn't want Bronwyn to tease her for gushing about Jackson. "He's incredible," she said quietly, a grin tugging at her mouth. "Let's just leave it at that."

Bronwyn whistled. "I believe you. Your smile is so wide it's blinding!"

To prevent herself from blurting out the truth, Grace popped a piece of watermelon into her mouth. She loved Bronwyn and hated keeping secrets from her, but she didn't feel comfortable discussing her sex life with her best friend. Jackson was special to her, important, and she didn't want to taint their relationship by revealing intimate details about him. It had been a month since Freezergate, but they'd spent so much time together it felt like years had passed since their infamous date at Lillian's, and Grace didn't want to betray his trust.

"What are you doing tonight?"

Jackson, she thought, hiding a smirk.

"Rodolfo's hanging out with his brothers, so I thought we could have a girl's night in."

"Sorry, but I have plans with Jackson. He's taking me to Little India for dinner."

"Great restaurant," Bronwyn said, vigorously nodding. "But can he afford it?"

"What's that supposed to mean?"

"He's not exactly rolling in dough and the entrees start at a hundred bucks."

"Of course he can," she snapped, struggling to control her temper. "He's not a gold digger, if that's what you're implying. Jackson's got plenty of money and he doesn't need mine."

"Jackson's hot, and I'm sure he's fantastic in bed, but don't fall for him. He's a player, just like Phillip, and he'll never, ever commit to you."

Grace wore a composed expression on her face, didn't argue, but inside she was seething. Bronwyn didn't know Jackson, and had no right to badmouth him.

"Things started off great with Philip, too, but we both know how that turned out," Bronwyn continued, her tone matter-of-fact. "Three months into your relationship he was hitting you up for money, demanding expensive gifts and using your Jag to pick up other women."

"Jackson's different. He's nothing like Phillip."

"I hope so, because I don't want to see you get hurt again."

Me, too, Grace thought, hanging her head. *I don't think my heart could take it.*

"Guys like Jackson don't change—"

"We're not serious, so you have nothing to worry about," she said with a shrug. "Except Rodolfo's bitchy mother ruining your big day!"

Bronwyn laughed and the sound of her high-pitched giggles made Grace smile.

"What are you wearing for your date?"

"I don't know. I haven't decided yet. Why?"

"Just make sure it's fabulous. Little India is the hottest new restaurant in town so you have to look amazing tonight." Bronwyn got up from the lounge chair and dragged Grace to her feet. "Let's head inside. I'll make lunch, then I'll help you get ready for your date."

Grace groaned. "Do I have a choice?"

"No, heifer, you don't. Time to go. Beauty waits for no one!"

Grace stood in front of the full-length bedroom mirror, her gaze narrowed, assessing her appearance. The sultry makeup, the peacock-blue dress, the gladiator sandals that drew attention to her long legs. Deciding her outfit was a winner, Grace smiled at her reflection, marveling at how sophisticated she looked in her designer ensemble.

Opening her jewelry box, she found her diamond hoop earrings. After Bronwyn left she'd taken a long, luxurious bubble bath, but as Grace entered her walk-in closet she heard her mother's voice in her ears and ditched the outfit Bronwyn had selected for her to wear.

"Always dress like you're going to meet your worst enemy," Rosemary had advised her numerous times. "And wear red lipstick. Men will find you irresistible."

With that thought in mind, she'd curled her hair and applied her favorite lipstick. The moment Grace put on the metallic sheath dress and peep-toe sandals she knew Jackson wouldn't be able to keep his hands off her. She wanted to impress him and couldn't wait to see the look on his face when she walked into Little India in her sexy outfit.

The home phone rang, interrupting her thoughts, and an unknown number appeared on the screen. "Hello?" she asked, hoping it wasn't a telemarketer.

"Grace, it's me. Don't hang up!"

Disgust curled her lips and seeped into her tone. "What do you want?"

"To see you. To apologize for ruining what we had."

"Phillip, I have nothing to say to you, so please leave me alone."

"I can't. We had something special once and I want you back."

His loud, strident voice pierced her eardrum, grating on her nerves. Why did Phillip have to be obnoxious? Why couldn't he respect her wishes and back off? When was he going to get it through his head they were over for good? Desperate to end their conversation, she said, "Save your breath because there's nothing you can say or do to change my mind. Bye."

"Baby, don't do this to me. We're magic together and I need you in my life."

"You should have thought of that before you deceived me."

"Hear me out," he said, sounding as cocky as ever, as if he was the one calling the shots. "I messed up. I admit it. Please find it in your heart to forgive me..."

Grace couldn't. Didn't have it in her. Phillip didn't deserve her and furthermore she had her eye on someone else—a hottie baker with a heart of gold. Grace couldn't go five minutes without thinking about Jackson and wanted to spend all of her free time with him. She was scared of being hurt again, but her heart was leading her straight to her biggest competitor.

"The Heritage Arts and Awards dinner is on Saturday and I want you to be my date."

"Why? So I can pay your way? No, thanks. I'm through being your meal ticket."

"Baby, let's talk about this. I miss you and I know you miss me."

Grace scoffed. "Yeah, about as much as I miss having pneumonia!"

"This is silly. I'm coming over. I need to see you. We have to talk face-to-face."

"Suit yourself, but I won't be here. I have a date."

"A—a date!" he stammered, his voice a pitiful squeak. "With who—"

"A *real* man who knows how to treat a woman." *And how to make my body sing*, she added silently, swiping her satin clutch off the dresser and tucking it under her arm. Men like Phillip—cocky, slick-talking types—were as common as flour in a bakery, but Jackson was one of a kind, and Grace wanted to be with him, not arguing with her ex on the phone.

"I don't want you dating other guys—"

"I don't care what you want," Grace snapped, wishing she could reach through the phone and whack him with her purse. "We're through, and so is this conversation. See ya!"

Grace dropped the cordless on the cradle and sailed through her bedroom door, thinking about her conversation with Phillip. He'd given her an idea. The Heritage Arts and Awards dinner recognized outstanding educators, artists and cultural leaders for their significant contributions to society, and she wanted to attend the black-tie event.

Fond memories flooded her mind. Three years earlier, she'd attended the awards show with her mother and they'd had the time of their lives. Drinking champagne. Dancing to old-school classics. Mingling with the beautiful people, handing out hugs and business cards. Her mother was gone, but she wanted to attend the event in Rosemary's honor. And she wanted Jackson to be her date. Grace was scared of going public with their relationship, knew her dad would be livid when he discovered she was dating the competition, but she adored Jackson and wanted the world to know they were a couple—especially his ex-girlfriends and female admirers.

Her cell phone buzzed and Grace fished it out of her purse. Reading Jackson's text message, she felt her heart skip a beat and a smile overwhelm her mouth.

Change of plans, beautiful. Meet me at home.

Anything for you, she thought, sailing through her bedroom door. Grace had never felt his good, this sexy and desirable, and Jackson was the reason why. He was always touching her, kissing her, telling her how beautiful and smart she was, and his words bolstered her confidence.

Grace unlocked her car, slid inside the driver's seat and started the engine. Minutes later, she was cruising down the street, singing along with the Sade song playing on the radio.

As she drove, a warm breeze flowed through the sunroof and her thoughts turned to Jackson. The more time they spent together, the more Grace desired him, wished he was her boyfriend and not just her lover. Isn't that why she was going to invite Jackson to the awards dinner? Because she wanted the whole world to know he was hers, and she was his? Initially, they'd only been interested in a sexual relationship, but deep down Grace wanted more, and hoped Jackson did, too.

Anxious to see him, Grace stepped on the gas and weaved in and out of traffic, driving with more finesse than a race car driver. Her speed climbed, and so did her pulse, thundering loudly in her ears. Grace hoped

Jackson had condoms at home because she wanted to make love, and a quickie before dinner was the perfect way to start the night.

Chapter 11

"Perfect timing. I just got back from the grocery store," Jackson said from the doorway of his house, his expression warm and welcoming, a broad grin on his lips. "Now we have everything we need to make a delicious meal *and* rum truffles!"

"I thought we were going to Little India for dinner."

"Why, when we can cook from the comfort of home?"

Hiding a grin, Grace stuck out her tongue. "Cheap-skate!"

Chuckling, Jackson pulled her into his open arms. "Baby, I want you all to myself tonight. I don't want to share you with anyone else, or compete for your attention."

His words, and his touch along her hips, made her heart soar like the birds in the sky.

"I missed you," he said, his husky voice thick with desire. "Come here."

Jackson kissed her, slowly, thoughtfully, as if he was savoring the taste of her mouth. His kiss excited her and his cologne aroused her senses, stirring powerful emotions inside her. Lust consumed her, making it impossible for Grace to control her sexual desires. She moaned into his mouth, linked her arms around his neck, loving his closeness.

He slipped his tongue into her mouth, hungrily mated with hers, devouring her. Moving closer, Grace playfully nibbled at the corners of his mouth, teasing and licking it. They were a perfect fit, an ideal match, and she relished being in his arms. In the bedroom, Jackson satisfied her every wish, and Grace was desperate for him, eager to feel him inside her one more time. Every night, after making love, they'd cuddle in bed, talking for hours, and those memories would stay with her forever.

"We better stop," he said between kisses, nuzzling his nose against hers. "I have onions sautéing on the stove and I don't want to burn the house down."

At the thought of their disastrous first date, Grace laughed out loud. "You're never going to let me live that down, are you?"

"Nope. Never!" Resting his hands on her hips, he steered her down the hallway and through the main floor. She loved the feel of Jackson's place, how spacious, bright and comfortable it was. Every time Grace looked at the mosaic paintings, handmade sculptures and dark wood carvings, she felt as if she'd stepped into a museum. His bachelor pad was filled with leather couches, low-hanging lights, silken drapes and every electronic device known to man. Grace noted how clean the living room was, how the floors and tables gleamed and sparkled, and suspected he had a female house-keeper.

Entering the kitchen, Grace inhaled the piquant aroma in the air. Hip-hop music was playing on the stereo system and the infectious beat of the song made Grace feel like dancing around the room. Mixing bowls filled with vegetables, packaged meat and expensive wine bottles sat on the countertop. "What are you making?"

"Not me, *we*," he amended, affectionately patting her hips. "We're making lentil soup, Tandoori chicken salad, lamb shakuti and coconut rice."

Laughing off his comment, she leaned into him, enjoying the warmth of his touch. "And for dessert?"

"Each other."

Another passionate kiss and her thoughts spun out of control. *I could definitely get used to this*, she decided, circling her arms around his waist. *I could stay here with Jackson forever.*

"I have something for you." Jackson strode into the pantry and flipped on the light.

Sliding onto one of the stools at the breakfast bar, Grace picked up the bottle of chili sauce and scanned the ingredients. Since meeting Jackson, she'd been eating out of control, and if she didn't cut back on the sweets she wouldn't be able to fit into her bridesmaid dress for Bronwyn's wedding, and her best friend would kill her for gaining weight.

"What do you think? Hilarious, right?"

Grace looked up, saw the apron Jackson was holding and burst out laughing, giggling until tears filled her eyes. It was fuchsia, covered in butcher knives, and the caption under the pocket read, I'm the Chef. If You

Don't Follow My Instructions, I'll Stab You! Moved by his thoughtfulness Grace beamed. "You know me so well. I love it."

Jackson smiled wider than a kid perched on Santa's lap. "I was hoping you'd say that."

"I'll cherish it forever."

"That's what I wanted to hear." He slipped the apron over her head, tied it and dropped a kiss on her cheek. "Why don't you chop up the vegetables while I prepare the lamb?"

"I—I can't. I haven't cooked since my mom died," she stammered, her heart threatening to beat out of her chest. "Every time I enter the bakery I relive the moment my mom slumped to the kitchen floor, moaning in pain, and I freeze up."

"Grace, I am so sorry for your loss. That must have been horrible."

"My friends and family think I should put the past behind me and resume baking, but I'm not strong enough. I just can't do it."

Jackson wrapped his arms around her, holding her tight. "Give yourself permission to grieve. It's the natural way of working through your pain and the only way to move forward."

His embrace made her feel comforted, as if she wasn't alone, and she adored him for it.

"Cry if you need to, yell, scream, do whatever it takes to feel better." His tone was full of compassion and sympathy. "And don't do anything you're not ready for, including baking."

"I miss creating new recipes and working with the staff, but I'm broken inside," she said, fighting the tears stinging her eyes. "I don't know how to live without her. My mom was my world, my everything, still is."

"Baby, you don't have to." Jackson rested a hand on her chest. "Your mom is right in here. In your heart. Forever. Her words are with you. Don't ever forget that."

Grace considered his advice. Jackson was right. Her mom *was* with her. She felt Rosemary's presence everywhere—at the bakery, at home, driving around town, even when she was at the gym. As he spoke, praising her for being strong in the face of adversity, her sadness lifted and her mood improved. Grace could always count on Jackson to make her feel better, to make her laugh and smile, and she appreciated his support.

"I want you to take it easy tonight. You've had a long week and you deserve to relax." Jackson swiped the remote control off the counter, handed it to Grace and gave her a peck on the lips. "You can deejay. Don't worry about dinner. I can handle it."

Feeling guilty, as if she was letting him down, she shook her head. "I can help. I'm fine."

"Trust me, I've got this."

"Have you cooked Indian food before?" she asked, noting the cookbooks strewn along the counter. "It's not as easy as it looks. Trust *me*. I learned the hard way several years ago."

"No, but I have all of the necessary ingredients, and as long as I follow Mariah's recipe to a T, everything will taste great." He added, "If it doesn't, I'll order a pizza!"

While Jackson cooked, they chatted about the Bite of Seattle festival, his brother's trip with his girlfriend to Snoqualmie Falls and Bronwyn's wedding.

Grace drummed her fingernails on the countertop, feeling restless and eager for something to do. Her eyes tracked Jackson around the kitchen, watching as he did his thing at the stove. He was a methodical cook, organized and exact in his approach, but Grace was so hungry she'd wolfed down an entire bag of carrots and feared dinner wouldn't be ready for hours.

"Cut the potatoes smaller. They'll cook faster," she advised. "And add more garlic to the soup. It will give the broth flavor and a rich, spicy taste."

Jackson nodded, but Grace knew he wasn't listening to her. He was too busy singing along with the radio, and his impersonation of the king of pop was so bad, Grace cupped her hands around her mouth and booed. "More cooking and less dancing."

He laughed, winking good-naturedly at her, and her heart swelled with happiness.

"Anything else, Ms. Bossy Pants?"

"Yes. Sprinkle some paprika on the lamb and don't forget the cumin. It's essential."

"Damn, you're worse than a backseat driver!"

"I wouldn't have to tell you what to do if you'd listen the first time."

"Since you're an expert, why don't you come over here and show me how it's done?"

"With pleasure!" Grace hopped off her stool, grabbed the wooden spoon from his hand and bumped him aside with her hip. "I've got this. Now, scram!"

Jackson raised his hands in the air and backed away from the stove. "I don't want any trouble. Just dinner!"

As Grace moved around the kitchen, happy images of her mom filled her mind. Rolling cinnamon buns. Icing cupcakes. Singing their favorite Cher song at the top of their lungs. Working side by side with Jackson, Grace realized she was creating wonderful new memories with him, and smiled to herself when he kissed her cheek for the second time in minutes. They talked about their families and past relationships, but Grace dodged his questions about Phillip. They were having a great time and she didn't want to ruin the night by discussing her ex.

"What qualities are you looking for in a guy?"

Grace turned off the stove. "He has to be thoughtful, sincere, loyal and romantic." Snapping her fingers, she fervently nodded. "And gainfully employed. If he doesn't have a j-o-b, he can't have me!"

"What's his name and what did he do?"

"What *didn't* he do?"

Jackson raised his eyebrows. "How did you meet?"

"Through friends. Phillip's brother was dating Bronwyn, so the four of us hung out a lot."

"Sounds cozy."

"It was. I met Phillip a couple months after my mom passed, and he helped fill the void in my life," Grace said sadly, with a heavy heart. "My dad told me Phillip was a gold digger who wanted to get his hands on my trust fund, but I didn't heed his warning."

"What went wrong?"

"Everything. He was a total gentleman when we first met, then he turned into a freakin' nightmare. He'd routinely ask for money and would give me the silent treatment if I refused. Phillip insisted on shopping and dining at premier restaurants, but expected me to pay."

Disgust darkened his face. "What a punk. You should have given him his walking papers the first time he asked you for money, because a real man would never mooch off his girl."

"That's not the worst of it."

"What could be worse than someone you love taking you for a ride?"

"Prior to meeting me, Phillip worked for the largest escort agency in Seattle."

Jackson whistled. "No shit. How did you find out about his past?"

"On my birthday. We ran into one of his 'friends' at the Hyatt, and their exchange piqued my curiosity. The woman was twice his age, dripping in diamonds, and practically threw herself at him. I did some digging, and thanks to Bronwyn I discovered the truth."

"Damn, that's terrible. I hope you dumped his ass, pronto."

"You know it! My mama didn't raise no fool." Yet Grace couldn't think about Philip without feeling like one. She couldn't believe how easily she'd believed his lies, and no longer trusted her own judgment. How could she have been so trusting and naive? If she could date the likes of Phillip Davies for nine months, what did that say about her?

Jackson uncorked the wine, filled two glasses and set them on a round silver tray.

"I can't believe how gullible I was," she complained, speaking her thoughts aloud. "I've always prided myself on being a smart, intelligent woman, but I never saw this coming."

"Don't beat yourself up. You did nothing wrong."

Eager to get the spotlight off of herself, she said, "Your turn. What do you want from a woman? Mind-blowing sex, ESPN privileges and a great steak?"

"Honesty, loyalty, and breakfast in bed from time to time would be nice."

"That's it?" Grace studied him, surprised by his confession. "You don't want much."

"I don't, but most of the women I meet are incapable of meeting my emotional and physical needs." Jackson wore a pensive expression on his face, as if his mind and heart were at odds, then shrugged. "I want to be with someone who understands me, and who I can trust. I want a lover and a best friend all rolled into one."

"Don't we all!" Grace picked up the salad bowl and patted Jackson affectionately on the cheek. "In the meantime, I'll settle for some help setting the table, so hurry up!"

Chapter 12

Candlelight flickered across the dining room, creating a romantic ambiance, but it was the sound of Grace's sultry laugh that put Jackson in an amorous mood. He couldn't take his eyes off her. He found himself remembering what they'd done last night at the Corbu Lounge and could almost hear her moans and groans in his ears now. It took every ounce of self-control he had to keep his hands in his lap and his butt in his seat.

"Thanks for inviting me over tonight." Grace stared at him over the rim of her glass, then took a sip of her wine. "You're great company, Jackson, and I enjoy spending time with you."

"And I with you, except when you're yelling at me in the kitchen!"

Grace gave him an exasperated look, as if she was annoyed with him, but Jackson could tell by her pursed lips that she was trying hard not to laugh.

"You should quit baking and take up acting. You're a natural! You'll win every award under the sun!

"Do you promise to be my leading lady?"

Grace beamed. "I'd love nothing more."

He raised her hand to his mouth and kissed it, allowing his lips to linger on her flesh. "That was the best meal I've had in a long time," he confessed, gesturing to his empty dinner plate. "You lied to me. You're not just a baker, you're an amazing cook, as well."

"Thanks, but I can't take all of the credit. My mom taught me everything I know about Indian cuisine, and if it wasn't for her patience and guidance I'd still be burning water!"

They laughed, moving closer to each other and intertwining fingers. Jackson yearned to love her, to stroke her body, wanted to make her scream his name. They'd made love every night that week, but since he didn't want Grace to think all he cared about was sex, he tore his gaze away from her mouth and deleted the explicit images from his mind.

Jackson was determined to keep his hands to himself, even if it killed him. They had more in common than just sex and he wanted to prove to Grace—and himself—that they could have fun outside of the bedroom. Though, if she made the first move he wouldn't stop her. Hell, who was he fooling? It would be a miracle if he made it through dessert without pouncing on her. Everything about Grace was a turn-on, and he wanted her every second of the day.

"How was practice?" she asked. "Is your team ready to defend their championship this season?"

"Not yet, but I'm confident they'll be in tip-top shape by opening night."

"That's because you're a great coach. The team is lucky to have you."

"I feel the same way about you." His hands were damp with sweat, cold and clammy, but he projected confidence. To Jackson, there was nothing better than being with Grace, and he wanted the world to know she was his girl. He moved closer to her, until their arms were touching. Feeling her warmth, her body against his, instantly calmed his nerves. "Diego's wife, Ana Sofia, is being honored at the Seattle Heritage Arts and Awards for her work with inner-city youth and I promised to attend the dinner to show my support. I know it's short notice, but I want you to be my date."

Jackson watched her, trying to gauge her reaction, but her expression was blank.

"If we attend the event together we'd be coming out publicly, so to speak," he continued, hoping he didn't sound as desperate as he felt. He wanted Grace by his side on Saturday night, didn't want to attend the event without her, and wished he'd asked her to be his date weeks ago instead of trying to hide their relationship from his friends and family. "Are you ready for that?"

"I think so," she said with a shy, endearing smile. "I can't wait to see you all dolled up, because your jeans-and-T-shirt look is getting a little tired!"

Jackson chuckled even though Grace was ribbing him about his wardrobe, and he didn't take offense. She'd said yes and that was all that mattered. "You sound like my mom."

"Is that a good thing or a bad thing?"

"That's a very good thing. I adore my mom and I'm not ashamed to admit it. My mother raised me to be a gentleman, taught me to appreciate, respect and protect women, and I wouldn't be the man I am today without her."

"Will your parents be at the awards show, as well?"

"No, they have a prior engagement, but you'll meet them, and the rest of my family, soon enough," Jackson promised, draping an arm around her shoulders. "I can't wait to show you off Saturday night. You're going to be the belle of the ball."

"And the females in attendance are *definitely* going to swoon over you."

"I don't care about anyone but you."

Her eyes smiled.

"I'm taking you to the Versace store this weekend. There's a red cut-out dress I have in mind for you and I know you're going to love it."

"You bake *and* shop?" she said, her tone filled with awe and wonder. "Be still, my heart. You *are* every woman's dream!"

They shared a laugh and another bottle of wine. Conversation was easy and comfortable, full of flirting, jokes and kisses, and Jackson realized for the first time in his life he was completely content with one woman, uninterested in every other girl. *Is Grace my future? Is she my soul mate? Can I trust her with my heart?* They'd only been dating for a few weeks, much too soon for him to declare his undying love, but he'd fallen hard for her. He didn't want to lose her to someone else, but instead of confessing his feelings, he snapped his mouth shut. Timing was everything, and Jackson didn't want to ruin their relationship by getting ahead of himself. He'd been burned before, betrayed by someone he'd cared deeply about, and was resolved to keep a lid on his emotions for now.

"I'm so excited about the roller derby tournament I'm counting down the days until I leave for Miami," Grace said, unable to sit still, practically bouncing up and down on her chair. "I'm psyched about it and so are my teammates."

"I want to hear all about it. When does it start? How long does it last?"

Animated and excited, Grace told him about the week-long competition on the east coast in August. "Last summer we got creamed, but not this year. If we work hard, we can win it all."

"You're going away for a week? That's a long time."

"You think so? I wanted to go for two weeks, but my teammates couldn't get the time off work. If I can convince Bronwyn to meet up with me, I'll definitely stay longer."

"Can I come?"

"As if!"

"Baby, I'm serious. I have plenty of vacation time, so let's make this trip happen."

Grace scoffed, dismissing his words with a flick of her hand. "You're all talk," she said, rolling her eyes to the ceiling. "We both know you're too busy with the bakery to join me in Miami, so drop the lovey-dovey act. You're not fooling anybody."

"What act? You're going to need something to do in the evenings, so why not *do* me?"

A smirk dimpled her cheeks and curled her lips. "Are you always this raunchy?"

"No, just when I'm with you."

Grace put the cover on the glass bowl and snapped it shut. "That's it," she quipped with a laugh. "No more rum truffles for you!"

The wall clock chimed and Jackson was surprised to see it was one in the morning. He lost track of time whenever Grace was around, and couldn't believe they'd been sitting in the dining room talking for three hours. Jackson couldn't recall ever being this enamored with a woman, but Grace Nicholas was the total package, and he loved spending time with her.

His gaze zeroed in on her, assessing her appearance. Her outfit was the perfect blend of naughty and nice, her dress so appealing he couldn't stop touching the soft material. Her mysterious aura made her irresistible, but it was her fiery wit that drew Jackson to her time and time again. Grace was a firecracker who kept him guessing, and just when he thought he'd figured her out she did something unexpected.

Jackson reflected on their relationship, could feel his grin widen as he remembered all the fun they'd had in recent weeks. Grace had treated him to a steak lunch one afternoon, surprised him with tickets to the football game at his alma mater after a rough day at the bakery and knocked his socks off when she'd shown up at his house in a black leather dress, sans underwear. Pushing him down on the couch, she'd freed his erection from his shorts, straddled him and rode him until he'd climaxed. She'd talked dirty to him, sucked and licked his ears as if they were coated in caramel and pumped her hips with more vigor than a horse jockey. Her behavior was outrageous, more explosive than a windmill dunk, and thinking about their fevered love-making made Jackson want more.

Sweat drenched his T-shirt, causing the lightweight material to cling to his skin. Thirsty, he picked up the water pitcher and filled his glass to the brim. Their eyes met, and time crawled to a stop. Desire flooded Jackson's body, leaving him speechless. His scalp tingled and blood shot to his groin. He'd seen that expression on her face before, knew exactly what Grace was thinking, what she wanted, what she needed, and made his move.

"Let's go upstairs," he proposed, rising to his feet. Her perfume washed over him, tickling his nostrils. She smelled like a tropical garden, fragrant and sweet, and her heady scent roused his senses. "I'll draw you a bath."

"You spoil me."

"I enjoy taking care of you. Are you complaining?"

"No, but I think it's time I return the favor."

"You're always doing nice things for me." To make her laugh, he patted her hips and joked, "But if you want to give me a massage, I won't object. You turned me out last night, and I have a crick in my neck to prove it!"

"I told you to lay still, but you wouldn't listen."

"You poured hot wax on my chest! What did you *expect* me to do!"

Giggling, she unbuckled his belt and unzipped his khaki pants.

"Grace, what are you doing?"

"Isn't it obvious? I'm thanking you for a wonderful evening."

Jackson pressed his eyes shut, groaned as her soft, delicate fingers seized his erection and worked their magic. His head fell back, rolled from side to side. It was impossible to think, to concentrate, when Grace was touching him, but he broke through the haze and met her eyes. "We've made love every night this week. Actually, every day since the first time in the locker room."

"Is that a problem?"

"No, but I don't want you to think all I care about is sex."

Her eyebrows rose and her lips parted in surprise, but she didn't speak.

"I want more than just your body, Grace. I want all of you. Your heart, your—"

Jackson heard the tremble in his voice, the vulnerability, and trailed off. He took a deep breath to steady his nerves, but it didn't help. His heart continued to pound in his ears, and his thoughts swirled like leaves in the wind. Why was it so hard for him to open up to her? Why couldn't he tell Grace the truth? That he'd fallen for her, and wanted them to be exclusive?

"Jackson, you're one of the sweetest, kindest people I've ever met, and I feel fortunate to have you in my life," she said. "I want you to know you're very special to me."

"I am? Prove it."

"I'm going to kiss you *here*," she said, stroking his shaft. "And you're going to love it."

Damn right I will. No one can ever compare to you.

"No shouting, okay, baby? I don't want your neighbors to call the cops again..."

Jackson cracked up. He'd never forget, for as long as he lived, the expression on Grace's face when Seattle's finest had showed up on his doorstep, demanding to have a look around. A week later, the incident still made him laugh.

"You know it's your fault the cops showed up, right?"

"If you say so," she cooed. "But *you're* the one who ripped off my dress and had your way with me."

Images from last Friday night filled his mind. They'd gotten carried away while playing poker, ended up having sex on the staircase and the next thing Jackson knew the cops were beating down his door. He'd done a lot of crazy things in his life, things he was ashamed of, but getting caught in the act with Grace wasn't one of them. They'd laughed about it, and made love again once the officers left.

"Jackson, you're right. I should leave before I get us in trouble—"

Grace spun around, but he grabbed her around the waist and pulled her to his chest. "You're not going anywhere. You're mine for the rest of the night."

"Just for tonight?" she whispered, brushing her lips against his mouth.

"How does forever sound?"

It wasn't a kiss; it was a sensuous assault. Grace devoured his mouth, kissing him with such hunger *his* knees buckled, and he slumped against the wall. Crushing her to him, he feasted on her lips, staked his claim with his tongue. It mated with hers, swirling and dancing around her minty fresh mouth.

Grace returned his kiss, matching his fire and intensity. He unzipped her dress, pushed it down her hips and tossed it aside, then made quick work of his clothes. Naked, their bodies pressed against each other, Jackson could feel desire radiating off her skin in waves. He sensed her excitement, how eager she was to please him, to love him, and sucked in a breath when she trailed kisses across his body, moving ever so slowly down his chest.

Licking his lips, he waited anxiously for Grace to make his fantasies a reality. She lowered herself to the floor, clutched his hips and drew his erection into her mouth, sucking it as if she was dying of thirst, and tingles stabbed his spine.

"Damn, baby, what are you doing to me?"

Grace twirled her tongue around the tip of Jackson's shaft, licking and teasing it. He sounded desperate, as if he was being tortured, but his face was covered in pleasure, the picture of pure bliss. Hearing his savage groans and grunts bouncing off the walls gave Grace a rush of adrenaline. She was the boss, in complete control, and it was a heady, exhilarating feeling.

Eager to please, she reached up and caressed his chest, tweaking his erect nipples. Having her way with him, calling the shots, was the ultimate turn-on. Grace decided right then and there, as Jackson thrusted himself deeper inside her mouth, that he was the only man for her, the only man she ever wanted to be intimate with. He was right about their relationship. It *was* about more than just great sex. They had great conversations, never ran out of topics to discuss, and confided in each other. More than anything, he made her feel supported, cherished, as if there was nothing he wouldn't do for her. The icing on the cake? The mind-blowing, toe-curling, earth-shattering sex. Jackson knew her body inside out, pleased her in every way, and no one would ever be able to take his place in the bedroom.

Gripping his shaft with her hands, she grazed her teeth along his length, nipping at it, licking and sucking. Grace enjoyed pleasing Jackson, loved being in control of his pleasure. He cupped her head, digging his nails into her hair, caressing and massaging her scalp.

"I don't know what I'd do if I lost you to someone else..."

Grace stared up at him, felt her eyes widen as he spoke openly about his deepest fears. Jackson was scared of losing her? Couldn't stomach the thought of seeing her with other guys? *But he's the one with numerous admirers, not me!* For some reason, his words turned her on, causing her to suck harder, faster, to lick his shaft as if it was a lollipop. Grace felt out of it, as if she was losing control.

Tremors shook Jackson's body and curses fell from his lips. His erection swelled inside her mouth, doubled in size, but he didn't climax. He yanked her to his chest and kissed her.

"Let's go upstairs." Soaking wet, desperate to feel him inside her, her body was vibrating with need. "I want you so bad it hurts."

"Screw it," he growled, lifting her onto the table. "I'm doing you right here, right now."

"No! You entertain in here, and—"

Jackson picked up his pants, retrieved a condom from the pocket and ripped it open. Within seconds, he rolled it onto his erection and positioned himself between her legs.

"You'll never be able to eat in here without thinking about us having sex."

A grin curled his lips. "I know. Isn't it great?"

"Baby, we can't do this. Your Chicago relatives are coming to visit at the end of the month and you're hosting a dinner party for them, remember?"

Jackson gave her a blank stare. "Yeah. So? What's the problem?"

"Let's go to your bedroom. We'll be more comfortable…"

Before Grace could finish her sentence, Jackson was inside her, moving, thrusting. She rocked against him, furiously pumping her hips. His hands explored her body, cupping and massaging her breasts, teasing her nipples with his thumbs, playing with the curls between her legs.

Passion swirled inside her, causing her to cry out. Kissing her, Jackson whispered sweet, soft words against her mouth. Clutching her hips, he dove into her, again and again and again.

"Deeper," she commanded, her words a breathless pant. "Deeper…faster…harder."

Jackson obliged, gave her everything she needed and more, moved his body with the skill of a trained dancer. "Baby, you like that? Is that what you want?"

"I don't like it—I love it… You're amazing."

Sweating profusely, her limbs sticky and hot, she stuck to his body like glue. Time passed with no end to their lovemaking in sight. It felt as if they'd been having sex for hours, but Grace didn't want Jackson to stop and told him she needed and wanted more. Grace couldn't get enough of him. She wanted to stay in his arms, loving him for the rest of the night. No one had ever loved her with such passion, and when Jackson hiked her legs in the air and sprayed kisses along her inner thighs, she lost it. Tingles tickled her spine and and an explosion erupted between her legs.

"Baby, turn around, I need you *bad*."

His command excited her, making her feel sexy and

desirable. Feeling weightless, lighter than air, Grace didn't have the energy to roll onto her stomach. It took supreme effort, but she focused her gaze on Jackson's face. His lips were moving, but Grace couldn't make out what he was saying. All she could hear was her erratic heartbeat ringing in her ears like a bell.

Inhaling sharply, Grace relished his scent. She'd lost her heart to Jackson the first time he'd ever kissed her, and weeks after Freezergate she was desperate for him, so turned on by their lovemaking she was chanting his name.

Her pulse quickened, and contractions rocked her body. Brilliant lights and colors exploded behind her eyes. A groan rose inside her throat, tumbling off her lips, as an orgasm reverberated through her core. It was heaven on earth, the cherry on top of the sundae, and she'd remember their thrilling, passionate night for the rest of her life.

The carnal pleasure of his kiss, the intensity of it, filled her with longing and desire. She raked her hands through his hair, clamped her legs possessively around his trim waist, met him thrust for thrust, proving she had the stamina to satisfy him.

"Damn, woman, are you trying to kill me?"

Satiated and sleepy, Grace closed her eyes and snuggled against him.

"Let's go upstairs. I have something to show you."

"Of course you do, but I need a nap before round two, so cool your heels, Drayson."

Chuckling, his hearty laugh filling the room, Jackson bent down, looped an arm around her waist and guided her up the staircase. In the master bedroom, he kissed her with such tenderness she melted against him and moaned into his mouth. And when they made love for the second time, wrapped up in each other's arms, Grace knew she'd never be the same again.

Chapter 13

Grace took the hand Jackson offered, stepped out of the Hummer limousine parked in front of the Marion Oliver McCaw Hall at Seattle Center and beamed when he pulled her close to his side, whispering compliments in her ear. It was early evening, but the air was still warm, the sun hot and the breeze humid. The wind carried the scent of flowers across the manicured grounds, and the soothing fragrance calmed Grace's nerves. Butterflies danced in her stomach, but one look at her handsome date and they dissipated.

"You're stunning, Grace, a vision of beauty," Jackson said proudly, his gaze sliding down her body. "I can't wait to get you home and rip this dress off of you."

"You paid big bucks for it, so I guess you can do what you want to it."

"Just the dress, or you, too?"

His touch along her hips made her heart soar and

her thoughts return to that afternoon. At three o'clock, he'd picked her up from the bakery—or rather a block away to avoid detection—and after hours of shopping they'd returned to his place to get ready for the awards dinner. But instead of getting dressed, they'd made love and consequently dozed off on the couch. If the limousine driver hadn't banged on the front door, waking them up, they'd still be fast asleep. It was a mad dash to get ready, but they'd left the house as scheduled. In the limousine, they'd laughed about their blunder, and thinking about how much fun they'd had that afternoon brought a girlish smile to her lips.

Gazing up at Jackson, Grace realized how much he meant to her. Their personalities complemented each other, they had great discussions about life and were open and honest with each other. Add to that, their chemistry was off the charts. Making love whenever the mood struck, whether they were washing his sports car, grilling in his backyard or taking a shower, was thrilling. And addictive. The more they had sex, the more Grace wanted him, and when he brushed his lips against her cheek she imagined herself pushing him back inside the limo, hiking up her dress and climbing on top of him.

"You look so sexy I won't be able to keep my hands off you."

"Likewise," she quipped, admiring his stylish attire. Jackson looked sharp in his navy blue suit, white shirt and striped Burberry tie, but his boyish smile was his best accessory. "I hope no one sinks their claws into you when I'm not looking."

"That will never happen." Cupping her chin, he

brushed his lips softly against her mouth. "I only have eyes for you."

Good, because I feel the same way. I don't want anyone but you.

Arms intertwined, they strode along the walkway, admiring the spectacular view of the Space Needle. McCaw Hall was decorated with colored lights, creating an ethereal ambiance, and fashionably dressed guests posed for pictures on the red carpet.

Open and inviting, the lobby was decorated with a tornado-like chandelier, attractive art pieces and high-end furniture. Servers, decked out in formal attire, carried trays of champagne and appetizers, and Jackson and Grace enjoyed sampling the complimentary food and beverages.

"Jackson Drayson, is that you?"

Grace spotted a voluptuous blonde in a black cocktail gown making eyes at Jackson, and narrowed her gaze. The woman had a Nokia camera in one hand and a cocktail glass in the other, and was smiling bright.

"Good evening," Jackson said, frowning. "Do I know you?"

The smile slid off her lips. "It's me. Delilah. Delilah Hasani…"

He wore a blank expression.

"We hung out in Miami last year. No, it was Vegas!" she shrieked, speaking a mile a minute. "I was working at the MGM Grand, and you were watching a boxing match with your friends. Or, was it the NBA finals? Geez, Louise, I can't remember…"

Listening to the blonde, her amusement growing, Grace sipped her champagne. She had nothing to worry about. The woman was no competition, and it was obvious Jackson was bored. He was staring at *her*, not the chatty stranger, and tightened his hold on her waist.

"If my memory serves me correctly, you're a flight attendant, right?" he asked.

"Your memory sucks! I'm a freelance photographer and I'm here on assignment."

"My bad," Jackson said in a contrite voice. "See you around. Don't work too hard—"

"How about a picture? You're a striking pair, definitely magazine-worthy."

"You're right. My girlfriend is stunning, isn't she?"

Jackson moved in close and kissed Grace on the cheek, causing her to giggle.

"One, two, three," the blonde counted from behind the camera lens.

The bulb flashed and after thanking Delilah, they continued through the lobby.

McCaw Hall was packed, filled with some of the most influential people in Seattle, and Grace hoped she didn't run into Ainsworth or his high-and-mighty parents. To please her father, she'd agreed to have lunch with the businessman on Monday afternoon, and Grace was dreading it. It was *her* life, and she had to stop letting her dad boss her around. Last week, she'd found a Realtor and was fervently searching for her dream place, somewhere she could call her own.

Entering the bright and spacious auditorium, they were greeted by a balding usher who led them to their first-tier seats. Walking down the aisle on Jackson's arm made Grace feel like a celebrity. People stared and gawked, and she knew every woman in the room wished they could trade places with her. Grace didn't blame them. Jackson was a catch, a perfect gentleman with a great personality and a big heart. He planned romantic dates for her, and surprised her with gifts when she least expected it. Sure, they disagreed at times, and argued about hot-button issues, but Grace wanted a future with Jackson, and hoped they could overcome their differences—namely her father. She'd planned to talk to him last night at dinner, but she'd lost her nerve when he'd badmouthed Lillian's bakery. Her dad was going out of town tomorrow to visit a sick friend in Spokane, but when he returned she'd come clean about her relationship with Jackson. Grace hoped he wouldn't lose his temper, or worse, disown her. The thought made her heart ache—

"Grace, I want you to meet Diego and his wife, Ana Sofia," Jackson said, clapping his friend on the back. "They cheat at poker, but they're still one of my favorite couples!"

"It's wonderful to meet you both and congratulations on your award, Ana Sofia."

Shaking hands with the couple, Grace noted how affectionate they were toward each other, and instantly liked them. Seated in his wheelchair at the end of the aisle, Diego gazed up at his wife with love in his eyes, and she was beaming at him.

"Thank you, Grace. It's great to finally put the name to a face, and what a beautiful face it is." Ana Sofia patted Jackson's cheek. "This guy's family, so take good care of him, okay?"

"I'll try my best, Ana Sofia, but I'm not going to lie. He's a handful!"

Chuckling, Diego fervently nodded. "Tell me something I don't know!"

The lights dimmed in the auditorium and the master

of ceremonies appeared on stage. Promising to meet up later during dinner, the couples took their seats.

"Your friends seem nice—"

"I'm a handful, huh?" Jackson whispered in her ear, his voice filled with mischief. "Wait until we get home. I'll show you just how *bad* I can be."

Grace was blown away. Not with the designer table linens or elaborate flower arrangements beautifying the Allen Foundation for the Arts room, but by how spectacular the awards show had been. Awards had been handed out, speeches had been made and the performances had moved Grace to tears. And now guests were ready to party.

Hunger pains stabbed Grace's stomach. A tantalizing aroma tickled her nose and she wet her lips in anticipation, knowing the food would be plentiful and delicious. Seated at a table with Ana Sofia, Diego and their family members, Grace laughed at their outrageous stories.

"Do you want something from the bar?" Jackson asked, gently rubbing her back.

"Yes, please. I'd love a strawberry daiquiri."

"I'm worried about getting you another alcoholic drink."

Puzzled, Grace gave him a sideways glance. "Why?"

"You know how you get when you drink," he whispered.

"No, I don't. How do I get?"

"Buck wild!"

Laughing, Grace snatched her napkin off the table and threw it at him.

"You look all sweet and innocent, but after a couple cocktails you turn into a freak."

"I do not," she argued, speaking only loud enough for him to hear.

"You're right. My bad. I must be confusing you with someone else." He cocked his head to the right, as if deep in thought, and stroked the length of his jaw. "Though you look a *lot* like the woman who jumped me in the shower and had her way with me this afternoon."

Her body flushed with heat as memories of their fervent lovemaking filled her mind. Grace stared at Jackson, thinking she'd jump him again in a heartbeat.

"Diego, go with Jack," Ana Sofia insisted, flapping her bejewelled hands in the air. "I want a vodka tonic and some more caviar, so please track down a server."

The men left and Ana Sofia wasted no time grilling Grace about Jackson. How did they meet? Were they in love? Were they going to get married? The high school art teacher had an infectious personality, and Grace enjoyed chatting with her, but dodged her intrusive questions.

"When Diego told me Jack was serious about someone, I didn't believe him," she confessed. "I've known Jack for years, but you're the only woman I've ever seen him fawn over and it's adorable. He's really into you, Grace, and it's great to see."

"But he was engaged before—"

"Yeah, but Mimi proposed, and it's not true love if the woman pops the question."

Grace laughed. "Really? Says who?"

"My *abuela*, and she's *never* wrong."

"Why did they break up?" she asked, filled with curiosity. "Was he unfaithful?"

Sadness touched her features. "No, he dumped Mimi because she—"

"Congratulations on your award, Ana Sofia!" a woman interrupted. "Everyone at Lakeside Upper School is thrilled for you. You're a shining example of what one can accomplish with dedication, perseverance and hard work..."

Several couples joined them, chatting excitedly about Ana Sofia's award, and Grace checked out of the conversation, instead searching the room for Jackson. She found him standing at the bar with a dark-skinned beauty of African descent, and rolled her eyes to the ceiling. What the hell? Did he have to flirt with everyone in the room? Had he forgotten that she was his date?

The woman placed a hand on his chest and Grace suspected they had been lovers. Her heart dropped and her shoulders sagged. Was there anyone in Seattle he hadn't slept with? Was she fooling herself? Would Jackson ever be able to commit to her, or would she always have to compete with the masses for his attention?

Needing a distraction, Grace took her cell phone out of her purse and scrolled through her newest text messages. Bronwyn wanted to have drinks tomorrow night, her dad had sent a message reminding her about Monday's staff meeting and Ainsworth wanted her to call him.

Her gaze wandered, landing again on Jackson. Grace strangled a groan as yet another woman was breathing down his neck. This one was tall, all boobs and ass, with a curly weave flowing down her back.

Hurling her cell into her purse, Grace considered leaving, but before she could head for the nearest exit Jackson was at her side, offering the cocktail she'd requested.

"Here you go."

"Took you long enough." Grace regretted the quip the moment it left her mouth. She sounded pitiful, and cringed with shame when Jackson gave her a puzzled look. Grace hated seeing him with other women, wanted him all to herself, but knew it would never be. This was their "coming out" party, not their engagement party, and she didn't want to ruin their date by acting possessive. "I shouldn't have said that. It's none of my business who you talk to."

He took her hands in his and kissed them. "Baby, it's not like that. Tanisha and Zoey are old friends, and nothing more. I asked you to be my date tonight because I wanted to show you off to the world. You're my girl, and don't you forget it."

Grace snuggled against him, enjoying his tender caress across her skin.

"You're gorgeous, you know that? The most beautiful woman in the room…"

Moved by his words, and the sincerity of his expression, she rested a hand on his face. As she leaned forward to kiss Jackson, a couple caught her eye and she froze. The woman in the silver, backless, gown was old enough to be Grace's mother, but it was the expression on the man's face that made Grace want to laugh. Phillip looked bewildered, as if he couldn't believe what he was seeing. His eyes were saucers, his mouth was wide open, and when he stumbled over his feet he spilled champagne on his tacky powder-blue suit.

Ignoring him, Grace closed her eyes and pressed her lips against Jackson's. It was a perfect kiss, fraught with passion and desire, and her body responded enthusiastically to him. Jackson pulled away before she'd had her fill of him, but Grace knew they'd have plenty of time to make love later and smiled at the thought.

"You're stunning and I want everyone to know you're mine," he murmured against her ear, his tone thick with desperation. "May I have this dance?"

His cologne wafted over her, ticking her flesh, exciting her like his kiss as he stood to his feet.

Feeling sexy, desirable and hot, Grace rose from her chair, and coiled an arm around his. "I thought you'd never ask," she said, unable to wipe the smile off her face.

"Are you having fun?"

"Absolutely. Thanks for inviting me, Jackson. I'm having a great time."

"That makes two of us. Now, let's show everyone how to get down and dirty!"

As Jackson took her in his arms and kissed her passionately on the lips, Grace wished their wonderful, magical night together would never end.

Chapter 14

"I thought you'd never get back." Jackson watched Mariah breeze into the bakery kitchen, smiling from ear to ear, and knew she'd been with Everett. These days the couple spent all their free time together, and it amazed him how girly his sister acted whenever her millionaire fiancé was around. "Where did Lover Boy take you for lunch?"

Mariah washed her hands in the sink and dried them with a tea towel. "The Sheraton, and my five-course meal was to die for, especially the dessert. White truffles are my favorite!"

"Is *that* why you've been gone for three hours?"

"Two, but who's counting?" she replied, smirking.

Jackson laughed. He couldn't believe how much his sister had changed since meeting Everett three months earlier. The businessman brought out the best in Mariah, made her smile like no one else, and Jackson admired the single dad for being an honest, stand-up guy.

"My turn. I'm starving." Jackson took off his apron, dropped it on the counter and lowered the temperature on the oven. "Do you mind checking on the mocha soufflés and whipping up another batch of raspberry scones? I was going to, but things got crazy after you left and Kelsey asked me to come out front and lend a hand."

"No, problem, Jack. Take as long as you need."

"Okay," he said with a wink. "See you in three hours!"

Jackson grabbed his BLT from the fridge and left the kitchen. Remembering he hadn't responded to Chase's earlier message, he sent his brother a text. Chase and Amber were finally back in Seattle and en route to the bakery. He couldn't believe his brother—the self-proclaimed workaholic who was obsessed with planning and strategizing— had actually taken a vacation. More shocking still, Jackson had met Grace and dumped every other girl. He wanted a future with Grace, could see them living together in wedded bliss, but he wanted to talk things over with Chase before he made any rash decisions. Grace was busy at the bakery—her earlier texts had said as much—but Jackson wanted to hear her voice. He dialed her cell number, waiting anxiously for her to pick up, but the call went straight to voice mail. "Baby, it's me. Call me when you get this. Love you…"

Jackson stared at his cell phone in disbelief, amazed at his bold declaration. He sat there for several seconds, thinking about what he'd done, and wondered what Grace would think when she heard his message. He'd never said "I love you" before, hadn't planned on blurting it out, but he didn't regret his confession. It was true. He *did* love her, and he wasn't afraid to admit it.

His stomach groaned and he tasted the sandwich Grace had made for him that morning. Jackson liked her being at his place, loved coming home to her at the end of the day, and wanted her around permanently. They cooked together, spent hours cuddled up on the couch watching TV, listening to music and playing board games. He couldn't imagine being with anyone else, and as Jackson reflected on the past few weeks he realized he was more positive and enthusiastic about life, and Grace was the reason why. She was the strongest woman he knew, not to mention the most beautiful, and Jackson wanted to grow old with her.

"I thought you could use a drink, so I brought you a mango lemonade. Enjoy!"

Jackson broke free of his thoughts, noticed the glass on the table and smiled at the fresh-faced barista. "Thanks, Kelsey. You're one in a million."

The intern beamed. "Anytime, boss. Holler if you need anything else."

Picking up the discarded newspaper on the table, he skimmed the headlines. Jackson flipped open the paper and his sandwich fell from his hands. He froze, as his gaze zeroed in on the advertisement on page two. "What the hell?" Sweetness Bakery had taken out a full-page ad for their new dessert, Chocolate Explosion, and it looked similar…no, exactly like the Draynut. Different name, but he'd bet every dollar in his bank account it tasted the same.

Jackson was so engrossed in his thoughts, gazing intently at the advertisement, he didn't realize Chase,

Amber and Mariah were standing beside his table until his sister waved her hands in front of his face.

Closing the newspaper, Jackson jumped to his feet and hugged the happy couple. He was pissed, but he forced a smile on his lips and spoke in a jovial tone. Until he spoke to Grace, he had to hide the truth about their relationship and the stolen recipe from his siblings. That, or go into hiding. "Welcome home," he said, clapping his brother on the back. "How was your trip? Did you have a good time?"

Chase wrapped his arms around Amber. "I was with my number-one girl. What do you think?"

"I wanted to stay another week, but duty calls," Amber said with a shrug.

"We had a great time, but it's good to be home." A frown darkened Chase's eyes, causing worry lines to wrinkle his forehead. "Trouble's brewing, and if we don't launch a counterattack we could be out of business by the end of the year."

Alarmed, perspiration wet his skin. Had Chase seen the ad in the *Seattle Times*?

Chase's next words confirmed he had. "Sweetness is advertising their new dessert on billboards all over town."

Mariah gasped. "On billboards? How can they afford that? They're super expensive."

"That's not the worst of it. Unfortunately, there's more..."

Jackson groaned inwardly, hanging his head as he listened to his brother discuss the radio advertisement he'd heard for Sweetness Bakery as he was driving to Lillian's minutes earlier.

"They're going all out to promote Chocolate Explosion because Bite of Seattle is next week," Chase explained. "They're trying to prove they're the best bakery in town, but they're not. That's why they're resorting to dirty tricks."

"This is wrong! How could they do this? They stole our recipe!"

In a state of shock, Jackson couldn't speak.

"What did you tell Grace about the Draynut?" Shouting her words, Mariah leveled a finger at him. "Did you show her the recipe? Is that how this happened?"

"Of course not! I'd never do that—"

"Then how did Sweetness get my recipe?" she demanded.

Amber frowned, scratching her head. "I'm lost. Who's Grace?"

"Jack's new girlfriend."

"Good one, Mariah." Chase chuckled. "No, really, who is she?"

"Jack met Grace Nicholas a couple days after you left for your trip, and he's been wooing her ever since. He took her to the Heritage Awards last Saturday, and the next morning their picture was splashed all over the internet and the local newspapers."

Chase scoffed. "Get out of here. You can't be serious. Jack does booty calls, not romantic dates."

"Chase, I wish I was. I told him to stop seeing her, but he wouldn't listen, and now look. She stole the Draynut recipe and screwed us over."

"No, she didn't," Jackson replied, annoyed that his sister was making false accusations about his girlfriend. Doubts crowded his mind, but he spoke with confidence. "Grace would never betray me, and furthermore, she's never been in the back of the shop."

"Of course she has! You guys got locked inside the storage room, remember, lover boy?"

"What?" Chase roared, his voice reverberating around the room. "Jack, are you out of your mind? How could you have done something so stupid? Are you trying to ruin us?"

Wearing a shaky smile, her gaze darting around the bakery, Amber clutched Chase's forearm and spoke quietly to him. "Baby, not here. Let's go talk in the kitchen."

Determined to get to the bottom of things, Jackson swiped his cell phone and the newspaper off the table. "I'll be back later."

Mariah slid in front of him to thwart his escape, but Jackson stepped past her.

"Where are you going?" Chase asked.

"To uncover the truth."

Jackson tried calling Grace from the car as he sped towards Sweetness Bakery, but her voice mail came on again. Why wasn't she answering her phone? They texted each other all day long, spoke on the phone, too, and he couldn't recall a time when he couldn't reach her.

Arriving at Sweetness Bakery, he found parking across the street. It was a small brick building, but what it lacked in size it more than made up for in character. Colorful signs and pictures hung in the front window, a chalkboard displayed the menu and a barista in a pumpkin costume stood in front of the store offering pedestrians sweet treats.

Standing at the intersection, waiting impatiently for the light to change, Jackson took off his sunglasses and stared through the shop window. No, he wasn't seeing things. Grace was sitting at a table with a buff, blond-haired man. It was her. No doubt about it. He recognized her outfit. That morning, as they were leaving his house, he'd complimented her, told her how beautiful she looked in her peach-colored dress, and she'd thanked him with a kiss.

Seeing Grace with another man was a shock to his system, leaving him dazed and confused. Is that why she wasn't answering his calls? Because she was too busy hanging out with G.I. Joe? All at once it hit him. The truth. The real reason Grace was spending time with him—so she could steal his family recipes.

Feeling stupid for ever trusting her, his heart ached with sadness. Looking back, Jackson realized he'd made a mistake befriending her. *What was I thinking? Why didn't I keep my distance? Guard my heart?*

Glancing up the road to ensure the coast was clear, Jackson jogged across the street and into Sweetness Bakery, anger shooting through his veins. Grace was so busy flirting with her tanned, blue-eyed date she didn't notice he'd entered the shop.

Didn't notice, or didn't care? his conscience jeered.

Jackson didn't know what he was angrier about—Grace stealing the Draynut recipe, or him catching her with another man. The latter, he decided, stalking toward the largest table inside the bright, sweet-smelling shop. "You guys look cozy," he said, faking a smile.

Her eyes widened, but Grace spoke in a calm voice. "Jackson, what are you doing here?"

"We need to talk *now*."

"This is not a good time."

"Why? Because you're busy cheating on me with this clown?"

Grace glared at him, as if *he* was the one out of line, and rose to her feet.

"How long has this been going on?"

G.I. Joe tossed his napkin on the table. "Who are you and what do you want?"

"I don't think we've met. I'm Jackson Drayson. Grace's boyfriend."

The color drained from the man's face and he coughed into his fist.

"Ainsworth, please excuse me. I'll be right back."

Jackson slid his hands into his pockets, didn't move, although Grace gestured for him to follow her. Everyone in the shop was staring at them but Jackson didn't care. He wasn't leaving until Grace told him the truth about the stolen Draynut recipe and her blond lover boy.

"Baby, let's talk outside," she whispered, giving him a pleading look. "It's not what you think, and you're getting worked up over nothing."

Grace reached for him, trying to touch his arm, but Jackson moved away.

"We can talk here. I have nothing to hide. Do you?"

"Jackson, please." Her gaze darted around the shop. "You're making a scene."

"Of course I'm making a scene! You betrayed me."

"Ainsworth is a family friend," she explained. "He's not my man. *You* are."

"Not anymore. We're through."

Her face fell and her bottom lip quivered.

"Dating you was a mistake. I don't know what I was thinking—"

"Where is this coming from... What did I do wrong?"

"Everything!" he shouted, unable to govern his temper. Jackson reached into his back pocket and pulled out the crumpled newspaper ad. "Did you think I wouldn't see this? That I was too stupid to put two and two together."

Grace stared at the advertisement, her eyes wide.

"I never should have befriended you, or taken a chance on love." Jackson knew he was shouting, heard the disgust in his voice, the pain, but he couldn't control his emotions. "You set me up and I was too blind to see it."

Tears filled her eyes. "That's not true! I didn't pursue you. *You* pursued me."

"And you made sure to capitalize on that, didn't you?

"I had nothing to do with this campaign and I didn't steal the Draynut recipe."

Her denial did nothing to soothe his feelings. Her words meant nothing to him. Guilt was written all over her face, clear to see, and Jackson knew his suspicions were right. "Tell me the truth. You owe me at least that."

"I just did."

"You won," he said with a shrug of his shoulders. "Happy now?"

"Baby, wait. Let's talk about this! We can fix this!"

With a heavy heart, Jackson turned and marched through the shop and out the door.

Grace called out to him, yelling his name, but he didn't look back.

Chapter 15

Grace opened the industrial oven inside the bakery kitchen, took out the metal pan with one hand and the cookie tray with the other. Since arriving at the shop at 5:00 a.m. that morning she'd baked dozens of mocha brownies, apple-cranberry tarts and hazelnut cookies, and although she'd been on her feet for hours Grace felt invigorated, not tired. Cooking dinner with Jackson weeks earlier had reminded Grace how much she loved being in the kitchen. She was devastated about their breakup, but she found comfort in baking her mother's favorite recipes.

To take her mind off Jackson she'd cleaned the shop from top to bottom, finished her monthly financial report and made her hard-working employees a continental breakfast when they'd arrived to work. The more Grace baked, the less upset she was.

Her thoughts returned to Monday afternoon. Jackson had marched into the bakery shouting accusations at her, and Grace shivered in horror at the memory of their argument. She'd felt as if she was in the eye of the storm and didn't know how to save herself. His insults had pierced her soul, broken her heart in two. With tears in her eyes, she'd watched Jackson storm out of the shop, jump into his car and speed off.

Forty-eight hours later, Grace still couldn't make sense of what had gone wrong, of how she'd lost the man she loved. She'd called Jackson numerous times over the last two days, but to no avail. After hearing his voice mail, and the words *I love you* fall from his mouth, she'd decided to go to his house. If not for Bronwyn talking her out of it, she would have driven to his place and forced him to talk to her. But that wasn't the answer. As much as she loved Jackson, and wanted to be with him, she was scared he'd hurt her, and didn't know what she'd do if he rejected her again. She felt sick over their argument, but Grace didn't know how to make things right.

Grace thought about her solitary breakfast that morning at home. She'd decided to write Jackson a letter, but crumpled it up and started over several times. Grace was hurt by his accusations, couldn't believe Jackson thought so little of her. She teared up as she remembered the hurtful things he'd said. Filled with sadness and despair, she'd changed her mind about reaching out to him. There was nothing to say. All she could do was learn from the situation, and move on with her life because Jackson hated her and he wasn't coming back.

Her phone buzzed and Grace fished it out of her apron pocket, hoping her new text message was from

Jackson. It wasn't. Disappointed, she slumped against the counter. She knew Bronwyn meant well, but her incessant quotes about love and hardships were depressing. Grace didn't need anyone to remind her she'd lost Jackson; the pain was constant, all-consuming, would be with her forever.

Grace pressed her eyes shut. Policing her thoughts, she chose not to dwell on her failed relationship with Jackson, or the promises they'd made to each other. Gathering herself, she wiped at her cheeks with the sleeve of her blouse. She didn't have time to cry. She had a bakery to run and couldn't spend the rest of the day hiding out in the kitchen having a pity party for one.

Her gaze landed on the black-and-white photograph hanging beside the kitchen door. Her mom was glowing in the image, beaming like a bride on her wedding day, and Grace owed it to her mom to pull herself together, and get back to work. She felt her mother's spirit around her, her aura, could hear her voice in her ears now and wanted to make her proud.

Entering the shop, holding the pastry trays, Grace smiled and greeted customers. It turned out Jackson was right. Chatting with the regulars, hearing their heartfelt stories about Rosemary, was uplifting, and Grace drew strength from their memories and words of encouragement.

"It's good to see you back in the kitchen!" a cop said with a broad smile.

"Welcome back, dear. We've missed you," an elderly woman exclaimed.

A mother of three whooped for joy. "I'll have a dozen

of your maple almond squares. I've *really* missed your baking!"

Grace glanced at the door and her stomach coiled into a knot. She thought the gentleman waiting in line was Jackson, but when she realized it wasn't, tears filled her eyes for the second time in minutes. *Get it together, Grace. You're losing it.* Taking a deep breath helped steady her nerves. The moment passed and she made quick work of replenishing the display shelves.

"Pumpkin, is that you?"

Hearing her dad's voice, Grace turned toward the kitchen. His eyes were bright, and seeing his toothy smile lifted her spirits and warmed her heart. "Hey, Dad! Welcome home."

"I heard you were in the kitchen baking up a storm, but I had to come see for myself." He kissed her forehead. "You couldn't have picked a better time to dust off your oven mitts. Bite of Seattle starts on Friday, and with you back at the helm we're going to crush the competition."

"Dad, we need to talk."

"Not now, pumpkin, I have an important meeting across town and I'm late."

"But you just got here." Recognizing she was being insensitive, Grace asked about his trip to Spokane. "How is Mr. Baldwin doing? Is he still in the hospital?"

"Yes, but the doctors expect him to make a full recovery," he explained. "Maybe next time I go visit, you can come."

"Sure, Dad. I'd like that. Mr. Baldwin is a sweet old man who tells great stories."

"I have to run. I forgot my briefcase so I dropped by to pick it up, but I can't stay."

Grace trailed her dad through the shop and down the hallway, speed-walking to keep up with him. No easy feat in a pencil skirt and high heels, but Grace wasn't letting him out of her sight until he came clean about the Chocolate Explosion. She'd sampled one yesterday, and sure enough it tasted like the Draynut. Did her dad have spies working at Lillian's? Had he paid someone to swipe the recipe? Were there others he planned to steal and pass off as his own?

"Dad, did you plant spies at Lillian's to steal the Draynut recipe?"

"You think they're the only ones who are creative?" A snarl curled his lips. "Well, they're not. Our staff worked damn hard creating the Chocolate Explosion, but you'd know that if you'd been here, instead of running around town with that Drayson boy."

Anguish squeezed her heart at the sound of Jackson's name.

"I had to hear about your relationship on the street!" Sadness flickered in his eyes, darkening his face, and his voice broke. "Do you have any idea how that made me feel?"

"Dad, I'm sorry. I was going to tell you, but it was never the right time—"

"You have no business dating that boy. He's a scoundrel just like Phillip."

"They're nothing alike. Jackson has a career, his own money and life goals."

"Why can't you date someone like Ainsworth? His family is worth *billions*."

"Good for them," she replied angrily. "I don't want Ainsworth. We have nothing in common."

He flapped his hands in the air, dismissing her words.

"Nonsense. You have everything in common. You're both smart, hard-working people from good families."

"Jackson is the only man I want. If I can't have him, I don't want anyone."

"I don't trust him, so break things off."

"It's over between us..." Saying the words aloud wounded her afresh. Jackson's face haunted her dreams at night, and she'd woken up that morning, longing to be back in his arms. "Jackson found out about the stolen Draynut recipe and he dumped me."

"Good. It makes things easier. Now you won't have to choose between us."

Stunned by his words, Grace stared at him in astonishment. She was done. Through letting her dad control her, and knew if she didn't take a stand now she'd never be independent.

He'd always warned her about men who'd try to take advantage of her, but she'd never imagined he'd be the one to hurt her the most. "I'm moving out of the house. It's time."

"But Grace—"

"But nothing, Dad. This is long overdue."

"Pumpkin, you can't go. I need you."

"And I need my independence, my freedom," she insisted, standing her ground. "If I don't move out you'll always treat me like a little girl, instead of a grown woman with a life of her own."

"Where is this coming from? Did the Drayson boy put you up to this?"

Filled with empathy, her heart overflowing with love, Grace wore a sympathetic smile. "Dad, I'm not leaving you. I'm spreading my wings, just like you did when you were my age."

"Fine, do what you want, but don't come running to me when you fall flat on your face."

"I won't," she said, meeting his gaze. "You and Mom have given me all the tools I need to be successful in life, and I won't let you down."

"Are you leaving Sweetness, too, or just me?"

"I'm committed to this shop, this community and our customers, and that won't change."

He released an audible sigh. "That's good to hear. And now that we have the Chocolate Explosion we can finally crush those jerks at Lillian's."

Seeing his narrowed gaze and the smug I'm-the-man expression on his face bothered her. Something clicked in Grace's mind, and she sensed her suspicions were right. He *had* planted someone at Lillian's. He'd never admit it to her, but it didn't matter. The writing was on the wall, and knowing her father was responsible for hurting the man she loved made Grace feel sick to her stomach. Sadly, things like this had happened before. Since her mother's death, she'd heard rumblings that her dad had engaged in dirty tactics to stay on top, but she'd ignored the rumors.

Not anymore. "I want to expand the business, and build shops nationwide, but if you steal another recipe from Lillian's, I'll quit."

"All's fair in love and war, *and* business."

"Mom wouldn't want this. If she was alive she'd be ashamed of you for stealing from our competitors." Grace couldn't hide her disgust. "And so am I."

Shame passed over his features, but Grace didn't stick around to hear his apology. Spinning around on her heels, she fled the office, willing the tears in her eyes not to fall.

Chapter 16

"I can't do this. I can't sit here and pretend every-thing's hunky-dory when I'm pissed…"

Utensils dropped, clanging against gold-rimmed plates, and an awkward silence fell across Graham and Nadia's lavishly decorated dining room. A couple of times a month, the Drayson family met for dinner, and although Jackson was miserable, he'd driven to his folks' place after his afternoon workout with his friends, hungry for his mother's delicious cooking.

"I'm so angry I feel like hitting something," Mariah continued, shouting her words.

Jackson closed his gaping mouth. His sister never raised her voice, so he was stunned by her outburst. "Sis, what's wrong? Did you and Everett have an argument or something?"

"No," she snapped, pointing her fork at him. "I'm mad at you."

"Me? What did I do?"

Mariah surged to her feet. "You screwed Lillian's over and that's not okay."

"Jack, Mariah, what's going on?" Nadia asked. "What's this all about?"

"Jack hooked up with our biggest competitor."

Eyebrows raised, his parents exchanged a worried look, and Jackson dropped his gaze to his plate. *Damn. Do we have to do this* now? *Can't I eat in peace?* Four days ago, his world had come crashing down around him, and he was still coming to terms with what had happened. Jackson tried to block the incident from his mind, but it didn't work. He'd fallen victim to anger on Monday, but now that he'd had time to reflect on his argument with Grace, he had doubts about her guilt. Snitching to her father was out of character for her. She wasn't the sneaky, deceptive type, and she didn't have a calculating bone in her body.

Remembering the things he'd said to her filled Jackson with shame. He only had himself to blame for his problems. *What have I done? Why didn't I give her a chance to explain instead of going off half-cocked? Is it too late to make amends?* Deciding it wasn't, he formulated a plan. Winning back Grace was a daunting task, but Jackson was up for the challenge. He wanted a future with her, needed her in his life, and didn't want to live another day without her. Nothing was going to keep them apart. Not even his family—

His mother's shrill voice cut into his thoughts and Jackson wondered how long he'd been daydreaming about Grace.

"Jack, is this true?" Even at home, surrounded by family, Nadia's makeup was perfect, every hair was in place and her floral designer dress was fresh off the Paris runway. "Have you been sleeping with the enemy?"

He dodged his mother's gaze, and her question. "Grace would never do the things Mariah is accusing her of."

"How would you know?" Chase asked. "It's not as if you guys are in a committed relationship. It's just sex. Three months from now you won't even remember her name."

"Chase, shut up. It isn't like that. Grace is different."

"Are you trying to sabotage the bakery?" Mariah asked.

"What kind of question is that?"

"A fair one," his brother argued. "Of all the women in Seattle you choose to hook up with our competitor. Why? Don't you have enough excitement in your life already?"

"You're a fine one to talk. You hooked up with the help."

Chase looked sour, and Jackson regretted taking a cheap shot at his big brother.

"Keep Amber out of this. She didn't steal the Dray-nut recipe—your booty call did."

Jackson shook his head. "This isn't fair. You guys both found love at Lillian's, so why are you ganging up on me for dating someone I met at the bakery?" His question was met with silence and Jackson knew he'd given his siblings something to think about. "I trust Grace. It's just not in her to be sneaky and deceitful."

His sister rolled her eyes to the ceiling, infuriating him, but Jackson fought back.

"You run the bakery, Mariah. Not me."

"What's that supposed to mean?"

"I'm not a puppet. I'm my own man," he said coolly. "I do what's best for me, not what you tell me to do, so back off."

"We're supposed to be a team!" Chase stood beside Mariah. "Have you forgotten that?"

Rising to his feet, he glared at his brother. "We are a team. I bust my butt every day to ensure everything runs smoothly at Lillian's, so don't you dare question my loyalty and dedication to the bakery."

"Then why did you tell her our secrets?" Mariah asked. "Who knows what else she's told her father about us, or how many other recipes she swiped when you weren't looking."

Chase wore a menacing look on his face. "You're jeopardizing our business, our reputations and our family name by sneaking around town with that woman."

His hands curled into fists. "Her name is Grace—"

"Who cares?" Mariah retorted. " I don't like her."

"Right now I don't like *you*, so we're in the same boat."

"Kids, that's enough." Standing, Graham gestured to their vacant chairs with a nod of his head. "Everyone have a seat. Things are getting out of hand."

"But, Dad—"

"Sit, Mariah. You, too, boys."

Jackson knew better than to argue with his dad and returned to his seat. He'd lost his appetite, had zero desire to eat, but he guzzled down his wine as if it was water. He glanced around the room, staring everywhere but at his family. The dining room was just off the kitchen area, a large, but cozy space with ivory walls, stained-glass windows overlooking the sprawling grounds, glittering chandeliers and decorative vases brimming with colored tulips. As beautiful as the room was, Jackson still felt trapped, as if he was in a jail cell, and he was anxious to leave.

"Draysons stick together," Graham said sternly, making eye contact with each one of them. "We don't tear each other down. *Ever.* Regardless of how bad things get."

Smoothing a hand over his mustache, his father gave him a pointed look. Jackson knew what his dad was thinking, knew he held him responsible for the argument with his siblings. Graham had never dated anyone besides Nadia, and had a hard time understanding why Jackson enjoyed playing the field. Though since meeting Grace he hadn't looked at another girl.

"Dad's right. Jack, I'm sorry. I never should have doubted you. Do you forgive me?"

Jackson cracked a sly smile. "I will, Mariah, if you do the early morning shift tomorrow!"

His sister laughed and Jackson chuckled, too, was relieved they were cool again.

"Watching you kids work together, and seeing all that you've accomplished with the bakery has made your father and I extremely proud."

Wide-eyed, Jackson stared at his mother in disbelief. "Really?" he said, unable to hide his surprise. "Three months ago you said I was squandering my life away at Lillian's, and embarrassing you, as well. You said, and I quote, 'Quit baking cakes, and get a real job.'"

"I owe you an apology, son." Nadia wiped at her eyes with the back of her hands. "Actually, I owe all of you an apology. I'm sorry for ever doubting your ability to succeed at Lillian's and for not supporting you. Can you find it in your hearts to forgive me?"

Mariah rubbed Nadia's back. "Of course, Mom. After all, you taught us everything we know about baking."

"I'll be proud to introduce my talented, successful children as master bakers at Sunday's charity gala and I'd also like to hire Lillian's to cater the event. Think you guys can make enough desserts to feed three hundred people?"

"What do you think, Jack? Can we?" Mariah asked with a small smile.

"In light of everything that's happened this week I should probably lay low. Maybe Kelsey or one of the other baristas can help you."

Chase clapped Jackson on the shoulder. "Man, get out of here. If not for you the bakery wouldn't be as popular as it is, and the competition wouldn't be stealing our recipes!"

Jackson hung his head, realizing how foolish he'd been to defend Grace to his family. Someone had stolen the Draynut recipe out of the recipe binder in the kitchen. Grace was the only person who had motive and opportunity. As much as he loved her and wanted to be with her, he had to keep his distance. His family was right; she'd tricked him, but he'd been too blind to see. *First Mimi and now Grace. Do I have the worst track record with women or what?*

"I was wrong. Grace is trouble, so I'm going to keep my distance. Let's pop the bubbly and celebrate. I'm single again!" he said dryly, raising his glass in the air.

"Jack, are you sure that's what you want?" his dad asked, his tone filled with concern. "It's obvious you care deeply about Grace, and it pains me to see you upset."

A bitter taste filled his mouth, coating his tongue, but he was man enough to admit his mistakes and speak the truth. "Chase and Mariah were right. I never should have pursued Grace. She's the enemy—"

"That's not what I said, bro."

"Chase, that's exactly what you said."

"Date her, just keep her out of the kitchen," Mariah said, piping up. "I trust you, Jackson, and if you believe in Grace then I believe in her, too. I'd never do anything to stand in the way of true love, and above all I want you to be happy."

"I don't have a problem with Grace, per se," Chase explained. "It's her father who worries me the most. From what I've heard, Doug Nicholas has no conscience, and will do anything to bury his competitors."

"You're dating Grace Nicholas, too?"

Jackson cranked his head to the right. "Mom, what are you talking about?"

"Meredith Ventura and I have mutual friends, and last week at the country club she went on and on about Grace Nicholas being the perfect woman for her son. Apparently, the two have been seeing each other for several weeks, and Ainsworth is completely smitten with her."

I never saw this coming. Not in a million years. Pain reverberated through Jackson's body. He saw the sympathetic expressions on his parents' faces, watched his siblings share a knowing look and slumped back in his chair. How could he have been so stupid? So blind? Grace had tricked him, and he'd played right into her hands.

"Bro, don't sweat it," Chase said. "You'll have another honey in no time."

To save face, Jackson winked and flashed a broad grin. But he knew in his heart he'd never find a woman as special as Grace.

Chapter 17

"This day is going from bad to worse," Grace grumbled as she spotted Mariah Drayson breeze through the front doors of Samson's Gym on Saturday afternoon. *Oh, brother, what now? What is she doing here? Shouldn't she be at Bite of Seattle?* Looking fit and trendy in her black Puma exercise gear, Mariah whipped off her sunglasses and glanced around the cardio room.

Hoping to avoid detection, Grace ducked behind the magazine stand, pretending to read the glossy tabloid covers. Once a week, Grace did a fitness class with her roller derby teammates, and while doing squats, high kicks and planks they strategized for matches. Her friends were already warming up in Studio A, and Grace didn't have the time or the energy to argue with Jackson's sister. She hadn't had a good night's sleep since Jackson dumped her, couldn't stop replaying their argument in her mind. Thoughts of him dominated her dreams at night, and the more she tried to censure her thoughts, the worse she felt.

Grace released a deep sigh, wondering if the pain in her heart would ever subside. She'd planned to attend Bite of Seattle that weekend, but after overhearing her father's twisted plan on Friday morning—to give away hundreds of Chocolate Explosion desserts to stick it to the Draysons—she'd changed her mind. She wanted nothing to do with hurting the man she loved.

Hoping her nemesis wouldn't find her, Grace bent down behind the water fountain and retied her neon pink sneakers. Approaching with the stealth of a burglar, Mariah sidled up beside her, blocking the sunshine streaming through the windows, but Grace refused to acknowledge her. The music inside the cardio room was deafening, blaring from the overhead speakers, but she heard Mariah's voice loud and clear.

"It's nice to see you again, Grace."

Grace choked on her tongue. *As if!* Mariah despised her, went out of her way to avoid her whenever she used to stop by Lillian's to see Jackson, and Grace thought she was a snob with no manners. Standing, she regarded the petite baker, making no attempt to hide her disdain.

"I was hoping to run into you at the Bite of Seattle this weekend, but you've been missing in action. Is, ah, everything okay?"

What do you think? Your brother dumped me and he won't return my calls. Of course I'm not okay! Scared her voice would crack if she spoke, Grace put her water bottle to her lips and took a long drink. "What are you doing here?"

Mariah frowned. "Excuse me? I've been coming to this gym for years."

"Then how come I've never seen you here before today?"

"Because my schedule is jam-packed and my amazing fiancé has been keeping me busy in the evenings. You know how it is. You start dating a great guy, then ditch your daily workouts to spend more time with him."

I know all too well, Grace thought sadly. *When I'm with Jackson nothing else matters.*

"I was hoping we could talk."

"I have nothing to say to you."

"Hear me out," Mariah pleaded.

"What do you want? My aerobics class just started and I don't want to miss it."

It was a lie, but Grace had nothing to say to Mariah and wanted her gone.

"We need to clear the air and I figured this was as good a place as any."

"I'm sure you know Jackson dumped me, so cut the nice-girl act, because I'm not buying it." Grace narrowed her gaze. "You're here to gloat, aren't you? Real mature, Mariah."

"That's not why I'm here."

A group of women approached and Grace stepped aside to let the trio pass. She wanted to leave, but something compelled her to stay. "Out with it, Mariah. I don't have all day."

"I won't lie. I've been suspicious of you ever since I caught you making out in the storage room fridge with my brother, but it was wrong of me to judge you because of your last name. I forgive you for stealing the Draynut recipe, but if you hurt Jack again I'll—"

"I didn't steal it!" Grace shouted, throwing her hands up in the air.

Her eyes widened with surprise and curiosity. "You didn't?"

"No. I've never even seen the recipe, nor do I want to."

"And that's the truth?"

"I love your…" Overcome with emotion, Grace trailed off speaking for fear of bursting into tears. "I adore your brother, and I'd never do anything to hurt him. He's special to me, and I only want the best for him."

Happiness covered Mariah's face. "Have you told Jack how you feel?"

"Yes, but he doesn't believe me, and that's okay. I get it."

Her smile faltered. "Get what? I'm confused."

"I'd never betray Jackson, but I'm pretty sure my father had something to do with stealing the recipe," she said sadly. "I'm Doug Nicholas's daughter, and that will never change so I'll stay on my side of the city, and you Draysons stay on yours. Problem solved."

"Not if you're miserable, and I suspect that you are. Just like my brother."

Grace had a million questions for Mariah, was dying to know how Jackson was doing, but she couldn't bring herself to ask. "I have to go."

"The Bite of Seattle ends tomorrow," Mariah said. "Jack's competing in the Bite Cook-Off at eleven o'clock. You should come out and cheer him on."

"Why? So he can insult me again? No, thanks."

"Jack loves you, Grace. I see it in his eyes every time he says your name."

"No, he doesn't." Haunted by the memory of their

breakup, a cold chill whipped through her body and she hugged her hands to her chest. "If he loved me he wouldn't have hurt me."

"Sometimes when people are upset they say things they don't mean."

Grace opened her mouth, realized she didn't have anything to say in response and slammed it shut. She had to admit that Mariah made a good point. Before their argument, Jackson had never yelled at her, let alone raised his voice, and had always been gentle with her. "Does Jackson know you're here? Talking to me right now?"

Mariah shook her head. "No way. He's been a sour-puss all week, so I've been staying *far* away from him. I can't help feeling responsible for his foul mood. My accusations built a wedge between you guys, and I'll do anything to make things right."

Grace believed her. She sounded sincere, and her face was filled with concern.

"I hope to see you tomorrow at Bite of Seattle," Mariah continued. "Come by the Lillian's booth. I'll make you a Draynut, free of charge. It's the least I can do. "

Hearing noises behind her, Grace glanced over her shoulder and smiled at her teammates. They beckoned to her from inside Studio A and she held up a hand, sig-naling she'd be there in five minutes.

"They look like a rough bunch." Mariah shivered. "Are they wrestlers?"

Grace laughed. "No, but don't mess with me or the Curvy Crashers will get you!"

"That's my cue to leave," she said with a laugh. "Will I see you tomorrow?"

"I don't know. I'll think about it."

"Fair enough. Enjoy your workout."

Grace watched Mariah exit the cardio room. Was she telling the truth? Did Jackson miss her? She shook her head, and the thought from her mind. It didn't matter. He hadn't answered her calls or texts, and after everything he'd put her through in the past week she'd started to think maybe their breakup was for the best. Her cell phone rang and Grace took it out of her pocket. "Hey, Bronwyn, what's up? I thought you were coming to class tonight."

"I changed my mind. Rodolfo wanted to check out the…"

Grace had to plug her left ear to hear what her best friend was saying. "You're where?" she asked, raising her voice to be heard above the noise on the phone line.

"Bite of Seattle. We sampled every booth and now we're so full we can't move. Help!"

"No worries. You guys have fun and I'll talk to you tomorrow—"

"Jackson's here."

"Of course he is," she said, speaking up in spite of the lump in the back of her throat. "He's part owner of Lillian's and a brilliant baker, as well. He *has* to be there."

"If you hurry you can make it down here before the festival ends at nine o'clock."

"I can't." Noting the time, she strode past the free weights towards Studio A. "Booty boot camp 101 is about to start and the girls are waiting for me."

"All right. I understand. I just wanted to give you a heads-up."

"A heads-up about what? What's going on? Is Jackson okay?"

"I'd say! He's surrounded by a bevy of beauties and they're literally eating out of the palm of his hand," Bronwyn reported, her tone thick with disapproval. "If he was my man I'd fly down here and tell the vultures to back off. But that's just me."

Grace forced a laugh to prevent tears from forming in her eyes. It was a lie. Jackson didn't miss her. Didn't want to reunite. If he did, he'd be with her instead of charming the masses at Bite of Seattle. "Girl, we'll talk tomorrow. Have a good night."

Ending the call, she entered Studio A. Her teammates cheered, and Grace rolled her eyes to the ceiling. The instructor, a slender Trinidadian woman with auburn twists, stood in front of the class, shouting instructions to the all-female group.

"Now that we're warmed up, it's time to get down!" the instructor shouted.

Having taken the class before, Grace followed along with ease. She was broken inside, couldn't stop thinking about Jackson with other women, but an odd thing happened as she danced and gyrated to the hip-hop music. Her mood improved, brightening as cherished memories of Jackson flooded her mind. He represented stability, love and family, and Grace wasn't ready to give up on their relationship yet. Tomorrow, she was going to come clean to Jackson about everything—her father's shady business practices, her friendship with Ainsworth, her dreams for their future—and hoped he'd still want her. Grace couldn't wait to see Jackson again, and thanks to his sister she knew exactly where to find him.

Chapter 18

Jackson slammed the driver's-side door, tucked his cell phone into his back pocket and fell into step beside Chase and Mariah. Attending Bite of Seattle, the three-day food festival held on the Seattle Center grounds, had been a Drayson family tradition for years, and as Jackson strolled down the street with his siblings, fond memories from his childhood warmed his heart.

The mood was jovial, the crowd thick, and there were enticing aromas in the air. Magicians did eye-popping tricks, cartoon characters posed for pictures with adoring, pint-sized fans and food vendors offered free samples to attract customers. Foodies of all ages wandered the grounds, desperate to get their hands on some mouth-watering grub—Jackson included. He'd skipped breakfast that morning, but planned to make a pit stop at the Lillian's booth before heading to the main stage. Jackson frowned. *Or maybe not.* The line was a mile long, but seeing customers devour their baked goods filled him with pride.

His gaze landed on a poster, suspended from a tree, and the smile slid off his face. Jackson couldn't go anywhere in the city without seeing signs for Chocolate Explosion, and every time he heard one of Sweetness Bakery's new radio ads he thought about Grace, remembering all of the good times they'd shared.

"We should head to the main stage," Chase said. "It's ten fifteen, and the cook-off starts at—"

"I know what time it starts," he snapped, cutting off his brother midsentence. "You don't have to remind me. I'm not a kid."

Chase stopped walking and stared him down. "You know what? You've been a jerk all week and I'm sick of it."

Riddled with guilt, Jackson hung his head. It wasn't his brother's fault Grace had screwed him over, so why was he taking his frustrations out on him? On everyone? He'd been irritable since breaking up with Grace, and everyone at the bakery was keeping their distance. Jackson didn't blame them. He was on edge, moody, but he didn't know how to pull himself out of his funk. On Thursday he'd coached his basketball team to victory, yesterday he'd gone to a movie with his dad and that morning he'd gone for a jog, but nothing helped. Every day without Grace was torture. Excruciating. What was wrong with him? How could he miss a woman who'd used him for her own selfish gain? Who'd been dating another guy their entire relationship?

"You made it!" Mariah shrieked.

His Chicago cousins, Belinda Drayson-Jones Anthony, Shari Drayson Robinson and Carter Drayson approached, smiling and waving, and the group exchanged hugs and fist bumps. "How is the family?" Jackson asked. "Everything good in Chi-town?"

"Couldn't be better," Shari said brightly. Five feet tall with a round face and ample curves, she looked model-pretty in her coral sundress, gold accessories and sandals. "Business is booming and our latest ad campaign is a roaring success!"

"We heard about the stolen Draynut recipe," Carter said, a scowl creasing his brow. Well-groomed, with short hair and brown eyes, the baker was like chocolate to most women: simply irresistible. Head over heels in love with his wife, Lorraine Hawthorne Hayes, he seemed oblivious to the women on the street staring at him. "Do you have any idea who the culprit is?"

Jackson shook his head, recalling how his great-aunt Lillian had posed the exact same question yesterday afternoon when they'd met at the bakery to discuss the stolen recipe. She'd interviewed the entire staff—including the cleaners and delivery guys—and her tough, hard-hitting questions had shocked everyone. Still, they had no leads.

"Chase, have you noticed an impact on sales since Sweetness debuted their Chocolate Explosion?" Curvy, with brown eyes and long straight hair, Belinda was the kind of woman who attracted male attention wherever she went. Hardworking and goal-oriented, the Chicago baker wasn't happy with herself—or anyone else—unless everything in her life was perfect, and since arriving in Seattle last night she'd made it her mission to uncover the truth.

"It's only been a short time, so it's too soon to tell, but—"

"I'm not worried," Jackson said, bumping elbows with Chase to make amends for snapping at him earlier. "We have the better product, the better staff and the smarter, sexier owners, so the competition doesn't stand a chance!"

Everyone laughed, fervently agreeing that Jackson was right.

"Seeing you together warms the cockles of my heart..."

Jackson raised an eyebrow. *Warmed her what?* His great-aunt Lillian Reynolds-Drayson appeared at his side, looking sophisticated and regal in her pastel pink suit, Chanel scarf and pearl stud earrings. The family matriarch of the Drayson clan was a thin woman with a full head of white hair, but at seventy-nine she showed no signs of slowing down.

"It's always been my fervent hope that each of you would not only succeed in life, but support one another, and I'm thrilled to see your bond growing. Nothing is more important than family. Never forget that."

Belinda and Shari each gave Jackson a one-arm hug and a smile tugged at his lips. His sister was right; his Chicago relatives weren't so bad. Since they'd opened Lillian's of Seattle several months ago, his cousins had been their biggest supporters, and Jackson appreciated their wisdom and guidance. Going forward, he'd make a concerted effort to spend more time with his cousins. They were family, and as Lillian had said earlier, they had to stick together.

"Jack, you're looking fetching this morning," Lillian said, patting his forearm. "It's time you took a bride, and I know just the girl. How do you feel about relocating to Chicago?"

I don't want anyone but Grace, he thought sadly, hating himself for wanting her. *I wish things had been different. I wish she'd loved me as much as I love her.* "I'm too busy at the bakery to date, Aunt Lillian. It's my number-one priority right now."

Her smile was as dazzling as the diamond broach pinned to her blazer. "I understand. I know how demanding work can be, and I'd hate to do anything to curtail the bakery's success."

"It must be something in the genes," Shari said, "Because I'm a workaholic, too, and proud of it!"

Everyone laughed. Jackson mouthed *thank you* to Shari and she winked. Glancing at the booth for Lillian's, which was busier than ever, he made a mental note to speak to Shari about his promotional ideas for the bakery after the cooking competition.

"Girls, how do I look?" Lillian asked, addressing her nieces. "I'd planned to wear a black Diane von Furstenberg sheath dress, but there's a stain on the hem and I didn't want to embarrass myself or the family by wearing something filthy..."

Jackson inhaled the sweet-smelling air, admired the radiant blue sky and reflected on the afternoon Grace had surprised him with a romantic picnic at Discovery Park. They'd fed each other, listened to R&B music on his cell phone, had even danced. The memories of that bright, sunny afternoon caused him to choke up. Would it always be this way? Would he ever get over Grace? Or, would he think about her every single day for the rest of his life?

"Are you ready to charm the Bite of Seattle crowd,

my dear boy?" asked Lillian. "It's time for the Bite Cook-Off, and I'd hate to keep our fans waiting."

Jackson didn't want to go to the main stage, wished he'd never agreed to be a celebrity chef or participate in the Bite Cook-Off with his great-aunt. She was the heart and soul of the business, not him, and he could kick himself for letting Chase and Mariah talk him into doing something he wasn't up to. "As ready as I'll ever be, Aunt Lillian, so let's do this!"

Twenty minutes later, Jackson and Lillian were standing to the left of the main stage. It was equipped with everything they'd need for the competition—utensils, cooking supplies, a microwave and even a state-of-the-art oven.

Jackson could feel the excitement in the air, and made up his mind to give the audience one hell of a show. It wasn't about him; it was about putting his family bakery on the map. Winning the baking competition and being crowned the Bite Cooks Master would definitely increase sales, and since it was the last day of the festival he had to bring his A game.

"Welcome to the Bite Cook-Off!" The female host stood onstage, waving at the audience. People were eating, talking and cheering, and the crowd was so large Jackson couldn't find their family members anywhere.

"Joining me onstage now are Lillian Reynolds-Drayson and Jackson Drayson," the host continued. "Jackson is one of the owners of Lillian's of Seattle, a fantastic new bakery in the Denny Triangle—and an offshoot of the famed Lillian's bakery in Chicago."

Offering his arm, Jackson helped Lillian up the steps and joined the host in the kitchen.

"I tried the Draynut this morning and thought I'd

died and gone to pastry heaven!" she shrieked. "Before we get started, tell the audience how Lillian's of Seattle came about, and some of the challenges you've faced being the new kid on the block, so to speak."

If you only knew! Jackson thought. All week there'd been a lot of buzz around town about Lillian's versus Sweetness, and if the public knew how real the fight was between the bakeries they'd be champing at the bit for all of the salacious details.

"Thank you for having us, Felicity. It's wonderful to be here," Jackson said, with a broad smile. "In the fifties, my great-aunt Lillian was a single mother with a hope and a dream. Working in a Chicago cafeteria, she'd bake special orders for her lunch customers, and when demand grew for her pastries, she quit the cafeteria and rented out a tiny storefront. From these modest beginnings grew a family dynasty."

The crowd cheered and whistled, and Lillian beamed with pride. "I'm thrilled about what my siblings and I have accomplished since the Seattle location opened earlier this year, and I'm excited about..." Jackson spotted a familiar face in the audience and lost his voice. Grace! She was standing at the edge of the crowd, staring at him, love shimmering in her eyes. She looked tired, as though she hadn't slept in weeks, but beautiful nonetheless. Her hair was curled, just the way he liked it, and her loose-flowing multi-colored dress made her look like a bohemian princess. *His* bohemian princess. The woman he loved was in the audience, and he had to speak to her. Now. Couldn't let this opportunity pass him by. Grace was the kind of woman who only came along once in a lifetime, and he didn't want to lose her. That didn't mean Jackson was cool with her dating other guys—he wasn't—but he was confident they could work things out.

"You're excited about…" the host prompted, her voice tinged with anxiety.

Jackson had dreamed about this moment all week, knew exactly what he'd do when he saw Grace again, but shocked himself—and probably everyone in the audience—by doing the unthinkable. He marched across the stage, jogged down the steps and weaved his way through the crowd toward Grace. Running toward him, she threw herself into his open arms.

Relief flooded Jackson's body. No, it was more than relief. It was joy, elation. Grace was back and they were going to work things out. His life *wasn't* over. In fact, it was just beginning.

"Do you have any idea how much I've missed you?" he murmured into her ear, inhaling her fragrant scent. "Baby, I'm sorry. I lost my temper, but I never meant to hurt you."

"I'm sorry, too. I should have told you about my dad, and Ainsworth, and—"

"Are you dating him?" Jackson held his breath. The word on the street was that Grace and Ainsworth were a hot new couple, and he was dying to know if it was true.

"No, Jackson, I'm not. He's a family friend, and nothing more," she said, reaching out and gently caressing his face "You're the only man I want, the only man I love. You have to believe me, baby."

He sighed, relieved the rumor mill had gotten it wrong.

"It was foolish of us to embark on a relationship we knew wouldn't work," Grace said.

Taking her hand, Jackson led her to a quiet corner of the grounds.

"Can I ask you something?"

Jackson nodded. "Of course. Ask me anything. I want everything to be out in the open."

"How could you think that I'd ever betray you?"

He didn't know what to say to her in his defense, couldn't find his voice.

"I thought we had something special, and now I don't know what to think."

"Grace, we *do* have something special."

"No, we don't. If we did you would have believed me when I said I didn't steal the Draynut recipe," she said. "Why didn't you give me the benefit of the doubt? An opportunity to defend myself?"

"Because the last time I gave someone the benefit of the doubt I got screwed."

"What happened?"

Jackson blew out a deep breath. He didn't want to talk about Mimi, but recognized he couldn't move forward with Grace until he opened up to her about his broken engagement and his ex-fiancée's deception. "Three months after Mimi proposed to me I discovered she'd learned my PIN number, and was helping herself to my poker winnings."

Moving closer to him, her face filled with concern, she slowly caressed his shoulders.

"Mimi denied it, of course. Swore on her mother's grave she never touched a dime and I foolishly believed her." He tried to govern his feelings, but his anger broke through and seeped into his tone. "I was embarrassed and wanted to put the incident behind me, but Chase forced me to meet with bank officials. Mimi wasn't on the video footage, but her ex-boyfriend was, so I knew they'd cooked up the scheme together."

"That's horrible, Jackson."

"I never recouped the eighty grand she stole, but that wasn't the worst part. My mom adored Mimi—hell, my entire family did—and she played with their emotions. To this day they think I was the one who messed up, and I don't have the heart to tell them the truth."

Laughter rippled through the crowd as his great-aunt filled in for him. No surprise. His aunt was loved by all, and made friends wherever she went. Having left Lillian in the lurch, Jackson knew he had to return to the stage, but first he had to smooth things over with the woman he loved. "Grace, I believe you. And, you're right, I never should have doubted you for a second. I was angry but deep down I knew you would never steal Lillian's recipes and pass them off as your own. That's not you."

Grace released an audible sigh. "Knowing that you believe me is a huge relief."

"You're my everything, Grace, and I don't want to lose you again."

She fell silent, and Jackson wondered what she was thinking.

"I don't have any proof, but I'm pretty sure my dad had something to do with the stolen Draynut recipe," she said quietly, biting her bottom lip. "I'm disappointed in him, and I hate what he did, but I'm still his daughter and I won't turn my back on him."

"I'm not asking you to."

Her eyes brightened with hope. "You're not?"

"No." Jackson pulled Grace into his arms and kissed her hair. "Baby, nothing is impossible. If we want to be together we'll find a way to make it work."

"The odds are against us."

"I don't care. You're my girl, and I'll move heaven and earth to be with you."

Grace smiled, and Jackson knew he was making progress with her.

"I want you to be my guest at tonight's charity gala. It's being held at the Four Seasons to commemorate the end of Bite of Seattle. All of the money raised will be donated to local charities," he explained. "Please say you'll come. I need you by my side, and I want you to meet my parents and the rest of my family."

She didn't respond, and he feared she was going to turn him down.

"I'll pay for your gown and I'll send a car service to pick you up, as well."

"No, thank you," Grace said, curls tumbling about her pretty face as she shook her head. "I have lots of designer dresses and I can drive myself. I have a Jaguar, you know!"

Jackson chuckled. "I have to get back onstage. I hope to see you later."

Reassured by her smile, he kissed her softly on the lips. Jackson could do anything he put his mind to, and as he jogged back to the stage he decided the charity ball was the perfect venue to prove his love to Grace.

Chapter 19

The glass-and-marble-filled lobby of the Four Seasons Hotel was packed with so many socialites, celebrities and influential businessmen Grace thought she was at a political convention. The luxury downtown hotel was only blocks away from the Space Needle, and the perfect venue for a black-tie event. Hundreds of people, decked out in tuxedos, floor-length gowns and diamonds, were milling about, networking and socializing.

Approaching the ballroom, Grace was shocked to see her dad pacing in front of the double doors. He had a troubled expression on his face and seemed oblivious to the stares he was receiving from silver-haired guests who reeked of old money. Casually dressed in a T-shirt and faded blue jeans, her dad looked out of place among Seattle's elite movers and shakers.

"Dad, what are you doing here?" Grace asked, approaching him. "Is everything okay?"

He stopped pacing, clutched her shoulders and stared deep into her eyes.

"What is it? You're scaring me."

"It was me. I did it."

Dread coated her stomach. "Did what?"

"I planted a college intern at Lillian's to steal the Draynut recipe."

Her heart plunged to her feet. Her dad had confirmed her suspicions, but instead of feeling relieved that he'd finally confessed, Grace felt worse. "Dad, no, how could you?"

"I'm embarrassed about what I did," he said, raking a hand over his hair. "It was foolish of me to think I could succeed by screwing Lillian's over, and I hope you'll find it in your heart to forgive me. I wanted to honor your mother's legacy, but went about it the wrong way."

Unable to speak, Grace swallowed hard.

"Pumpkin, I've thought a lot about your promotional ideas, and I think it's time we implement some of them." Taking her hand in his, he spoke with pride. "Poetry Fridays and Talent Night Saturdays will be a hit. I know it."

"I agree. We're going to knock 'em dead!" Grace smiled, to prove to her dad he had her support, but her heart was full of sadness. What would Jackson do when the truth came out? Would he still love her? Would his family make him choose between them and her?

"I caught a glimpse of you with Jackson Drayson this morning at Bite of Seattle. It's obvious you love him, and seeing you happy and content makes me happy."

Sensing a presence, Grace glanced around the lobby. Jackson appeared at her side and she sucked in a shaky breath. How much had he heard? What did he know? He looked debonair in his crisp black tuxedo, and smelled of sandalwood, her favorite masculine scent. Seeing Jackson decked out in designer threads, Grace was reminded of the Heritage Awards dinner weeks earlier, and smiled at the memory of that romantic, passionate night.

"I'm Jackson Drayson, Mr. Nicholas. It's an honor to finally meet you."

"Grace had nothing to do with stolen recipe. I paid Kelsey Andrews to steal it," he blurted out. "I know it was a rotten thing to do, so I'm canceling the Chocolate Explosion ad campaign and pulling the dessert from our menu."

"It takes a strong man to not only admit his mistakes, but to make amends for it," Jackson said. "I appreciate the gesture, Mr. Nicholas, and I'm sure my family will, too."

"Jackson, what are you going to do about Kelsey?" Grace asked. "I know how much you like her, and she's been a huge help to you the last few months."

"I'm going to fire her, and anyone else who helped her. Loyalty means everything to me, and now I know she can't be trusted."

Troubled, Grace fidgeted with her hands. She hated what her father had done, and wished there was something she could do to make it up to Jackson and his siblings.

"Take good care of my daughter, Jackson."

"I will, sir. You have my word."

Grace hugged her dad and kissed his cheek. "Thanks, Dad. I love you."

"I love you, too, pumpkin. Have fun tonight."

Wearing a sad smile, he strode through the lobby, out of the hotel doors and into the balmy summer night.

Grace had no words. Her father's deception saddened her, and she feared the Draysons would hold his mistakes against her.

"I love your dress."

"What? This old thing?" she joked, striking a pose.

Jackson chuckled and happiness bloomed inside her heart. Wanting to impress him, she'd selected an empire waist gown with crystals along the bodice, and paired it with satin high heels. Admiration shone in his eyes and Grace knew she'd chosen wisely.

"You look like an ebony princess."

"Why, thank you, Mr. Drayson. That's *just* the look I was going for."

"I'm so glad you're here. I was scared you wouldn't come."

"I'm scared, too, Jackson, but I'm willing to break the rules with you."

"How ironic," he said, a pensive expression on his face. "Because seeing you in this stunning white dress makes me want to get all traditional with you."

Her ears tingled. "Wh-what are you saying?"

"What if we eloped, and relocated to New York?"

"Elope?" Grace squeaked. "We can't elope."

"Of course we can. I know it seems sudden, but it feels right. *We* feel right."

His words, and his smile, touched her heart.

"It's not as if I was born to be a baker," he continued. "I've had lots of great careers over the years, and I've never had trouble finding a job. Furthermore, you've always dreamed of moving to the Big Apple, and I want to make your dreams come true."

Mindful of his feelings, Grace chose her words carefully. "I want to marry you, but we can't elope to New

York. It's important to me to have our friends and family there, and I don't want to upset the people we love by shutting them out of the biggest day of our lives."

"I never looked at it that way," he said.

"Furthermore, I don't want to be the reason why you pull out of Lillian's of Seattle." Caressing his face, she tenderly stroked his chiseled features. "Don't you want to see what you could accomplish if you stuck with the bakery for a while?"

"I intend to stick with you forever." Jackson wore an impish smile. Gazing at her, he drew her to him, wrapping his arms possessively around her waist.

"Baby, I can't wait to see what you do with the bakery. You've been successful at the things you've done short-term, so imagine what you could accomplish at the bakery over time. What we could accomplish together if we worked as a team."

"I know one thing I'd like to accomplish with you…"

"Do tell," she cooed, loving their playful banter and the broad, sexy grin on his mouth.

"I'm staying in the penthouse suite, so let's go upstairs and break as many rules as we can think of." He added, "And, this time we won't have to worry about the boys in blue showing up!"

"I'd love to, but *first* I have to meet your parents. I've wanted to meet them for quite some time and this is the perfect opportunity, don't you think?"

"Damn, I wish you weren't so responsible!" Jackson gave her a peck on the lips, then straightened to his full height and offered his forearm. "Ready to meet my family?"

Grace wet her lips with her tongue, wishing her throat wasn't bone-dry. Their arrival at the charity gala was sure to raise a few eyebrows, but she didn't care what anyone thought and snuggled against her man. "I'd love to. Lead the way."

With floor-to-ceiling windows providing spectacular views of Elliott Bay and Puget Sound, the grand ballroom held a magical, enchanted feel. The turquoise water, tall, majestic mountains and pinkish-orange sunset in the background were breathtaking. Professional athletes, TV personalities and celebrity impersonators were on hand signing autographs, and caricature artists sketched images of guests. The five-piece band was performing a Frank Sinatra song, but the atmosphere was as loud and as cheerful as a high school pep rally. Couples kissed and laughed, and animated conversation filled the room.

"Wow, I've never seen this many famous faces in one place before," Grace exclaimed, marveling at all of the big names in attendance. "Your mom must have a lot of connections."

"You've seen one celebrity, you've seen them all."

Incredulous, Grace swatted his forearm. "Oh, stop. The only reason you're not schmoozing with the cast of *Models of Miami* is because the line at their table is out the door."

"Why would I want to hang out with a bunch of catty reality stars when I have you?" Jackson asked, his tone as seductive as his gaze. "You're the total package and I know how lucky I am to have a woman like you in my life. That's why I'll never take you for granted."

It was a struggle to keep a straight face, but she gave him a pointed look and hitched a hand to her hips. "You're trying to get in my panties again, aren't you, Drayson?"

"No." Reaching out, he drew his fingers across her cheek, lovingly and tenderly caressing her skin. "These past few weeks with you have been incredible, the best of my life, and if we never make love again it wouldn't change how I feel about you."

Touched by his words, she wanted to wrap her arms around him and kiss him until she was breathless, but they had an audience, and Grace didn't want to offend his family. The Drayson clan was spread out across two tables and everyone was staring at them. The last thing she wanted to do was upset his loved ones, so she wisely kept her hands at her sides, and off his muscled body.

"Grace, this is my family," Jackson announced, gesturing to the wide-eyed, fashionably dressed group. "Family, this is my girlfriend, Grace Nicholas."

Shaking hands with everyone at the table, Grace admired how suave the men looked, how beautiful the women were and how friendly everyone was, especially Jackson's parents. Energized by their enthusiasm, she clasped Jackson's hand and smiled up at him, deeply grateful they'd been given a second chance at love.

"Grace, it's a pleasure to finally meet you," Nadia said brightly. "My son is completely smitten with you, and it's obvious why."

Graham stepped forward and nodded in greeting. "We've heard a lot of great things about you, and we look forward to getting to know you better."

"Thank you, Mr. and Mrs. Drayson. It's an honor to be here, and I appreciate the warm welcome."

Lillian tapped a gold, dainty spoon against her champagne flute and everyone gathered around her, moving in close to hear what she had to say. "Opening Lillian's of Seattle was the smartest decision I've ever made," she confessed with a proud smile. "Not only has it exceeded my expectations and created a bond across the generations, it helped toward repairing the breach that occurred between Oscar and Henry many moons ago..."

Grace caught Mariah staring at her and giggled when Jackson's sister waved frantically.

"Chase, Mariah and Jackson came together to open the best new bakery on the west coast, and in the process found their soul mates, and I couldn't be happier for them." Raising her flute in the air, her gaze landed on her husband of fifty-five years, Henry Drayson. "A good marriage is like a plum pudding. Only those who make it *really* know what goes into it, so work as a team, and never lose sight of your love."

"To true love!" Henry shouted. "May the fairy tale never end!"

"To true love!" the Drayson clan bellowed in one voice, clinking glasses.

Jackson squeezed Grace's hand and she beamed at him, convinced her heart would burst with love and happiness. Feeling her eyes tear up, she circled her arms around his waist, and rested her head on his chest. His closeness and his dreamy cologne set her body on fire, and Grace couldn't wait to get Jackson upstairs to his suite. He must have read her thoughts because he gestured to the ballroom doors, causing Grace to giggle. "I love you, Jackson."

"And, I love you," he whispered. "You'll never have to question my love, and I'll cherish you every day for the rest of our lives, as long as we both shall live."

Jackson stepped forward, dropped to one knee, and clasped Grace's left hand, sending shock waves through her body. *This can't be happening*, she thought. Her knees were knocking together, threatening to give way. *I* must *be dreaming!*

Gazing up at her with love in his eyes, Jackson slid a pear-shaped diamond ring onto her fourth finger, and squeezed her hand.

Emotion clogged her throat, and the room swam out of focus, spinning around her. It was hard to stay in the moment, but she blocked out everything around them and listened intently to what Jackson had to say.

"The first time we met you gave me attitude, and even dissed my pistachio cupcakes, but I didn't let that stop me from pursuing you. I knew in my heart you were the only one for me."

Remembering their infamous meeting weeks earlier at Lillian's made Grace smile. It felt like they'd known each other for years, rather than a few months. She was more comfortable with Jackson than anyone else she'd ever dated and wanted to spend all of her free time with him. He made her laugh, treated her with respect and showered her with love and affection. It was easy to love him, and she did, with every ounce of her being.

"Grace, I love you, with all that I am, and I always will. You will always be the only woman for me," he declared. "I love your wit, your sense of humor, how smart and sophisticated you are..."

His words touched her deeply, filling her with pride.

"You're everything to me," he said, his tone earnest and sincere. "The spring in my step, the beat of my heart, the sprinkles on my cupcake."

Giggling, she couldn't help but laugh at his joke.

"I knew I wanted to marry you the first time we kissed, and my feelings for you have only gotten stronger since Freezergate."

Grace heard chuckles and whistles behind her, and knew Jackson's family had heard about the night they spent in the bakery storage room.

"I've never loved anyone the way I love you and I want us to create more wonderful memories together. I'll bake for you, cheer you on at your roller derby games and whisk you off to New York to watch your beloved Knicks. Marry me, baby, and I promise you won't regret it."

Grace wanted to shout "yes" from the top of her lungs, but it felt like her lips were glued together. Bursting with excitement, she wrapped her arms around his neck, holding him tight.

"The noise is deafening in here," he said, brushing his nose playfully against hers, his hands affectionately patting her hips. "Was that a 'yes'? Will you marry me?"

Grace noticed, for the first time, that the band had stopped playing and everyone in the room was watching them. Smiling through her tears, she fervently nodded her head, and snuggled against him. "When we're together I feel complete, and there's nothing I'd love more than becoming your lawfully wedded wife. I can't wait to become Mrs. Jackson Drayson!"

"How does a Christmas Day wedding sound?"

"Like heaven on earth," she said, tears spilling down her cheeks.

Grace wished her parents were there to celebrate the joyous occasion, but she sensed her mother's presence in the room, and would call her dad later to share her good news.

"I love you," she whispered. "Thank you for believing in me, and for giving me a second chance. You've made me the happiest woman in Seattle!"

A proud smile covered his face. "I aim to please," he said with a wink.

Pressing her lips to his mouth, Grace kissed her new fiancé slowly, deeply, proving to the world that Jackson Drayson—her one-time rival, and biggest competitor— was indeed the man of her dreams.

* * * * *

BEST FRIEND BRIDE

KAT CANTRELL

One

Jonas Kim would typically describe himself as humble, but even he was impressed with the plan he'd conceived to outwit the smartest man he knew—his grandfather. Instead of marrying Sun, the nice woman from a prominent Korean family, a bride Grandfather had picked out, Jonas had proposed to Viviana Dawson. She was nice, too, but also his friend and, more importantly, someone he could trust not to contest the annulment when it came time to file it.

Not only was Viv amazing for agreeing to this ridiculous idea, she made excellent cupcakes. It was a win all the way around. Though he could have done without the bachelor party. So not his thing.

At least no strippers had shown up. Yet.

He and his two best buddies had flown to Vegas this morning and though Jonas had never been to the city of sin before, he was pretty sure it wouldn't take much to have naked women draped all over the suite. He could think of little he'd like less. Except for marrying Sun. That he would hate, and not only because she'd been selected on his behalf. Sun was a disaster waiting to happen that would happen to someone else because Jonas was marrying Viv tomorrow in what would go down as the greatest favor one friend had ever done for another.

"Sure you wanna do this?" Warren asked as he popped open the bottle of champagne.

Also a bachelor party staple that Jonas could have done without, but his friends would just laugh and make jokes about how Jonas needed to loosen up, despite being well aware that he had been raised in an ultra-conservative family. Grandfather had a lot of traditional ideas about how a CEO should act, and Jonas hadn't landed that job, not yet. Besides, there was nothing wrong with having a sense of propriety.

"Which part?" Jonas shot back. "The bachelor party or inviting you morons along?"

Hendrix, the other moron, grinned and took his glass of champagne from Warren. "You can't get married without a bachelor party. That would be sad."

"It's not a real wedding. Therefore, one would assume that the traditions don't really have to be observed."

Warren shook his head. "It is a real wedding. You're going to marry this woman simply to get out of having a different bride. Hence my question. Are you sure this is the only way? I don't get why you can't just tell your grandfather thanks but no thanks. Don't let him push you around."

They'd literally been having the exact same argument for two weeks. Grandfather still held the reins of the Kim empire closely to his chest. In Korea. If Jonas had any hope of Grandfather passing those reins to him so he could move the entire operation to North Carolina, he had to watch his step. Marrying a Korean woman from a powerful family would only solidify Jonas's ties to a country that he did not consider his home.

"I respect my elders," Jonas reminded Warren mildly. "And I also respect that Sun's grandfather and my grandfather are lifelong friends. I can't expose her or it might disrupt everything."

Sun had been thrilled with the idea of marrying Jonas; she had a secret—and highly unsuitable—lover she didn't want anyone to find out about and she'd pounced on the idea of a husband to mask her affair. Meanwhile, their grandfathers were cackling over their proposed business merger once the two families were united in marriage.

Jonas wanted no part of any of that. Better to solve the problem on his own terms. If he was already married, no one could expect him to honor his grandfather's agreement. And once the merger had gone through, he and Viv could annul their marriage and go on with Jonas's integrity intact.

It was brilliant. Viv was the most awesome person on the planet for saving his butt from being burned in this deal. Tomorrow, they'd say some words, sign a piece of paper and poof. No more problems.

"Can you guys just be happy that you got a trip to Vegas out of this and shut up?" Jonas asked, and clinked glasses with the two men he'd bonded with freshman year at Duke University.

Jonas Kim, Hendrix Harris and Warren Garinger had

become instant friends when they'd been assigned to the same project group along with Marcus Powell. The four teenagers had raised a lot of hell together—most of which Jonas had watched from the sidelines—and propped each other up through everything the college experience could throw at them. Until Marcus had fallen head over heels for a cheerleader who didn't return his love. The aftermath of that still affected the surviving three members of their quartet to this day.

"Can't. You said no strippers," Hendrix grumbled, and downed his champagne in one practiced swallow. "Really don't see the point of a bachelor party in Las Vegas if you're not going to take full advantage of what's readily available."

Jonas rolled his eyes. "Like you don't have a wide array of women back in Raleigh who would get naked for you on demand."

"Yeah, but I've already seen them," he argued with a wink. "There are thousands of women whose breasts I've yet to ogle and I've been on my best behavior at home. What happens in Vegas doesn't affect my mom's campaign, right?"

Hendrix's mom was running for governor of North Carolina and had made him swear on a stack of Bibles that he would not do anything to jeopardize her chances. For Hendrix, that meant a complete overhaul of his social life, and he was feeling the pinch. So far, his uncanny ability to get photographed with scantily clad women hadn't surfaced, but he'd just begun his vow of chastity, so there was plenty of opportunity to cause a scandal if he really put his mind to it.

"Maybe we could focus on the matter at hand?" Warren suggested, and ran his fingers through his wavy brown hair as he plopped down on the love seat near the floor-to-ceiling glass wall of the Sky Suite they'd booked at the Aria. The dizzying lights of Vegas spread out in a panoramic view sixty stories below.

"Which is?"

Warren pointed his glass at Jonas. "You're getting married. Despite the pact."

The pact.

After the cheerleader had thoroughly eviscerated Marcus, he'd faded further and further away until eventually, he'd opted to end his pain permanently. In the aftermath of his death, the three friends had sworn to never let love destroy them as it had Marcus. The reminder sobered them all.

"Hey, man. The pact is sacred," Jonas said with a scowl. "But we never vowed to remain single the rest of our lives. Just that we'd never let a woman take us down like that. Love is the problem, not marriage."

Once a year, the three of them dropped whatever they were doing and spent the evening honoring the memory of their late friend. It was part homage, part reiteration of the pact. The profoundly painful incident had affected them in different ways, but no one would argue that Warren had taken his roommate's suicide harder than anyone save Marcus's mother.

That was the only reason Jonas gave him a pass for the insult. Jonas had followed the pact to the letter, which was easier than he'd ever let on. First of all, a promise meant something to him.

Second, Jonas never got near a woman he could envision falling in love with. That kind of loss of control... the concept made his skin crawl. Jonas had too much to lose to let a woman destroy everything he'd worked for.

Warren didn't look convinced. "Marriage is the gateway, my friend. You can't put a ring on a woman's finger and expect that she won't start dreaming of romantic garbage."

"Ah, but I can," Jonas corrected as he let Hendrix top off his champagne. "That's why this plan is so great. Viv knows the score. We talked about exactly what was going to happen. She's got her cupcake business and has no room for a boyfriend, let alone a permanent husband. I wouldn't have asked her to do this for me if she wasn't a good friend."

A friend who wasn't interested in taking things deeper. That was the key and the only reason Jonas had continued their friendship for so long. If there was even a possibility of getting emotional about her, he'd have axed their association immediately, just like he had with every other woman who posed a threat to the tight rein he held on his heart.

Hendrix drank straight from the champagne bottle to get the last few drops, his nearly colorless hazel eyes narrowed in contemplation as he set the empty bottle on the coffee table. "If she's such a good friend, how come we haven't met her?"

"Really? It's confusing to you why I'd want to keep her away from the man voted most likely to corrupt a nun four years in a row?"

With a grin, Hendrix jerked his head at Warren. "So Straight and Narrow over there should get the thumbs-up. Yet she's not allowed to meet him either?"

Jonas shrugged. "I'll introduce you at the ceremony tomorrow."

When it would be unavoidable. How was he supposed to explain that Viv was special to a couple of knuckleheads like his friends? From the first moment he'd met her, he'd been drawn to her sunny smile and generosity.

The little bakery near the Kim Building called Cupcaked had come highly recommended by Jonas's admin, so he'd stopped in to pick up a thank-you for his staff. As he'd stood in the surprisingly long line to place his order, a pretty brown-haired woman had exited from the back. She'd have captured his interest regardless, but when she'd stepped outside to slip a cupcake to a kid on the street who'd been standing nose pressed to her window for the better part of fifteen minutes, Jonas couldn't resist talking to her.

He'd been dropping in to get her amazing lemon cupcakes for almost a year now. Sometimes Viv let him take her for coffee to someplace where she didn't have to jump behind the counter on the fly, and occasionally she dropped by the Kim Building to take Jonas to lunch.

It was an easy, no-pressure friendship that he valued because there was no danger of him falling in too deep when she so clearly wasn't interested in more. They weren't sleeping together, and that kind of relationship wouldn't compute to his friends.

Didn't matter. He was happy with the status quo. Viv was doing him a favor and in return, he'd make it up to her with free business consulting advice for the rest of her life. After all, Jonas had singlehandedly launched Kim Electronics in the American market and had grown revenue to the tune of $4.7 billion last year. She could do worse than to have his undivided attention on her balance sheet whenever she asked, which he'd gladly make time for.

All he had to do was get her name on a marriage

certificate and lie low until his grandfather's merger went through. Then Viv could go back to her single cupcake-baker status and Jonas could celebrate dodging the bullet.

Warren's point about marriage giving a girl ideas about love and romance was pure baloney. Jonas wasn't worried about sticking to the pact. Honor was his moral compass, as it was his grandfather's. Love represented a loss of control that other men might fall prey to, but not Jonas. He would never betray his friends or the memory of the one they'd lost.

All he had to do was marry a woman who had no romantic feelings for him.

Viviana Dawson had dreamed about her wedding day a bunch of times and not once had she imagined the swirl in her gut, which could only be described as a cocktail of nerves and *holy crap*.

Jonas was going to be her husband in a few short minutes and the anticipation of *what if* was killing her.

Jonas Kim had asked her to marry him. *Jonas.* The man who had kept Viv dateless for almost a year because who could measure up to perfection? Nobody.

Oh, sure, he'd framed it all as a favor and she'd accepted under the premise that they'd be filing for annulment ASAP. But still. She'd be Mrs. Kim for as long as it lasted.

Which might be short indeed if he figured out she had a huge crush on him.

He wasn't going to figure it out. Because *oh, my God.* If he did find out…

Well, he couldn't. It would ruin their friendship for one. And also? She had no business getting into a serious relationship, not until she figured out how to do and be whatever the opposite was of what she'd been doing and being with men thus far in her adult dating life.

Her sisters called it clingy. She called it committed. Men called it quits.

Jonas was the antidote to all that.

The cheesy chapel wasn't anything close to the venue of her fantasies, but she'd have married Jonas in a wastewater treatment plant if he'd asked her to. She pushed open the door, alone and not too happy about it. In retrospect, she should have insisted one of her sisters come to Vegas with her. Maybe to act as her maid of honor.

She could really use a hand to hold right about now, but no. She hadn't told any of her sisters she was getting married, not even Grace, who was closest to her in age and had always been her confidante. Well, until Grace had disappeared into her own family in much the same fashion as their other two sisters had done.

Viv was the cute pony in the Dawson family stable of Thoroughbreds. Which was the whole reason Viv hadn't mentioned her quickie Vegas wedding to a man who'd never so much as kissed her.

She squared her shoulders. A fake marriage was exactly what she wanted. Mostly.

Well, of course she wanted a real marriage eventually. But this one would get her into the secret club that the rest of the married Dawson sisters already belonged to. Plus, Jonas needed her. Total win across the board.

The chapel was hushed and far more sacrosanct than she'd have expected in what was essentially the drivethrough lane of weddings. The quiet scuttled across her skin, turning it clammy. She was really doing this. It had all been conceptual before. Now it was real.

Could you have a nervous breakdown and recover in less than two minutes? She didn't want to miss a second of her wedding. But she might need to sit down first.

And then everything fell away as she saw Jonas in a slim-fitting dark suit that showcased his wiry frame. His energy swept out and engulfed her, as it always had from that first time she'd turned to see him standing outside her shop, his attention firmly on her instead of the sweet treats in the window.

Quick with a smile, quicker with a laugh, Jonas Kim's beautiful angular face had laced Viv's dreams many a night. He had a pretty rocking body, too. He kept in great shape playing racquetball with his friends, and she'd spent hours picturing him shirtless, his chest glistening as he swung a racket. In short, he was a truly gorgeous individual who she could never study long enough to sate herself.

Jonas's dark, expressive eyes lit up as he caught sight of her and he crossed the small vestibule to sweep her into a hug. Her arms came up around his waist automatically. How, she had no idea, when this was literally the first time he'd ever touched her.

He even smelled gorgeous.

And now would be a great time to unstick her tongue from the roof of her mouth. "Hey."

Wonderful. They'd had spirited debates on everything from the travesty of pairing red wine with fish to the merits of the beach over the mountains. Shakespeare, *The Simpsons*. But put her in the arms of the man she'd been salivating over for months and the power of speech deserted her.

He stepped back. Didn't help. And now she was cold.

"I'm so glad you're here," he said, his smooth voice

ruffling all her nerve endings in the most delicious way. Despite being born in North Carolina, he had almost no accent. Good thing. He was already devastating enough.

"Can't have a wedding with no bride," she informed him. Oh, thank God, she could still talk, Captain Obvious moment aside. "Am I dressed okay for a fake marriage?"

His intense eyes honed in on her. "You look amazing. I love that you bought a new dress for this."

Yeah, that was why she passed up the idiots who hit on her with lame lines like "Give me your number and I'll frost your cupcakes for you." Jonas paid attention to her and actually noticed things like what she wore. She'd picked out this yellow dress because he'd mentioned once that he liked the color.

Which made it all the more strange that he'd never clued in that she had a huge thing for him. She was either better at hiding it than she'd had a right to hope for, or he knew and mercifully hadn't mentioned it.

Her pulse sped out of control. He didn't know, she repeated silently. Maybe a little desperately.

There was no way he could know. He'd never have asked her to do this marriage favor otherwise.

She'd been faking it this long. No reason to panic.

"I wanted to look good," she told him. *For you.* "For the pictures."

He smiled. "Mission accomplished. I want you to meet Warren."

Jonas turned, absently putting his arm around her and oh, that was nice. They were a unit already, and it had seemed to come so naturally. Did he feel it, too?

That's when she realized there was another man in the vestibule. Funny, she hadn't even noticed him, though she supposed women must fawn all over him, with those cheekbones and that expensive haircut. She held out her hand to the friend Jonas had talked endlessly about. "Nice to meet you. Jonas speaks very highly of you."

"Likewise," Warren said with a cryptic glance at Jonas. "And I'm sure whatever he's told you is embellished."

Doubtful when she didn't need Jonas's help to know that the energy drink company his friend ran did very well. You couldn't escape the logo for Flying Squirrel no matter where you looked.

Jonas waved that off with a smirk. "Whatever, man. Where's Hendrix?"

"Not my turn to babysit him." Warren shrugged, pulling out his phone. "I'll text him. He'll be here."

Somehow, Jonas seemed to have forgotten his arm was still around Viv's waist and she wasn't about to remind him. But then he guided her toward the open double doors that led to the interior of the chapel with firm fingers. Well, if this almost-intimacy was part of the wedding package, she'd take it.

"I'm not waiting on his sorry ass," Jonas called over his shoulder. "There are a thousand more couples in line behind us and I'm not losing my spot."

Warren nodded and waved, still buried in his phone.

"Some friends," Jonas murmured to her with a laugh, his head bent close. He was still taller than her even when she wore heels, but it had never been as apparent as it was today, since she was still tucked against his side as if he never meant to let go. "This is an important day in my life and you see how they are."

"I'm here." For as long as he needed her.

Especially if he planned to put his arm around her a whole bunch more. His warm palm on her waist had oddly settled her nerves. And put a whole different kind of butterfly south of her stomach.

Wow, was it hot in here or what? She resisted the urge to fan herself as the spark zipped around in places that *could not* be so affected by this man's touch.

His smile widened. "Yes, you are. Have I mentioned lately how much I appreciate that? The slot for very best friend in the whole world has just become yours, since clearly you're the only one who deserves it."

As reminders went, it was both brutal and necessary. This was a favor. Not an excuse for a man to get handsy with her.

Fine. Good. She and Jonas were friends, which was perfect. She had a habit of pouring entirely too much of herself into a man who didn't return her level of commitment. Mark had stuck it out slightly longer than Zachary, and she didn't like to think about how quickly she'd shed Gary and Judd. A sad commentary on her twenties that she'd had fewer boyfriends than fingers on one hand.

A favor marriage was the best kind because she knew exactly how it would end. It was like reading the last page of the book ahead of time, and for someone who loved surprise flowers but hated surprise discussions that started with "we have to talk," the whole thing sounded really great.

No pressure. No reason to get clingy and drive Jonas away with her neediness. She could be independent and witty and build her confidence with this marriage. It was a practice run with all the best benefits. He'd already asked her to move into his penthouse on Boylan

Avenue. As long as she didn't mess up and let on how much she wanted to cling to every last inch of the man, it was all good.

Back on track, she smiled at the friend she was about to marry. They were friends with benefits that had nothing to do with sex. A point she definitely needed to keep in the forefront of her brain.

A lady in a puke-green suit approached them and verified they were the happy couple, then ran down the order of the ceremony. If this had been a real marriage, Viv might be a little disappointed in the lack of fanfare. In less than a minute, traditional organ music piped through the overhead speakers and the lady shoved a drooping bouquet at Viv. She clutched it to her chest, wondering if she'd get to keep it. One flower was enough. She'd press it into a book as a reminder of her wedding to a great man who treated her with nothing but kindness and respect.

Jonas walked her down the aisle, completely unruffled. Of course. Why would he be nervous? This was all his show and he'd always had a supreme amount of confidence no matter the situation.

His friend Warren stood next to an elderly man holding a Bible. Jonas halted where they'd been told to stand and glanced at her with a reassuring smile.

"Dearly beloved," the man began and was immediately interrupted by a commotion at the back. Viv and Jonas both turned to see green-suit lady grappling with the door as someone tried to get into the room.

"Sir, the ceremony has already started," she called out to no avail as the man who must be Hendrix Harris easily shoved his way inside and joined them at the front.

Yep. He looked just like the many, many pictures she'd seen of him strewn across the media, and not just because his mother was running for governor. Usually he had a gorgeous woman glued to his side and they were doing something overly sensual, like kissing as if no one was watching.

"Sorry," he muttered to Jonas. His eyes were bloodshot and he looked like he'd slept in his expensively tailored shirt and pants.

"Figured you'd find a way to make my wedding memorable," Jonas said without malice, because that's the kind of man he was. She'd have a hard time being so generous with someone who couldn't be bothered to show up on time.

The officiant started over, and in a few minutes, she and Jonas exchanged vows. All fake, she chanted to herself as she promised to love and cherish.

"You may kiss the bride," the officiant said with so little inflection that it took a minute for it to sink in that he meant *Jonas* could kiss *her*. Her pulse hit the roof.

Somehow, they hadn't established what would happen here. She glanced at Jonas and raised a brow. Jonas hesitated.

"This is the part where you kiss her, idiot," Hendrix muttered with a salacious grin.

This was her one chance, the only time she had every right to put her lips on this man, and she wasn't missing the opportunity. The other people in the room vanished as she flattened her palms on Jonas's lapels. He leaned in and put one hand on her jaw, guiding it upward. His warmth bled through her skin, enlivening it, and then her brain ceased to function as his mouth touched hers.

Instantly, that wasn't enough and she pressed forward, seeking more of him. The kiss deepened as his lips aligned properly and oh, yes, that was it.

Her crush exploded into a million little pieces as she tasted what it was like to kiss Jonas. That nice, safe attraction she had been so sure she could hide gained teeth, slicing through her midsection with sharp heat. The dimensions of sensation opened around her, giving her a tantalizing glimpse of how truly spectacular it would feel if he didn't stop.

But he did stop, stepping back so quickly that she almost toppled over. He caught her forearms and held her steady…though he looked none too steady himself, his gaze enigmatic and heated in a way she'd never witnessed before.

Clearly that experience had knocked them both for a loop. What did you say to someone you'd just kissed and who you wanted to kiss again, but really, that hadn't been part of the deal?

"That was nice," Jonas murmured. "Thanks."

Nice was not the word on her mind. So they were going to pretend that hadn't just happened, apparently.

Good. That was exactly what they should do. Treat it like a part of the ceremony and move on.

Except her lips still tingled, and how in the world was Jonas just standing there holding her hand like nothing momentous had occurred? She needed to learn the answer to that, stat. Especially if they were going to be under the same roof. Otherwise, their friendship—and this marriage—would be toast the second he clued in to how hot and bothered he got her. He'd specifically told her that he could trust her because they were *friends* and he needed her to be one.

"I now pronounce you husband and wife," the officiant intoned, completely oblivious to how the earth had just swelled beneath Viv's feet.

Jonas turned and led her back up the aisle, where they signed the marriage license. They ended up in the same vestibule they'd been in minutes before, but now they were married.

Her signature underneath Jonas's neat script made it official, but as she'd expected, it was just a piece of paper. The kiss, on the other hand? That had shaken her to the core.

How was she going to stop herself from angling for another one?

"Well," Hendrix said brightly. "I'd say this calls for a drink. I'll buy."

Two

Jonas had never thought of his six-thousand-square-foot penthouse condo as small. Until today. It was full of Viviana Dawson. Er, *Kim*. Viviana Kim. She'd officially changed her name at the Department of Motor Vehicles, and soon, she'd have a new driver's license that said she had the legal right to call herself that. By design. His sense of honor wouldn't permit him to outright lie about his relationship with Viv; therefore, she was Mrs. Kim in every sense of the word.

Except one.

The concept was surreal. As surreal as the idea that she was his wife and he could introduce her as such to anyone who asked.

Except for himself apparently because he was having a hard time thinking of her that way no matter how many times he repeated the word *wife* when he glimpsed her through the archway leading to the kitchen. Boxes upon boxes covered every inch of the granite countertops, and though she'd been working on unpacking them for an hour, it looked like she'd barely made a dent.

He should quit skulking around and get in there to help. But he hadn't because he couldn't figure out how to manage the weird vibe that had sprung up between them.

That *kiss*.

It had opened up a Pandora's box that he didn't know how to close. Before, he'd had a sort of objective understanding that Viv was a beautiful woman whose company he enjoyed.

Ever since the ceremony, no more. There was a thin veil of awareness that he couldn't shake. But he needed to. They were living together as *friends* because she'd agreed to a favor that didn't include backing her up against the counter so he could explore her lush mouth.

He liked Viv. Add a previously undiscovered attraction and she was exactly the kind of woman he'd studiously avoided for nearly a decade. The kind he could easily envision taking him deeper and deeper until he was emotionally overwhelmed enough to give up everything.

The problem of course being that he couldn't stop calling her, like he usually did with women who threatened his vow. He'd married this one.

He was being ridiculous. What was he, seventeen? He could handle a little spark between friends, right? Best way to manage that was to ignore it. And definitely not let on that he'd felt something other than friendly ever since kissing her.

All he and Viv had to do was live together until he could convince his grandfather to go through with the merger anyway. Once the two companies signed agreements, neither would back out and Jonas was home free. Since he was covering Viv's rent until then, she could move back into her apartment at that point.

This plan would work, and soon enough, he could look back on it smugly and pinpoint the exact moment when he'd outsmarted his grandfather.

Casually, he leaned on the exposed-brick column between the dining room and the kitchen and crossed his arms like everything was cool between them. It *would* be cool. "What can I do?"

Viv jerked and spun around to face him, eyes wide. "You scared me. Obviously."

Her nervous laugh ruffled his spine. So they were both feeling the weirdness, but it was clearly different weirdness on her side than on his. She was jumpy and nervous, not hot and bothered. He had not seen that coming. That was…not good. "Sorry. I didn't mean to. We've both been living alone for so long that I guess we have to get through an adjustment period."

Which was the opposite of what he'd expected. They'd always been so relaxed with each other. How could they get back to that?

She nodded. "Yes, that's what I've been telling myself."

Was it that bad? Her forlorn voice tripped something inside him and it was not okay that she was uncomfortable around him now. "Best way to adjust is to spend time together. Let me help you put away these…" He grabbed a square glass dish from the counter. "Pans?"

"Pyrex." She smiled and it seemed like it came easier. "I can't imagine you care anything about where I put my bakeware."

He waggled his brows. "That depends on whether that's something you use to make cupcakes or not."

Her cupcakes weren't like the store-bought ones in the hard plastic clamshells. Those tasted like sugared flour with oily frosting. Viv's lemon cupcakes—a flavor he'd never have said he'd like—had a clean, bright taste like she'd captured lemonade in cake form.

"It's not. Casseroles."

"Not a fan of those." He made a face before he thought better of it.

Maybe she loved casseroles and he was insulting her taste. And her cooking skills. But he'd never said one word about her whipping up dinner for him each night, nor did he expect her to. She knew that. Right?

They had so much to learn about each other, especially if they were going to make this marriage seem as real as possible to everyone, except select few people they could trust, like Warren and Hendrix. If word got back to his grandfather that something wasn't kosher, the charade would be over.

And he'd invested way too much in this marriage to let it fail now.

His phone beeped from his pocket, and since the CEO never slept, he handed over the glass dish to check the message.

Grandfather. At 6:00 a.m. Seoul time. Jonas tapped the message. All the blood drained from his head.

"Jonas, what's wrong?" Viv's palm came to rest on his forearm and he appreciated the small bit of comfort even as it stirred things it shouldn't.

"My grandfather. My dad told him that we got married." Because Jonas had asked him to. The whole point had been to circumvent his grandfather's arranged-marriage plan. But this—

"Oh, no. He's upset, isn't he?" Viv worried her lip with her teeth, distracting him for a moment.

"On the contrary," Jonas spit out hoarsely. "He's thrilled. He's so excited to meet you, he got on a plane last night. He's here. In Raleigh. Best part? He talked my dad into having a house party to welcome you into the family. This weekend."

It was a totally unforeseen move. Wily. He didn't believe for a second that his grandfather was thrilled with Jonas's quick marriage or that the CEO of one of the largest conglomerates in Korea had willingly walked away from his board meetings to fly seven thousand miles to meet his new granddaughter-in-law.

This was something else. A test. An "I'll believe it when I see it." Maybe Grandfather scented a whiff of the truth and all it would take was one slipup before he'd pounce. If pressed, Jonas would feel honor bound to be truthful about Viv's role. The marriage could be history before dark.

A healthy amount of caution leaped into Viv's expression. "This weekend? As in we have two days to figure out how to act like a married couple?"

"Now you're starting to see why my face looks like this." He swirled an index finger near his nose, unbelievably grateful that she had instantly realized the problem. "Viv, I'm sorry. I had no idea he was going to do this."

The logistics alone... How could he tell his mom to give them separate bedrooms when they were essentially still supposed to be in the honeymoon phase? He couldn't. It was ludicrous to even think in that direction when what he should be doing was making a list of all the ways this whole plan was about to fall apart. So he could mitigate each and every one.

"Hey."

Jonas glanced up as Viv laced her fingers with his as if she'd done it many times, when in fact she hadn't. She shouldn't. He liked it too much.

"I'm here," she said, an echo of her sentiment at the wedding ceremony. "I'm not going anywhere. My comment wasn't supposed to be taken as a 'holy cow how are we going to do this.' It was an 'oh, so we've got two days to figure this out.' We will."

There was literally no way to express how crappy that made him feel. Viv was such a trouper, diving into this marriage without any thought to herself and her own sense of comfort and propriety. He already owed her so much. He couldn't ask her to fake intimacy on top of everything else.

Neither did he like the instant heat that crowded into his belly at the thought of potential intimate details. *He* couldn't fake intimacy either. It would feel too much like lying.

The only way he could fathom acting like he and Viv were lovers would be if they were.

"You don't know my grandfather. He's probably already suspicious. This house party is intended to sniff out the truth."

"So?" She shrugged that off far too easily. "Let him sniff. What's he going to find out, that we're really legally married?"

"That the marriage is in name only."

To drive the point home, he reached out to cup Viv's

jaw and brought her head up until her gaze clashed with his, her mouth mere centimeters away from his in an almost-kiss that would be a real one with the slightest movement. She nearly jumped out of her skin and stumbled back a good foot until she hit the counter. And then she tried to keep going, eyes wide with…something.

"See?" he said. "I can't even touch you without all sorts of alarms going off. How are we going to survive a whole weekend?"

"Sorry. I wasn't—" She swallowed. "I wasn't expecting you to do that. So clearly the answer is that we need to practice."

"Practice what?" And then her meaning sank in. "Touching?"

"Kissing, too." Her chest rose and fell unevenly as if she couldn't quite catch her breath. "You said we would best get through the adjustment period by spending time together. Maybe we should do that the old-fashioned way. Take me on a date, Jonas."

Speechless, he stared at her, looking for the punch line, but her warm brown eyes held nothing but sincerity. The idea unwound in his gut with a long, liquid pull of anticipation that he didn't need any help interpreting.

A date with his wife. No, with Viv. And the whole goal would be to get her comfortable with his hands on her, to kiss her at random intervals until it was so natural, neither of them thought anything of it.

Crazy. And brilliant. Not to mention impossible.

"Will you wear a new dress?" That should not have been the next thing out of his mouth. *No* would be more advisable when he'd already identified a great big zone of danger surrounding his wife. But *yes* was the only answer if he wanted to pull off this plan.

She nodded, a smile stealing over her face. "The only caveat is no work. For either of us. Which means I get dessert that's not cupcakes."

Oddly, a date with Viv where kissing was expected felt like enough of a reward that he didn't mind that addendum so much, though giving up cupcakes seemed like a pretty big sacrifice. But as her brown eyes seared him thoroughly, the real sacrifice was going to be his sanity. Because he could get her comfortable with his hands on her, but there was no way to get *him* there.

The date would be nothing but torture—and an opportunity to practice making sure no one else realized that, an opportunity he could not pass up. Having an overdeveloped sense of ethics was very inconvenient sometimes.

"It's a deal. Pick you up at eight?"

That made her laugh for some reason. "My bedroom is next door to yours, silly. Are we going to have a secret knock?"

"Maybe." The vibe between them had loosened gradually to where they were almost back to normal, at least as far as she was concerned. Strange that the concept of taking Viv on a date should be the thing to do it. "What should it be?"

Rapping out a short-short-pause-short pattern, she raised her brows. "That means we're leaving in five minutes so get your butt in gear."

"And then that's my cue to hang out in the living room with a sporting event on TV because you're going to take an extra twenty?"

Tossing her head, she grinned. "You catch on fast. Now, I have to go get ready, which means you get to unload the rest of these boxes."

Though he groaned good-naturedly as she scampered out of the kitchen, he didn't mind taking over the chore. Actually, she should be sitting on the couch with a drink and a book while he slaved for hours to get the house exactly the way she liked it. He would have, too, simply because he owed her for this, but she'd insisted that she wanted to do it in order to learn where everything was. Looked like a date was enough to trump that concept.

As the faint sound of running water drifted through the walls, he found spots in his cavernous kitchen for the various pieces Viv had brought with her to this new, temporary life. Unpacking her boxes ended up being a more intimate task than he'd anticipated. She had an odd collection of things. He couldn't fathom the purpose of many of them, but they told him fascinating things about the woman he'd married. She made cupcakes for her business but she didn't have so much as one cupcake pan in her personal stash. Not only that, each item had a well-used sheen, random scrapes, dents, bent handles.

Either she'd spent hours in her kitchen trying to figure out what she liked to bake the most or she'd cleaned out an estate sale in one fell swoop. He couldn't wait to find out, because what better topic to broach on a date with a woman he needed to know inside and out before Friday night?

As he worked, he couldn't help but think of Viv on the other side of the walls, taking a shower. The ensuing images that slammed through his mind were not conducive to the task at hand and it got a little hard to breathe. He should not be picturing her "getting ready" when, in all honesty, he had no idea what that entailed. Odds were good she didn't lather herself up and spend extra time stroking the foam over her body like his brain seemed bent on imagining.

What was his *problem*? He never sat around and fantasized about a woman. He'd never felt strongly enough about one to do so. When was the last time he'd even gone on a date? He might stick Warren with the workaholic label but that could easily be turned back on Jonas. Running the entire American arm of a global company wasn't for wimps, and he had something to prove on top of that. Didn't leave a lot of room for dating, especially when the pact was first and foremost in his mind.

Of course the women he dated always made noises about not looking for anything serious and keeping their options open. And Jonas was always completely honest, but it didn't seem to matter if he flat-out said he wasn't ever going to fall in love. Mostly they took it as a challenge, and things got sticky fast, especially when said woman figured out he wasn't kidding.

Jonas was a champion at untangling himself before things went too far. Before *he* went too far. There were always warning signs that he was starting to like a woman too much. That's when he bailed.

So he had a lot of one-night stands that he'd never intended to be such. It made for stretches of lonely nights, which was perhaps the best side benefit of marriage. He didn't hate the idea of having someone to watch a movie with on a random Tuesday night, or drinking coffee with Viv in the morning before work. He hoped she liked that part of their marriage, too.

Especially since that was all they could ever have between them. It would be devastating to lose her friendship, which would surely happen if they took things to the next level. Once she found out about the pact, either she'd view it as a challenge or she'd immediately shut down. The latter was more likely. He'd hate either one.

At seven forty he stacked the empty boxes near the door so he could take them to the recycling center in the basement of the building later, then went to his room to change clothes for his date.

He rapped on Viv's door with the prescribed knock, grinning as he pictured her on the other side deliberately waiting for as long as she could to answer because they'd made a joke out of this new ritual. But she didn't follow the script and opened the door almost immediately.

Everything fled his mind but her as she filled the doorway, her fresh beauty heightened by the colors of her dress. She'd arranged her hair up on her head, leaving her neck bare. It was such a different look that he couldn't stop drinking her in, frozen by the small smile playing around her mouth.

"I didn't see much point in making you wait when I'm already ready," she commented. "Is it okay to tell you I'm a little nervous?"

He nodded, shocked his muscles still worked. "Yes. It's okay to tell me that. Not okay to be that way."

"I can't help it. I haven't been on a date in…" She bit her lip. "Well, it's been a little while. The shop is my life."

For some reason, that pleased him enormously. Though he shouldn't be so happy that they were cut from the same workaholic cloth. "For me, too. We'll be nervous together."

But then he already knew she had a lack in her social life since she'd readily agreed to this sham marriage, telling him she was too busy to date. Maybe together,

they could find ways to work less. To put finer pleasures first, just for the interim while they were living
together. That could definitely be one of the benefits
of their friendship.

She rolled her eyes. "You're not nervous. But you're
sweet to say so."

Maybe not nervous. But something.

His palms itched and he knew good and well the
only way to cure that was to put them on her bare arms
so he could test out the feel of her skin. It looked soft.

Wasn't the point of the date to touch her? He had
every reason to do exactly that. The urge to reach out
grew bigger and rawer with each passing second.

"Maybe we could start the date right now?" she suggested, and all at once, the hallway outside her room
got very small as she stepped closer, engulfing him in
lavender that could only be her soap.

His body reacted accordingly, treating him to some
more made-up images of her in the shower, and now
that he had a scent to associate with it, the spike through
his gut was that much more powerful. And that much
more of a huge warning sign that things were spiraling
out of control. He just couldn't see a good way to stop.

"Yeah?" he murmured, his throat raw with unfulfilled need. "Which part?"

There was no mistaking what she had in mind when
she reached out to graze her fingertips across his cheek.
Nerve endings fired under her touch and he leaned into
her palm, craving more of her.

"The only part that matters," she whispered back.
"The part where you don't even think twice about getting close to me. Where it's no big thing if you put your
arm around my waist or steal a kiss as I walk by."

If that was the goal, he was failing miserably because it was a big thing. A huge thing. And getting bigger as she leaned in, apparently oblivious to the way her lithe body brushed against his. His control snapped.

Before he came up with reasons why he shouldn't, he pulled her into his arms. Her mouth rose to meet his and, when it did, dropped them both into a long kiss. More than a kiss. An exploration.

With no witnesses this time, he had free rein to delve far deeper into the wonders of his wife than he had at the wedding ceremony.

Her enthusiastic response was killing him. *His* response was even worse. How had they been friends for so long without ever crossing this line? Well, he knew how—because if they had, he would have run in the other direction.

He groaned as her fingers threaded through his hair, sensitizing everything she touched. Then she iced that cake with a tentative push of her tongue that nearly put him on his knees. So unexpected and so very hot. Eagerly, he matched her sweet thrust with his own. Deeper and deeper they spiraled until he couldn't have said which way was up. Who was doing the giving and who was greedily lapping it up.

He wanted more and took it, easing her head back with firm fingers until he found the right angle to get more of her against his tongue. And now he wanted more of her against his body.

He slid a hand down the curve of her spine until he hit a spot that his palm fit into and pressed until her hips nestled against his erection. Amazing. Perfect.

The opposite of friendly.

That was enough to get his brain in gear again. This

was not how it should be between them, with all this raw need that he couldn't control.

He ended the kiss through some force of will he'd never understand and pulled back, but she tried to follow, nearly knocking herself off balance. Like she had at the ceremony. And in a similar fashion, he gripped her arms to keep her off the floor. It was dizzying how caught up she seemed to get. A rush he could get used to and shouldn't.

"Sorry," he said gruffly. "I got a little carried away."

"That's what was supposed to happen," she informed him breathlessly, "if we have any hope of your grandfather believing that we're deliriously happy together."

Yeah, that wasn't the problem he was most worried about at this moment. Viv's kiss-swollen lips were the color of raspberries and twice as tempting. All for show. He'd gotten caught up in the playacting far too easily, which wasn't fair to her. Or to his Viv-starved body that had suddenly found something it liked better than her cupcakes.

"I don't think anyone would question whether we spark, Viv," he muttered.

The real issue was that he needed to kill that spark and was pretty certain that would be impossible now.

Especially given the way she was gazing up at him with something a whole lot hotter than warmth in her brown eyes. She'd liked kissing him as much as he'd liked it. She might even be on board with taking things a step further. But they couldn't consummate this marriage or he could forget the annulment. Neither did he want to lead her on, which left him between a rock and an extremely hard place that felt like it would never be anything but hard for the rest of his life.

"In fact," he continued, "we should really keep things platonic behind closed doors. That's better for our friendship, don't you think?"

He'd kissed his wife and put his hands on her body because she'd told him to. And he was very much afraid he'd do it again whether it was for show or not unless he had some boundaries. Walking away from Viv wasn't an option. He had to do something that guaranteed he never got so sucked into a woman that she had power over his emotional center.

Thankfully, she nodded. "Whatever works best for you, Jonas. This is your fake marriage."

And how messed up was it that he was more than a little disappointed she'd agreed so readily?

Three

Viv hummed as she pulled the twenty-four-count pan from the oven and stuck the next batch of Confetti Surprise in its place. Customers thronged the showroom beyond the swinging door, but she kept an eye on things via the closed-circuit camera she'd had installed when she first started turning a profit.

Couldn't be too careful and besides, it made her happy to watch Camilla and Josie interact with the cupcake buyers while Viv did the dirty work in the back. She'd gotten so lucky to find the two college-aged girls who worked for her part-time. Both of them were eager students, and soon Viv would teach them the back-office stuff like bookkeeping and ordering. For now, it was great to have them running the register so Viv could focus on product.

Not that she was doing much focusing. Her mind

wandered constantly to the man who'd kissed her so passionately last night.

Jonas had been so into the moment, so into her, and it had been heady indeed. Score one for Viv to have landed in his arms due to her casual suggestion that they needed to "practice." Hopefully he'd never clue in that she jumped when he touched her because he zapped a shock of heat and awareness straight to her core every dang time, no matter how much she tried to control it.

Of course, he'd shut it all down, rightfully so. They were friends. If he'd been interested in more, he would have made a move long before now.

Didn't stop her from wishing for a repeat.

A stone settled into her stomach as three dressed-to-the-nines women breezed through the door of her shop. On the monitor, she watched her sisters approach the counter and speak to Josie, oblivious to the line of customers they'd just cut in front of. Likely they were cheerfully requesting to speak with Viv despite being told countless times that this wasn't a hobby. She ran a business, which meant she didn't have time to dash off with them for tea, something the three housewives she shared parentage with but little else didn't seem to fully grasp.

Except she couldn't avoid the conversation they were almost certainly here for. She'd finally broken down and called her mother to admit she'd gotten married without inviting anyone to the wedding. Of course that news had taken all of five minutes to blast its way to her sisters' ears.

Dusting off her hands, Viv set a timer on her phone and dropped it into her pocket. Those cupcakes in the oven would provide a handy out if things got a little intense, and knowing Hope, Joy and Grace, that was likely. She pushed open the swinging door and pasted a smile on her face.

"My favorite ladies," she called with a wave and crossed the room to hug first Grace, her next-oldest sister, then Joy and Hope last. More than a few heads turned to check out the additions to the showroom. Individually, they were beautiful women, but as a group, her sisters were impressive indeed, with style and elegance galore.

Viv had been a late-life accident, but her parents tried hard not to make her feel like one. Though it was obvious they'd expected to have three children when they couldn't come up with a fourth virtue to name their youngest daughter. She'd spent her childhood trying to fit in to her own family and nothing had changed.

Until today. Finally, Viviana Kim had a new last name and a husband. Thanks to Jonas and his fake marriage deal, she was part of the club that had excluded her thus far. Just one of many reasons she'd agreed.

"Mom told us," Hope murmured, her social polish in full force. She was nothing if not always mindful of propriety, and Viv appreciated it for once, as the roomful of customers didn't need to hear about Viv's love life. "She's hurt that you ran off to Vegas without telling anyone."

"Are you happy?" Grace butted in. She'd gotten married to the love of her life less than a year ago and saw hearts and flowers everywhere. "That's the important thing."

"Mom said you married Jonas Kim," Joy threw in before Viv could answer, not that she'd intended to interrupt before everyone had their say. That was a rookie mistake she'd learned to avoid years ago. "Surely his family would have been willing to make a discreet contribution to the ceremony. You could have had the wedding of the year."

Which was the real crime in Joy's mind—why spend *less* money when you could spend more, particularly when it belonged to someone else? Joy's own wedding had garnered a photo spread in *Bride* magazine five years ago, a feat no other Raleigh bride had scored since.

It had been a beautiful wedding and Joy had been a gorgeous bride. Of course, because she'd been so happy. All three of her sisters were married to handsome, successful men who treated them like royalty, which was great if you could find that. Viv had made do with what had been offered to her, but they didn't have to know that. In fact, she'd do everything in her power not to tip off her sisters that her marriage was anything but amazing. Was it so wrong to want them to believe she'd ended up exactly where she'd yearned to be for so long?

"Also, he's Korean," Hope added as if this might be news to Viv. "Mom is very concerned about how you'll handle the cultural differences. Have you discussed this with him?"

That was crossing a line. For several reasons. And Viv had had enough. "Jonas is American. He was born in the same hospital as you, so I'm pretty sure the cultural differences are minimal. Can you just be happy for me and stop with the third degree?"

All three women stared at her agape, even Grace, and Viv was ashamed at how good the speech had made her feel. She rarely stood up to the steamroller of her sisters, mostly because she really did love them. But she was married now, just like they were, and her choices deserved respect.

"Jonas does make me happy," she continued, shooting Grace a smile. "But there's nothing to be concerned about. We've known each other for about a year and our relationship recently grew closer. That's all there is to it."

Despite the fact that it was absolute truth, prickles swept across her cheeks at the memory of how *close* they'd gotten last night.

An unconvinced expression stole over Hope's face. As the oldest, she took her role as the protector seriously. "We still don't understand why the secrecy. None of us even remember you so much as mentioning his name before."

"Of course we know who he *is*," Joy clarified. "Everyone in Raleigh appreciates that he's brought a global company to this area. But we had no idea you'd caught his eye."

Viv could read between those lines easily enough. She didn't wear nine-thousand-dollar Alexander McQueen suits to brunch and attend the opera with a priceless antique diamond necklace decorating her cleavage. "He's been coming in to buy cupcakes for quite some time. We go to lunch. It's not that big of a mystery."

Did it seem like a mystery to others? A lick of panic curled through her stomach. She couldn't ruin this for Jonas. If other people got suspicious because she wasn't the type of woman a billionaire CEO should want to marry, then everything might fall apart.

Breathe. He'd made that decision. Not her. He'd picked Viv and anyone who thought she wasn't good enough for him could jump in a lake.

"But he married you." Grace clapped her hands, eyes twinkling. "Tell us how he proposed, what you wore at the wedding. Ooooh, show us pictures."

Since his proposal had begun with the line "This is going to sound crazy, but hear me out," Viv avoided that subject by holding out her left hand to dazzle her sisters with the huge diamond and then grabbing her phone to thumb up the shots Warren had taken at Jonas's request. The yellow of her dress popped next to Jonas's dark suit and they made an incredibly striking couple if she did say so herself. Mostly because she had the best-looking husband on the planet, so no one even noticed her.

"Is that Hendrix Harris in the shot?" Hope sniffed and the disapproval on her face spoke volumes against the man whose picture graced local gossip rags on a regular basis.

"Jonas and Hendrix are friends," Viv said mildly as she flipped through a few more pictures that mercifully did not include North Carolina's biggest scandalmonger. "They went to Duke together. I'll try not to let him corrupt me if we socialize."

As far as she could tell, Hendrix had scarcely noticed her at the wedding, and he'd seemed preoccupied at the cocktail lounge where they'd gone to have drinks after the ceremony. The man was pretty harmless.

"Just be careful," Hope implored her, smoothing an invisible wrinkle from her skirt. "You married Jonas so quickly and it appears as if he may have some unsavory associations. I say this with love, but you haven't demonstrated a great track record when it comes to the men you fall for."

That shouldn't have cut so deeply. It was true. But still.

"What Hope means is that you tend to leap before you look, Viv," Grace corrected, her eyes rolling in their sister's direction, but only Viv could see the show of support. It soothed the ragged places inside that Hope's comment had made. A little.

"It's not a crime to be passionate about someone." Hands on her hips, Viv surveyed the three women, none of whom seemed to remember what it was like to be single and alone. "But for your information, Jonas and I were friends first. We share common interests. He gives me advice about my business. We have a solid foundation to build on."

"Oh." Hope processed that. "I didn't realize you were being so practical about this. I'm impressed that you managed to marry a man without stars in your eyes. That's a relief."

Great. She'd gotten the seal of approval from Hope solely because she'd skirted the truth with a bland recitation of unromantic facts about her marriage. Her heart clenched. That was the opposite of what she wanted. But this was the marriage she had, the one she could handle. For now. Tomorrow, Jonas would take her to his father's house to meet his grandfather and she hoped to "practice" being married a whole lot more.

Thankfully, she'd kept Jonas in the dark about her feelings. If he could kiss her like he had last night and not figure out that she'd been this close to melting into a little puddle, she could easily snow his family with a few public displays of affection.

It was behind closed doors that she was worried about. That's where she feared she might forget that her marriage was fake. And as she'd just been unceremoniously reminded, she had a tendency to get serious way too fast, which in her experience was a stellar way to get a man to start looking for the exit.

That was the part that hurt the most. She wanted to care about someone, to let him know he was her whole world and have him say that in return. It wasn't neediness. She wasn't being clingy. That's what love looked like to her and she refused to believe otherwise.

But she'd yet to find a man who agreed with her, and Jonas was no exception. They had a deal and she would stick to it.

The house Jonas had grown up in lay on the outskirts of Raleigh in an upscale neighborhood that was homey and unpretentious. Jonas's father, who had changed his name to Brian when he became a legal US citizen upon marrying his American wife, hadn't gone into the family business, choosing to become a professor at Duke University instead.

That had left a hole in the Kim empire, one Jonas had gladly filled. He and Grandfather got along well, likely because they were so similar. They both had a drive to succeed, a natural professionalism and a sense of honor that harbored trust in others who did business with Kim Electronics.

Though they corresponded nearly every day in some electronic form, the time difference prevented them from speaking often, and an in-person visit was even rarer. The last time Jonas had seen Grandfather had been during a trip to Seoul for a board meeting about eighteen months ago. He'd invited his parents to come with him, as they hadn't visited Korea in several years.

"Are you nervous?" Jonas glanced over at Viv, who had clutched her hands together in her lap the second the car had hit Glenwood Avenue. Her knuckles couldn't get any whiter.

"Oh, God. You can tell," she wailed. "I was trying so hard to be cool."

He bit back a grin and passed a slow-moving mini-van. "Viv, they're just people. I promise they will like you."

"I'm not worried about that. Everyone likes me, especially after I give them cupcakes," she informed him loftily.

There was a waxed paper box at her feet on the floor-board that she'd treated as carefully as a newborn baby. When he'd reached for it, she'd nearly taken his hand off at the wrist, telling him in no uncertain terms the cupcakes were for her new family. Jonas was welcome to come by Cupcaked next week and pick out whatever he wanted, but the contents of that box were off-limits.

He kind of liked Bossy Viv. Of course he liked Sweet Viv, Uncertain Viv, Eager-to-Help Viv. He'd seen plenty of new facets in the last week since they'd moved in together, more than he'd have expected given that they'd known each other so long. It was fascinating.

"What are you worried about then?" he asked.

"You know good and well." Without warning, she slid a hand over his thigh and squeezed. Fire rocketed up his leg and scored his groin, nearly doubling him over with the sudden and unexpected need.

Only his superior reflexes kept the Mercedes on the road. But he couldn't stop the curse that flew from his mouth.

"Sorry," he muttered but she didn't seem bothered by his language.

"See, you're just as bad as me." Her tone was laced with irony. "All that practice and we're even jumpier than we were before."

Because the practice had ended before he started peeling off her clothes. Ironic how his marriage of convenience meant his wife was right there in his house—conveniently located in the bedroom next to his. He could hear her moving around between the walls and sometimes, he lay awake at night listening for the slightest movement to indicate she was likewise awake, aching to try one of those kisses with a lot less fabric in the way.

That kind of need was so foreign to him that he wasn't handling it well.

"I'm not jumpy," he lied. "I'm just…"

Frustrated.

There was no good way to finish that sentence without opening up a conversation about changing their relationship into something that it wasn't supposed to be. An annulment was so much less sticky than a divorce, though he'd finally accepted that he was using that as an excuse.

The last thing he could afford to do was give in to the simmering awareness between them. Jonas had convinced himself it was easy to honor the pact because he really didn't feel much when it came to relationships. Sure, he enjoyed sex, but it had always been easy to walk away when the woman pushed for more.

With Viv, the spiral of heat and need was dizzyingly strong. He felt too much, and Marcus's experience was like a big neon sign, reminding him that it was better never to go down that path. What was he supposed to do, stop being friends with Viv if things went haywire between them? Neither was there a good way to end their relationship before the merger.

So he was stuck. He couldn't act on his sudden and fierce longing to pull this car over into a shadowy bower of oak trees and find out if all of Viv tasted like sugar and spice and everything nice.

"Maybe we shouldn't touch each other," he suggested.

That was a good solution. Except for the part where they were married. Married people touched each other. He bit back the nasty word that had sprung to his lips. Barely.

"Oh." She nodded. "If you think that won't cause problems, sure."

Of course it was going to cause problems. He nearly groaned. But the problems had nothing to do with what she assumed. "Stop being so reasonable. I'm pulling you away from your life with very little compensation in return. You should be demanding and difficult."

Brilliant. He'd managed to make it sound like touching her was one of the compensation methods. He really needed to get out of this car now that he had a hyper-awareness of how easily she could—and would—reach out to slide a hand full of questing fingers into his lap.

Viv grinned and crossed her arms, removing that possibility. "In that case, I'm feeling very bereft in the jewelry department, Mr. Kim. As your wife, I should be draped in gems, don't you think?"

"Absolutely." What did it say about how messed up he was that the way *Mr. Kim* rolled off her tongue turned him on? "Total oversight on my part. Which I will rectify immediately."

The fourteen-carat diamond on her finger was on loan from a guy Jonas knew in the business, though the hefty fee he'd paid to procure it could have bought enough bling to blind her. Regardless, if Viv wanted jewelry, that's what she'd get.

They drove into his parents' neighborhood right on time and he parked in the long drive that led to the house. "Ready?"

She nodded. "All that talk about jewelry got me over my nerves. Thanks."

That made one of them.

His mom opened the door before they'd even hit the stone steps at the entryway, likely because she'd been watching for the car. But instead of engulfing Jonas in the first of what would be many hugs, she ignored her only child in favor of her new daughter-in-law.

"You must be Viviana," his mother gushed, and swept Viv up in an embrace that was part friendly and part *Thank you, God, I finally have a daughter.* "I'm so happy to meet you."

Viv took it in stride. "Hi, Mrs. Kim. I'm happy to meet you, too. Please call me Viv."

Of course she wasn't ruffled. There was so little that seemed to trip her up—except when Jonas touched her. All practicing had done was create surprisingly acute sexual tension that even a casual observer would recognize as smoldering awareness.

He was currently pretending it didn't exist. Because that would make it not so, right?

"Hi, Mom," he threw in blithely since she hadn't even glanced in his direction.

"Your grandfather is inside. He'd like to talk to you while I get to know Viviana. Tell me everything," she said to her new daughter-in-law as she accepted the box of cupcakes with a smile. "Have you started thinking about kids yet?"

Jonas barely bit back another curse. "Mom, please. We just got here. Viv doesn't need the third degree about personal stuff."

Right out of the gate with the baby questions? Really? He'd expected a little decorum from his mom. In vain, obviously, and a mistake because he hadn't had a chance to go over that with Viv. Should they say they didn't want children? That she couldn't have any?

He and Viv clearly should have spent less time "practicing" and more in deep conversation about all aspects of potential questions that might come up this weekend. Which they'd have to rectify tonight before going to bed. In the same room.

His mother shot him a glare. "Grandchildren are not personal. The hope of one day getting some is the only reason I keep you around, after all."

That made Viv laugh, which delighted his mother, so really, there was nothing left to do but throw up his hands and go seek out Grandfather for his own version of the third degree.

Grandfather held court in the Kim living room, talking to his son. The older Jonas's dad got, the more he resembled Grandfather, but the similarities ended there. Where Brian Kim had adopted an American name to match his new homeland, Kim Jung-Su wore his Korean heritage like the badge of honor it was.

Kim Electronics had been born after the war, during a boom in Korean capitalism that only a select few had wisely taken advantage of. Jonas loved his dad, but Grandfather had been his mentor, his partner as Jonas had taken what Jung-Su had built and expanded it into the critical US market. They'd created a chaebol, a family-run conglomerate, where none had existed, and they'd done it together.

And he was about to lie to his grandfather's face solely to avoid marrying a disaster of a woman who might cause the Kim family shame.

It was a terrible paradox and not for the first time he heard Warren's voice of reason in his head asking why he couldn't just tell Grandfather the truth. But then he remembered that Sun's grandfather and Jonas's grandfather had fought in the war together and were closer than brothers. Jonas refused to out Sun and her unsuitable lover strictly for his own benefit. No, this way was easier.

And it wasn't a lie. He and Viv were married. That was all anyone needed to know.

Grandfather greeted Jonas in Korean and then switched to English as a courtesy since he was in an English-speaking house. "You are looking well."

"As are you." Jonas bowed to show his respect and then hugged his dad, settling in next to him on the couch. "It's a pleasure to see you."

Grandfather arched a thick brow. "An unexpected pleasure I assume? I wanted to meet your new wife personally. To welcome her into the family."

"She is very honored. Mom waylaid her or she'd be here to meet you, as well."

"I asked your mother to. I wanted to speak with you privately."

As if it had been some prearranged signal, Jonas's

dad excused himself and the laser sights of Jung-Su had zero distractions. The temperature of the room shot up about a thousand degrees. One misstep and the whole plan would come crashing down. And Jonas suddenly hated the idea of losing this tenuous link with Viv, no matter how precarious that link was.

"Now, then." Grandfather steepled his hands together and smiled. "I'm very pleased you have decided to marry. It is a big step that will bring you many years of happiness. Belated congratulations."

Jonas swallowed his surprise. What was the wily old man up to? He'd expected a cross-examination designed to uncover the plot that Grandfather surely suspected. "Thank you. Your approval means a lot to me."

"As a wedding gift, I'd like to give you the Kim ancestral home."

"What? I mean, that's a very generous gesture, Grandfather." And crafty, as the property in question lay outside of Seoul, seven thousand miles away from North Carolina. Jonas couldn't refuse or Grandfather would be insulted. But there was an angle here that Jonas couldn't quite work out.

"Of course I'd hoped you'd live in it with Sun Park, but I understand that you cannot curb the impulses of the heart."

Jonas stared at his grandfather as if he'd suddenly started speaking Klingon. The impulses of the heart? That was the exact opposite of the impression he'd wanted to convey. Sure, he'd hoped to convince everyone that they were a couple, but only so that no one's suspicions were aroused. Solid and unbreakable would be more to his liking when describing his marriage, not *impulsive* and certainly not because he'd fallen madly in love.

This was the worst sort of twist. Never would he have thought he'd be expected to sell his marriage as a love match. Was that something that he and Viv were going to have to practice, too? His stomach twisted itself inside out. How the hell was he supposed to know what love looked like?

Regardless of the curveball, it was the confirmation Jonas had been looking for. Grandfather was on board with Viv, and Jonas had cleared the first hurdle after receiving that ominous text message the other day. "I'm glad you understand. I've been seeing Viv for almost a year and I simply couldn't imagine marrying anyone else."

That much at least was true, albeit a careful hedge about the nature of his intentions toward Viv during that year. And thankfully they'd become good enough friends that he felt comfortable asking her to help him avoid exactly what he'd suspected Grandfather had in mind. Apparently throwing Sun in his path *had* been an attempt to get Jonas to Korea more often, if not permanently. It was counter to Jonas's long-term strategy, the one he still hadn't brought to Grandfather because the merger hadn't happened yet. Once Park Industries and Kim Electronics became one, they could leverage the foothold Jonas had already built in America by moving the headquarters to North Carolina, yet keep manufacturing in Korea under the Park branch.

It was also the opportune time to pass the reins, naming Jonas the CEO of the entire operation. The dominoes were in much better position now, thanks to the huge bullet Viv had helped him dodge without upsetting anyone. It was…everything.

Grandfather chatted for a few more minutes about his plans while in the US, including a request for a tour of the Kim Building, and then asked Jonas to introduce him to Viv.

He found her in the kitchen writing down her cupcake recipe for his mother.

"You got her secret recipe already, Mom?" Jonas asked with a laugh. "I guess I don't have to ask whether everyone is getting along."

His mother patted his arm. "You obviously underestimate how much your wife cares for you. I didn't even have to ask twice."

Viv blushed and it was so pretty on her, he couldn't tear his gaze from her face all at once, even though he was speaking to his mom. "On the contrary, I'm quite aware of how incredibly lucky I am that Viv married me."

"You didn't have to ask me *that* twice either," Viv pointed out. "Apparently I lack the ability to say no to anyone with the name Kim."

An excellent point that he really wished she hadn't brought up on the heels of his discovery of how much he enjoyed it when she called him Mr. Kim. All at once, a dozen suggestions designed to get her to say yes over and over sprang to his lips. But with his mom's keen-eyed gaze cutting between the two of them, he needed to get himself under control immediately.

"Come and say hi to my grandfather," he said instead, and she nodded eagerly.

She was far too good to him. For the first time, it bothered him. What was she getting out of this farce?

Some advice about how to run her business? That had seemed inadequate before they'd gotten married. Now? It was nearly insulting how little he was doing for her.

She had to have another reason for being here. And all at once, he wanted to know what it was.

Four

Ten minutes into dinner, Jonas figured out his grand-father's angle. The wily old man was trying to drive him insane with doubt about pulling off this ruse, especially now that he had *impulses of the heart* echoing through his head. Jonas was almost dizzy from trying to track all the verbal land mines that might or might not be strewn through random conversational openers.

Even "pass the butter" had implications. Grandfather hated butter.

And if Grandfather failed at putting Jonas in the loony bin, Viv was doing her part to finish the job, sitting next to him looking fresh and beautiful as she reminded him on a second-by-second basis that she was well within touching distance. Not just easily accessible. But *available* to be touched. It was *expected*. Would a loving husband sling his arm across the back of her chair? Seemed reasonable.

But the moment he did it as he waited for his mom to serve the kimchi stew she'd made in honor of Grandfather's visit, Viv settled into the crook of his elbow, which had not been his intent at all. She fit so well, he couldn't help but let his arm relax so that it fully embraced her and somehow his fingers ended up doing this little dance down her bare arm, testing whether the silkiness felt as good all the way down as it did near her shoulder.

It did.

"...don't you think, Jonas?"

Blinking, Jonas tore his attention away from his wife's skin and focused on his dad. "Sure. I definitely think so."

"That's great," Brian said with a nod and a wink. "It wasn't a stretch to think you'd be on board."

Fantastic. What in the world had he just agreed to that had his father winking, of all things? Jonas pulled his arm from around Viv's shoulders. At this point, it seemed like everyone was convinced they were a couple and all the touching had done nothing but distract him.

Viv leaned in, her hand resting on his thigh. It was dangerously close to being in his lap. One small shift would do it, and his muscles strained to repeat the experience. But before he could sort her intention, she murmured in his ear, "We're playing Uno later. As a team. You'll have to teach me."

Card games with a hard-on. That sounded like the opposite of fun. But at least he knew what he'd absently agreed to, and shot Viv a grateful smile. Her return smile did all sorts of things that it shouldn't have, not the least of which was give him the sense that they were coconspirators. They were in this farce together and he appreciated that more than he could say. At least they could laugh about this later. Or something.

Grandfather was watching him closely as he spooned up a bite of stew, and Jonas braced for the next round of insanity. Sure enough, Grandfather cleared his throat.

"Will you and your bride be starting a family soon?"

Not this again and from his grandfather, too? Obviously Jonas's mother had a vested interest in the answer strictly because she wanted babies to spoil, but Grandfather wasn't asking for anything close to that reason. It was all part of the test.

"Not soon," he hedged because family was important to the Kims. It was a source of frustration for both his parents and his grandparents that they'd only had one child apiece, and Jonas imagined they'd all be thrilled if he said Viv wanted a dozen. "Viv owns a bakery and it's doing very well. She'd like to focus on her career for a while."

Yes. That was the reason they weren't having kids right away. Why had he been racking his brain over that? Except now he was thinking about the conversation where he had to tell everyone that while he cared about Viv, they were better as friends, so the marriage was over. While it soothed his sense of honor that it was the truth, he'd never considered that the annulment would upset his family.

"We're having her cupcakes for dessert," his mother threw in with a beaming smile. "They look scrumptious."

Perfect segue and took some heat off a subject that Jonas suddenly did not want to contemplate. "The lemon are my favorite. One bite and that was when I decided I couldn't let Viv get away."

The adoring glance she shot him thumped him in the gut. The little secret smile playing about her lips worked in tandem, spreading tendrils of heat through him in ways that should be uncomfortable at a table full of Kims who were all watching him closely. But the sensation was too enjoyable to squelch.

"Honestly, that was when I knew he was special," Viv admitted, and Jonas nearly did a double take at the wistful note in her voice. "He appreciates my cupcakes in a way regular customers don't. A lot goes into the recipes and I don't just mean my time. It's a labor of love, born out of a desire to make people happy, and I can see on his face that I've done that. Most customers just devour the thing without stopping to breathe, but Jonas always takes one bite and immediately stops to savor it. Then he tells me how great it is before taking another bite."

Well, yeah, because he could taste the sunshine in it, as if she'd somehow condensed a few rays and woven them through the ingredients. How could he not take his time to fully appreciate the unique experience of a Viviana Dawson cupcake?

Jonas blinked, dragging his lids down over his suddenly dry eyes. He didn't do that *every* time, not the way she was describing it, as if a cupcake held all that meaning.

He glanced at his mom, who looked a little misty.

"That sounds like a magical courtship," she said.

"Oh, it was," Viv agreed enthusiastically. "It was like one of those movies where the hero pretends he only wants the cupcakes when he comes into the shop, but it's really to see the baker. But I always knew from the first that the way to his heart was through my frosting."

His mother laughed and Jonas checked his eye roll because the whole point was to sell this nonsense. Everyone was eating it up, no pun intended, so why mess with the ridiculous story Viv was spinning?

Except the whole thing made him uncomfortable.

Surely his grandfather wouldn't appreciate hearing his successor described with such romanticism. If anything, Viv could help Jonas's case by telling everyone how hard he worked and how difficult it was to pry him away from his cell phone when they went to lunch.

He sighed. She couldn't say that. It would be a big, fat lie. When he did anything with Viv, he always switched his phone to do not disturb. He loved listening to stories about her sisters, or a new recipe she was working through. But it didn't mean he was gaga over her like a besotted fool.

Yet…that's what he needed his grandfather to buy, as difficult as it was to envision. Grandfather hadn't accepted Jonas's marriage to Viv because she'd helped him increase profits or created an advantageous business alliance. Viv was an *impulse of the heart*.

How had he gotten caught in the middle of trying to prove to his grandfather that Jonas was a committed, solid CEO candidate, while also attempting to convince him that he and Viv had fallen in love? And Jonas had no illusions about the necessity of maintaining the current vibe, not after his grandfather smiled over Viv's enthusiastic retelling of what would probably forever be called the Cupcake Courtship. It was madness.

"Will you bring your wife to Seoul to visit the Kim ancestral home?" Grandfather asked in the lull. "It's yours now. Perhaps you'll want to redecorate?"

Jonas nearly groaned. He hadn't had four seconds

to mention the gift to Viv. Her eyebrows lifted in silent question and he blessed her discretion.

"We're actually looking for a house together in Raleigh," Jonas improvised much more smoothly than he would have guessed he could. Viv's eyebrows did another reach-for-the-sky move as he rushed on. "So probably we won't make it to Korea anytime soon. But we do both appreciate the gift."

Nothing like a good reminder that Jonas's home was in America. The future of the company lay here, not in Seoul. The more he could root himself in North Carolina, the better. Of course the answer was to buy a property here. With Viv. A new ancestral home in North Carolina. Then his statement to his grandfather wouldn't be a lie.

"Yes, thank you so much, Mr. Kim," Viv said sweetly. "We'll discuss our work schedules and find a mutual time we can travel. I would be honored to see your ancestral home. Mrs. Kim, perhaps you'd advise me on whether the decor needs refurbishing?"

Jonas's mom smiled so widely that it was a wonder she didn't crack her face. "That's a lovely idea. I would be thrilled to go to lunch and discuss the house, as I've always loved the locale."

Speechless, Jonas watched the exchange with a very real sense of his life sliding out of control and no way to put on the brakes. In the last two minutes, he'd managed to rope himself into shopping for a house in Raleigh, then traveling to Korea so Viv could visit Seoul with the express intent of redecorating a house neither of them wanted...with his mom. What next?

"While you're in Korea," Grandfather said, and his tone was so leading that everyone's head turned toward him, "we should discuss taking next steps toward increasing your responsibilities at Kim Electronics. The board will look very favorably on how you've matured, Jonas. Your accomplishments with the American market are impressive. I would be happy to recommend you as the next CEO when I retire."

The crazy train screeched to a halt in the dead center of Are You Kidding Me Station. *Say something. Tell him you're honored.*

But Jonas's throat froze as his brain tried to sort through his grandfather's loaded statements.

Everything he'd worked for had just been handed to him on a silver platter—that Viv was holding in her delicate fingers. The implications were staggering. Grandfather liked that Jonas was married. It was a huge wrinkle he had never seen coming.

Now he couldn't annul the marriage or he'd risk losing Grandfather's approval with the board. How was he supposed to tell Viv that the favor he'd asked of her had just been extended by about a year?

And what did it mean that his insides were doing a secret dance of happiness at getting to keep Viv longer than planned?

The spare bedroom lay at the end of a quiet hall and had its own en suite bathroom. Nice. Viv wasn't too keen on the idea of wandering around in her bathrobe. At least not outside the bedroom. Inside was another story.

Because Jonas was on this side of the closed door. Time to ramp it up.

If she hoped to build her confidence with a man, there was no better scenario to play that out than this one, especially since she already knew they were attracted to each other And headed for a divorce. None of this was real, so she could practice without fear.

She shivered as her gorgeous husband loosened his tie and threw himself onto the bed with a groan. *Shivered.* What was that but a commentary on this whole situation?

"Bad day, sweetie?" she deadpanned, carefully keeping her voice light. But holy cow, Jonas was so sexy with his shirtsleeves rolled up and his bare feet crossed at the ankle as he tossed an elbow over his eyes.

"That was one of the most difficult dinners I've ever endured," he confessed, as if there was nothing odd about being in a bedroom together with the door closed, while he lounged on the bed looking like a commercial for something sensual and expensive.

"Your family is great." She eased onto the bed because she wanted to and she could. It wasn't like there were a ton of other seats in the cute little bedroom. Well, except for the matching chairs near the bay window that flanked an inlaid end table. But she didn't want to sit way over there when the centerpiece of the room lay on the bed.

As the mattress shifted under her weight, he peeked out from beneath his elbow, his dark eyes seeking hers. "You're only saying that to be nice. You should stage a fight and go home. It would serve me right to have to stay here and field questions about the stability of our marriage."

As if she'd ever do that when the best part of this fake marriage had just started. She was sharing a bedroom with Jonas Kim and he was her husband and the night was rife with possibilities.

There came the shiver again and it was delicious.
Careful.

This was the part where she always messed up with men by seeming too eager. Messing up with Jonas was not happening. There was no do-over.

Of course, scoring with Jonas had its issues, too. Like the fact that she couldn't keep him. This was just practice, she reminded herself. That was the only way she could get it together.

"I'm not staging a fight." She shook her head and risked reaching out to stroke Jonas's hair in a totally casual gesture meant to soothe him, because after all, he did seem pretty stressed. "What would we fight about? Money?"

"I don't know. No." The elbow came off his face and he let his eyes drift closed as she ran her fingers over his temples. "That feels nice. You don't have to do that."

Oh, yes. She did. This was her chance to touch Jonas in a totally innocuous way and study her husband's body while he wasn't aware.

"It's possible for me to do something because I want to instead of out of a sense of obligation, you know."

He chuckled. "Point taken. I'm entirely too sensitive to how big a favor this is and how difficult navigating my family can be."

Stroking his hair might go down as one of the greatest pleasures of her life. It was soft and silky and thick. The inky strands slid across her fingertips as she buried them deep and rubbed lightly against his scalp, which earned her a groan that was amazingly sexy.

"Relax," she murmured, and was only half talking to herself as her insides contracted. "I don't find your family difficult. Your mom is great and I don't know if you know this or not, but your grandfather does not in fact breathe fire."

"He gave us a house." His eyes popped open and he glanced over at her, shrinking the slight distance between them. "There are all sorts of underlying expectations associated with that, not the least of which is how upset he's going to be when I have to give it back."

She shrugged, pretending like it wasn't difficult to get air into her lungs when he focused on her so intently. "Don't give it back. Keep it and we'll go visit, like we promised."

"Viv." He sat up, taking his beautiful body out of reach, which was a shame. "You're being entirely too accommodating. Were you not listening to the conversation at dinner? This is only going to get more complicated the longer we drag it out. And we *are* going to be dragging it out apparently."

Normally, this would be where she threw herself prostrate at a man's feet and wept with joy over the fact that he wasn't calling things off. But she wasn't clingy anymore. Newly Minted Independent Viv needed to play this a whole different way if she wanted to get to a place where she had a man slavishly devoted to her. And she would not apologize for wishing for a man who loved her so much that he would never dream of calling the duration of their marriage "dragging it out."

"You say that like being married to me is a chore," she scolded lightly. "I was listening at dinner. I heard the words *CEO* and *Jonas* in the same sentence. Did you? Because that sounded good to me."

"It is good. For me. Not you. I'm now essentially in the position of using you to further my career goals for an extended period of time. Not just until the merger happens. But until my grandfather retires and fully transitions the role of CEO to me. That could take months. A year."

Oh, God. A whole year of living with Jonas in his amazing loft and being his wife? That was a lot of practicing for something that would never be real. How could she possibly hide her feelings for Jonas that long? Worse, they'd probably grow stronger the longer she stayed in his orbit. How fair was it to keep torturing herself like this?

On the flip side, she'd promised to do this for Jonas as a favor. As a *friend*. He wasn't interested in more or he'd have told her. Practice was all she could reasonably expect from this experience. It had to be enough.

"That's a significant development, no doubt. But I don't feel used. And I'm not going anywhere."

Jonas scowled instead of overflowing with gratitude. "I can't figure out what you're getting out of this. It was already a huge sacrifice, even when it was only for a few weeks until my grandfather got his deal going with Park. Now this. Are you dying of cancer or something?"

She forced a laugh but there was nothing funny about his assumptions. Or the fact that she didn't have a good answer for why she didn't hate the idea of sticking around as long as Jonas would have her. Maybe there was something wrong with that, but it was her business, not his. "What, like I'm trying to check off everything on my bucket list before I die and being married to Jonas Kim was in the top three? That's a little arrogant, don't you think?"

When he flinched, she almost took it back, but that's how Newly Minted Viv rolled. The last thing he needed to hear was that being married to him occupied the top spot on all her lists. And on that note, it was definitely time to put a few more logs on the pile before she set it on fire.

"Running a cupcake business is hard," she told him firmly. "You've built Kim Electronics from the ground up. You should know how it is. You work seventy hours a week and barely make a dent. Who has time for a relationship? But I get lonely, same as anyone. This deal is perfect for me because we can hang out with no pressure. I like you. Is that so hard to believe?"

Good. Deflect. Give him just enough truth to make it plausible.

His face relaxed into an easy grin. "Only a little. I owe you so much. Not sure my scintillating personality makes up for being stuck sharing a bedroom with me."

"Yeah, that part sucks, all right," she murmured, and let her gaze trail down his body. What better way to "practice" being less clingy than to get good and needy and then force herself to walk away? "We should use this opportunity to get a little more comfortable with each other."

The atmosphere got intense as his expression darkened, and she could tell the idea intrigued him.

"What? Why? We've already sold the coupledom story to my family. It's a done deal and went way better than I was expecting. We don't have to do the thing where we touch each other anymore."

Well, that stung. She'd had the distinct impression he liked touching her.

"Oh, I wish that was true." She stuck an extra tinge of dismay into her tone, just to be sure it was really clear that she wasn't panting after him. Even though she was lying through her teeth. "But we still have all of tomorrow with your family. And you're planning to meet mine, right? We have to sell that we're hopelessly in love all over again. I'm really concerned about tongues wagging. After all, Joy's husband knows everyone who's anyone. The business world is small."

Jonas's eyes went a little wide. "We just have to sell being married. No one said anything about love."

"But that's why people get married, Jonas." Something flickered through his expression that looked a lot like panic. And it set a bunch of gears in motion in her head. Maybe they should be using this time to get matters straight instead of doing a lot of touching. Because all at once, she was really curious about an important aspect of this deal that she'd thus far failed to question. "Don't you think so?"

"That people should only get married if they're in love? I don't know." But he shifted his gaze away so quickly that it was obvious he had something going on inside. "I've never been married before."

That was a careful way to answer the question. Did that mean he had been in love but not enough to marry the girl? Or he'd never been in love? Maybe he was nursing a serious broken heart and it was too painful to discuss. "Your parents are married. Aren't they in love?"

"Sure. It's just not something I've given a lot of thought to."

"So think about it." She was pushing him, plain and simple, but this was important compatibility stuff that she'd never questioned. Everyone believed in love. Right? "I'm just wondering now why you needed a fake wife. Maybe you should have been looking for someone to fall in love with this whole time instead of taking me to lunch for a year."

He hadn't been dating anyone, this she knew for a fact because she'd asked. Multiple times. Her curiosity on the matter might even be described as morbid.

"Viv." His voice had gone quiet and she liked the way he said her name with so much texture. "If I'd wanted to spend time with someone other than you over the last year, I would have. I like you. Is that so hard to believe?"

Her mouth curved up before she could catch it. But why should she? Jonas made her smile, even when he was deflecting her question. Probably because he didn't think about her "that way" no matter how hot the kiss outside her bedroom had been. One-sided then. They were friends. Period. And she should definitely not be sad about that. He was a wonderful, kind man who made not thinking wicked thoughts impossible the longer they sat on a bed together behind closed doors.

Yeah, she could pretend she was practicing for a relationship with some other man all she wanted. Didn't change the fact that deep in her heart Viv wished she could be the person Jonas would fall madly in love with.

But she knew she couldn't keep Jonas. At least she was in the right place to fix her relationship pitfalls.

Now, how did one go about seducing a man while giving him the distinct impression she could take him or leave him?

Five

The bed in Jonas's mother's guest room must have razor blades sewn into the comforter. It was the only explanation for why his skin felt like it was on fire as he forced himself to lie there chatting with Viv as if they really were a real married couple having a debrief after his family's third degree.

They *were* a real married couple having a chat.

If only she hadn't brought up the *L* word. The one concept he had zero desire to talk about when it came to marriage. Surely Viv knew real married couples who didn't love each other. It couldn't be that huge of a departure, otherwise the divorce rate would be a lot lower.

But they were a married couple, albeit not a traditional one behind closed doors. If they were a traditional married couple, Jonas would be sliding his fingers across the mattress and taking hold of Viv's thigh so he could brace her for the exploration to come. His lips would fit so well in the hollow near her throat. So far, she hadn't seemed to clue in that every muscle beneath his skin strained toward her, and he had no idea how she wasn't as affected by the sizzling awareness as he was.

They were on a bed. They were married. The door was closed. What did that equal? Easy math—and it was killing him that they were getting it so wrong. Why wasn't he rolling his wife beneath him and getting frisky with breathless anticipation as they shushed each other before someone heard them through the walls?

"Since we like each other so much, maybe we should talk about the actual sleeping arrangements," she suggested. "There's not really a good way to avoid sharing the bed and we're keeping things platonic when no one's around."

Oh, right, because this was an exercise in insanity, just like dinner. He really shouldn't be picturing Viv sliding between cool sheets, naked of course, and peeking up at him from under her lashes as she clutched the pale blue fabric to her breasts.

"I can sleep on the floor," he croaked. She cocked a brow, eyeing him as if she could see right through his zipper to the hard-on he wasn't hiding very well. "I insist. You're doing me a favor. It's the least I can do."

"I wasn't expecting anyone to sleep on the floor. We're friends. We can sleep in the same bed and keep our hands off each other. Right?" Then she blinked and something happened to her eyes. Her gaze deepened, elongating the moment, and heat teased along the edges of his nerve endings. "Unless you think it would be too much of a temptation."

He swallowed. Was she a mind reader now? How had she figured out that he had less than pure thoughts about sharing a bed with his wife? How easy it would be to reach out in the middle of the night, half-asleep, and pull her closer for a midnight kiss that wouldn't have any daylight consequences because nothing counted in the dark.

Except everything with Viv counted. That was the problem. They had a friendship he didn't want to lose and he had taken a vow with Warren and Hendrix that he couldn't violate.

"No, of course not," he blurted out without checking his emphatic delivery. "I mean, definitely it'll be hard—" *Dear God.* "Nothing will be hard! Everything will be…" *Not easy. Don't say easy.* "I have to go check on…something."

Before he could fully internalize how much of an ass he was making of himself, he bolted from the bed and fled the room, calling over his shoulder, "Feel free to use the bathroom. I'll wait my turn."

Which was a shame because what he really needed was a cold shower. Prowling around the house like a cat burglar because he didn't want to alert anyone he'd just kicked himself out of his own newlywed bedroom, Jonas poked around in his dad's study but felt like he was intruding in the hallowed halls of academia.

He and his dad were night and day. They loved each other, but Brian Kim wasn't a businessman in any way, shape or form. It was like the entrepreneurial gene had skipped a generation. Put Brian in a lecture hall and he was in his element. In truth, the only reason Jonas had gone to Duke was because his father was on faculty and his parents had gotten a discount on tuition. They'd refused to take a dime of Grandfather's money since Brian hadn't filled a position at Kim Electronics.

If his dad had taken a job at any other university, Jonas never would have met Warren, Hendrix and Marcus. His friendship with those guys had shaped his twenties, more so than he'd ever realized, until now.

The funeral had been brutal. So hard to believe his friend was inside that casket. His mom had held his hand the entire time and even as a twenty-one-year-old junior in college who desperately wanted to be hip, he hadn't let go once. Marcus had been down in the dumps for weeks, but they'd all shrugged it off. Typical male pride and bruised feelings. Who hadn't been the victim of a woman's fickle tastes?

But Marcus had been spiraling down and none of them had seen it. That was the problem with love. It made you do crazy, out-of-character things. Like suicide.

Jonas slid into his dad's chair and swiveled it to face the window, letting the memory claw through his gut as he stared blindly at the koi pond outside in the garden. There was no shame in having missed the signs. Everyone had. But that reassurance rang as hollow today as it had ten years ago. What could he have done? Talked sense into the guy? Obviously the pain had been too great, and the lesson for Jonas was clear: don't let a woman get her hooks into you.

That was why he couldn't touch Viv anymore. The temptation wasn't just too much. It was deadly. Besides, she was his friend. He'd already crossed a bunch of lines in the name of ensuring his family bought into the marriage, but it was all just an excuse to have his cake and eat Viv, too.

Bad, bad thing to be thinking about. There was a part of him that couldn't believe Viv would be dangerous to his mental state. But the risks were too great, especially to their friendship. They'd gone a whole year without being tempted. What was different now? Proximity? Awareness? The fact that he'd already kissed her and couldn't undo the effect on his body every time he got within touching distance of her?

That one.

Sleeping with her in the bed was going to be torture. He really didn't know if he had it in him. Probably the best thing to do was sleep on the couch in the living room and set an alarm for something ridiculous like 5:00 a.m. Then he could go for a jog and come back like he'd slept in Viv's bed all night long. Of course he'd never jogged in his life…but he could start. Might burn off some of the awareness he couldn't shake.

That was the best plan. He headed back to the bedroom they shared to tell her.

But when he eased open the door and slipped inside, she was still in the bathroom. He settled onto the bed to wait, next to her open suitcase. There was literally no reason for him to glance inside other than it was right there. Open. With a frothy bunch of racy lingerie laid out across the other clothes.

Holy crap. Jonas's eyes burned the longer he stared at the thin straps and drapes of lace. Was that the *top*? Viv's breasts were supposed to be covered by that? Something that skimpy should be illegal. And red. But the lace was lemon yellow, the color of the frosting Viv slathered all over the cupcakes she always brought him when they had lunch. His mouth watered at the thought of tasting Viv through all that lace. It would be easy. The pattern would show 90 percent of her skin.

The little panties lay innocuously to the side as if

an afterthought. Probably because there wasn't enough lace making up the bottom half of the outfit to rightfully call them panties. He could picture them perfectly on his wife's body and he could envision slowly stripping them off even more vividly.

Wait. What was Viv doing with such smoking-hot lingerie?

Was she planning to wear it for *him*? His brain had no ability to make sense of this revelation. She'd brought lingerie. To wear. Of course the only man in the vicinity was Jonas. Who else would she be wearing it for?

That was totally against the rules.

And totally against what he was capable of giving her in this marriage. She might as well drape herself in hearts and flowers. Viv clearly thought love was a recipe for marriage. Stir well and live happily ever after. He wasn't the right ingredient for that mix.

The sound of running water being shut off rattled through the walls. Viv had just emerged from the shower. He should get the hell out of that bedroom right now. But before he could stand, she walked out of the bathroom holding a towel loosely around her body. Her *naked* body. She was still wet. His gaze traced the line of one drop as it slid down her shoulder and disappeared behind the towel.

"Oh. I didn't know you'd come back," she announced unnecessarily as he was reasonably certain she wouldn't have waltzed into the room mostly naked if she'd known he was sitting on the bed.

"Sorry," he muttered, and meant to avert his eyes but the towel had slipped a little, which she'd done nothing to correct.

Maybe she wanted him to catch a glimpse of her perfect breasts. Not that he knew for sure that they were perfect. But the little half-moon slices peeking above the towel flashed at him more brightly than a neon sign, and his whole body went up in flames.

Anything that powerful at only a quarter strength had to be perfect in its entirety.

"Did you want to take a turn in the bathroom?" she asked casually. Still standing there. Wet. In a towel. Naked.

"Uh, sure." He didn't stand. He should cross the room and barricade himself in the bathroom, where it wouldn't matter if she'd used all the hot water because the shower needed to be glacial.

"Okay. Can you give me two minutes? I need to dry my hair." And then she laughed with a little peal that punched him the gut. "Normally I would wrap it up in the towel but there are only two and I didn't want to hog them all."

Then she pulled on the edge of the towel, loosening it from the column it formed around her body and lifted the tail end to the ends of her dripping hair. A long slice of skin peeked through the opening she'd unwittingly created and the answering flash of heat that exploded in his groin would have put him on his knees if he'd been standing. Good thing he hadn't moved.

"You should get dressed," he suggested, but she didn't hear him because his voice wasn't working. Besides, *dressed* could have a lot of different meanings, and the frothy yellow concoction in her suitcase appeared to be the next outfit of choice. If she hadn't been planning to slip it on, it wouldn't be on top, laid out so carefully.

Oh, man. Would she have been wearing it when he got into bed later? No warning, just bam!

He should pretend he hadn't seen the yellow concoction. How else could he find out if that had been her plan? That had to be her plan. Please, God, let it be her plan.

He was so hard, it was a wonder his erection hadn't busted out of his zipper.

Clearing his throat, he tested out speaking again. "I can come back."

That, she heard. "Oh, you don't have to. Really, I've taken way too long already. We're sharing and I'm not used to that. The shower was lovely and I couldn't help standing there under the spray, just letting my mind drift."

Great. Now his mind was drifting—into the shower with her as she stood there. Naked. Letting the water sluice down her body, eyes closed with a small, rapturous smile gracing her face.

He groaned. What was he doing to himself?

"Are you okay?" Her attention honed in on him and she apparently forgot she wasn't wearing anything but a damp towel because she immediately crossed the room to loom over him, her expression laced with concern.

It would take less than a second to reach out and snag her by the waist, pulling her down into his lap. That towel would fall, revealing her perfect breasts, and they'd be right there, ripe and available to taste. No yellow concoction needed. But that would be criminal. She should get to wear her newlywed lingerie if she wanted.

"Oh." Viv blushed all at once, the pink stain spreading across her cheeks, and Jonas could not tear his eyes off her face. But she was staring at the open suitcase. "You didn't see that ridiculous thing Grace gave me, did you?"

She picked up the yellow lacy top and held it up to her body, draping it over the towel one-handed, which had the immediate consequence of smooshing her breasts higher. "Can you imagine me wearing this?"

With absolute, brilliant clarity.

"I don't know what she was thinking," Viv continued as if his entire body wasn't poised to explode. "'Open this with Jonas,' she says with a sly wink. I thought it was going to be a joke, like a gravy boat, and besides, this isn't a real marriage, so I didn't think you'd actually want to help open gifts. Sorry I didn't wait for you."

She rolled her eyes with another laugh that did not help things down below.

"That's okay. Next time." What was he saying? *Sure, I'll help open future gifts full of shockingly transparent clothing that would make a porn star blush?* "Your sister meant well. She doesn't know we're not sleeping together."

Or rather they weren't yet. In a scant few minutes, they'd be in the bed. Together. Maybe some sleeping would occur but it wasn't looking too likely unless he got his body cooled down to something well below its current thermonuclear state.

"Well, true. But obviously she expects us to be hot and heavy, right? I mean, this is the kind of stuff a woman wears for a man who can't keep his hands off her." Suddenly, she swept him with a glance that held a glittery sort of challenge. "We should probably practice that, don't you think?"

"What?" he squawked. "You want me to practice not being able to keep my hands off you?"

Actually, he needed to practice self-control, not the other way around. Restraint was the name of the game. Perfect. He could focus on that instead of the fact that the lingerie had been a gift, not a carefully crafted plan to drive him over the brink.

It was a testament to how messed up he was that he couldn't squelch his disappointment.

She nodded. "My sister just got married not too long ago and she's pretty open with me about how hot the sex is. I think she envisions all newlyweds being like that."

"That doesn't mean she expects us to strip down in your parents' foyer," he countered a little too forcefully. Mostly because he was envisioning how hot *this* newlywed couple could be. They could give Grace and her husband a run for her money, all right.

No. No, they could not.

Viv was not wearing the yellow lacy gateway to heaven for him tonight or any night. She wasn't challenging him to out-sex her sister's marriage. There was no sex at all in their future because Viv had a career she cared about and really didn't have time for a man's inconvenient attraction. Even if the man was her husband. Especially if the man was her husband who had promised to keep things platonic.

Of course he'd done that largely for himself. He'd never experienced such a strong physical pull before and he wasn't giving in to it no matter how badly he wanted to. There was a slippery edge between keeping himself out of trouble so he could honor his promise to his late friend and maintaining his integrity with Viv and his family about the nature of his marriage.

On that note, he needed to change the subject really fast. And get his rampant need under control before he lost everything.

Viv couldn't quite catch her breath. Her lungs ached to expand but the towel was in a precarious spot. If she breathed any deeper, it would slip completely from her nerveless fingers.

Though based on how long it was taking Jonas to clue in that this was a seduction scene, maybe throwing her boobs in his face would get the point across.

God, she sucked at this. Obviously. The girls on TV made it look so simple. She'd bet a million dollars that if this scene had happened on *Scandal*, the seductress would already be in the middle of her third orgasm.

Maybe she *should* have opened the wedding gift with Jonas instead of laying it out so he could find it. For some reason, she'd thought it would give him ideas. That he'd maybe take the lead and they could get something going while they had the perfect setup to indulge in the sparks that only burned hotter the longer they didn't consummate their marriage.

How was she supposed to prove she could be the opposite of clingy with a man she wanted more than oxygen if he wouldn't take her up on the invitation she'd been dangling in his face?

"Instead of practicing anything physical," Jonas said, "we should get our stories straight. We're not going to be hanging out with your family anytime soon but mine is just on the other side of the door. I don't want any missteps like the one at dinner where we didn't plan our responses ahead of time and somehow ended up promising to go to Korea."

"I don't mind going to Korea, Jonas. I would love to see it."

He shook his head with bemusement. "It's a sixteen-hour trip and that's only if there's a not a horribly long line in customs, which even a Kim cannot cut through. Trust me, I'm doing you a favor by not taking you."

How had they shifted from talking about hot sex to visiting his grandfather? That was not how this was supposed to go.

"Well, we have plenty of time to talk about our stories, too," she said brightly. "And the good news is that my hair is almost dry so the bathroom is yours. I like to read before going to sleep so I'll just be here whenever you're ready."

"Oh. Um…" Jonas glanced at the bed and back at her. "Okay. I was thinking about sleeping on the couch and setting an alarm—"

"You can't do that," she cut him off in a rush. That would ruin everything. "What if someone gets up for a midnight snack? Also, the couch would be so uncomfortable. Sleep here. I insist."

She shooed him toward the bathroom and the moment he shut the door, she dragged air into her lungs in deep gulps as she dropped the towel and twisted her hair into a modified updo at her crown, spilling tendrils down her cheeks. Then she slithered into the shameless yellow teddy and panties set that she'd picked out with Grace yesterday. Strictly so she could rub it in that she had a hot husband to wear it for, of course. And then she'd had Grace gift wrap it. The sly wink had been all her sister's idea, so she really hadn't fibbed much when she'd related the story to Jonas.

The lace chafed at her bare nipples, sending ripples

of heat through her core. The panties rode high and tight, the strings threading between her cheeks. Not a place she was used to having pressure and friction, but it was oddly exciting.

No wonder women wore this stuff. She felt sexy and more than a little turned on just by virtue of getting dressed. Who knew?

The sound of running water drifted through the walls as Jonas went through his nightly routine. She dove into bed and pulled up the covers until they were tight around her shoulders. Wait. That wasn't going to work. Experimentally, she draped the sheet across her chest like a toga, and threw her shoulders back. Huh. The one breast looked spectacular in the low-cut lace teddy, but the other one was covered up, which didn't seem like the point. Inching the sheet down, she settled into place against the pillow until she was happy with how she looked.

That was a lot of skin on *display*. Much more than she was used to. The lace left little to the imagination.

Surely this would be enough to entice Jonas into making the most of this opportunity to share a bedroom.

Light. She leaped up and slammed down the switch, leaving only the bedside lamp illuminated and leaped back under the covers. The doorknob to the bathroom rattled and she lost her nerve, yanking the sheet back up to cover the yellow lace until X-ray vision would be the only way Jonas could tell what she was wearing. He strode into the room.

Oh, God. Was a more delicious man ever created in the history of time? He'd untucked his button-down and the tail hung casually below his waist. Plenty of access for a woman to slide her hands underneath. There was a gaping hole where his tie had been. A V framed a slice of his chest and he'd rolled his sleeves up to midforearm. It was the most undressed she'd ever seen him and her pulse quickened the closer he came.

This gorgeous creature was about to strip all that off and *get into bed*. With her. This was such a bad idea. Alluring and aloof was not in her wheelhouse and at that moment, she wanted Jonas with a full body ache that felt completely foreign and completely right at the same time.

"I thought you were going to be reading," he said, and stopped in the middle of the room as if he'd hit an invisible wall.

So close. And yet so far.

She shook her head, scrambling for a plausible excuse when she'd just said that was what she planned to do. Couldn't hold an e-reader and pretend you weren't wearing sexy lingerie that screamed *put your hands on me* at the same time.

In retrospect, that might have been a nice scene. She could have been reading with the tablet propped up on her stomach, which would have left her torso completely bare without making it look like she'd set up the scene that way. Dang it. Too late now.

"I couldn't find anything that held my attention."

"Oh. Okay."

And then the entire world fell away along with most of her senses as Jonas started unbuttoning his shirt. It was a slow, torturous event as he slipped the buttons free and each one revealed more of his beautiful body.

Thank God she hadn't stuck a book in front of her face. Otherwise she'd have missed the Jonas Striptease.

She glanced up to see his dark eyes on hers. Their

gazes connected and she had the distinct impression he hadn't expected her to be watching him undress. But he didn't seem terribly unhappy about the audience, since he kept going. She didn't look away either.

He let the shirt fall, revealing first one shoulder, then the other. It shouldn't have been such a shock to see the indentations of muscles in his biceps as his arms worked off the shirt. She knew he hit the gym on a regular basis. They'd been friends for a year and talked about all manner of subjects. Sometimes he told her about his workout routine or mentioned that he'd switched it up and his arms were sore. Little had she realized what a visual panorama had been in store for her as a result.

"I feel like I should be wearing something sparkly underneath my pants," Jonas said with wry amusement. "Would it be possible for you to not watch me?"

"Oh. Um…sure." Cheeks on fire, she flipped over and faced the wall, careful to keep the sheet up around her neck. With the motion, it stretched tight. More mummy than Marilyn Monroe, but this was her first seduction. Surely even a woman like Marilyn had a few practice runs before she got it right. This one was Viv's.

And she needed a lot of practice, clearly, since she'd been caught staring and made Jonas uncomfortable at the same time. The whisper of fabric hitting the carpet made her doubly sorry she hadn't been facedown in a book when he came out of the bathroom because she could easily have pretended to be reading while watching the slow reveal out of the corner of her eye.

The bed creaked and the mattress shifted with Jonas's weight. "Still think this is a good idea?"

"I never said it was a good idea," she shot back over her shoulder. "I said our friendship could take it."

Which wasn't a given now that he was so close and so male and so much the subject of her fantasies that started and ended in a bed very much like this one. And she'd been forced to miss half of it due to Jonas's inconvenient sense of propriety. Well, he was done undressing now, right? This was her seduction and she wanted to face him. Except just as she rolled, he snapped off the bedside lamp, plunging the room into darkness.

"Good night," Jonas said, his voice sinfully rich in the dark.

The covers pulled a little as he turned over and settled into position. To go to sleep.

As mood killers went, that was a big one. She'd totally botched this.

Okay. Not totally. This was just a minor setback, most likely because she was trying to play hard to get, which was not as easy as it sounded, and frankly, not her typical method of operation. Plus? This was not a typical relationship. Jonas needed to keep her around, so by default this wasn't going to go like it had with her ex-boyfriends.

She had to approach this like a new recipe that hadn't quite turned out because she'd gone against her instincts and added an ingredient that she didn't like. And if she didn't like it, what was the point?

This was her cupcake to bake. Being the opposite of clingy and needy had only gotten her a disinterested husband—and rightfully so. How was he even supposed to know she wished he'd roll back over and explore the lingerie-clad body she'd hidden under the covers like a blushing virgin bride? Viv wasn't the kind of woman to inspire a man to slavish passion or it would have happened already.

She had to be smart if she couldn't be a femme fatale.

She blinked against the dark and tried not to focus on how the sound of Jonas breathing fluttered against her skin in a very distracting way. Somehow she was going to have to announce her interest in taking things to the next level in big bold letters without also giving him the impression she couldn't live without him. Though perhaps that last part wouldn't be too difficult; after all, she'd already been pretending for a year.

Six

After the weekend of torture, Jonas went to work on Monday with renewed determination to get his grandfather moving on the Park Industries merger. The sooner the ink was dry on that deal, the better. Then Jonas could get over his irritation that his marriage to Viv was what had tipped the scales toward his grandfather's decision to retire.

Grandfather recognized Jonas's accomplishments with Kim Electronics. Deep down, he knew that. But it rankled that the conversation about naming Jonas as the next CEO had come about *after* Grandfather had met Viv.

Didn't matter. The subject had come up. That was enough. And Jonas intended to make sure the subject didn't get dropped, because if he was forced to stay married to Viv, he should get something out of it. An Academy Award wouldn't be out of line after the stellar performance he'd turned in at his parents' house. How he'd acted like he'd been sleeping all night while lying next to his wife was still a mystery to him and he was the one who'd pulled it off.

Her scent still haunted him at odd moments. Like now. This conference call he'd supposedly been participating in had gotten maybe a quarter of his attention. Which was not a good way to prove he deserved the position of CEO.

But it was a perfect way to indulge in the memory of the sweet way she'd curled up next to him, her even breathing oddly arousing and lulling at the same time. He'd expected it to be weird the next morning, like maybe they wouldn't look each other in the eye, but Viv had awoken refreshed and beautiful, as if she'd gotten a great night's sleep. He pretended the same and they settled into an easy camaraderie around his parents that hadn't raised a single brow.

At least that part was over. Viv's mom and dad had invited them for dinner on Friday and he was plenty nervous about that experience. It would probably be fine. As long as he didn't have to act like he couldn't keep his hands off Viv. Or act like he didn't want to touch her. Actually, he'd lost track of *what* he was supposed to be doing. Hence the reason he hated lying. The truth was so much easier.

But when he got home that evening after a long day that had included a two-hour debrief with Legal regarding the merger proposal, Viv was sitting on the couch with two glasses of wine. She smiled at him and he felt entirely incapable of faking anything. Especially if it came down to pretending he didn't want to be with her.

His answering smile broadened hers and that set off

all sorts of fireworks inside that should have been a big fat warning to back off, but he was tired and there was absolutely nothing wrong with having a glass of wine with his friend Viv after work. That was his story and he was sticking to it.

"Are we celebrating something?" he asked as he hung his work bag on the hook near the refrigerator.

"Yes, that I can in fact open a bottle of wine all by myself." She laughed with that little peal he'd never noticed before he'd married her, but seemed to be a common occurrence lately. Or had she always laughed like that and he'd been too stuck in his own head to notice how warm it was?

"Was that in question?" He took the long-stemmed glass from her outstretched fingers and eased onto the couch next to her. Instantly, that turned into a big mistake as her scent wrapped around him. It slammed through his gut and his arm jerked, nearly spilling the wine.

For God's sake. This ridiculousness had to stop, especially before Friday or the second family trial by fire would end in a blaze.

"I'm just not talented in the cork-pulling arena," she answered casually as if she hadn't noticed his idiocy. "My skills start and end with baking."

Yes. Baking. They could talk about cupcakes while he got back on track. "Speaking of which, I wasn't expecting you home. Doesn't the shop stay open until seven on Mondays?"

She smiled. "You've been memorizing my work schedule? That's sweet. Josie is closing up for me. I wanted to be here when you got home."

"You did? Why?"

Because I couldn't stay away, Jonas. You're so much more interesting to me than cupcakes, Jonas. I want to strip you naked and have my wicked way with you, Jonas.

There came her gorgeous laugh again. He couldn't hear it enough, especially when he was in the middle of being such a doofus. If she was laughing, that was a good thing. Otherwise, he'd owe her an apology. Not that she could read his thoughts, thank God.

"I wanted to see you. We're still friends, right?"

Oh, yeah. "Right."

"Also, I wasn't kidding when I said my sisters are going to have an eagle eye on our relationship this Friday." Viv sipped her wine, her gaze on his over the rim. "We're still a little jumpy around each other. I'm not sure why, but sharing a bed didn't seem to help."

Huge mystery there. Maybe because his awareness level had shot up into the stratosphere since he'd woken up with a woman whom he hadn't touched one single time. Or it could be because he'd been kicking himself over his regret ever since. He shouldn't regret not touching her. It was the right move.

"No, it didn't help," he muttered. "That wasn't ever going to be the result of sleeping together platonically."

She nodded sagely. "Yes, I realized that sometime between then and now. Don't worry. I have a new plan."

"I wasn't worried. What is it?"

"We're trying too hard. We need to dial it back and spend time as friends. We were comfortable around each other then. It can totally be that way again."

That sounded really great to him. And also like there was a catch he couldn't quite see. Cautiously he eyed her. "What, like I take you to lunch and we just talk about stuff?"

"Sure." She shrugged and reached out to lace her fingers through his free hand. "See, we can hold hands and it doesn't mean anything. I'm just hanging out with my friend Jonas, whom I like. Hey, Jonas, guess what?"

He had to grin. This was not the worst plan he'd ever heard. In fact, it was pretty great. He'd missed their easy camaraderie and the lack of pretension. Never had she made him feel like he should be anything other than himself when they hung out. "Hey, Viv. What?"

"I made reservations at this new restaurant in Cary that sounds fab. It's Thai."

"That's my favorite." Which she well knew. It was hers, too. He took the first deep breath in what seemed like hours. They were friends. He could dang well act like one and stop nosing around Viv like a hormonal teenager.

"Drink your wine and then we'll go. My treat."

"No way. You opened the bottle of wine. The least I can do is spring for dinner."

"Well, it was a major accomplishment," she allowed, and clinked her glass to his as he held out the stemware. "I'm thrilled to have it recognized as such."

And the evening only got better from there. Jonas drove Viv to the restaurant and they chattered all the way about everything and nothing, which he'd have called a major accomplishment, too, since he managed to concentrate on the conversation and not on the expanse of Viv's bare leg mere inches from his hand resting on the gearshift. The food was good and the service exceptional.

As they walked in the door of the condo later, Jonas paused and helped Viv take off her jacket, then turned to hang it up for her in the foyer coat closet.

"I have to say," he called over his shoulder as he slid the hanger into place. "Dinner was a great idea."

He shut the door and Viv was still standing there in the foyer with a small smile.

"It's the best date I've been on in a long time," she said. "And seems like the plan worked. Neither of us is acting weird or jumpy."

"True." He'd relaxed a while back and didn't miss the edginess that had plagued him since the wedding ceremony. He and Viv were friends and that was never going to change. That was the whole reason he'd come up with this idea in the first place. "We may not set off the fire alarms when we visit with your family on Friday, but we can certainly pull off the fact that we like each other, which is not something all married couples can say."

That was fine with him. Better that way anyway. His reaction to the pull between him and Viv was ridiculous. So unlike him. He had little experience with something so strong that it dug under his skin, and he'd handled it badly.

Fortunately, he hadn't done anything irreversible that would have ruined their friendship. Though there'd been more than a handful of moments in that bed at his parents' that he'd been really afraid it was going to go the other way.

But then she stepped a little closer to him in the foyer, waltzing into his space without hesitation. The foyer was just a small area at the entrance of the condo with a coat closet and nothing more to recommend it. So there was little else to take his attention off the woman who'd suddenly filled it with her presence.

"We've been friends a long time," she said, and it was such a strange, unnecessary comment, but he nodded anyway because something had shifted in the atmosphere.

He couldn't put his finger on it. The relaxed, easy vibe from the restaurant had morphed into something else—a quickened sense of anticipation that he couldn't explain, but didn't hate. As if this really was a date and they'd moved on to the second part of the evening's activities.

"We've done a lot of firsts in the last little while," she continued, also unnecessarily because he was well aware that he'd shifted the dynamic of their relationship by marrying her.

"Yeah. Tonight went a long way toward getting us back to normal. To being friends without all the weirdness that sprang up when I kissed you."

That was probably the dumbest thing he could have said. He'd thrown that down between them and it was like opening the electrical panel of a television, where all the live components were exposed, and all it would take was one wrong move to fry the delicate circuitry.

Better to keep the thing covered.

But it was too late. Her gaze landed square on his mouth as if she was reliving the kiss, too. Not the nice and unexpectedly sweet kiss at the wedding ceremony. But the hot, tongue-on-tongue kiss outside her bedroom when they'd been practicing being a couple. The necessity of that practice had waned since his family had bought the marriage hook, line and sinker. Sure, they still had to get through her family, but he wasn't worried about it, racy lingerie gifts aside.

Now the only reason to ever kiss Viv again would be because he couldn't stop himself.

Which was the worst reason he could think of. And keep thinking about, over and over again.

"I don't think it was weirdness, Jonas," she murmured.

Instantly, he wished there was still some circumstance that required her to call him Mr. Kim. Why that was such a turn-on remained a mystery to him. But really, everything about Viv was a turn-on. Her laugh. Her cupcakes. The way her hair lay so shiny and soft against her shoulders.

"Trust me, it was weird," he muttered. "I gave myself entirely too many inappropriate thoughts with that kiss."

And that was the danger of being lulled back into a false sense of security with the sociable, uneventful dinner. He'd fallen into friendship mode, where he could say anything on his mind without consequence.

The admission that had just come out of his mouth was going to have consequences.

Her smile went from zero to sixty in less than a second and all at once, he wasn't sure the consequences were going to be anything close to what he'd envisioned. She waltzed even closer and reached up to adjust his tie in a provocative move that shouldn't have been as affecting as it was.

The tie hadn't needed adjusting. The knot was precisely where he'd placed it hours ago when he'd gotten dressed for work. It slid down a few centimeters and then a few more as she loosened it.

Loosened it. As if she intended to take it off.

But she stopped short of committing, which was good. Really…good. He swallowed as she speared him with her contemplative gaze, her hands still at his collar in an intimate touch. She was so close he could pull her into his arms if he wanted to.

He wanted to. Always.

Dinner hadn't changed that.

"The thing is, Jonas," she said. "I've had some thoughts, too. And if yours are the same as mine, I'm trying to figure out why they're inappropriate."

She flattened her hands on his lapels. The pressure sang through him and it would feel even better if he didn't have a whole suit jacket and two shirts between her palms and his skin.

The direction of this conversation floored him. And if she kept it up, the floor was exactly where they were going to end up.

"What are you saying, Viv?" he asked hoarsely, scrambling to understand. "That you lie awake at night and think about that kiss, aching to do it again?"

She nodded and something so powerful swept through his body that he could hardly breathe. This was the opposite of what should be happening. She should be backing off and citing her inability to focus on a man and her career at the same time. She was too busy, too involved in her business to date. This was the absolute he'd banked on for long agonizing hours, the thing that was keeping him from indulging in the forbidden draw between them.

Because if he gave in, he'd have no control over what happened next. That certainty had already been proven with what little they'd experimented so far. More would be catastrophic.

And so, so fantastically amazing.

"After tonight, I'm convinced we're missing an opportunity here," she said, her voice dripping with something sensual that he'd never have expected from his sunny friend Viviana Dawson. *Kim.*

Viv wasn't his friend. She was his wife. He'd been ignoring that fact for an entire day, but it roared back to the forefront with an implication he couldn't ignore. Except he didn't know what it meant to him, not really. Not just a means to an end, though it was an inescapable fact that she'd married him as a favor.

And he wanted to exploit that favor to get her naked and under him? It was improper, ridiculous. So very illicit that his body tightened with thick anticipation.

"What opportunity is that?" he murmured, letting his gaze flick over her face, searching for some sign that the answer about to come out of her mouth *was not* a green light to get naked.

Because he'd have a very difficult time saying no. In fact, he couldn't quite remember why he should say no. He shouldn't say no. If nothing else, taking this next step meant he wasn't lying to anyone about their marriage.

Her limpid brown eyes locked on to his. "We're both too busy to date. And even if we weren't, I have a feeling that 'oh, by the way, I'm married' isn't a great pickup line. You said it yourself. We spark. If our friendship can take a kiss, maybe it can take more. We should find out."

More. He liked the word *more* a lot. Especially if her dictionary defined it as lots and lots of sex while maintaining their friendship. If things got too intense, he could back off with no harm, no foul. It was like the absolute best of all worlds.

Unless that wasn't what she meant.

Clarification would be in order, just to be sure they were speaking the same language. "More?"

"Come on, Jonas." She laughed a little breathlessly and it trilled through him. "Are you going to make me spell it out?"

"Yes, I absolutely am," he growled, because the whole concept of Viv talking dirty to him was doing things to his insides that he was enjoying the hell out of. If he'd known dinner was *this* kind of date, he'd have skipped dessert. "I want to be crystal clear about what's on the table here."

Instead of suggesting things Jonas could do to her— all of which he'd immediately commit to memory so he didn't miss a single one—she watched him as she hooked the neckline of her dress and pulled it to the side. A flash of yellow seared his vision as his entire body tensed in recognition.

"I'm wearing my sister's gift," she murmured, and that admission was as much of a turn-on as any dirty talk. Maybe more so because he'd been fantasizing about that scrap of yellow lace for a million years.

"I bet it looks amazing on you."

"Only one way to find out," she shot back and curled her fingers around his lapels to yank him forward.

He met her mouth in a searing kiss without hesitation. All of his reservations melted in an instant as he sank into her, shaping her lips with his as he consumed her heat, letting it spread deep inside.

Why had he resisted this? Viv didn't want anything from him, didn't expect an emotional outpouring or even anything permanent. This was all going to end at some point and thus didn't count. No chance for romantic nonsense. No declarations of love would ever be forthcoming—on either side. Jonas's sense of honor would be intact, as would his sworn vow to Warren and Hendrix.

Instead of two friends pretending to be a married couple having sex, they were going to be married friends who *were* having sex. Living the truth appealed to him enormously. Desire swept through him as he got great handfuls of Viv's skin under his palms and everything but his wife drained from his mind.

Viv would have sworn on a truckload of Bibles that the kiss outside her bedroom last week had been the hottest one she'd ever participate in.

She'd have been wrong.

That kiss had been startling in its perfection. Unexpected in its heat. It had gotten her motor humming pretty fast. She'd been angling for another one just like that. Thank God she hadn't gotten her wish.

This kiss exploded in her core like a cannon. Desire crackled through the air as Jonas backed her up against the wall, crowding her against it with his hard body, demanding that her every curve conform to him. Her flesh rapidly obeyed. She nearly wept with the glory of Jonas pressed against her exactly as she'd fantasized hundreds of times.

He angled her jaw with his strong fingers until he got her situated the way he apparently wanted and then plunged in with the wickedest of caresses. His tongue slicked across hers so sensuously that she moaned against it, would have sagged if he hadn't had her pinned to the wall.

His hands nipped at her waist, skimmed upward and

hooked both sides of the neckline. The fabric tore at the seams as he separated it from her shoulders, and she gasped.

"I need to see you," he murmured fiercely. "I'll buy you two to make up for this one."

And with that, the dress came apart in his hands. He peeled it from between them, following the line of the reveal with his hot mouth, laving at her exposed flesh until he caught the silk strap of the yellow teddy in his teeth, scraping the sensitive hollow of her shoulder.

The sensation shot through her center with tight, heated pulls. *Oh, my.* His fingers tangled in the strap, binding his palm to her shoulder as he explored the skin beneath the yellow lace with his tongue, dipping and diving into the holes of the pattern. Then his lips closed around her nipple through the fabric and her whole body jerked. Hot, wet heat dampened the scrap between her legs. The awareness that Jonas had drenched her panties so quickly only excited her more.

What had happened to the kind, generous man she'd been so intent on seducing? He'd become a hungry, untamed creature who wanted to devour her. She loved every second. His tongue flicked out to tease her nipple, wetting the lace, and it was wickedly effective. Moans poured from her throat as her head thunked back against the wall.

All at once, he sank to his knees and trailed his lips across the gap between the top and the bottom of her sexy lingerie set, murmuring her full name. *Viviana.* The sound of it rang in her ears as he worshipped her stomach with his mouth, and it was poetry.

Her thighs pressed together, seeking relief from the ache his touch had created, and she arched into his lips, his hands, crying out as his fingers worked under the hem of her soaked panties. The gorgeous man she'd married glanced up at her from his supine position, his gaze so wickedly hot that she experienced a small quake at that alone, but then he slid one finger along her crease, teasing her core until she opened wider, begging him to fill her.

He did. Oh, how he did, one quick motion, then back out again. The exquisite friction burned through her core a second time and she cried out.

"Please, Jonas" dripped from her mouth with little gasping sighs and she whimpered as she pleaded with him for whatever he planned to give her next.

She didn't know she could be this wanton, that the man she'd married could drive her to neediness so easily. It was so hot that she felt the gathering of her release before she was ready for the exquisite torture to end. No way to hold back. She crested the peak and came with hard ripples against Jonas's fingers. The orgasm drained her of everything but him.

Falling apart at his hands was better than what she'd dreamed of, hoped for, imagined—and then some. And it still wasn't over.

He nipped at her lace-covered sex and swept her up in his arms, still quaking, to carry her to his bedroom. Blindly, she tried to clear her senses long enough to gain some semblance of control. Why, she wasn't sure, but being wound up in Jonas's arms wearing nothing but wet lace while he was still fully dressed felt a lot like she'd surrendered more than she'd intended to.

But he wasn't finished with the revelations.

He laid her out on the comforter and watched her as he stripped out of his suit jacket and tie. She shivered long and hard as he began unbuttoning his shirt, but she didn't dare blink for fear of missing the greatest show on earth—the sight of her husband shedding his clothes. For her. Because she'd finally gotten him to see reason.

They were friends. What better foundation was there to get naked with someone than because you liked each other? It was sheer brilliance, if she did say so herself. The fact that she'd been racking her brain over how to best get to this place when the answer had been staring her in the face for a year? She'd rather not dwell on that.

Good thing she had plenty else to occupy her mind. That beautiful torso of his came into sight, still covered by a white undershirt that clung to his biceps and lean waist, and she wanted to touch him so badly her fingers tingled. But then his hands moved to his belt and she didn't move. Couldn't. Her lungs rattled with the need to expand. Slowly, the belt loosened and he pulled it from the loops. After an eternity, it dropped to the floor, followed shortly by the pants, and then came the pièce de résistance. Jonas stripped off his undershirt and worked off his boxers in the most spectacular reveal of all. Better than Christmas, her birthday and flipping the sign in Cupcaked's window to Open for the first time.

Her husband's body was gorgeous, long, lean. Vibrating with need that hungrily sniffed out hers as he crawled onto the bed and onto her, easily knocking her back to the mattress, covering her body with his.

And then she wasn't so coherent after that. His arms encircled her as easily as his dominant presence did. His kiss claimed her lips irrevocably, imprinting them with his particular brand of possession, the likes of which she'd never known. Never understood could exist.

The sensuous haze he dropped her into was delicious

and she soaked it in, content to let him take his time as he explored her body with his hands more thoroughly than she'd have imagined possible when she still wore the yellow lace. She was so lost in him that it took her a minute to remember that she could indulge herself, too, if she wished.

Viv flattened her palms to his chest, memorizing the peaks and valleys of his body, reveling in the heat under her fingertips. She slid downward to cup his buttocks, shifting to align their hips because the ache at her core had only been awakened, not sated, and he had precisely what she needed.

He groaned deep in his throat as she circled against his thick, gorgeous erection, grinding her hips for maximum impact. The answering tilt of his hips enflamed her. As did the quickening of his breath.

"I need to be inside you," he murmured. "Before I lose my mind."

Rolling with her in his arms, he reached one hand out to sling open the bedside table and extracted a box of condoms with ruthless precision. In seconds, he'd sheathed himself and rolled back into place against her.

His thumb slid into the indentation in her chin, levering her head up to lock his hot-eyed gaze onto her as he notched himself at her entrance.

The tip of his shaft tormented her, sensitizing everything it touched as he paused in the worst sort of tease.

"Jonas," she gasped.

"Right here, sweetheart. Tell me what you want."

"Everything." And she couldn't take it back, no matter how much of a mistake it was to admit that she wasn't the kind of woman who could be in the midst of such passion and hold back.

Except she wasn't entirely sure he meant for her to as he gripped her hip with his strong fingers, lifted and pushed in with a groan, spreading her wide as he filled her. The luscious solid length of him stretched her tight, and before she could question it, one tear slipped from the corner of her eye. It was a testament to the perfection of how he felt moving inside her, how wholly encompassing the sensations were that washed over her as Jonas made love to her.

And she was ten kinds of a fool if she thought she could keep pretending this was practice for her next relationship.

"Amazing. Beautiful. Mine." Words rained down on her from Jonas's mouth as he increased the tempo. "I can't believe how this feels...you're so wet, so silky. I can't stop. Can't hold back."

For a woman who had never incited much more than mild interest in a man, to be treated to this kind of evidence that she was more than he could take—it was everything. "Give it all to me."

Unbelievably, there *was* more and he gave it to her, driving her to a soaring crescendo that made her feel more alive than anything in her memory. No longer was this bed a proving ground to show she could be with a man and not pour all of herself into him. He demanded her participation, wrung every drop of her essence out of her body.

She gladly surrendered it. Jonas was it for her, the man she'd married, the man she'd wanted for so very long.

As they both roared toward a climax, she had half a second to capture his face in her palms and kiss him with all the passion she could muster before they both shattered. She swallowed his groan and took the shudders of his body, absorbing them into hers even as she rippled through her own release. Everything was so much bigger, stronger, crisper than she'd have ever imagined and his mouth under hers curved into a blissful smile that her soul echoed.

And as he nestled her into his arms for a few badly needed moments of recovery time, she bit her lip against the wash of emotions that threatened to spill out all over their friendship.

She'd told him their relationship could take this. Now she had to stick to her promise. How in the world she was going to keep him from figuring out that she was in love with him?

Seven

For the second day in a row, Jonas struggled to maintain his composure at work. It was for an entirely different reason today than it had been yesterday. But still. His wife swirled at the center of it and he wasn't sure what to do with that.

Last night had been legendary. Off the charts. Far more explosive than he would have ever guessed—and he'd spent a lot of time contemplating exactly how hot things with Viv could be.

She'd surpassed everything he'd ever experienced. Even here in his somewhat sterile office that had all the hallmarks of a CEO who ran a billion-dollar global company, his loins tightened the second he let his thoughts stray. She'd made him thoroughly question what he knew about how it could be between a man and a woman. How it could be between Jonas and Viv, more importantly, because he had a feeling they weren't done.

How could they be done? He'd barely peeled back the first layer of possibilities, and he was nothing if not ravenous to get started on the second and third layers. Hot Viv. Sensual Viv. The list could be endless.

Instead of drooling like an idiot over the woman he'd married, Jonas squared his shoulders and pushed the erotic images from his mind. The merger with Park was still just a nebulous concept and no one had signed anything. This was the deal of the century, and Jonas had to get it done before anyone thought twice about marriage alliances. Sun Park's grandfather could still pull the plug if he'd had his heart set on a much more intimate merger. Thus far, Jonas had done little but meet with Legal on it.

Four hours later, he had sketched out a proposed hierarchy for the business entities, worked through the human resources tangle of potential duplicate positions and then run the numbers on whether the Kim Building could support the influx of new people. His grandfather would be coming by soon to take a tour and this was exactly the data Jonas needed at his fingertips. Data that would solidify his place as the rightful CEO of Kim Electronics, with or without an *impulse of the heart* on his résumé.

So that was still a sore spot apparently. Jonas tried to shrug it off and prepare for his grandfather's arrival, but wasn't at all surprised that Jung-Su showed up twenty minutes early. Probably a deliberate move to see if Jonas was prepared.

He was nothing if not ready, willing and able to prove

that he was the right choice. He'd been preparing to be his grandfather's successor since college.

He strolled to the reception area, where his admin had made Grandfather comfortable. Technically Jung-Su was the boss of everyone in this building, but he hadn't visited America in several years. Jonas held the helm here and he appreciated that Grandfather didn't throw his weight around. They had professional, mutual respect for each other, which Jonas had to believe would ultimately hold sway.

Jung-Su glanced up as Jonas came forward, his weathered face breaking into a polite smile. Grandfather stood and they shook hands.

"Please follow me," Jonas said, and indicated the direction. "I'd like to show you the executive offices."

Jung-Su nodded and inclined his head, but instead of following Jonas, he drew abreast and walked in lockstep toward the elevator. Over the weekend, they'd done a lot of sitting down and Jonas hadn't noticed how much his grandfather had shrunk. Jonas had always been taller and more slender to his grandfather's stocky build, but more so now, and it was a visual cue that his grandfather had aged. As much as Jonas had focused on getting his grandfather comfortable with passing the mantel, he'd given little thought to the idea that becoming the next CEO of the global company meant his mentorship with Jung-Su would be over.

"Tell me," Grandfather said as they reached the elevator. "How is your lovely wife?"

"She's…" *A vixen in disguise.* Not the kind of information his grandfather was looking for with the innocuous question. "Great. Her shop is constantly busy."

And Viv had ducked out early to take him on the ride

of his life last night. For the first time, he wondered if she'd planned the evening to end as it had or if it had been as spontaneous on her part as it had been on his. Maybe she'd been thinking about getting naked since the weekend of torture, too. If so, he liked that she'd been similarly affected.

They rode two floors up to the executive level. As they exited, Jonas and Jung-Su nodded to the various employees going about the business of electronics in a beehive of activity.

"You've mentioned your wife's business frequently," his grandfather commented just outside the boardroom where Jonas conducted the majority of his virtual meetings. "Doesn't she have other interests?"

The disapproval in his grandfather's voice was faint. "You don't understand. Her bakery is much more than just a business. It's an extension of her."

Cupcakes had been a mechanism to fit in among her older, more accomplished sisters, as she'd told him on numerous occasions. But it had morphed from there into a business that she could be proud of. Hell, it was a venture *he* was proud of.

"Anyone can pull a package of cupcake mix off the shelf at the grocery store," Jonas continued, infusing as much sincerity into his speech as he could. His grandfather had no call to be throwing shade at his wife's profession. "That's easy. Viv spends hours in her kitchen doing something special to hers that customers can't get enough of."

"It seems as if you are smitten by her cupcakes, as well," Grandfather commented with a tinge of amusement.

Jonas forced a return smile that hopefully didn't look

as pained as he suspected it did. *Smitten.* He wasn't smitten with Viv and it rankled that he'd managed to convince his grandfather that he was. Cupcakes, on the other hand—no pretending needed there. "Of course I am. That's what first drew me to her."

Like it was yesterday, he recalled how many times he'd found excuses to drop by Cupcaked to get a glimpse of Viv in those first few weeks after meeting her. Often she was in the back but if she saw him, she popped out for a quick hi, ready with a smile no matter what she had going on in the kitchen. That alone had kept him coming back. There was always someone in the office with a birthday or anniversary, and cupcakes always made an occasion more festive.

"Ah, yes, I recall that conversation at dinner where she mentioned you pretended to go there for her cupcakes but were really there to see her."

"It was both," he corrected easily since it was true. He could own that he liked Viv. They were friends.

Who'd seen each other naked.

Before he could stop it, images of Viv spilled through his mind.

The rush of heat to his body smacked him, sizzling across his skin so fast he had little chance of reeling it back. But he had to. This was the most inappropriate time to be thinking about his wife wearing that see-through yellow lacy concoction strictly for his benefit.

"Pardon me for a moment," Jonas croaked, and ducked into the executive washroom to get himself under control. Or as close to it as he could with an enormous erection that showed no signed of abating.

And while he stood in front of the mirror concentrating on his breathing and doing absolutely nothing constructive, he pulled out his phone to set a reminder to drop by the jewelry store on the way home. Viv had expressly asked for jewels as compensation for the favor she was doing him. She needed something pretty and ridiculously expensive.

Thinking of her draped in jewelry he'd bought wasn't helping.

After the longest five minutes of his life, Jonas finally got the tenting mostly under control. No one had noticed. Or at least that's what he tried to tell himself. His staff didn't walk around with their eyes on his crotch.

The biggest hit was to Jonas's psyche. How had he let Viv get under his skin like that? It was unacceptable. If nothing else, he needed to maintain his professionalism during this period when his grandfather's support meant everything. There were other contenders for Jung-Su's job, such as vice presidents who lived in Korea and had worked alongside the CEO for thirty years. Some of Mr. Park's staff could rise to the top as worthy heads of a global company, and those under the Park umbrella arguably had more experience running the factories that would come into play with the merger.

Jonas had to reel it back with Viv. Way back. There was no excuse for falling prey to baser urges and he definitely didn't want to find out what happened next if he kept going down this path. That was one absolute he trusted—the less he let a woman get tangled up in his emotions, the better.

Resolute, Jonas returned to find his grandfather in deep discussion with Jonas's chief financial officer, a man without whom Kim Electronics would suffer in the American market.

Perfect. This was an opportunity to guide the discussion to Jonas's accomplishments as well as those of his staff, who were a reflection of his ability to run the Americas branch. Back on track, Jonas smiled at the two men and jumped into the conversation as if he hadn't just had a minor freak-out over an incontrollable urge to drive straight home and bury himself in his wife.

That wasn't happening. Boundaries needed to happen. Jonas didn't have the luxury of letting his wife dig further under his skin. But when he got home later that night, it was to an empty house, and boundaries didn't seem like such a fun plan.

More disappointed than he had a right to be, Jonas prowled around the enormous condo to be sure Viv hadn't tucked herself away in a corner to read or watch TV. *Nada.* He glanced at his watch. It was well after seven. She must have gotten caught up at the shop. Totally her right to work late. They didn't answer to each other.

For a half second, he contemplated walking the four blocks to Cupcaked. Strictly so he could give Viv her gift, of course. But that smacked of eagerness to see her that he had no intention of admitting to. So instead, he flopped on the couch and scrolled through his never-ending inbox on his phone, desperate for something to take his mind off the resounding silence in the condo. Wow, was it quiet. Why had he never noticed that before? The high ceilings and exposed beams usually created an echo that reminded him of a museum, but he'd have to be making noise for that echo to happen.

Viv had made a lot of noise last night, but he hadn't been paying a whole lot of attention to whether the sounds of her gasps and sighs had filled the cavernous part of the loft. And now he was back to thinking about his wife, her gorgeous body and why she wasn't currently naked in his lap.

He scowled. They'd done zero to establish how their relationship would progress after last night. They should have. *He* should have. Probably the smartest thing would have been to establish that last night was a onetime thing. He couldn't keep having meltdowns at work or moon around over whether Viv planned to hang out with him at night.

He should find something else to do. Like… He glanced around the condo, suddenly at a loss. Prior to getting married, what had he done on a random Tuesday when he was bored?

Nothing. Because he was rarely bored. Usually he had work and other stuff to occupy him. *Friends.* Of course the answer was to ping his friends. But Warren didn't respond to his text message and Hendrix was in New York on a business trip.

Viv's key rattled in the lock. Finally. He vaulted off the couch to greet her, totally not okay with how his pulse quickened at the prospect of seeing her and completely unsure how to stop it.

As she came through the door, her smile widened as she spied Jonas standing in the hall, arms crossed, hip casually cocked out against the wall.

"Hi," she said, halting just short of invading his space. "Were you waiting for me?"

No sprang to his lips before he thought better of it. Well, he couldn't really deny that, now, could he? If he'd stayed sprawled on the couch and given her a casual "what's up?" as she strolled through the door, he might have had a leg to stand on. Too late.

"Yeah," he admitted, and held up the shiny blue foil bag clutched in his fingers. "I have something for you."

Her eyes widened as she held out her hand to accept the bag. The most delicious smell wafted between them, a vanilla and Viv combo that made him think of frosting and sex and about a million other things that shouldn't go together but did—like marriage and friendship.

Why couldn't he greet his wife at the door if he felt like it? It wasn't a crime. It didn't mean anything.

The anticipation that graced her smile shouldn't have pleased him so much. But he couldn't deny that it whacked him inside in a wholly different way than the sultry smile she'd laid on him last night, right before she informed him that she had on yellow lingerie under her clothes.

Which was not up for a repeat tonight. Boundaries should be the first order of business. Viv had sucked him down a rabbit hole that he didn't like. Well, he *liked* it. It just didn't sit well with how unbelievably tempting she was. If she could tempt him into letting go of his professionalism, what other barriers could she knock down? The risk was not worth it.

But then she opened the box, and her startled gasp put heat in places that he should be able to control a hell of lot better.

"Jonas, this is too much," she protested with a laugh and held out the box like she expected him to take it back or something.

"Not hardly. It's exactly right." Before she got ideas in her head about refusing the gift that had taken him thirty minutes to pick out, he plucked the diamond necklace from its velvet housing and undid the clasp so he could draw it around her neck. "Hush, and turn around."

She did and that put him entirely too close to her sweet flesh. That curve where her shoulder flared out called to him. Except it was covered by her dress. That was a shame.

Dragging her hair out of the way, she waited for him to position the chain. He let the catch of the necklace go and the ten-carat diamond dropped to rest against her chest, just above the swell of her breasts. Which were also covered, but he knew precisely where they began.

His lips ached to taste that swell again. Among other things. Palms flat across her back, he smoothed the chain into place, but that was really just an excuse to touch her.

"If you're sure," she murmured, and she relaxed, letting her body sink backward until it met his and heat flared between them.

"Oh, I'm sure." She'd meant about the diamond. Probably. But his mouth had already hit the bare spot she'd revealed when she'd swept her long brown hair aside and the taste of Viv exploded under his tongue.

Groaning, he let his hands skim down her waist until he found purchase and pulled until their bodies nested together tighter than spoons in a drawer. The soft flesh of her rear cradled the iron shaft in his pants, thickening his erection to the point of pain. He needed a repeat of last night. Now.

He licked the hollow of her collarbone, loving the texture under his tongue. More Viv needed. Her answering gasp encouraged him to keep going.

Gathering handfuls of her dress, he yanked it from between them and bunched it at her waist, pressing harder into the heat of her backside the moment he bared it. His clothes and a pair of thin panties lay between him and paradise, and he wanted all that extraneous fabric gone.

She arched against him as his fingers cruised along the hem of her drenched underwear and he took that as agreement, stripping them off in one motion. Then he nudged her legs wider, opening her sex, and indulged them both by running a fingertip down the length of her crease. Her hands flew out and smacked the wall and she used it to brace as she ground her pelvis into his.

Fire tore through his center and he needed to be inside her with an uncontrollable urge, but the condoms were clear across the cavernous living area in his bedside table. He couldn't wait. Viv cried out his name as he plunged one then two fingers into her center, groaning at the slick, damp heat that greeted him. She was so wet, so perfect.

As he fingered her, she shuddered, circling her hips in a frenzied, friction-induced madness that pushed him to the brink. Her hot channel squeezed his fingers and that was nearly all she wrote. Did she have a clue how much he wanted to yank his zipper down, impale her and empty himself? Every muscle in his body fought him and his will crumbled away rapidly. Reaching between them, he eased open his belt.

But then she came apart in his arms, huffing out little noises that drove him insane as she climaxed. His own release roared to the forefront and all it would take was one tiny push to put him over the edge. Hell, he might not even need a push. Shutting his eyes against the strain, he drew out her release with long strokes that made her whimper.

She collapsed in his arms as she finished and he

held her upright, murmuring nonsense to her as she caught her breath.

"Let me take you to bed," he said, and she nodded, but it was more of a nuzzle as she turned her cheek into his.

To hell with boundaries.

He hustled her to his room, shed his clothes and hers without ripping anything this time—because he was in control—and finally she was naked. Sultry smile in place, she crawled onto the bed and rolled into a provocative position that begged him to get between her legs immediately and hammer after his own release. But despite being positive the only thing he could possibly do next was get inside her as fast as humanly possible, he paused, struck immobile all at once.

That was *his wife* decked out on the bed.

The sight bled through him, warming up places inside dangerously fast. Places that weren't what he'd call normal erogenous zones. And that's when he realized his gaze was on her smile. Not her body.

What was wrong with him? A naked woman was on display for his viewing pleasure. He forced his gaze to her breasts, gratified when the pert tips pebbled under his watchfulness. That was more like it. This was about sex and how good two people could make each other feel.

With a growl, he knelt on the bed and kissed his way up her thigh. He could absolutely keep his hands off her if he wanted to. He had total control over his desires, his emotions. There was nothing this woman could do to drive him to the point of desperation, not in bed and certainly not out of it. To prove it, he pushed her thighs open and buried his face between them.

She parted for him easily, her throaty cry washing over him as he plunged his tongue into her slickness. That wet heat was *his*. He'd done that to her and he lapped at it, groaning as her musky scent flooded his senses. The ache in his groin intensified into something so strong it was otherworldly. He needed to feel her tight, slick walls close around him, to watch her face as it happened. He needed it, but denied himself because she didn't own his pleasure. He owned hers.

Her hips rolled and bucked. He shoved his mouth deeper into her center as she silently sought more, and he gave it to her. Over and over he worked his lips and tongue against her swollen flesh until she bowed up with a release that tensed her whole body. And then she collapsed against the mattress, spilling breathy, satisfied sighs all over him. Only then did he permit his own needs to surge to the surface.

Fingering on a condom that he'd retrieved from the drawer, he settled over her and indulged his intense desire to kiss her. She eagerly took his tongue, sucking it into her hot mouth, and he groaned as he transferred her own taste back to her. Their hips came together, legs tangling, and before he could fully register her intent, she gathered him up in her tight fist and guided him into the paradise at her core.

A strong urge to fill her swelled. But he held on by the scrabbly edge of his fingertips, refusing to slam into her as he ached to do. Slowly, so slowly that he nearly came apart, he pushed. Her slickness accepted him easily, wringing the most amazing bliss from a place he scarcely recognized. The deeper he sank, the better it felt.

Her gaze captured his and he fell into her depths.

She filled him, not the other way around. How was that physically possible? He couldn't fathom it, but neither could he deny it. Or halt the rush of Viviana through his veins as she streamed straight to his heart in a kill shot that flooded all four chambers at once.

And then there was nothing but her and the unbelievable feel of her skin against his, her desire soaking through his pores in an overwhelming deluge. He meant to hold back, determined to prove something that escaped him as she changed the angle. Somehow that allowed him to go deeper, push harder. Her cries spurred him on, and unbelievably, she took it higher, sucking him under into a maelstrom of sensation and heightened pleasure.

When her hips began pistoning in countermeasure to his, it nearly tore him in two. Delirious with the need to come, he grabbed one of her legs and pushed at the knee, opening her wider so he had plenty of room to finger her at the source of her pleasure. Two circular strokes and she climaxed, squeezing him so tight that it tripped the wire on his own release.

Bright pinpoints of light streamed behind his eyes as he came so hard that he would have easily believed he'd crossed over into an alternate dimension. In this new dimension, he could let all the things crowding through his chest spill out of his mouth. But those things shouldn't exist in any universe.

If he didn't acknowledge them, they didn't exist. Then he wouldn't be breaking his word.

As his vision cleared and his muscles relaxed, rendering him boneless, he collapsed to the mattress, rolling Viv into his arms.

The heavy diamond swung down from the chain he'd

latched around her neck, whacking him on the shoulder. He fingered it back into place silently, weighing out whether he could actually speak or if that spectacular orgasm had in fact stolen his voice.

"I get the sense you've been saving up," Viv commented huskily, her lips moving against his chest, where her face had landed after he'd nestled her close. Probably he shouldn't have done that, but he liked coming down from a post-lovemaking high with her in his arms.

"It's been a while," he allowed. "I mean, other than last night, obviously."

Her mouth curved up in a smile. "Both times were amazing. I could get used to this."

He could, too. That was enough to get the panic really rolling. "We should probably talk about that."

To soften the blow, he threaded some of her pretty, silky hair through his fingers. That felt so nice, he kept going, running all the way down her head to her neck and back again.

"Mmm," she purred, pressing into his fingers, which were somehow massaging her with little strokes that she clearly liked. "I'm listening."

"We're still friends, right?" Pathetic. That hadn't been what he'd intended to say at all, but now that it was out there…it was exactly what he wanted to know. He wanted to hear her say that having an amazing encounter that he'd felt to his soul hadn't really affected her all that much. Then he could keep lying to himself about it and have zero qualms.

"Sure."

She kissed his chest right above his nipple and then flicked her tongue across the flat disk. Flames erupted under his skin, fanning outward to engulf his whole body, including his brain, because he suddenly couldn't recall what he'd been so convinced he needed to establish.

Then she slung a leg over his, nestling her thigh against the semi-erection that grew a lot less semi much faster than he would have credited, considering how empty he'd have sworn he was already.

"Geez, Viv." He bit back the curse word that had sprung to his lips. "You're insatiable."

Not that he was complaining. Though he should be saying something that sounded a lot like "Let's dial it back about one hundred and eighty degrees."

"You make me that way," she said throatily. "I've been celibate for like a billion years and that was totally okay, but all of a sudden, you kiss me and I can't think. I just want to be naked with you 24/7."

"Yeah?" he growled. That pretty much mirrored his thoughts perfectly. "That can be arranged."

No. No, it could not.

He had a merger to manage. Reins to pick up from his grandfather. What was he talking about, letting Viv coerce him into a day-and-night screw fest? That sounded like a recipe for disaster, especially given how strong his reactions to her were. They needed to cool it off.

"We can't." She sighed. "I've got a mountain of paperwork and Josie requested the rest of the week off so she can study for final exams. As nice as this is, we should probably back off for a while. Don't you think?"

"Absolutely not." Wrong answer. *Open your mouth and take it back.* "We're doing fine winging it. Aren't we? There's no pressure. If you come home from work hot and needy and want to strip down in the foyer to let me take care of you, I'm perfectly fine with that."

In fact, he'd gladly etch that date on his planner with a diamond drill bit. Mental note: buy Viv more jewelry and more racy lingerie. If he really tried, he could space out the gifts, one a night for oh, at least two weeks.

She arched a brow. "Really? This isn't feeling a little too real?"

His mood deflated. And now he was caught in a trap of his own making. He couldn't lie to Viv, but neither could he admit that it had been feeling too real since the ceremony. The same one he'd tried to sell to Warren and Hendrix as a fake wedding when Warren had clued in immediately that there was nothing fake about any of this.

This was what he got for not nodding his head the second the words *back off* came out of her mouth.

"See, the thing is," he began and would have sworn he'd been about to say that being friends with no benefits worked better for him. But that's not what happened. "I need this to be real. I don't have to pretend that I'm hot for you, because I am. We don't have to sell that we're burning up the sheets when we have dinner with your family on Friday. Why not keep going? The reasons we started this are still true. Unless I've dissatisfied you in some way?"

"Oh, God. No!" Her hand flew to her mouth. "Not in the slightest. You're the hottest lover I've ever had, bar none."

That pleased him enormously. "Then stop talking about easing off. We can be casual about it. Sometimes you sleep in my bed. Sometimes you don't. No rules. We're just friends who're having really great sex."

"That sounds like a plan."

She shrugged like she could take it or leave it, which raked across his spine with a sharpness that he didn't like. She obviously wasn't feeling any of the same things he was. She'd been a half second from calling it quits. Would have if he hadn't stopped her.

"Great." And somehow he'd managed to appease his sense of honor while agreeing to continue sleeping with his wife in what was shaping up to be the hottest affair he'd ever had.

It was madness. And he couldn't wipe the grin off his face.

Eight

If there was a way to quit Jonas, Viv didn't want to know about it.

She should be looking for the exit, not congratulating herself on the finest plea for remaining in a man's bed that had ever been created in the history of time. She couldn't help it. The scene after the most explosive sexual encounter of her life had been almost as epic. Jonas had no idea how much it had killed her to act so nonchalant about ending things. He'd been shocked she'd suggested backing off. It had been written all over his face.

That kept her feeling smug well into the dawn hours the next morning. She rolled toward the middle of the bed, hoping to get a few minutes of snuggle time before work. Cold sheets met her questing fingers. Blinking an eye open, she sought the man she'd gone to sleep with.

Empty. Jonas had gotten out of bed already. The

condo was quiet. Even when she was in her bedroom, she could hear the shower running through the pipes in the ceiling—a treat she normally enjoyed, as she envisioned the man taking a shower in all his naked glory.

Today, she didn't get that luxury, as Jonas was clearly already gone. Profoundly disappointed that he hadn't kissed her goodbye, said goodbye or thought about her at all, she climbed out from under the sheets and gathered up her clothes for the return trek to her bedroom.

It was fine. They'd established last night that there were no rules. No pressure. When he'd gotten on board with convincing her that they could keep sleeping together—which she still couldn't quite believe she'd orchestrated so well—she'd thought that meant they were going to spend a lot of time together. Be goofy and flirty with each other. Grow closer and closer until he looked up one day and realized that friendship plus marriage plus sex equaled something wonderful, lasting and permanent. Obviously she'd thought wrong.

The whole point had been to give him the impression she wasn't clingy. That Independence was her middle name and she breezed through life just fine, thanks, whether she had a man or not. Apparently he'd bought it. *Go me.*

The sour taste wouldn't quite wash from her mouth no matter how much mouthwash she used. After a long shower to care for her well-used muscles, Viv wandered to the kitchen barefoot to fight with Jonas's espresso machine. She had a machine at Cupcaked but Jonas's was a futuristic prototype that he'd brought home from work to test. There were more buttons and gizmos than on a spaceship. Plus, it hated her. He'd used it a couple of times and made it seem so easy, but he had a natural affinity with things that plugged in, and the machine had his name on it, after all. Finally, she got a passably decent latte out of the monstrosity.

She stood at the granite countertop to drink it, staring at the small, discreet Kim Electronics logo in the lower right-hand corner of the espresso machine. Jonas's name had been emblazoned on her, too, and not just via the marriage license and subsequent trip to the DMV to get a new driver's license. He'd etched his name across her soul well before they'd started sleeping together. Maybe about the third or fourth time they'd had lunch.

Strange then that she could be so successful with snowing him about her feelings. It had never worked with any man before. Of course, she'd never tried so hard to be cool about it. Because it had never mattered so much.

But now she wasn't sure what her goal here really was. Or what it should be. Jonas had "talked" her into keeping sex on the menu of their relationship. She'd convinced him their friendship could withstand it. Really, the path was pretty clear. They were married friends with benefits. If she didn't like that, too bad.

She didn't like it.

This wasn't practice for another relationship and neither was it fake, not for her. Which left her without a lot of options, since it was fake to Jonas.

Of course, she always had the choice to end things. But why in the world would she want to do that? Her husband was the most amazing lover on the planet, whose beautiful body she could not get enough of. He bought her diamonds and complimented her cupcakes. To top it all off, Viv was *married*. She'd been after that holy grail for ages and it had felt really nice to flash her ring at her sisters when they'd come to the shop last week. It was the best possible outcome of agreeing to do this favor for Jonas.

Convinced that she should be happy with that, she walked the four blocks to Cupcaked and buried herself in the kitchen, determined to find a new cupcake flavor to commemorate her marriage. That was how she'd always done things. When something eventful occurred, she baked. It was a way of celebrating in cake form, because wasn't that the whole point of cake? And then she had a cupcake flavor that reminded her of a wonderful event.

The watermelon recipe she'd been dying to try didn't turn out. The red food coloring was supposed to be tasteless but she couldn't help thinking that it had added something to the flavor that made the cupcake taste vaguely like oil. But without it, the batter wasn't the color of watermelon.

Frustrated, she trashed the whole batch and went in search of a different food coloring vendor. Fruitless. All her regular suppliers required an industrial sized order and she couldn't commit to a new brand without testing it first.

She ended up walking to the market and buying three different kinds off the shelf. For no reason, apparently, as all three new batches she made didn't turn out either. Maybe watermelon wasn't a good cupcake flavor. More to the point, maybe she shouldn't be commemorating a fake marriage that was real to her but still not going to last. That was the problem. She was trying to capture something fleeting that shouldn't be immortalized.

After the cupcake failure, her mood slid into the dumps. She threw her apron on the counter and stayed out of the kitchen until lunch, when she opened for business to the public. On the plus side, every display case had been cleaned and polished, and the plate-glass window between Cupcaked and the world had not one smudge on it. Camilla wouldn't be in until after school, so Viv was by herself for the lunch rush, which ended up being a blessing in disguise.

Wednesday wasn't normally a busy day, but the line stretched nearly out the door for over an hour. Which was good. Kept her mind off the man she'd married. Josie had the rest of the week off, and Viv had approved it thinking she and Camilla could handle things, but if this kind of crowd was even close to a new normal, she might have to see about adding another part-time employee. That was a huge decision, but a good sign. If she couldn't have Jonas, she could have her cupcakes. Just like she'd always told him.

After locking the bakery's door, tired but happy with the day's profits, she headed home. On the way, she sternly lectured herself about her expectations. Jonas might be waiting in the hall for her to come in the door like he had been last night. Or he might not. Her stomach fluttered the entire four blocks regardless. Her husband had just been so sexy standing there against the wall with a hot expression on his face as if he planned to devour her whole before she completely shut the door.

And then he pretty much had, going down on her in the most erotic of encounters. She shuddered clear to her core as she recalled the feel of that first hot lick of his tongue.

Oh, who was she kidding? She couldn't stop hoping he'd be waiting for her again tonight. Her steps quickened as she let herself anticipate seeing Jonas in a few minutes.

But he wasn't in the hall. Or at home. That sucked.

Instead of moping, she fished out her phone and called Grace. It took ten minutes, but eventually her sister agreed to have dinner with Viv.

They met at an Italian place on Glenwood that had great outdoor seating that allowed for people watching. The maître d' showed them to a table and Grace gave Viv a whole three seconds before she folded her hands and rested her chin on them.

"Okay, spill," she instructed. "I wasn't expecting to see you before Friday. Is Jonas in the doghouse already?"

"What? No." Viv scowled. Why did something have to be wrong for her to ask her sister to dinner? Besides, that was none of Grace's business anyway. Viv pounced on the flash of green fire on her sister's wrist in a desperate subject change. "Ooooh, new bracelet? Let me see."

The distraction worked. Grace extended her arm dutifully, her smile widening as she twisted her wrist to let the emeralds twinkle in the outdoor lighting. "Alan gave it to me. It's an anniversary present."

"You got married in April," Viv said.

"Not a wedding anniversary. It's a...different kind of anniversary."

Judging by the dreamy smile that accompanied that admission, she meant the first time she and Alan had slept together, and clearly the act had been worthy of commemorating.

Viv could hardly hide her glee. It was going to be one of *those* discussions and she *finally* got to participate. "Turns out Jonas is big on memorializing spectacular sex, too."

"Well, don't hold back. Show and tell." Grace waggled her brows.

Because she wanted to and she could, Viv fished the diamond drop necklace from beneath her dress and let it hang from her fingers. Not to put too fine a point on it, but hers was a flawless white diamond in a simple, elegant setting. Extremely appropriate for the wife of a billionaire. And he'd put it around her neck and then given her the orgasm of her life.

The baubles she could do without and had only mentioned jewelry in the car on the way to Jonas's parents' house because he'd pushed her to name something he could do for her. She hadn't really been serious. But all at once, she loved that Jonas had unwittingly allowed her to stand shoulder to shoulder with her sister when it came to talking about whose marriage was hotter.

"Your husband is giving you jewelry already?" Grace asked, and her tone was colored with something that sounded a lot like she was impressed. "Things must be going awfully well."

"Oh, yeah, of course," Viv commented airily and waved her hand like she imagined a true lady of the manor would. "We didn't even make it out of the foyer where he gave it to me before his hands were all over me."

Shameless. This was the raciest conversation she'd ever had with anyone except maybe Jonas, but that didn't count. She should be blushing. Or something. Instead she was downright giddy.

"That's the best." Grace's dreamy smile curved back into place. "When you have a man who loves you so much that he can't wait. I'm thrilled you finally have that."

Yeah, not so much. Her mood crashed and burned as reality surfaced. Viv nodded with a frozen expression that she hoped passed for agreement.

Obviously Grace knew what it felt like to have a man dote on her and give her jewelry because he cared, not because they were faking a relationship. Grace could let all her feelings hang out as much as she wanted and Alan would eat it up. Because they were in love.

Something that felt a lot like jealousy reared its ugly head in the pit of Viv's stomach. Which was unfair and petty, but recognizing it as such didn't make it go away.

"Jonas was worth waiting for," she said truthfully, though it rankled that the statement was the best she could do. While Viv's husband might rival her sister's in the attentive lover department, when it came to matters of the heart, Grace and Alan had Viv and Jonas beat, hands down.

"I'm glad. You had a rough patch for a while. I started to worry that you weren't going to figure out how stop putting a man's emotional needs ahead of yours. It's good to see that you found a relationship that's on equal footing."

Somehow, Viv managed to keep the surprise off her face, but how, she'd never know. "I never did that. What does that even mean?"

"Hon, you're so bad at putting yourself first." Grace waved the waiter over as he breezed by and waited until he refilled both their wineglasses before continuing. "You let everyone else dictate how the relationship is going to go. That last guy you dated? Mark? He wanted to keep things casual, see other people, and even though that's not what you wanted, you agreed. Why did you do that?"

Eyebrows hunched together, Viv gulped from her newly filled wineglass to wet her suddenly parched throat. "Because when I told him that I wanted to be exclusive, he said I was being too possessive. What was I supposed to do, demand that he give me what I want?"

"Uh, *yeah*." Grace clucked. "You should have told him to take a hike instead of waiting around for him to do it for you."

"It really didn't take that long," she muttered, but not very loud, because Grace was still off on her tangent.

Her sister was right. Viv should have broken up with Mark during that exact conversation. But on the heels of being told she was "clingy," "controlling" and "moving too fast" by Zachary, Gary and Judd respectively, she hadn't wanted to rock the boat.

Why was it such a big deal to want to spend time with a man she was dating? It wasn't clingy. Maybe it was the wine talking, but Grace's point wasn't lost on Viv—she shouldn't be practicing her independence but finding a different kind of man. One who couldn't stand being apart from her. One who texted her hearts and smiley faces just to let her know he was thinking of her. One who was in love with her.

In other words—not Jonas.

The thought pushed her mood way out of the realm of fit for company. Dinner with Grace was a mistake. Marrying Jonas had been a mistake. Viv had no idea what she was doing with her life or how she was going to survive a fake marriage she wished was real.

"I just remembered," she mumbled. "I have to…do a thing."

Pushing back from the table, Viv stood so fast that her head spun. She'd planned to walk home but maybe a cab would be a better idea.

"What?" Grace scowled. "You called me. I canceled drinks with the ladies from my auxiliary group. How could you forget that you had something else?"

Because Viv wasn't perfect like Grace with the perfect husband who loved her, and frankly, she was sick of not getting what she wanted. "Jonas has scrambled my wits."

Let her sister make what she would out of that. Viv apologized and exited the restaurant as quickly as she could before she started crying. After not seeing Jonas this morning and the watermelon-slash-red-food-coloring disaster and the incredibly busy day at the store and then realizing that she had not in fact gotten to join the club her sisters were in, crying was definitely imminent.

The icing on the cake happened when she got home and Jonas was sprawled on the couch watching TV, wearing jeans with a faded Duke T-shirt that clung to his torso like a second skin.

His smile as he glanced up at her was instant and brilliant and that was all it took to unleash the waterworks.

With tears streaming down her face, Viv stood in the foyer of the condo she shared with Jonas until whatever point in the future he decided to pull the plug on their marriage and it was all suddenly not okay.

"Hey, now. None of that." Jonas flicked off the TV and vaulted to his feet, crossing the ocean of open space between the living room and the foyer in about four strides.

He didn't hesitate to gather Viv in his strong arms, cradling her against his chest, and dang it, that T-shirt was really soft against her face. It was a testament to how mixed-up she was that she let him guide her to the leather couch and tuck her in against his side as he held her while softly crooning in his baritone that she'd heard in her sleep for aeons.

What was wrong with her that she was exactly where she wanted to be—in his arms? She should be pushing away and disappearing into her bedroom. No pressure, no love, no nothing.

"What's wrong, sweetheart?" he asked softly into her hair. "Bad day at work?"

"I wasn't at work," she shot back inanely, sniffling oh so attractively against his shoulder.

"Oh. Well, I wondered where you were when you weren't here."

"You weren't here either," she reminded him crossly. "So I went to dinner with Grace."

He pulled back, the expression on his face both confused and slightly alarmed. "Did we have plans that I forgot about or something? Because if so, I'm sorry. I didn't have anything on my calendar and my grandfather asked me to take him to the airport. I texted you."

He had? And how desperate would it appear to pull out her phone to check? Which was totally dumb anyway. It was obvious he was telling her the truth, which he didn't even have to do. God, she was such a mess. But after he'd disappeared this morning and then she'd come home to an empty house and...so what? He was here now, wasn't he? She was making a mountain out of a molehill.

"It's okay, we didn't have plans. You called it. Bad

day at work," she said a bit more brightly as she latched on to his excuse that wasn't even a lie. Sales had been good, sure, but Cupcaked meant more to her than just profits. "I tried out a new recipe and it was a complete failure."

All smiles again, Jonas stroked her hair and then laid a sweet kiss on her temple. "I hate days like that. What can I do to fix it?"

About a hundred suggestions sprang to her mind all at once, and every last one could easily be considered X-rated. But she couldn't bear to shift the current vibe into something more physical when Jonas was meeting a different kind of need, one she'd only nebulously identified at dinner. This was it in a nutshell—she wanted someone to be there for her, hold her and support her through the trials of life.

Why had she gotten so upset? Because Jonas hadn't fallen prostrate at her feet with declarations of undying love? They were essentially still in the early stages of their relationship, regardless of the label on it. Being married didn't automatically mean they were where Grace and her husband were. Maybe Viv and Jonas were taking a different route to get to the same destination and she was trying too hard.

Also known as the reason her last few relationships hadn't worked out.

"You're already fixing it," she murmured as his fingers drifted to her neck and lightly massaged.

Oh, God, that was a gloriously unfulfilled need, too. After a long day on her feet, just sitting here with Jonas as he worked her tired muscles counted as one of the highest points of pleasure she'd experienced at his hands. Her eyelids drifted closed and she floated.

"Did I wake you up this morning?" he asked after a few minutes of bliss.

"No. I was actually surprised to find that you were gone." Thank God he'd lulled her into a near coma. That admission had actually sounded a lot more casual than she would have expected, given how his absence had been lodged under skin like a saddle burr all day.

"That's good." He seemed a lot more relieved than the question warranted. "I'm not used to sleeping with someone and I was really worried that I'd mess with your schedule."

What schedule? "We slept in the same bed at your parents' house."

"Yeah, but that was over the weekend when no one had to get up and go to work. This is different. It's real life and I'm nothing if not conscious that you're here solely because I asked you to be. You deserve to sleep well."

Warmth gushed through her heart and made her feel entirely too sappy. What a thoroughly unexpected man she had married. "I did sleep well. Thank you for being concerned. But I think I slept so well because of how you treated me before I went to sleep. Not because you tiptoed well while getting dressed."

He did treat her like a queen. That was the thing she'd apparently forgotten. They were friends who cared about each other. Maybe he might eventually fall in love with her, but he certainly wouldn't if she kept being obsessive and reading into his every move.

Jonas chuckled. "Last night was pretty amazing. I wasn't sure you thought so. I have to be honest and tell you that I was concerned I'd done something to make you angry and that's why you weren't here when I got home after taking my grandfather to the airport. I could have called him a car."

"No!" Horrified, she swiveled around to face him, even though it meant his wonderful hands slipped from her shoulders. "We just talked about no pressure and I was—well, I just thought because you weren't here…"

Ugh. How in the world was she supposed to explain that she'd gone out to dinner with Grace because of a hissy fit over something so ridiculous as Jonas not being here because he'd taken his grandfather to the airport? Maybe instead of using the excuse that she'd missed his text messages, she should tell him how she felt. Just flat out say, *Jonas, I'm in love with you.*

"We did talk about no pressure," Jonas threw out in a rush. "And I'm definitely not trying to add any. I like our relationship where it is. I like *you*. It's what makes the extra stuff so much better."

Extra stuff. She absorbed that for a second. Extra stuff like deeper feelings he didn't know he was going to uncover? Extra stuff like being there for each other?

"I value our friendship," she said cautiously, weighing out how honest she could be. How honest she wanted to be given how she managed to screw up even the simplest of relationship interactions.

And just as she was about to open her mouth and confess that she appreciated the extra stuff, too, maybe even tell him that she had a plethora of extra stuff that she could hardly hold inside, he smoothed a hand over her hair and grinned. "I know. I'm being all touchy-feely and that's not what we signed up for. Instead, let's talk about Cupcaked."

"Um…okay?" He'd literally switched gears so fast, she could scarcely keep up.

That was him being touchy-feely? Jonas wasn't one to be gushy about his feelings and usually erred on the side of being reserved; she knew that from the year of lunches and coffee. Clearly, he was uncomfortable with the direction of the discussion. She definitely should not add a level of weirdness, not on top of her storming in here and having a minor meltdown.

This was her relationship to make or break. All at once, it became so obvious what she should be focusing on here.

No, this wasn't practice for the next man she dated. She was practicing for *this* one. If she hoped to get to a point where they were both comfortable with declarations of love, she had to tread carefully. While she didn't think Jonas was going to divorce her if she moved too fast, neither did she have a good handle on how to be less intense.

She needed to back off. Way off. Otherwise, she was going to freak him out. And suddenly she could not fathom giving up this marriage under any circumstances.

"I'd love to talk about Cupcaked," she said with a smile. "Seems like you owe me some advice."

"Yes, exactly." His return smile bordered on relieved. "You've been so patient and I'm a selfish jerk for not focusing on your career when that's the one thing you're getting out of this deal."

"The sex is nice, too," she teased. Look at that. She could be cool.

Jonas shot her a wicked once-over. "That's what makes you so perfect. We can hang out as friends, but if I wanted to, say, slip my hand under your dress, you'd gladly climb in my lap for a little one-on-one time. It's the best."

She shrugged to cover how his compliment had thrilled her to the marrow. "I promised it wouldn't make things weird."

Now she'd stick to that. At the end of the day, Cupcaked *was* important to her. She'd just have to make sure that eventually Jonas realized that he was important to her, as well.

Jonas ducked out of a meeting on Friday with a guilty conscience. While he knew Viv would understand if he put off a thorough analysis of her business plan, he wasn't okay with ignoring his promise. Unfortunately, Park had come through with some amendments to the merger agreement Jonas had drafted, which had taken his time and attention for the whole of the week.

The moment he stepped outside the Kim Building, the sunshine raised his spirits. He was on his way to see his wife at Cupcaked, which oddly would mark the first time he'd graced the store since they'd gotten married. Before the wedding, he found excuses to drop by on a frequent basis. But now he didn't have to. The cupcake baker slept in his bed and if he wanted to see her, all he had to do was turn his head.

It was pretty great. Or at least that's what he'd been telling himself. In reality, the look on Viv's face when she'd told him she valued their friendship had been like a big fat wake-up call. Basically, she was telling him no pressure worked for her regardless of how hot he could get her with nothing more than a well-placed caress.

Well, that *was* great. He didn't have any desire to pressure her into anything. But he couldn't deny that he might like to put more structure around things. Would she think it was weird if he expected her to be his plus-one for events? His admin was planning a big party for the whole company to commemorate the anniversary of opening the Kim Americas branch. He wanted Viv by his side. But it was yet another favor. If they were dating instead of married he wouldn't think twice about asking her.

Everything was backward and weird and had been since that no-pressure discussion, which he'd initiated because he needed the boundaries. For no reason apparently. Viv so clearly wasn't charging over the imaginary lines he'd drawn in the sand. In fact, she'd drawn a few lines of her own. Yet how could he change those lines when Viv had gotten so prickly about the subject? In fact, she'd already tried to call off the intimate aspects of their relationship once. He needed to tread very carefully with her before he got in too deep for them both.

When he got to Cupcaked, the door was locked. Not open yet. He texted Viv that he was outside and within thirty seconds, she'd popped out of the kitchen and hurried to the plate-glass door with a cute smile.

"I didn't know you were coming by," she commented unnecessarily since he was well aware it was a surprise. After she let him in, she locked the door and turned, her brown hair shining in the sunlight that streamed through the glass.

Something was wrong with his lungs. He couldn't breathe. Or think. All he could do was soak in the most beautiful woman he'd ever seen in his life. And all of his good intentions designed to help her with her business flew out the window in a snap.

Without hesitation, he pulled her into his arms and kissed her. She softened instantly and the scent of vanilla and Viv wound through his senses, robbing him of the ability to reason, because the only thing he could think about was getting more of her against him.

Almost as if she'd read his mind, she opened under his mouth, eagerly deepening the kiss, welcoming the broad stroke of his tongue with her own brand of heat. Slowly she licked into his mouth in kind, teasing him with little flutters of her fingers against his back.

That was not going to work. He wanted to feel her fingers against his flesh, not through the forty-seven layers of clothing between them.

Walking her backward, he half kissed, half maneuvered her until they reached the kitchen, and then he spun her through the swinging door to the more private area, where the entire city of Raleigh couldn't see them.

Her mouth was back on his without missing a beat, and he pushed her up against the metal counter, trapping her body with his. Her sweet little curves nestled into the planes of his body and he wasn't sure if he could stand how long it was taking to get her naked.

The zipper of her dress took three tries to find and then slid down easily, allowing him to actually push the fabric from her shoulders instead of ripping it, a near miracle. There was something about her that drove him to a place he didn't recognize, and it bothered him to be this crazy over her. But then her dress slipped off, puddling to the floor, and he forgot about everything but her as she unhooked her bra, throwing it to the ground on top of her dress.

Groaning, he looked his fill of her gorgeous breasts, scarcely able to believe how hard and pointy they were from nothing other than his gaze. Bending to capture one, he swirled his tongue around the perfection of her nipple and the sound she made shot through his erection like an arrow of heat.

"Hurry," she gasped. "I'm about to come apart."

Oh, well, that was something he'd very much like to witness. In a flash, he pushed her panties to her ankles and boosted her up on the counter. Spreading her legs wide, he brushed a thumb through her crease and, yes, she was so ready for him.

She bucked and rolled against his fingers, her eyes darkening with the pleasure he was giving her, and he wanted her more than anything he could recall. As much as he'd like to do any number of things to bring her to climax, there was one clear winner. Ripping out of his own clothes in record time, he stepped back between her thighs and hissed as she nipped at his shoulder.

"Tell me you have a condom," she commanded, and then smiled as he held it up between his fingers.

He'd stashed a couple in his wallet and he really didn't want to examine that particular foresight right now. Instead, he wanted to examine the wonders of Viv and sheathed himself as fast as humanly possible, notching himself at the slick entrance to her channel. Her wet heat welcomed him, begged him to come inside, but he paused to kiss her because that was one of his favorite parts.

Their tongues tangled and he got a little lost in the kiss. She didn't. She wrapped her legs around him, heels firm against his butt, and pushed him forward, gasping as he slammed into her. So that's how she wanted it. Two could play that game.

He engulfed her in his arms and braced her for a demanding rhythm, then gave it to her. She took each and every thrust eagerly, her mouth working the flesh at his throat, his ear, nipping sensuously. *He* was the one about to come apart.

Viv flew through his soul, winging her essence into every diameter of his body. Wiggling a hand between their slick bodies, he fingered her at the source of her pleasure, gratified when she cried out. Her release crashed against his, shocking him with both the speed and intensity.

She slumped against him, still quaking as she held on. He was busy losing the entire contents of his body as everything inside rushed out in a flash to fill her. Fanciful to be sure since there was a barrier preventing anything of the sort. But she'd wrung him out, taken everything and more, and he couldn't have stopped the train as it barreled down the track, even if he wanted to. Why would he want to?

He turned his head, seeking her lips, and there they were, molding to his instantly. Viv was amazing, a woman he liked, cared for deeply even, and they had the most spectacular chemistry. He could hardly fathom how much he still wanted her four seconds after having her. It was everything he said he wanted.

Except the warmth in his chest that had nothing to do with sex wasn't supposed to be there. He wasn't an idiot. He knew what was happening. He'd let her in, pretending that being friends gave him a measure of protection against falling for her. Instead, he'd managed to do the one thing he'd sworn he'd never do—develop feelings for someone who didn't return them.

This was a huge problem, one he didn't have a good solution for. One he could never let her know he was facing because he'd promised not to pressure her.

Best thing would be to ignore it. It wasn't happening if he didn't acknowledge it. And then he wouldn't be lying to her or dishonoring the pact he'd made with his friends, neither of which could ever happen. If he didn't nurture these fledging tendrils of disaster that wound through his chest, he could kill them before they ruined everything.

Actually, the best thing would be to stop being around Viv so much. *Without* letting on to her that he was deliberately creating distance.

The thought hurt. But it was necessary for his sanity.

Nine

Jonas helped Viv off the metal countertop that she'd have to bleach within an inch of its life and pray the fourteen different health-code violations never came to light.

It had been worth it. Whenever Jonas got like that, so into her and excited and feverish as if he'd die if he didn't have her that instant…that was the best part of this fake marriage. Men were never that gaga over her. Except this one. And she secretly loved it. She couldn't tell him. What would she say?

Slow and steady wins the race, she reminded herself. Not-Clingy was her new middle name and she was going to own it. Even if it killed her not to blubber all over him about how it was so beautiful it hurt when he was inside her.

They spent a few minutes setting their clothes back

to rights, no small feat without a mirror. She gladly helped Jonas locate his missing tie and then buttoned his suit jacket for him when he forgot.

"Gorgeous," she commented after slipping the last button into its slot and perusing the final product of her husband in his power suit that she immediately wanted to strip him out of again.

He grinned. "Yes, you are."

Great, now she was blushing, judging by the prickles in her cheeks. Dead giveaway about the things going on inside that she'd rather keep a secret.

"Now, stop distracting me," he continued. "I'm here to get started on my promise to review your books. Lead me to them."

Oh. For some reason, she'd thought he'd come by strictly to have an explosive sexual encounter in her bakery. But in reality, he was here for business reasons. That took a little of the wind from her sails though it shouldn't have. Of course he'd honor his promise to help her, despite absolutely no prompting on her part. "Sure, my office is in the back. We can squeeze in there."

She led him to the tiny hole in the wall where she paid bills and ordered inventory. It wasn't much, not like the Kim Building, where Jonas had an entire office suite expressly designed for the CEO. But she wasn't running a billion-dollar electronics company here, and they both knew that.

He didn't complain about the lack of comfort and space, easily sliding into the folding chair she pulled from behind the door and focusing on her with his dark eyes. "Let me see your balance sheet."

Dutifully, she keyed up her accounting software and ran the report, then pushed the monitor of her ancient computer toward him so he could see it. His gaze slid down the columns and back up again. Within a moment, he'd reviewed the entire thing and then launched into a dizzying speech about how her asset column was blah blah and her inventory was blah blah something else. After five minutes of nodding and understanding almost nothing of what he said, she held up a hand.

"Jonas, while I appreciate your attention on this, you lost me back around 'leveraging your cash.' Can we take a step back and focus on the goal of this?"

She knew what her goal was. Spend time with Jonas. But clearly he'd taken the idea of helping her seriously.

"Sure, sorry." He looked chagrined and adorable as he ran a hand through his hair. "I shouldn't have gone so deep into financial strategy that quickly. Maybe I should ask you what *your* goal is since your career is the most important thing to you. What do you want to see happen with Cupcaked?"

Oh, yeah, right. Her career. The thing she'd sold to him as the reason she didn't date. "I haven't really thought about it."

Should she be thinking about it? She wasn't rich by any stretch, but she made enough and got to bake cupcakes for a living. What else was there?

"Okay." His smile broadened. "I hear you saying that you need help coming up with a five-year plan. Part of that should include a robust marketing strategy and expansion."

Expansion? Her eyebrows lifted almost by themselves. "Are you suggesting I could become a chain?"

The idea seemed so far-fetched. She just made cupcakes and had no ambitions beyond being able to recognize regular customers. But she didn't hate the idea of seeing more Cupcaked signs around Raleigh. Maybe even in Chapel Hill or by the university. The thought of owning a mini-cupcake empire made her smile. Poor substitute for Jonas. But not a terrible one.

"I'm not suggesting it. I'm flat out saying if that's what you want, I will make it happen for you. Sky's the limit, Mrs. Kim." He waggled his brows. "You should take as much advantage of me as you possibly can. Ask for anything."

Mrs. Kim. What if she told him that she'd like to ask him to call her that for the rest of her life? What would he say?

Before she could open her mouth, he launched into another long litany of things to consider for her shop and his gleeful tone told her he was having fun helping her think through the items that might appear on her five-year plan. They talked about any number of ideas from branded cupcake mix to be sold in grocery stores to licensing her flavors to other cupcake bakeries.

Frankly, the discussion was fun for her, too. Partially because she was having it with Jonas and she loved watching his mind churn through the possibilities. But she couldn't deny a certain anticipation regarding the leaps and bounds Cupcaked could take through the doors her husband might open for her.

Camilla popped in to say hi and make sure Viv was okay with her opening the bakery to customers. Viv nodded her assent and dove back into the fascinating concept of franchising, of which Jonas admitted having only a rudimentary knowledge, but he knew way more than she did. She wanted to know more.

His phone rang and he lifted a finger in the universal "one minute" gesture, jabbering away to the caller with a bunch of terms that sounded vaguely legal. Eventually, he ended the call and stood.

"I'm so sorry, but I have to get back to the world of electronics."

She waved off his apology. "You've been here for two hours. I know you're busy. I should give Camilla a hand anyway. If today is anything like the rest of the week, she'll need the help."

Jonas laid a scorching kiss on her and left. Dazed and more than a little hot and bothered, she lost herself in cupcakes until the day got away from her. As planned, she and Jonas went to dinner at her parents' house that night. Given that he shot her smoking-hot glances when he thought no one was watching, and her sisters were nothing if not eagle-eyed when it came to potential gossip, she didn't think they had anything to worry about when it came to revelations about the nature of their marriage.

Or rather, the revelations weren't going to be publicized to the rest of the world. Just to Jonas. As soon as she figured out when she could start clueing him in to the idea that friendship wasn't the only thing happening between them, of course. This was the problem with playing it cool. She wasn't sure when to bring up concepts like *love*, *forever* and *no divorce*.

She bided her time and didn't utter a peep when Jonas carried her to his bed after the successful dinner with her parents. He spent extra time pleasuring her, claiming that tomorrow was Saturday so she had plenty of opportunity to sleep later. Not that she was complaining about his attention. Or anything else, for that matter. Her life was almost perfect.

On Monday, she learned exactly how many people in

the business world jumped when her husband said jump. By nine o'clock, she had appointments lined up every day for the entire week with accounting people, retail space experts and a pastry chef who had ties with the Food Network. A marketing consultant arrived shortly thereafter and introduced herself as Franca, then parked herself in Viv's office, apparently now a permanent part of her staff, as she'd informed Mrs. Kim, courtesy of Mr. Kim.

Franca lived to talk, as best Viv could work out between marathon strategy sessions that filled nearly every waking hour of the day. And some of the hours Viv would have normally said were for sleeping. At midnight, Franca sent a detailed list of the short-term and long-term goals that they'd discussed and asked Viv to vet it thoroughly because once she approved, the list would form the basis of Cupcaked's new five-year plan. Which would apparently be carved in stone.

By Friday, Viv hadn't spent more than five minutes with Jonas. They slept in the same bed, but sometimes he climbed into it well after she had, which was quite a feat since she hadn't hit the sheets until 1:00 a.m. most nights. He'd claimed her busyness came at a great time for him because he was able to focus on the merger with Park Industries without feeling guilty for ignoring her. The hours bled into days and she'd never been so exhausted in her life.

It sucked. Except for the part where sometimes Jonas texted her funny memes about ships passing in the night or had a dozen tulips delivered to the shop to commemorate their one-month anniversary. Once he popped up with Chinese takeout for dinner as a "forced" break for them both. He gave her his fortune cookie and told her a story about how one of the ladies in his procurement department had gone into labor during a meeting. Those stolen moments meant the world to her because she could almost believe that he missed her as much as she missed him.

The pièce de résistance came when the pastry chef she'd met with a couple of weeks ago contacted her via Franca to let her know that he'd loved her cupcakes and gotten her a spot on one of the cupcake shows on the Food Network. Agape, Viv stared at Franca as the tireless woman reeled off the travel plans she'd made for Viv to fly to Los Angeles.

"I can't go to Los Angeles," Viv insisted with a head shake. "I have a business to run."

Franca tapped her phone on Viv's new desk. "Which will become nationally known once you appear on the show."

She'd had Viv's office completely redone and expanded at Jonas's expense and the top-of-the-line computer that had replaced the old one now recessed underneath the surface of the desk with the click of a button. It was very slick and gave them a lot more working space, which Franca used frequently, as she spread brochures and promo items galore across the top of it at least twice a week.

"How long would I be gone?" Viv asked. Josie and Camilla had never run the bakery by themselves for a whole day, let alone several. They needed her. Or did they? She was often in the back strategizing with Franca anyway. They had four or five irons in the fire at any given time and the woman was indefatigable when it came to details. There was literally nothing she couldn't organize or plan and often took on more of a personal assistant role for Viv.

"Depends on whether you make the first cut." Franca shrugged and flipped her ponytail behind her back, a move she made when she was about to get serious. "It's a competition. You lose the first round, you come home. You win, you stay. I would advise you to win."

Viv made a face. "You're talking days."

"Sure. I hope so anyway. We're going to launch the new website with online ordering at the same time. It'll be an amazing kick start to the virtual storefront."

Sagging a little, Viv gave herself about four seconds to pretend she was going to refuse when in reality, she couldn't pass up the opportunity. It really didn't matter if she won or not because it was free advertising and all it would cost her was some time away from Jonas. Whom she rarely saw awake anyway.

"When do I leave?"

Franca grinned like she'd known the direction Viv would end up going the whole time. "I'll get the rest of the arrangements settled and let you know."

With a nod, Viv texted the news to Jonas, who instantly responded with at least four exclamation marks and a *congrats* in all caps. Funny, they were basically back to being friends with no benefits, thanks to her stupid career. She had all the success she'd lied to Jonas about wanting and none of the happiness that she'd pretended would come along with it.

Worse, if she hadn't been so busy, she'd be sitting around the condo by herself as Jonas worked his own fingers to the bone. This was really, really not the marriage she'd signed up for.

Or rather it was absolutely the one she'd agreed to but not the one she wanted.

The day before she was supposed to fly to Los Angeles for the taping, Viv came home early to pack. Shockingly, Jonas was sitting on the couch still decked out in his gorgeous suit but on the phone, as he nearly always was anytime she'd been in the same room with him lately.

For half a second, she watched him, soaking in his pretty mouth as it formed words. Shuddered as she recalled what that mouth could do to her when he put his mind to it. God, she missed him. In the short amount of time they'd been married, they'd gone from zero to sixty to zero again. She'd prefer a hundred and twenty.

She waved, loath to interrupt him, but before she could skirt past him to her bedroom, where her clothes still were since she'd never really "moved in" to Jonas's room, he snagged her by the hips and settled her on the couch near him as he wrapped up his phone call.

Tossing his phone on the glass-and-steel conglomeration that he called a coffee table, he contemplated her with the sort of attention she hadn't experienced in a long while. It was delicious.

"You're going to LA in the morning?" he said by way of greeting, and picked up her hand to hold it in his, brushing his thumb across her knuckles.

"Yeah. I don't know for how long. Franca left the plane ticket open-ended." The little strokes of his thumb stirred something inside that had been dormant for a million years. He'd been so distant lately. Dare she hope that they might be coming back together?

No reason she had to let him be the instigator. She lifted his hand to her mouth and kissed it, but he pulled away and sat back on the couch. "That sounds like fun. I hope you have a good time."

Cautiously, she eyed him. Why had he caught her before she left the room if he hadn't been after spending time with her? "Is everything okay? I wasn't expecting you to be here."

"I...came home on purpose. To see you," he admitted. "Before you left."

Her heart did a funny a little dance. But then why all the weird hot and cold? He obviously cared about her—but how much? Enough? She had no idea because they never talked about what was really going on here.

It was high time they had it out. She was leaving for LA in the morning and they rarely saw each other. She had to make this small opportunity work.

"I'm glad. I missed you." There. It was out in the open.

But he just smiled without a hint of anything. "I miss hanging out with you, too. We haven't had coffee in ages."

Or sex. The distinction between the two was legion and she didn't think for a minute that he'd misspoken or forgotten that they'd been intimate. It was a deliberate choice of words. "We haven't had a coffee relationship in ages."

His expression didn't change. "I know. It's been crazy. We're both so busy."

"By design, feels like."

That got a reaction, but why, she couldn't fathom. She watched as unease filtered through his gaze and he shifted positions on the couch, casually folding one leg over the other but also moving away from her. "We're both workaholics, that's for sure."

"I'm not," she corrected. "Not normally. But I've been dropped into an alternate reality where Franca drives me fourteen hours a day to reach these lofty goals that don't represent what I really want out of life."

Jonas frowned, his gaze sweeping over her in assessment. "You're finally getting your career off the ground. She's been keeping me apprised and I've been pleased with the direction she's taking you. But if you're not, we should discuss it. I can hire a different marketing expert, one that's more in line—"

"It's not the direction of the marketing," she broke in before he called in yet another career savant who would be brilliant at taking her away from her husband. "It's that I was happier when Cupcaked was a little bakery on Jones Street and we had sex in the foyer."

Something flitted through his gaze that she wished felt more like an invitation. Because she would have stripped down right here, right now if that had gotten the reaction she'd hoped for. Instead, his expression had a huge heaping dose of caution. "We agreed that we'd take that part as it came. No pressure. You're focusing on your career, just like I am. If Franca's not guiding you toward the right next level, then what do you want her to do?"

"I want her to go away!" Viv burst out. "She's exhausting and so chipper and can do more from 10:00 p.m. to midnight than a general, two single moms and the president combined. I want to have dinner with you, and lie in bed on a Saturday morning and watch cartoons with my head on your shoulder. I want you to rip my dress at the seams because you're so eager to get me naked. Most of all, I don't want to think about cupcakes."

But he was shaking his head. "That's not me. I'm not the kind of guy who rips a woman's dress off."

"But you are. You did," she argued inanely because what a stupid thing to say. He was totally that man and she loved it when he was like that. "I don't understand why we were so hot and heavy and then you backed off."

There came another shadow through his gaze that darkened his whole demeanor. "Because we're friends and I'm nothing if not interested in preserving that relationship."

"I am, too," she shot back a little desperately. This conversation was sliding away from her at an alarming pace, turning into something it shouldn't be, and she wasn't sure how that had happened. Or how to fix it. "But I'm also not happy just being friends. I love the text messages and I'm thrilled with what you've done for my business. But it's not enough."

"What are you saying?" he asked cautiously, his expression blank.

"That I want a real marriage. A family. I want more than just cupcakes."

Jonas let the phrase soak through him. Everything inside shifted, rolling over. In six words, Viv had reshaped the entire dynamic between them, and the effects might be more destructive than a nuclear bomb.

His chest certainly felt like one had gone off inside. While he'd been fighting to keep from treating Viv to a repeat of the dress-ripping incident, she'd been quietly planning to cut him off at the knees. Apparently he'd been creating distance for no reason.

Viv's gorgeous face froze when he didn't immediately respond. But what was he supposed to say?

Oh, that's right. *What the hell?*

"Viv, I've known you for over a year. We've been married for almost five weeks. For pretty much the entire length of our acquaintance, you've told me how important your career is to you. I have never once heard you mention that you wanted a family. Can you possibly expand on that statement?"

The weird vibe went even more haywire and he had the impression she regretted what she'd said. Then, she dropped her head into her hands, covering her eyes for a long beat. The longer she hid from him, the more alarmed he got. What was she afraid he'd see?

"Not much to expand on," she mumbled to her palms. "I like cupcakes, but I want a husband and a family, too."

Which was pretty much what she'd just said, only rephrased in such a way as to still not make any sense. "Let me ask this a different way. Why have you never told me this? I thought we were friends."

Yeah, that was a little bitterness fighting to get free.

How well did he really know the woman he'd married if this was just now coming out after all this time? After all the intimacies that they'd shared?

The lick of temper uncurling inside was completely foreign. He'd asked her to marry him strictly because he'd been sure—*positive* even—that she wasn't the slightest bit interested in having a long-term relationship.

Otherwise, he never would have asked her to do this favor. Never would have let himself start to care more than he should have.

His anger fizzled. He could have been more forthcoming with his own truths but hadn't for reasons that he didn't feel that self-righteous about all at once.

"I never told you because it...never came up." Guilt flickered in her tone and when she lifted her face from her hands, it was there in her expression, too. "I'm only telling you now because you asked."

Actually, he hadn't. He'd been sorting through her comments about the marketing consultant he'd hired, desperately trying to figure out if Viv and Franca just didn't get along or if the references he'd received regarding the consultant's brilliance had been embellished. Instead, she'd dropped a whole different issue in his lap. One that was knifing through his chest like a dull machete.

Viv wanted a real husband. A family. This fake marriage was in her way. *Jonas* was in her way. It was shattering. Far more than he would have said.

He didn't want to lose her. But neither could he keep her, not at the expense of giving her what she really wanted. Obviously he should have given more weight to the conversation they'd had at his parents' house about love being a good basis for marriage. Clearly that was what she wanted from a husband.

And he couldn't give her that, nor was she asking him to. He'd made a promise that he'd never let a woman have enough sway to affect his emotions. Judging by the swirl of confusion beneath his breastbone, it was already too late for that.

If she just hadn't said anything. He could have kept pretending that the solution to all his problems was to keep her busy until he figured out how to make all his inappropriate feelings go away.

But this…he couldn't ignore what he knew was the right thing to do.

"Viv." Vising his forehead between his fingers, he tried like hell to figure out how they'd gotten so off track. "You've been telling me for over a year that your career sucked up all your time and that's why you didn't date. How were you planning to meet said husband?"

"I don't know," she shot back defensively. "And cupcakes are important to me. It's just not the only thing, and this marathon of business-plan goals kind of solidified that fact for me. I love the idea of sharing my recipes with a bigger block of customers. But not at the expense of the kind of marriage I think would make me happy. I want—need—to back off."

Back off. From him, she meant. Jonas blinked as something wrenched loose in his chest, and it felt an awful lot like she'd gripped his heart in her fingers, then twisted until it fell out. "I understand. You deserve to have the kind of marriage you want and I can't give that to you."

Her face froze, going so glacial all at once he scarcely recognized her.

"You've never thought about having a real marriage?" she asked in a whisper.

Not once. Until now. And now it was all he could think about. What was a real marriage to her? Love, honor and cherish for the rest of her days? He could do two out of three. Would she accept that? Then he could keep her friendship, keep this marriage and… how crappy was that, to even contemplate how far he could take this without breaking his word to anyone? It was ridiculous. They should have hashed out this stuff long ago. Like before they got married. And he would have if she'd told him that she harbored secret dreams of hearts and googly eyes. Too bad that kind of stuff led to emotional evisceration when everything went south.

Like now.

"Viv." She shifted to look at him, apparently clueing in that he had something serious to say. "I married you specifically because I have no intention of having a real marriage. It was deliberate."

Something that looked a lot like pain flashed through her gaze. "Because I'm not real marriage material?"

A sound gurgled in his throat as he got caught between a vehement denial and an explanation that hopefully didn't make him sound like an ass.

"Not because you're unlovable or something." God, what was wrong with him? He was hurting her with his thoughtlessness. She'd spilled her guts to him, obviously because she trusted him with the truth, and the best he could do was smash her dreams? "I care about you. That's why we're having this conversation, which we should have had a long time ago. I never told you about Marcus."

Eyes wide, she shook her head but stayed silent as he spit out the tale of his friend who had loved and lost and then never recovered. When he wound it up with the tragedy and subsequent pact, she blinked away a sheen of tears that he had no idea what to do with.

"So you, Warren and Hendrix are all part of this… club?" she asked. "The Never Going to Fall in Love club?"

It sounded silly when she said it like that. "It's not a club. We swore solemn vows and I take that seriously."

She nodded once, but confusion completely screwed up her beautiful face. "I see. Instead of having something wonderful with a life partner, you intend to stick to a promise you made under duress a decade ago."

"No," he countered quietly. "I intend to stand by a promise I made, period. Because that's who I am. It's a measure of my ethical standards. A testament to the kind of man I want to be."

"Alone? That's the kind of man you want to be?"

"That's not fair." Why was she so concerned about his emotional state all at once? "I don't want to be alone. That's why I like being married to you so much. We have fun together. Eat dinner. Watch TV."

"Not lately," she said pointedly, and it was an arrow through his heart. If he was going to throw around his ethics like a blunt instrument, then he couldn't very well pretend he didn't know what she meant.

"Not lately," he agreed. "I'd like to say it's because we've both been busy. But that's not the whole truth. I...started to get a little too attached to you. Distance was necessary."

The sheen was back over her eyes. "Because of the pact. You've been pulling back on purpose."

He nodded. The look on her face was killing him, and he'd like nothing more than to yank her into his arms and tell her to forget that nonsense. Because he wanted his friend back. His lover. His everything.

But he couldn't. In the most unfair turnabout, he'd told her about the pact and instead of her running in the other direction like a lot of women, *he* was the one shutting down. "It was the only way I could keep you as my wife and honor the promises I made to myself and to my friends. And to you. I said no pressure. I meant to keep it that way. Which still stands, by the way."

She laughed, but he didn't think it was because she

found any of this funny. "I think this is about the lowest-pressure marriage on the planet."

"You misunderstand. I'm saying no pressure to stay married."

Her gaze cut to him and he took the quick, hard punch to the gut in stride without letting on to her how difficult it had been to utter those words.

Take them back. Right now.

But he couldn't.

"Jonas, we can't get divorced. You'd lose your grandfather's support to take over his role."

The fact that she'd even consider that put the whole conversation in perspective. They were friends who cared about each other. Which meant he had to let her go, no matter how hard it was. "I know. But it's not fair to you to stay in this marriage given that you want something different."

"I do want something different," she agreed quietly. "I have to go to LA. I can't think about any of this right now."

He let her fingers slip from his, and when she shut herself in her bedroom, the quiet click of the door burst through his chest like a gunshot to the heart. He wished he felt like congratulating himself on his fine upstanding character, but all he felt like doing was crawling into bed and throwing a blanket over his head. The absence of Viv left a cold, dark place inside that even a million blankets couldn't warm.

Ten

The trip to LA was a disaster. Oh, the cooking show was fine. She won the first round. But Viv hated having to fake smile, hated pretending her marriage wasn't fake, hated the fakeness of baking on camera with a script full of fake dialogue.

There was nothing real about her, apparently. And it had been slowly sapping her happiness away until she couldn't stand it if one more person called her Mrs. Kim. Why had she changed her name? Even that was temporary until some ambiguous point in the future.

Well, there was one thing that was real. The way she felt about Jonas, as evidenced by the numbness inside that she carried 24/7. Finally, she had someone to care about and *he* cared about *her*. Yay. He cared so much that he was willing to let her out of the favor of being married to him so she could *find someone else*.

How ironic that she'd ended up exactly where she'd intended to be. All practiced up for her next relationship, except she didn't want to move on. She wanted Jonas, just like she had for over a year, and she wanted him to feel the same about her.

The cooking show, or rather the more correctly labeled entertainment venue disguised as a cupcake battle, wrapped up the next day. Viv won the final round and Franca cheered from the sidelines, pointing to her phone, where she was presumably checking out the stats on Cupcaked's new digital storefront. Every time the show's camera zoomed in on Viv's face, they put a graphic overlay on the screen with her name and the name of her cupcake bakery. Whatever results that had produced made Franca giddy, apparently.

It was all too overwhelming. None of this was what she wanted. Instead of cooking shows, Viv should have been spending fourteen hours a day working on her marriage. The what-ifs were all she could think about.

On the plane ride home, Franca jabbered about things like click-through rates, branding and production schedules. They'd already decided to outsource the baking for the digital storefront because Viv's current setup couldn't handle the anticipated volume. Judging by the numbers Franca was throwing out, it had been a good decision.

Except for the part where none of this was what Viv wanted. And it was high time she fixed that.

When she got home, she drafted a letter to Franca thanking her for all of her hard work on Viv's behalf but explaining that her career was not in fact the most important thing in her life, so Franca's services were no longer needed. The improvements to Cupcaked were great and Viv intended to use the strategies that they'd both developed. But she couldn't continue to invest so much energy into her business, not if she hoped to fix whatever was broken in Jonas's head that made him think that saying a few words a decade ago could ever compare with the joy of having the kind of marriage she'd watched her sisters experience. Viv had been shuffled to the side once again and she wasn't okay with that.

Jonas came home late. No surprise there. That seemed to be the norm. But she was not prepared to see the lines of fatigue around his eyes. Or the slight shock flickering through his expression when he caught sight of her sitting on the couch.

"Hey," he called. "Didn't know you were back."

"Surprise." Served him right. "Sit down so we can talk."

Caution drenched his demeanor and he took his time slinging his leather bag over the back of a chair. "Can it wait? I have a presentation to the board tomorrow and I'd like to go over—"

"You're prepared," she told him and patted the cushion next to her. "I've known you for a long time and I would bet every last cupcake pan I own that you've been working on that PowerPoint every spare second for days. You're going to kill it. Sit."

It was a huge kick that he obeyed, and she nearly swooned when the masculine scent of her husband washed over her. He was too far away to touch, but she could rectify that easily. When it was time. She was flying a little blind here, but she did know one thing—she was starting over from scratch. No familiar ingredients. No beloved pan. The oven wasn't even heated up yet.

But she had her apron on and the battle lines drawn. Somehow, she needed to bake a marriage until it came out the way she liked.

"What's up? How was the show?" he asked conversationally, but strictly to change the subject, she was pretty sure.

"Fine. I won. It was fabulous. I fired Franca."

That got his attention. "What? Why would you do that?"

"Because she's too good for me. She needs to go help someone run an empire." She smiled as she gave Jonas a once-over. "You should hire her, in fact."

"Maybe I will." His dark eyes had a flat, guarded quality that she didn't like. While she knew academically that she had to take a whole different track with him, it was another thing entirely to be this close but yet so far.

"Jonas, we have to finish our conversation. The one from the other day."

"I wasn't confused about which one you meant." A brief lift of his lips encouraged her to continue, but then the shield between them snapped back into place. "You've decided to go."

"No. I'm not going anywhere." Crossing her arms so she couldn't reach out to him ranked as one of the hardest things she'd done. But it was necessary to be clear about this without adding a bunch of other stuff into the mix. "I said I was going to do you this favor and as strongly as you believe in keeping your word, it inspires me to do the same. I'm here for the duration."

Confusion replaced the guardedness and she wasn't sure which one she liked less. "You're staying? As my wife?"

"And your friend." She shrugged. "Nothing you said changed anything for me. I still want the marriage I envision and I definitely won't get that if I divorce you."

Jonas flinched and a million different things sprang into the atmosphere between them. "You're not thinking clearly. You'll never meet someone who can give you what you want if you stay married to me."

"For a smart man, you're being slow to catch on." The little noise of disgust sounded in her chest before she could check it. But *men*. So dense. "I want a real marriage with *you*, not some random guy off the street. What do you think we've been doing here but building this into something amazing? I know you want to honor your word to your friends—"

"Viv." The quiet reverberation of her name stopped her cold and she glanced at him. He'd gone so still that her pulse tumbled. "It's not just a promise I made to my friends. I have no room in my life for a real marriage. The pact was easy for me to make. It's not that I swore to never fall in love. It's that I refuse to. It's a destructive emotion that leads to more destruction. That's not something I'm willing to chance."

Her mouth unhinged and she literally couldn't make a sound to save her life. Something cold swept along her skin as she absorbed his sincerity.

"Am I making sense?" he asked after a long pause.

That she could answer easily. "None. Absolutely no sense."

His mouth firmed into a long line and he nodded. "It's a hard concept for someone like you who wants to put your faith and trust in someone else. I don't. I can't. I've built something from nothing, expanded Kim Electronics into a billion-dollar enterprise in the American market, and I'm poised to take that to the next level. I cannot let a woman nor the emotions one might introduce ruin everything."

She'd only thought nothing could make her colder than his opening statement. But the ice forming from this last round of crazy made her shiver. "You're lumping *me* in that category? *I'm* this nebulous entity known as 'woman' who might go Helen of Troy on your business? I don't even know what to say to that."

Grimly, he shook his head. "There's nothing to say. Consider this from my perspective. I didn't even know you wanted anything beyond your career until a couple of days ago. What else don't I know? I can't take that risk. Not with you."

"What?" Her voice cracked. "You're saying you don't trust me because I didn't blather on about hearts and flowers from the first moment I met you?"

Pathetic. Not-clingy hadn't worked. In fact, it might have backfired. If she'd just told him how she felt from the beginning, she could have used the last five weeks to combat his stupid pact.

Something white-hot and angry rose up in her throat. Seriously, this was so unfair. She couldn't be herself with *anyone*. Instead there were all these rules and games and potholes and loopholes, none of which she understood or cared about.

"Viv." He reached out and then jerked his hand back before touching her, as if he'd only just realized that they weren't in a place where that was okay. "It's not a matter of trust. It's…me. I can't manage how insane you make me."

She eyed him, sniffling back a tsunami of tears. "So

now I make you crazy? Listen, buster, I'm not the one talking crazy here—"

A strangled sound stopped her rant. Jonas shook his head, clearly bemused. "Not crazy. Give me a break. I was expecting you to walk out the door, not grill me on things I don't know how to explain. Just stop for a second."

His head dropped into his hands and he massaged his temples.

"Insane and crazy are the same thing."

"I mean how much I want you!" he burst out. "All the time. You make me insane with wanting to touch you, and roll into you in the middle of the night to hold you. Kiss you until you can't breathe. So, yeah, I'll give you that. It makes me crazy. In this case, it does mean the same thing."

Reeling, she stared at him, dumbstruck, numb, so off balance she couldn't figure out how to make her brain work. What in the world was wrong with *any* of that?

"I don't understand what you're telling me, Jonas."

"It's already way too much." He threw up his hands. "How much worse will it get? I refuse to let my emotions control me like that."

This was awful. He was consciously rejecting the concept of allowing anything deeper to grow between them. Period. No questions asked. She let that reality seep into her soul as her nails dug into her palms with little pinpricks of pain that somehow centered her. If this was his decision, she had to find a way to live with it.

"So, what happens next?" she whispered. "I don't want a divorce. Do you?"

At that, he visibly crumpled, folding in on himself as if everything hurt. She knew the feeling.

"I can't even answer that." His voice dipped so low that she could scarcely make it out. "My grandfather asked me to come to Korea as soon as possible. He got some bad news from his doctor and he's retiring earlier than expected."

"Oh, no." Viv's hand flew to her mouth as she took in the devastation flitting through Jonas's expression. "Is he going to be okay?"

"I don't know. He wants you to come. How can I ask that of you?" His gaze held a world of pain and indecision and a million other things that her own expression probably mirrored. "It's not fair to you."

This was where the rubber met the road. He wasn't asking her to go, nor would he. He was simply stating facts and giving the choice to her. If she wanted to claim a real marriage for herself, she had to stand by her husband through thick and thin, sickness and health, vows of honor and family emergencies.

This was the ultimate test. Did she love Jonas enough to ignore her own needs in order to fulfill his? If nothing else, it was her sole opportunity to do and be whatever she wanted in a relationship. Her marriage, her rules. If she had a mind to cling like Saran Wrap to Jonas, it was her right.

In what was probably the easiest move of the entire conversation, she reached out to lace her fingers with his and held on tight. "If you strip everything else away, I'm still your wife. Your grandfather could still pass his support to someone else if he suspects something isn't right between us. If you want me to go, I'll go."

Clearly equal parts shocked and grateful, he stared at her. "Why would you do that for me?"

She squared her shoulders. "Because I said I would." No matter how hard it would be.

Jonas kept sneaking glances at Viv as she slept in the reclined leather seat opposite his. She'd smiled for nearly ten minutes after claiming a spot aboard the Kim private jet that Grandfather had sent to Raleigh to fetch them. It was fun to watch her navigate the spacious fuselage and interact with the attentive staff, who treated her like royalty. Obviously his grandfather had prepped them in advance.

But after the initial round of post-takeoff champagne, Viv had slipped back into the morose silence that cloaked them both since their conversation. He'd done everything in his power to drive her away so he didn't hurt her and what had she done? Repacked the suitcase that she'd just pulled off a conveyor belt at the airport hours before and announced she was coming with him to Korea. No hesitation.

What was he going to do with her?

Not much, apparently. The distance between them was nearly palpable. Viv normally had this vibe of openness about her as if she'd never met a stranger and he could talk to her about anything. Which he had, many times. Since he'd laid down the law about what kind of marriage they could have in that desperate bid to stop the inevitable, there might as well have been an impenetrable steel wall between them.

Good. That was perfect. Exactly what he'd hoped for. He hated it.

This purgatory was exactly what he deserved, though. If Viv wasn't being her beautiful, kind, amazing self, there was no chance of his emotions engaging.

Or rather, engaging further. He was pretty sure there was a little something already stirring around inside. Okay a lot of something, but if he could hold on to that last 50 percent, he could still look Warren and Hendrix in the eye next time they were in the same room.

If he could just cast aside his honor, all of this would be so much easier.

Seoul's Incheon Airport spread out beneath them in all its dazzling silvery glory, welcoming him back to Korea. He appreciated the birthplace of his father and the homeland of his grandfather. Seoul was a vibrant city rich in history with friendly people who chattered in the streets as they passed. It was cosmopolitan in a way that Raleigh could never be, but Jonas preferred the more laid-back feel of his own homeland.

"It's beautiful," Viv commented quietly as the limo Grandfather had sent wound through the streets thronged with people and vehicles.

"I'll take you a few places while we're here," he offered. "You shouldn't miss Gyeongbokgung Palace."

They could walk through Insa-dong, the historic neighborhood that sold art and food, then maybe breeze by the Seoul Tower. He could perfectly envision the delighted smile on her face as she discovered the treasures of the Eastern world that comprised a portion of his lineage. Maybe he'd even find an opportunity to take her hand as they strolled, and he could pretend everything was fine between them.

But Viv was already shaking her head. "You don't have to do that. I don't need souvenirs. You're here for your grandfather and I'm here for you."

That made him feel like crap. But it was an inescapable fact that she'd come because he needed her.

Warmth crowded into his chest as he gazed at her, the beauty of Seoul rushing past the limousine window beyond the glass.

"Why?" he asked simply, too overcome to be more articulate.

Her gaze sought his, and for a brief moment, her normal expressiveness spilled onto her face. Just as quickly, she whisked it away. "No matter what, you're still my friend."

The sentiment caught in his throat. Her sacrifice and the unbelievable willingness to be there for him would have put him on his knees if he wasn't already sitting down. Still might. It didn't make any sense for her to be so unselfish with her time, her body, her cupcakes even without some gain other than the righteous promise of *friendship*. "I don't believe that's the whole reason."

A tiny frown marred her gorgeous mouth and he wished he could kiss it away. But he didn't move. This was something he should have questioned before they got on the plane.

"Is this another conversation about how you don't trust me?" she asked in a small voice.

Deserved that. He shook his head. "This is not a trust issue. It's that I don't understand what you're getting out of all of this. I've always wondered. I promised you that I would help you with your business since you claimed that as your passion. Then you politely declined all the success my efforts have produced. I give you the option to leave and you don't take it. Friendship doesn't seem like enough of a motivator."

Guilt crowded through her gaze. What was that all about? But she looked away before he got confirmation that it was indeed guilt, and he had a burning need to understand all at once.

The vows he'd taken with Warren and Hendrix after Marcus's death seemed like a pinky swear on the playground in comparison to Viv's friendship standards, yet he'd based his adult life on that vow. If there was something to learn from her about the bonds of friendship, he'd be an instant student.

Hooking her chin with his finger, he guided her face back toward his, feathering a thumb across her cheek before he'd barely gotten purchase. God, she felt so good. It was all he could do to keep from spreading his entire palm across her cheek, lifting her lips into a kiss that would resolve nothing other than the constant ache under his skin.

He'd enjoy every minute of the forbidden, though.

Since she still hadn't answered, he prompted her. "What's your real reason, Viv? Tell me why you'd do this for me after all I've said and done."

She blinked. "I agreed to this deal. You of all people should know that keeping your word is a choice. Anyone can break a promise but mine to you means something."

That wasn't it, or rather it wasn't the full extent. He could tell. While he appreciated her conviction, she was hedging. He hadn't expanded Kim Electronics into the American market and grown profits into the ten-figure range by missing signs that the person on the other side of the table wasn't being entirely forthcoming. But she wasn't a factory owner looking to make an extra million or two or a parts distributor with shady sources.

She was his wife. Why couldn't he take what she said at face value and leave it at that?

Because she hadn't told him about wanting a real

marriage, that was why. It stuck under his rib cage, begging him to do something with that knowledge, and the answer wasn't pulling her into his arms like he wanted to. He should be cutting her free by his choice, not hers.

Yet Viv was quietly showing him how to be a real friend regardless of the cost. It was humbling, and as the limo snaked through the crowded streets of Seoul toward his grandfather's house, his chest got so tight and full of that constant ache he got whenever he looked at Viv that he could hardly breathe.

Caught in the trap of his own making, he let his hand drop away from her face. He had a wife he couldn't let himself love and two friends he couldn't let himself disappoint. At what point did Jonas get what he wanted? And when had his desire for something more shifted so far away from what he had?

There was no good answer to that. The limo paused by his grandfather's gates as they opened and then the driver pulled onto the hushed property draped with trees and beautiful gardens. The ancestral home that Grandfather had given Jonas and Viv lay a kilometer down the road up on a hill. Both properties were palatial, befitting a businessman who entertained people from all over the world, as Jung-Su did. As Jonas would be expected to do when he stepped into Grandfather's shoes. He'd need a wife to help navigate the social aspects of being the CEO of a global company.

But the painful truth was that he couldn't imagine anyone other than Viv by his side. He needed *her*, not a wife, and for far more reasons than because it might or might not secure the promotion he'd been working toward. At the same time, as much as he'd denied that his questions were about trust, he was caught in a horrible catch-22. Trust *was* at the root of it.

Also a trap of his own making. He was predisposed to believe that a woman would string him along until she got tired of him and then she'd break his heart. So he looked for signs of that and pounced the moment he found evidence, when in reality, he'd have to actually give his heart to a woman before it could be broken. And that was what he was struggling to avoid.

Grandfather's *jibsa* ushered them into the house and showed them to their rooms. A different member of the staff discreetly saw to their needs and eventually guided Jonas and Viv to where his grandfather sat in the garden outside, enjoying the sunshine. The garden had been started by Jonas's grandmother, lovingly overseen until her death several years ago. Her essence still flitted among the mugunghwa blooms and bellflowers, and he liked remembering her out here.

His grandfather looked well, considering he'd recently been diagnosed with some precursors to heart disease and had begun rounds of medication to reverse the potential for a heart attack.

"Jonas. Miss Viviana." Grandfather smiled at them each in turn and Viv bent to kiss his cheek, which made the old man positively beam. "I'm pleased to see you looking well after your flight. It is not an easy one."

Viv waved that off and took a seat next to Jung-Su on the long stone bench. His grandfather sat on a cushion that was easier on his bones but Viv didn't seem to notice that she was seated directly on the cold rock ledge. Discreetly, Jonas flicked his fingers at one of the many uniformed servants in his grandfather's employ, and true to form, the man returned quickly with another cushion for her.

She took it with a smile and resituated herself, still chatting with Grandfather about the flight and her impressions of Korea thus far. Grandfather's gaze never left her face and Jonas didn't blame him. She was mesmerizing. Surrounded by the lush tropical beauty of the garden and animated by a subject that clearly intrigued her, she was downright breathtaking. Of course, Jonas was biased. Especially since he hadn't been able to take a deep breath pretty much since the moment he'd said *I do* to this woman.

"Jonas. Don't hover." Grandfather's brows came together as he shot a scowl over the head of his new granddaughter-in-law. "Sit with us. Your lovely wife was just telling me about baking cupcakes on the American television show."

"Yes, she was brilliant," Jonas acknowledged. But he didn't sit on the bench. The only open spot was next to Viv and it was entirely too much temptation for his starving body to be that near her.

"Jonas is too kind." Viv's nose wrinkled as she shook her head. "The show hasn't even aired yet."

"So? I don't have to see it to know that you killed it." Plus, she'd told him she'd won, like it was no big deal, when in fact, it was. Though the result was hardly shocking. "*Brilliant* is an understatement."

Viv ducked her head but not before he caught the pleased gleam in her eye. He should have told her that already and more than once. Instead, he'd been caught up in his own misery. She deserved to hear how wonderful she was on a continual basis.

"It's true," he continued. "She does something special with her recipes. No one else can touch her talent when it comes to baking."

Grandfather watched them both, his gaze traveling back and forth between them as if taking in a fascinating tennis match. "It's very telling that you are your wife's biggest fan."

Well, maybe so. But what it told, Jonas had no idea. He shrugged. "That's not a secret."

"It's a sign of maturity that I appreciate," his grandfather said. "For years I have watched you do nothing but work and I worried that you would never have a personal life. Now I see you are truly committed to your wife and I like seeing you happy. It only solidifies my decision to retire early."

Yeah. *Committed* described Jonas to a T. Committed to honor. Committed to making himself insane. Committed to the asylum might well be next, especially since his grandfather was so off the mark with his observation. But what was he supposed to do, correct him?

"It's only fair," Viv murmured before Jonas could formulate a response. "I'm his biggest fan, as well."

"Yes, I can see that, too," Jung-Su said with a laugh.

He could? Jonas glanced at Viv out of the corner of his eye in case there was some kind of sign emanating from her that he'd managed to miss. Except she had her sights firmly fixed on him and caught him eyeing her. Their gazes locked and he couldn't look away.

"You're a fan of workaholic, absentee husbands?" he asked with a wry smile of his own. Might as well own his faults in front of God and everyone.

"I'm a fan of your commitment, just like your grandfather said. You do everything with your heart. It's what I first noticed about you. You came into the shop to get cupcakes for your staff, and every time, I'd ask you 'What's the occasion today?' and you always knew the smallest details. 'It's Mrs. Nguyen's fiftieth birthday' or 'Today marks my admin's fourth anniversary working for me.' None of my other customers pay attention to stuff like that."

He shifted uncomfortably. Of course he knew those things. They'd been carefully researched excuses to buy cupcakes so he could see Viv without admitting he was there to see her. Granted, she'd already figured that out and blathered on about it to his parents during their first official married-couple dinner. Why bring that up again now?

"That's why he'll make the best CEO of Kim Global," she said to his grandfather as an aside. "Because he cares about people and cares about doing the right thing. He always keeps his word. His character is above reproach and honestly, that's why I fell for him."

That was laying it on a bit thick, but his grandfather just nodded. "Jonas is an honorable man. I'm pleased he's found a woman who loves him for the right reasons."

Except it was all fake. Jonas did a double take as Viv nodded, her eyes bright with something that looked a lot like unshed tears. "He's an easy man to love. My feelings for him have only grown now that we're married."

Jonas started to interrupt because…come on. There was playacting and there was outright lying to his grandfather for the sake of supporting Jonas's bid to become the next CEO. But as one tear slipped from her left eye, she glanced at him and whatever he'd been about to say vanished from his vocabulary. She wasn't lying.

He swallowed. Viv was in love with him? A band

tightened around his lungs as he stared at her, soaking in the admission. It shouldn't be such a shock. She looked at him like that all the time. But not seconds after saying something so shocking, so provocative *out loud*. She couldn't take it back. It was out there, pinging around inside him like an arrow looking for a target.

A servant interrupted them, capturing Grandfather's attention, and everything fell apart as it became apparent that they were being called for dinner. Jonas took Viv's hand to help her to her feet as he'd done a hundred times before but her hand in his felt different, heavier somehow as if weighted with implications. She squeezed his hand as if she knew he needed her calming touch.

It was anything but calming. She was in love with him. The revelation bled through him. It was yet another thing that she'd held back from him that changed everything. He worked it over in his mind during dinner, longing to grab her and carry her out of this public room so he could ask her a few pointed questions. But Grandfather talked and talked and talked, and he'd invited a few business associates over as well, men Jonas couldn't ignore, given that the whole reason he was in Korea was to work through the transition as his grandfather stepped down.

Finally all the obstacles were out of the way and he cornered his wife in their room. She glanced up as he shut the door, leaning against it as he zeroed in on the woman sitting on the bed.

"That went well," she commented, her gaze cutting away from his. "Your grandfather seems like he's in good spirits after his diagnosis."

"I don't want to talk about that." He loved his grandfather, but they'd talked about his illness at length before Jonas had left the States, and he was satisfied he knew everything necessary about Jung-Su's health. Jonas's wife, on the other hand, needed to do a whole lot more talking and he needed a whole lot more understanding. "Why did you tell my grandfather that you're in love with me?"

"It just kind of…came out," she said. "But don't worry, I'm pretty sure he bought it."

"I bought it," he bit out. "It wasn't just something you said. You meant it. How long have you been in love with me?"

She shrugged. "It's not a big deal."

"It is a big deal!" Frustrated with the lack of headway, he crossed the room and stopped short of lifting her face so he could read for himself what she was feeling. But he didn't touch her, because he wanted her to own up to what was really going on inside. For once. "That's why you married me. Why you came to Korea. Why you're still here even though I told you about the pact."

That's when she met his gaze, steady and true. "Yes."

Something wonderful and beautiful and strong burst through his heart. It all made a lot more sense now. What he'd been calling friendship was something else entirely.

Now would be a *really* good time to sit down. So he did. "Why didn't you tell me? That's information that I should have had a long time ago."

"No, Jonas, it's not." She jammed her hands on her hips. "What does it change? Nothing. You're determined to keep your vow to your friends and I can't stop being in love with you. So we're both stuck."

Yes. *Stuck*. He'd been between a rock and a hard place for an eternity because he couldn't stop being in love with her either.

He'd tried. He'd pretended that he wasn't, called it friendship, pushed her away, stayed away himself, thrown his honor down between them. But none of it had worked because he'd been falling for her since the first cupcake.

Maybe it was time to try something else.

"Viv." He stood and waited until he had her full attention. But then when she locked gazes with him, her expressive eyes held a world of possibilities. Not pain. Not destruction. None of the things that he'd tried to guard against.

That was the reason she should leave. Instead of feeling stuck, she should divorce him simply because he was a moron. The character she'd spoken of to his grandfather didn't include being courageous. He was a coward, refusing to acknowledge that avoiding love hadn't saved him any heartache. In fact, it had caused him a lot more than he'd credited. Had caused Viv a lot, too.

Worse, he'd avoided the wonderful parts, and ensured that he'd be lonely to boot. And what had he robbed himself of thus far? Lots of sex with his wife, a chance to have a real marriage and many, many moments where she looked at him like she was looking at him right now. As if he really was worthy of her devotion, despite his stupidity.

He'd had plenty of pain already. Avoiding the truth hadn't stopped that. The lesson here? No more pretending.

"Tell me," he commanded. "No more hiding how you really feel. I want to hear it from you, no holds barred."

"Why are you doing this?" Another tear slipped down her face and she brushed it away before he could, which seemed to be a common theme. She had things inside that she didn't trust him with and he didn't blame her.

"Because we haven't been honest with each other. In fact, I'd say my behavior thus far in our marriage hasn't been anything close to honorable, and it's time to end that. You know what? I should go first then." He captured her hand and held it between his. "Viv. You're my friend, my lover, my wife, my everything. When I made a vow to never fall in love, it was from a place of ignorance. Because I thought love was a bad thing. Something to be avoided. You taught me differently. And I ignored the fact that I took vows with you. Vows that totally overshadow the promise I made to Warren and Hendrix before I fully understood what I was agreeing to give up. I'm not okay with that anymore. Not okay with pretending. What I'm trying to say, and not doing a very good job at, is that I love you, too."

Like magic, all of his fear vanished simply by virtue of saying it out loud. At last, he could breathe. The clearest sense of happiness radiated from somewhere deep inside and he truly couldn't fathom why it had taken him so long to get to this place.

Viv eyed him suspiciously instead of falling into his waiting arms. "What?"

He laughed but it didn't change her expression. "I love you. I wouldn't blame you if you needed to hear it a hundred more times to believe me."

Her lips quirked. "I was actually questioning the part where you said you weren't doing a good job explaining. Because it seemed pretty adequate to me."

That seemed like as good an invitation as any to sweep her into his arms. In a tangle, they fell back against the mattress, and before he could blink, she was kissing him, her mouth shaping his with demanding little pulls, as if she wanted everything inside him. He didn't mind. It all belonged to her anyway.

Just as he finally got his hands under her dress, nearly groaning at the hot expanse of skin that he couldn't wait to taste, she broke the kiss and rolled him under her.

That totally worked for him. But she didn't dive back in like his body screamed for her to. Instead, she let him drown in her warm brown eyes as she smiled. "What's going to happen when we get home and you have to explain to Warren and Hendrix that you broke your word to them?"

"Nothing. Because that's not what I'm going to say." He smoothed back a lock of her hair that had fallen into her face, and shifted until her body fell into the grooves of his perfectly. This position was his new favorite. "We made that pact because we didn't want to lose each other. Our friendship isn't threatened because I finally figured out that I'm in love with you. I'll help them realize that."

"Good. I don't want to be the woman who came between you and your friends."

"You couldn't possibly. Because you're the woman who *is* my friend. I never want that to change."

And then there was no more talking as Viv made short work of getting them both undressed, which was only fair since she was on top. He liked Take Charge Viv almost as much as he liked In Love with Him Viv.

She was everything he never expected when he fell in love with his best friend.

Epilogue

Jonas walked into the bar where he'd asked Warren and Hendrix to meet him. He'd tried to get Viv to come with him, but she'd declined with a laugh, arguing that the last person who should be present at the discussion of how Jonas had broken the pact was the woman he'd fallen in love with.

While he agreed, he still wasn't looking forward to it. Despite what he'd told Viv, he didn't think Warren and Hendrix were going to take his admission lightly.

His friends were already seated in a high-backed booth, which Jonas appreciated given the private nature of what he intended to discuss. They'd already taken the liberty of ordering, and three beers sat on the table. But when he slid into the booth across from Warren, Hendrix cleared his throat.

"I'm glad you called," Hendrix threw out before

Jonas could open his mouth. "I have something really important to ask you both."

Thrilled to have an out, Jonas folded his hands and toyed with his wedding band, which he did anytime he thought about Viv. He did it so often, the metal had worn a raw place on his finger. "I'm all ears, man."

Warren set his phone down, but no less than five notifications blinked from the screen. "Talk fast. I have a crisis at work."

Hendrix rolled his eyes. "You always have a crisis. It's usually that you're not there. Whatever it is can wait five minutes." He let out a breath with a very un-Hendrix-like moan. "I need you guys to do me a favor and I need you to promise not to give me any grief over it."

"That's pretty much a guarantee that we will," Warren advised him with cocked eyebrow. "So spill before I drag it out of you."

"I'm getting married."

Jonas nearly spit out the beer he'd just sipped. "To one woman?"

"Yes, to one woman." Hendrix shot him a withering glare. "It's not that shocking."

"The hell you say." Warren hit the side of his head with the flat of his palm. Twice. "I think my brain is scrambled. Because I'd swear you just said you were getting married."

"I did, jerkoff." Hendrix shifted his scowl to Warren. "It's going to be very good for me."

"Did you steal that speech from your mom?" Warren jeered, his phone completely forgotten in favor of the real-life drama happening in their booth. "Because it sounds like you're talking about eating your veggies, not holy matrimony."

"You didn't give Jonas this much crap when he got married," Hendrix reminded him as Warren grinned.

"Um, whatever." Jonas held up a finger as he zeroed in on the small downturn of Hendrix's mouth. "That is completely false, first of all. You have a short memory. And second, if this is like my marriage, you're doing it for a reason, one you're not entirely happy about. What's this really about?"

Hendrix shrugged, wiping his expression clear. "I'm marrying Rosalind Carpenter. That should pretty much answer all of your questions."

It *so* did not. Warren and Jonas stared at him, but Warren beat him to the punch. "Whoa, dude. That's epic. Is she as much a knockout in person as she is in all those men's magazines?"

He got an elbow in his ribs for his trouble, but it wasn't Warren's fault that there were so many sexy pictures of Rosalind Carpenter to consider.

"Shut up. That's my fiancée you're talking about."

Jonas pounded on the table to get their attention. "On that note…if the question is will we be in the wedding party, of course we will." They had plenty of time to get the full story. After Jonas steered them back to the reason why he'd called them with an invitation for drinks. "Get back to us when you've made plans. Now chill out while we talk about my thing."

"Which is?" Warren gave him the side-eye while checking his messages.

"I broke the pact."

The phone slipped out of Warren's hand and thunked against the leather seat. "You did what? With Viv?"

Jonas nodded and kept his mouth shut as his friends lambasted him with their best shots at his character, the depths of his betrayal and the shallowness of his definition of the word *vow*. He took it all with grace because he didn't blame them for their anger. They just needed to experience the wonders of the right woman for themselves and then they'd get it.

When they were mostly done maligning him, Jonas put his palms flat on the table and leaned forward. "No one is more surprised by this than me. But it's the truth. I love her and I broke the pact. But it's not like it was with Marcus. She loves me back and we're happy. I hope you can be happy for us, too. Because we're going to be married and in love for a long time."

At least that was his plan. And by some miracle, it was Viv's, too.

"I can't believe you're doing this to us," Warren shot back as if he hadn't heard a word Jonas said. "Does keeping your word mean nothing to you?"

"Integrity is important to me," he told them without blinking. "That's why I'm telling you the truth. Lying about it would dishonor my relationship with Viv. And I can't stop loving her just to stick to a pact we made. I tried and it made us both miserable."

"Seems appropriate for a guy who turns on his buddies," Hendrix grumbled.

"Yeah, we'll see how you feel after you get married," Jonas told him mildly. Hendrix would come around. They both would eventually. They'd been friends for too long to let something like a lifetime of happiness come between them, strictly over principle.

Warren griped about the pact for another solid five minutes and then blew out a breath. "I've said my piece and now I have to go deal with a distribution nightmare. This is not over."

With that ominous threat, Warren shoved out of the booth and stormed from the restaurant.

Hendrix, on the other hand, just grinned. "I know you didn't mean to break the pact. It's cool. Things happen. Thank God that'll never be me, but I'm happy that you're happy."

"Thanks, man." They shook on it and drank to a decade of friendship.

When Jonas got home, Viv was waiting in the foyer. His favorite. He flashed her the thumbs-up so she would know everything was okay between him and his friends—which it would be once Warren calmed down—then wrapped Viv in his arms and let her warmth infuse him. "I have another favor to ask."

"Anything."

No hesitation. That might be his favorite quality of hers. She was all in no matter what he asked of her—because she loved him. How had he gotten so lucky? "You're not even going to ask what it is?"

She shrugged. "If it's anything like the last favor, which landed me the hottest husband on the planet, by the way, why would I say no? Your favors are really a huge win for me so…"

Laughing, he kissed her and that made her giggle, too. His heart was so full, he worried for a moment that it might burst. "Well, I'm not sure this qualifies as a win. I was just going to ask you to never stop loving me."

"Oh, you're right. I get nothing out of that," she

teased. "It's torture. You make me happier than I would have ever dreamed. Guess I can find a way to put up with that for the rest of my life."

"Good answer," he murmured, and kissed his wife, his lover, his friend. His everything.

* * * * *

CAPPUCCINO KISSES

YAHRAH ST. JOHN

To my love and friend, Freddie Blackman.

Chapter 1

"Welcome to the Lillian's of Seattle grand opening," Lillian Drayson, founder of the renowned Chicago bakery told the large crowd gathered in her second location. "We Draysons—" she turned to look at her grand-niece, Mariah, and grand-nephews Chase and Jackson "—are excited to open up this new bakery in the Denny Triangle section of town. It's a vibrant location with a plethora of professional and residential communities whose members will enjoy the delicious baked goods the Drayson family has been providing to the Chicago area for over forty years, and will now to the city of Seattle."

Applause erupted as the entire Seattle Drayson family cheered on Lillian, the matriarch, whose name they proudly represented at the new bakery.

Mariah Drayson stood away from the crowd and surveyed her family as she sampled one of the salted caramel cupcakes from the back of the room. She knew she shouldn't be eating another cupcake given that she'd already had one earlier that afternoon, but she had a tendency to eat when she was nervous. Opening her own bakery with her brothers was definitely something to make her worry. She'd used every penny of her divorce settlement from her ex-husband, Richard Hems, to cover her share, but deep down Mariah knew the venture would be worthwhile in the end. After the divorce, she'd chosen to go back to her maiden name. She was happy she did because Lillian's was a family business run by Draysons.

At age seventy-nine, her aunt Lillian was a force to be reckoned with, and when she'd decided to open a second location last summer, Mariah and her brothers had been initially reluctant. Mariah had been coming off the heels of a divorce and didn't know anything about running a bakery. Sure, she had a flair for baking after the summers she'd spent in Chicago learning at Lillian's knee, and during her self-imposed hiatus from work while she and her ex-husband had tried to become pregnant, but this was different.

Aunt Lillian would be entrusting her name, her brand, to the three of them. After much discussion, however, Mariah and her siblings had figured that each of them brought something different to the table. As well as being the best baker, she knew advertising and marketing. Chase, the numbers man, would keep track of the bakery's finances. Then there were was Jackson, bringing up the rear as a businessman and social media guru, and with a knack for cakes. Mariah smiled as she remembered how Lillian's of Seattle had been born.

The bakery was a labor of love for all of them, and they'd mutually agreed that Aunt Lillian should give the speech at the grand opening and ribbon cutting ceremony. It was her namesake, after all, and she was highly admired across the country after the Chicago Draysons had won the You Take the Cake competition three years ago on national television.

"Can you believe we did it, sis?" Jackson asked from her side.

Mariah hazarded a glance at her charming, handsome brother, who was two years her senior. Lillian's was the first time he'd actually stuck with a job longer than a few months. Though he'd done well at the private school all three siblings had attended, Jack was easily bored. He'd had numerous entrepreneurial successes, but as soon as they began to blossom, he would sell them. Would this time be any different? Mariah sure hoped so.

"No, I can't," she finally answered. After they'd found a location and Chase had worked out the finances, the bakery had come together, allowing them to open now, in early spring.

Jackson glanced her way. "Don't look so surprised, Mariah. With your baking skills, Chase's business acumen and my charm, we have what it takes to make this place a success." He swung his arms wide and motioned to the packed bakery, which was filled with family, friends, the news media and people who loved baked goodies. "We'll show them that we're as good as they are."

Mariah followed her brother's gaze and saw it resting on Belinda, Carter and Shari Drayson, their cousins from Chicago. "Why are you so mistrustful of them?"

"'Cause," Jackson said, "you know Grandpa Oscar always says they can't be trusted."

"We—" Mariah pointed between the two of them "—have no beef with our cousins. If Grandpa Oscar and Great-Uncle Henry have issues over money, that doesn't mean we should. Belinda, Shari and Carter have been nothing but gracious to us and have helped us in the kitchen."

The three had flown in from Chicago several days earlier to help make pies, cakes and tortes for the grand opening. They'd been in the kitchen baking and sweating as much as the rest of them. And Carter, being the skilled artisan cake maker he was, had created several works of art that were proudly displayed in their windows this very moment.

"That's because they probably thought we were inept," Jackson replied. "I mean, Shari's running Lillian's of Chicago. She probably wanted to make sure we weren't going to mess anything up that might get thrown back on her."

"Well, we didn't," Mariah stated. "And this is a success. Can't we just be happy today of all days?"

"Happy about what?" Chase came over and joined their huddle, wrapping his arms around their shoulders.

Mariah glanced up at her six-foot-four brother. He, too, was easy on the eyes, but in a studious way thanks to the wire-rimmed glasses, dress shirt and khaki pants he always wore while at the bakery. "We were just talking about what a great turnout this is, and I was reminding Jackson that we should be thankful so many people came out to support us."

"Yeah, I can't believe how packed it is," Chase commented. "It's a good start, but we put a lot of capital into the place and it's going to be a while before we see a return on our investment."

Mariah frowned. "Is money all you think about?"

"Yes." Jackson laughed and answered for him.

"Shh," Chase said, as a reporter posed a question to Aunt Lillian at the podium.

"Mrs. Drayson, coming into Seattle is a risky move for you, is it not?" the young Caucasian man asked, with a microphone pointed up at Aunt Lillian.

"How so?"

"Well, Sweetness Bakery has ruled the Seattle market for years," the man replied. "Other bakeries have tried to make inroads in the past and no one has been able to break into the market. What makes Lillian's any different?"

"Lillian's is different," she responded, "because we are a small family-owned business. I can promise the citizens of Seattle that they will enjoy the same high-quality baked goods as I make in my own kitchen, and that any customer would find in my flagship location on the Magnificent Mile in Chicago. That's what puts us a notch up over the rest."

Jackson stepped forward into the crowd and clapped loudly. "That about does it for the speeches, folks. Please come over and sample the delicious offerings we've laid out today, as I think our products will speak for themselves." He ushered everyone toward the tables.

"Well said, Jackson." Aunt Lillian gave him a wink as her husband, Great-Uncle Henry, helped her off the podium. "Come on over here. And Chase, Mariah, you come up here, too, for some photos." She beckoned them all forward.

Mariah smiled at the command in the older woman's voice. She placed the half-eaten cupcake on a nearby counter and blotted her mouth with a napkin. She wished she could touch up her lipstick, but had to comfort herself with the fact that at least she wouldn't have icing all over her mouth. "Coming…" She put on a bright smile and walked over in her brown peep-toe pumps toward the group.

After all the baking she'd done during the last three days, her smudged attire wouldn't do, so Mariah had gone home for a quick shower and change of clothes. She hadn't known what to wear for such a grand event and had erred on the side of chic elegance. She'd slid into a tailored denim pocket skirt and coral shirt teamed with a brown belt, and put a cream blazer over her outfit before rushing back to the bakery.

She'd arrived just in time to see her parents' noses wrinkle as they walked into bakery. Graham and Nadia Drayson were ultraconservative, especially her mother, and they didn't understand why she, Chase and Jackson had agreed to waste their money on such a foolish investment. Her father was a traditionalist who had made much of his sizable wealth in real estate, and fully expected one of her brothers to follow in his footsteps, but they'd chosen their own path.

Lillian's of Seattle wasn't some harebrained scheme. It was a family business, and with Aunt Lillian's seal of approval, they would steadily build on the brand. And why shouldn't they? Their cousins Carter and Drake, with their best friend, Malik, Belinda's husband, had already successfully branched off from the family business with their Brothers Who Bake blog and successful cookbooks. They'd even gone on tours and there was discussion of a potential television series.

Why shouldn't the Seattle Draysons get in on the action? When Mariah had presented the idea to Jackson, he was on board immediately. Chase had taken a little more convincing. He'd been working for a successful accounting firm and wasn't all that eager to give up that hefty paycheck, but eventually she and Jack had convinced him that with their aunt's support, it was a sound investment.

Mariah smiled as she, Lillian, Chase and Jackson posed for multiple pictures. Some were taken of them behind the display and a few others were outside in front of the stenciled Lillian's of Seattle sign. Mariah was trying her best to grin from ear to ear, even though her cheeks hurt, when she saw a sexy fine man strolling up the sidewalk toward them. He was clean-shaven, with a short haircut, and was nearly as tall as Chase. He wore a tailored gray suit with a checkered dress shirt and blue tie. Everything about him screamed money, which only enhanced his sex appeal. It was definitely the man who made the clothes, not the other way around.

Mariah didn't know who he was and wasn't altogether sure she wanted to, because the torrid sensations he was causing to flow through her body to the place between her thighs was making her feel flush all over.

He stopped when he reached them and paused for several seconds as he surveyed Mariah up and down, before opening the glass storefront door and walking inside Lillian's.

"Mariah!" Jackson called.

"What?" she asked, exasperated by the interruption.

"One more picture," the photographer said, when she turned back around after staring at the sexy stranger. Mariah forced herself to focus on the task at hand, and smiled buoyantly.

When the session was over, Jackson whispered in her ear as she quickly headed to the front door. "What's wrong with you?"

She glanced back at him. "Nothing. Why?"

"You just look funny, is all," he commented as he followed her inside.

"Well, I'm fine," Mariah replied. Or so she hoped. She glanced around the bakery for the mystery man. It was easy to find him in the crowd, because he commanded attention. She gulped. Her breath hitched and heart lurched into an excited rhythm. Damn! From across the room he was openly admiring her, and she didn't like the way he made her feel with just one hungry gaze. Her entire being yearned for something she couldn't quite name, didn't want to name. Why was this man having such a profound effect on her?

* * *

Everett Myers was intrigued. Not just by the new pastry shop that had just opened, but by the beautiful siren he'd seen standing outside by the sign. Who was she? And how could he meet her?

He'd come to find out if Lillian's was as good as the critics claimed, but as soon as he'd walked toward the group and photographer standing outside, he'd liked what he'd seen. Smooth caramel-toned skin, a pert little nose and straight honey-blond hair had Everett licking his lips. It wasn't as if she was dressed provocatively, either. She was stylish and classic in a cream blazer over a coral top, but it was the sexy blue jean skirt hugging her behind, allowing him to make out her curves, that had him standing at attention. She had to be in the neighborhood of mid-twenties, which suited him just fine. *God, what's wrong with me?* he wondered.

Deep down, he knew what. It had been a long time, too long, since he'd felt this way. Sure, she'd seen him when he approached, but since she'd reentered the establishment, she'd been doing her best to ignore him.

Everett wasn't used to being ignored. With him being six foot two, it was impossible not to see him coming. Plus, everyone in Seattle knew who he was. The Myers Hotel chain was synonymous with luxury and class, and had been a staple in the urban community for nearly thirty years. If people didn't know him personally, they knew of him or knew his name. He supposed that's why he was irked that the young woman who'd caught his eye was doing her best to feign ignorance at his blatant appreciation of her.

Just at that moment, the beautiful siren turned and glanced toward him. He flashed her a smile, but she quickly looked away. Damn, had he really lost his charm? He had been off the market the last nine years. He'd married Sara, his college sweetheart, when he was only twenty-one, and their son, Everett Jr.—EJ for short—was born soon after. But five years ago a tragic accident had taken Sara's life.

It wasn't easy being a widowed father at the grand old age of thirty, but he was doing his best to provide a loving, stable home for EJ. Up until now, he hadn't been eager to give EJ a new mom. Had he had opportunities? Heck, yeah! When he'd been single, Everett had often had women propositioning him, but as soon as he'd been widowed it got worse. They were all too eager to find out exactly how many zeros were in his bank account.

Or was he being too cynical? Maybe they just pitied him and felt his then three-year-old son needed a mother. And maybe EJ did back then, but Everett hadn't had it in him to even think about marrying again. He wasn't sure he could stand losing someone else he loved. And so he'd remained a bachelor the last five years, and quite frankly, had been content with the single life. Until now.

Determinedly, he strode over to where the gorgeous woman stood, speaking to a small group of people. She glanced up when he approached, but said nothing.

Instead, the man beside her, who had to be at least two inches taller than Everett, called out to him, "Everett Myers!" He held out his hand. "Pleasure to have you here."

Everett had no choice but to accept the fervent handshake. "And you are?"

"Chase Drayson," the tall man answered. "Part owner of Lillian's."

Everett caught the word *part* and looked the siren whom he'd fancied from across the room directly in the eye. Except now, standing so close to her, he found she was even more striking. "And you, would you be a part owner, as well?"

Her eyebrows furrowed. "Yes, but how could you tell?"

Everett inclined his head toward the door. "You were outside taking photos earlier, and I couldn't help but notice you."

His observation caused her to blush and she lowered her eyes, but that didn't stop the tall man from continuing the conversation, even though Everett wished he would go away and give them some privacy so he could get to know her better.

"We're all part owners," Chase offered. "Mariah, myself and our brother, Jackson, over there," He motioned to a man across the room surrounded by a group of young female customers sampling pastries from a platter he held.

"Mariah..." Everett let her name dangle on his lips. "It's nice to meet you." He offered her his hand.

Something shifted in the air between them. Something Everett hadn't felt in a long time. Awareness. Sexual awareness of another person, but not just *any* person. Her. It was several moments before she finally accepted his hand with a smile. "Pleasure to meet you."

A current of electricity passed between them at the slight touch, but then, as if Everett had imagined it, it was gone.

"What brings you by our little establishment?" Chase inquired.

Everett breathed in deeply. Clearly, her brother wasn't getting the hint that he wanted to be alone with his sister, so he needed to be blunt. "Perhaps I can explain to Mariah?" he asked, holding out his arm. "As she gives me a tour?"

Chase glanced at his sister and then back at Everett, and understanding finally dawned. "Oh, of course, I'll go mingle with the other guests. Have fun, sis." He gave her wink as he strode away.

Everett sighed. Thankfully, they were alone. "So—"

he grasped her delicate hand and slid it in the crook of his arm "—Mariah Drayson, what's your role here at Lillian's?" he asked, as she led him around the bakery.

When she glanced up at him with those brilliant brown eyes, Everett's stomach flip-flopped.

"I'm not only part owner, but head baker, as well." Mariah walked over to one of the tables holding a spread of pastries, muffins and scones. She reached for a petite orange scone and offered it to him.

"Really?" He arched an eyebrow as he accepted it. When he took a bite it was so moist and delicious, he couldn't help but groan out loud.

She blushed at his near-sexual response. "Does that surprise you?"

His brow furrowed. "Hmm. I guess so. You don't strike me as the domesticated type."

"That's because you don't know me," Mariah responded.

"I'd like to remedy that," Everett replied smoothly as he drew closer to her. "How about sharing a meal with me sometime?" Had he really just asked her out, with no preamble or finesse? He hoped she would say yes.

Chapter 2

Mariah coughed audibly. Had she heard him correctly? Had this impossibly gorgeous man with sexy dimples just asked her out? Her chest expanded as she responded to his close proximity. She could feel the heady attraction between them as her heart thumped loudly in her chest. It was as if he was magnetically pulling her toward him. "Excuse me?"

"You heard me," Everett said with a smile, as he reached for another piece of heaven on that platter. He popped it in his mouth and chewed as he watched her intently. He was clearly waiting on an answer.

"I—I can't," she finally answered. Awareness of him prickled across her skin and made her uncomfortable.

"Why not?"

"Are you always this persistent?"

"When someone is trying to avoid me, I am."

"And I'm trying to avoid you?"

He smiled. "You know you are. And there's no need. I don't bite."

Mariah wasn't so sure about that. Everett Myers looked like just the sort of man she should steer clear of. He radiated a sexual magnetism so potent that she shifted, restless on her feet.

"I'm waiting," he said, folding his arms across his amazingly broad chest. His voice was slow and seductive.

Mariah couldn't help but notice how defined he was. With his football player physique, he looked as if he spent a great amount of time at the gym, pumping iron. Everett Myers was sinfully sexy and he smelled equally divine. His cologne, spicy and woodsy, was tantalizing her senses, so much so that she had to step away.

"I've only been divorced a short time and I'm not ready to jump back into the dating pool."

His eyes followed her every movement. "That's too bad, but perhaps you'll change your mind."

"I doubt that."

"If you can't tell, I'm pretty persistent," Everett replied.

"I've noticed. You ran my poor brother off with that look you gave him."

Everett grinned unabashedly. "Did I? I just wanted some time alone with you."

"I'm sorry to have wasted your time, since I'm not on the market. But my pastries are," Mariah replied, "and you seem to like the scones. Can I get a variety box for you to take home? We have orange, lemon, triple berry and blueberry. Or perhaps something chocolate? Like an éclair?"

"Ah, the lady is changing the subject," Everett said, as she moved away from him toward the register.

She gave him her friendliest smile. "I'm starting a new business, Mr. Myers, and my focus has to be on making it a success."

He nodded. "I can appreciate that."

She frowned.

"No, I can," he declared. "Ensuring that my family's legacy continues is important to me, since my father left running the hotels to me."

"Omigod!" Mariah clapped her hand to her mouth. "You're Everett Myers."

He adjusted his tie and smiled with his eyes as she realized exactly who he was. "That's right."

"Of Myers Hotels," Mariah finished, as understanding dawned. "I'm sorry, I didn't realize…"

"Would that have changed your answer?"

"About?"

"Dating me?"

Mariah snorted. "No, it wouldn't."

He let out a full and masculine laugh. "I guess I'm a bit rusty, as I have been out of practice."

"Better luck next time."

He took a step backward. "Are you saying that I might have the opportunity to redeem myself and get another chance with you?"

"N-no. No." Mariah shook her head. "You misunderstood me."

"Did I?"

"Y-yes." She tucked her hair behind her ear. "Are you always this infuriating?"

"Only with you." He smiled.

Mariah let out a deep sigh. "You should really work on accepting the word *no*."

"Oh, I can," Everett said. "But I don't think that's why you turned me down."

"What do you mean?"

"I think you're afraid," he said, searching her eyes. "Because you felt the sparks between us as much as I did, but you're too afraid to act on it yet. And that's fine. I can wait. I'm a patient man when it comes to getting what I want."

"Why, of all the arrogant things—"

He pointed to the display. "I'll definitely have some of those delicious crumpets you fed me earlier."

He gave her a wink and Mariah's stomach lurched. Resisting Everett Myers was not going to be easy. But for her own peace of mind she knew she would have to, because her poor heart could not withstand being broken again.

After Everett Myers walked away with his box of pastries, Mariah was perplexed. How was it that he could sense her unease in such a short time? Usually she kept her emotions in check, so much so that even her family didn't know what was she thinking or feeling. Why? Because she was always looking out for their needs above her own. Even though she was the youngest, Mariah had always taken care of her older brothers. She'd been wired that way.

It had annoyed her ex-husband that she was so selfless. He'd always tell her to do more for herself, and she had. The one thing she'd always wanted was a baby. So when they'd had trouble conceiving early on in their marriage, she'd done everything in her power to ensure their success.

She'd spent three of the five years of their marriage in the pursuit of parenthood—a chase that went nowhere. At first she'd been unconcerned by her inability to conceive, but as each month passed, Mariah became further discouraged. When the doctor finally suggested aggressive fertility treatments, Rich hadn't been on board. He'd told Mariah he would be happy if it was just the two of them, but she'd always dreamed of motherhood and hadn't been willing to throw in the towel. The treatments caused a strain on her marriage, however, and Mariah didn't exactly help the situation by quitting her high-stress job for her phantom baby.

Instead, she'd watched everything she ate, even gave up caffeine and alcohol, as the doctors instructed. But nothing worked. Eventually Rich had had enough and told her their marriage was over. She'd thrown adoption on the table, but he had long ago given up on them, and they decided to separate amicably. Rich had even agreed to pay alimony, which had allowed Mariah to contribute her share of the bakery start-up.

"Mariah, there you are," Belinda Drayson-Jones said when she found her hiding behind the register. "You've been a hard woman to catch up with today."

"I'm sorry, cuz," Mariah said as she watched Everett interact with Chase, who couldn't resist stopping the hotelier before he could exit the bakery. Mariah was sure Chase was trying to pick his brain about some business deal, because her brother was all about the numbers.

Her cousin glanced behind her to find the object of Mariah's attention. "I'm not," she responded. "If that's who had you occupied."

Mariah blinked and returned her attention to Belinda. She was happy that her cousin had flown from Chicago for the grand opening of the bakery. They'd grown close during her marriage, when Mariah and Rich had lived in Chicago. "What did you say?"

Belinda chuckled. "Someone is sure infatuated. Who is that?"

"Just a guy who asked me out."

"Did he? And what was your answer?" she asked, leaning forward with eager interest.

"I told him no, of course," Mariah answered, stepping from behind the counter, even though she couldn't help hazarding a glance at Everett. When she did, she caught him staring at her, too, so she quickly looked away. "You know I'm not ready to jump into dating. It's only been a year since Rich and I separated."

"True," Belinda said. "But if you're honest with yourself, you'll admit your marriage was over well before then and was just limping along."

Mariah frowned deeply. "Thanks a lot, Belinda."

"I'm not trying to hurt you, baby girl." Her cousin reached for her hand and gave it a squeeze, "But you know I speak the truth."

"I suppose, but it's hard to hear nonetheless."

Belinda nodded. "I know. But it's time you start your life over, Mariah. You can't continue looking back at the past."

"How can I not, when my past could affect my future?" Mariah asked, as she watched Everett Myers leave Lillian's.

"Because marriages fail every day." Belinda fell silent for several long moments before saying. "Let me ask you something. Would you have left Rich if he hadn't left you?"

Mariah shook her head. "No, I wouldn't."

"Why?"

"Because I thought that if I just persevered for the both of us, it would get better."

"Did you ever think that perhaps Richard wasn't meant for you?"

"And he is?" Mariah pointed to the door Everett had just exited.

"No, but you have to get back on the horse eventually."

"That's easy for you to say," Mariah responded. "You're married to Malik and you guys are wonderful together."

"It didn't start out like that," Belinda said. "I fought my attraction to Malik, but in the end, I couldn't deny it."

"Yeah, well, there may have been some initial sparks

with Everett, but I need some time to sort through my feelings and my life without jumping back into the relationship foray."

"Who said anything about a relationship?" Belinda replied. "But a date is harmless. What could it hurt?"

Mariah rubbed her chin. A date with anyone other than alpha male Everett Myers might be harmless. But Mariah's sixth sense told her he would be anything but.

"Daddy, you're home!" EJ shouted when Everett stepped through the door of his penthouse apartment several hours later. Everett placed the box of scones from Lillian's on the side table.

"I'm sorry, Mr. Myers," his housekeeper said, rushing after the boy.

"It's okay, Margaret." He halted her, raising his hand. "You go on with your day while EJ and I catch up."

"Sure thing, Mr. Myers," the housekeeper said as she headed off toward the back of the apartment.

He lifted his eight-year-old son into his arms and ruffled his curly hair. He'd inherited the soft curls from his mother, along with that impish grin he was sporting right now. EJ reminded Everett of Sara, and it sometimes made him sad that she wasn't here to see their son grow up. Other times, it reminded him just how lucky he was.

"How's my boy?" Everett asked as he carried him to his study.

"I'm good," EJ answered, looking down at him.

"How was school?" He lowered EJ to the floor and then sat in his recliner to hear about his son's day, while EJ sat on the adjacent ottoman. It was their daily routine and a way for Everett to catch up on what happened.

"Fine, but I need you to sign off on a field trip." EJ produced a slip of paper from his back pocket.

"When's this?" Everett asked. Although he had a busy schedule as president of Myers Hotels and his own business, Myers Coffee Roasters, he made a point of attending EJ's field trips as a chaperone when his schedule permitted.

"At the end of the month."

"Sounds like fun. I'll be there."

"Aww, Dad," EJ sighed. "You don't have to come every time."

Everett frowned. "You don't want me to come?" He was crushed. He thought these were moments EJ would treasure, because Everett made time for him despite his busy schedule.

"It's not that…"

"Then what is it?"

EJ lowered his head and was silent.

"Well? I'm waiting."

His son's curly head popped up. "It's just that I don't want the other kids to think I'm uncool because my dad is a chaperone."

Everett smiled as he breathed a sigh of relief. He knew there would be a time when he would have to pump the brakes, pull back and not be so overprotective, but he'd thought that was a few years away. He was wrong. "If I promise to be a 'cool dad,' can I still come? What do you say?"

"Okay, but only if you promise not to embarrass me."

Everett chuckled as he held out his hand for a father-son handshake. "Sounds like a deal to me. By the way, I brought a treat for you."

"Oh, yeah? What'd you bring me?" EJ asked.

Everett rose from the recliner. "I'll be right back." He returned moments later holding the box of goodies from Lillian's. "I brought you these." He handed it to EJ. With the bakery's signature label on the top and the deliciously sweet aroma of fresh baked goodies emanating from within, he knew EJ would be in heaven.

His son's large, dark brown eyes opened wide with interest and he started to open the box, but Everett slapped his hand away.

"After dinner," he said. "Miss Margaret would kill me if I allowed you to eat that beforehand."

"Can't I have just one?" EJ gave him his best puppy dog look.

"Sorry, kid," Everett said. "That doesn't work on me, but good try. I promise we'll have them after dinner."

"All right," EJ replied. "How was your day, Dad?"

Everett was surprised sometimes when his son inquired after him. He was supposed to be the parent, not the other way around. But Everett suspected that EJ was curious why pretty much all he did was work, then come home most nights. Everett didn't have a social life to speak of.

Occasionally he went out on a date with someone his parents or friends fixed him up with, but most of those fizzled when the women realized he wasn't interested in marriage or commitment. They assumed he was in the market for a wife and mother for EJ, but were sorely disappointed by the end of the evening, or in some case by the second or third date, when they realized he wasn't budging.

It wasn't as if he was still mourning for Sara. He'd finally gotten over the tragic loss and had picked up the pieces of his life. He just hadn't been sure he was ready for another serious commitment, until today, when he'd seen Mariah Drayson. He wasn't sure why meeting the woman had him reevaluating his stance on marriage and commitment, but he was.

"Dad's day was good," Everett finally responded. "I

found that new bakery." He pointed to the box. "Has me thinking of new ideas."

"Like what?" EJ sat cross-legged on the ottoman and propped his head in his hands with rapt attention.

"Like expanding our coffee business at the bakery."

The idea had come to him almost immediately as he'd watched the large crowd at the bakery. What if he offered Myers coffee there for folks to buy along with their pastries? It would be a win-win for both firms, but especially Lillian's. Having the Myers brand for purchase on-site would only authenticate Lillian's promise that they offered the best and highest quality of products, given that Myers coffee was available only in high-end restaurants and coffee shops throughout Seattle.

"Sounds cool, Dad."

"Thanks, son." Everett smiled. "How about we get cleaned up and have some dinner?"

"Sounds like a plan."

Everett only hoped that Mariah and her brothers approved of his idea. It was good business and it would also give him the opportunity to spend some time with Mariah and get to know her better. He knew his play was somewhat obvious, but if she wouldn't agree to have dinner with him as a man, perhaps he could appeal to her as a business colleague. Time would tell.

"It was a wonderful turnout," Shari Drayson told Mariah after all the guests had gone and they were cleaning up after the grand opening. "I'm sure Lillian's of Seattle will be a great success."

"Thank you." Mariah smiled from ear to ear. It was great to hear such high praise from her cousin, given that Lillian had entrusted the flagship location to Shari several years ago. Mariah greatly respected Shari not only as baker, but as a businesswoman. When she'd lived in Chicago, Mariah had sat in on one of the family board meetings, and she could see it wasn't easy wrangling with all those personalities and big egos. But Shari did it with ease. Heck, she made it look simple, when Mariah knew it was the opposite.

Her cousin Belinda hadn't been happy with Lillian's decision for Shari to run Lillian's of Chicago. Mariah had always suspected that Belinda was Aunt Lillian's favorite because she'd followed behind their aunt when she was a child and was always in the bakery as her helper. And even though Mariah was closer in age to Shari, she'd always favored Belinda, who was several years older, and she'd wanted to be just like her. Belinda had a great sense of style, dressed in designer duds and never went out of the house without her makeup on. It also hadn't helped that Shari had gotten pregnant when she was in college, and had a son, Andre, while Mariah had been unable to conceive. Why was it so easy for some women to conceive without even trying, while she desperately wanted a baby and had struggled to get pregnant?

"Mariah?"

"Hmm…?" She drifted out of her reverie.

"I was asking about your parents," Shari said. "They didn't seem excited by the opening."

Mariah nodded. "They don't really support our endeavor, but that's fine. I intend to prove them wrong. Show them that Chase, Jackson and I have what it takes to get the job done."

"That's admirable," Shari said. "But I have to tell you it'll be a challenge, especially having two brothers involved."

"Because I'm a woman?" Mariah offered.

Shari nodded. "Sometimes it's hard for men to take direction from a woman."

"Was it like that for you in Chicago?"

Shari chuckled. "That and then some," she replied, "Everyone thought Carter, as the oldest grandchild, would have been chosen to run Lillian's, but instead Grandma picked me. Why? Because I have the business acumen, with my degree, and the creativity, thanks to the cake mix idea I came up with, to run the front of the house at Lillian's while Carter runs the back. And it's also why she chose you for the helm here."

Mariah smiled. "How do you manage running the front of the house and baking? Because you make it look easy." She'd already felt herself somewhat stressed at the prospect, even though she found it incredibly rewarding, more so than she ever had when she'd worked as an advertising executive.

"It's about balance," Shari said, "Trust me, it's not easy running the bakery business and being a wife and mother, especially now."

"Why now?" Mariah inquired. Unlike Jack, she had a healthy curiosity about her Chicago cousins and was eager to learn more about them.

Shari rubbed her stomach and then looked into Mariah's eyes with a huge grin, "Grant and I are expecting our second child. We're about to make Andre a big brother."

All the air in the room seemed to vanquish, as if sucked out by a backdraft in a fire, and Mariah thought she might expire on the spot. Not that she didn't wish Shari every happiness, but this was the last thing she wanted to hear.

Yet there was nothing she could do except stand there and fake a smile, because Shari was still speaking.

"We didn't want to announce it yet," she was saying,

"until I was in my second trimester, but I think it's safe now to tell the family."

Mariah pasted a smile onto her face even though deep down she knew it was less than genuine. She so desperately wanted to be in Shari's place, pregnant with her own child, but it wasn't in the cards for her. "That's wonderful, Shari. I'm very happy for you."

"Anyway, it looks like we're just about finished up here." Her cousin glanced around the nearly empty kitchen.

"Yes, it would appear that way," Mariah responded.

Carter had already quietly sneaked off, no doubt to call his wife, Lorraine Hawthorne-Hayes Drayson, who was at home with their twin boys in Chicago. Not only was Lorraine a twin herself, but apparently twins ran in her family. Given that Carter had been a committed bachelor, it had surprised the family when he'd wasted no time starting a family with the former debutante, whose career as one of Chicago's most sought-after artists allowed her to stay at home with their boys.

Mariah had hoped to spend more time with Belinda, but she had somehow disappeared, too. She was probably trying to catch Malik at the bakery, since he and her brother Drake were holding down the fort in Chicago.

"Let's get out of here." Mariah headed toward the door, with Shari on her heels, and turned off the lights.

As she locked up the bakery, it was hard for her to believe that she'd actually done it. She'd started her own business with her brothers' help. Now what?

Chapter 3

Mariah was the first to arrive at the bakery the next morning. Unlike Chase, who had a set morning routine of cardio and weight training, followed by a healthy breakfast, or Jackson, who was no doubt rolling out of bed late because he'd spent the night having too much fun with some unsuspecting female, Mariah didn't have any of those options. She was alone.

It wasn't that she liked it that way. She'd loved being married and all that it had meant. She'd loved being Mrs. Richard Hems and being part of a couple, a unit and a partnership. She'd always thought her marriage would last. How wrong she'd been, Mariah thought as she opened the back door of the bakery.

She couldn't focus on that now. She knew it wasn't healthy to keep looking back; she had to focus on other things. Namely, on baking all the breakfast goods that she hoped would be necessary for the morning rush. Aunt Lillian believed in providing the freshest baked products each day, so any unpurchased item was given away to a local shelter at the end of the night.

Mariah quickly turned on the lights, grabbed her apron hanging on a hook nearby, and headed toward the kitchen to get down to business.

Two hours later, she was wrist deep in flour when her brother Jack finally deigned to gift her with his presence. She'd already prepared the first batch of pastries, from cinnamon and pecan rolls to Danishes and croissants, for the breakfast rush. She was now starting on the triple berry, blueberry, lemon and orange scones that were a big part of their menu selection.

"Look who finally decided to join me," Mariah said, as he slowly made his way to the sink to wash his hands.

"Don't start, Ri," he replied, using his nickname for her. When he was finished, he grabbed a paper towel and dried his hands.

Mariah quirked her brow. "You were supposed to be here—" she glanced at her watch "—hours ago. I needed help. I haven't even started on the muffins yet."

"I'm sorry, okay?" Jackson responded as he quickly grabbed several mixing bowls and ingredients for the muffins from the cabinets and refrigerator.

She was surprised that for once he offered an apology instead of an excuse. "I presume you were with one of your admirers from the grand opening?" Mariah selected a handful of dough and set it on the already floured counter. She rolled the dough and used a scone cutter to cut out the pieces before placing them on a greased cookie sheet.

Jackson gave her a sly smile. "A gentleman never kisses and tells."

"Well, a certain gentleman needs to set his alarm so he's not late again. I can't do this without you," Mariah replied.

"Duly noted. What's got your panties in a twist?"

"Nothing."

Jackson stopped mixing the dry ingredients and looked at his sister.

Could he see that she hadn't really slept that well? The strain of the previous day had caught up to Mariah. She couldn't pinpoint exactly what had made her uneasy. Was it their parents' less than enthusiastic response to the bakery opening? Or perhaps it was meeting that sexy stranger who'd caught her eye from the second she'd seen him strolling down the sidewalk, and turning down his offer of a date? Or maybe it was Shari revealing that she was pregnant yet again, when Mariah's hopes of mother-hood had been repeatedly dashed year after year during her five-year marriage? Maybe it was a combination of all three causing her lack of sleep. In any event, she'd been up with the roosters.

"You're frowning," Jackson said. "Did something happen last night? Did you go out with Everett Myers?"

Mariah spun around to face him. "Why would you ask such a thing?"

Her brother shrugged. "I don't know. Maybe 'cause the guy was really feeling you and cock-blocked anyone from getting close to you during the party."

Mariah chuckled. She hadn't realized that was what he was doing, but he had made his intentions clear, especially when he'd grasped her arm and damn near demanded she give him a tour of the bakery.

"C'mon," Jackson said, "I know it's been a long time since you've been on that horse—the dating horse, that is—but even you can recognize a man's interest in you." When she didn't respond right away, he asked, "Can't you?"

Mariah let out a long, exasperated sigh. "Of course I can. I'm not blind."

"Then why didn't you give the brother a chance?" Jackson inquired.

"I'm just not ready yet."

"Will you ever be?"

Luckily, Mariah didn't have to answer that question because the buzzer on the oven sounded, signaling that her second batch of pastries was ready. She scooted over to remove the delicious treats from the stove, effectively ending their conversation.

They didn't have a chance to pick up where they left off because their third baker arrived. Nancy Alvarez was a middle-aged woman with a background in the bakery business, and she knew her stuff. It had taken some convincing to talk Nancy into working for them, but once Mariah had sweetened the deal by making it part-time, with Mariah taking the early morning shift, she'd acquiesced.

Among the three of them, they were able to get a lot accomplished, and were ready to open their doors at 7:00 a.m. for the breakfast rush.

Since she'd been the first to arrive, Mariah left Jackson and Nancy in the kitchen while she attended to the front of the house. Customers slowly trickled in, wanting delicious baked goods, but eventually business took off and the morning sped by.

Mariah was surprised when Jackson came to relieve her for a short break, so she could get off her feet and have a cup of much-needed coffee.

Mariah went into the office and took a seat. She pulled off her comfortable flats and rubbed her aching arches. She hadn't truly realized just how exhausting running a bakery could be, affecting not just her sleeping routine, but her feet.

Owning and operating a bakery was hard work. The hours were long and the work tiring, but Mariah believed without risk there would be no reward.

Chase hadn't arrived yet. He typically didn't show up until 9:00 a.m., and Mariah envied his banker's hours from nine to five. He'd soon be scouring the pile of bills she'd seen sitting on his desk—invoices for the inventory of ingredients and equipment that it took to run Lillian's. Money was constantly going out and they would need to start pouring some back in to ensure the firm's viability.

She was leaning back in the chair, strategizing on an advertising campaign that would help boost business, when Jackson poked his head into the room. "You have a visitor."

"Who is it?" she asked, looking up, but he was already gone.

Mariah sighed. She didn't have time for visitors. She needed to come up with a plan to get Lillian's name out there. The reporter yesterday had been right when he'd indicated that Sweetness Bakery had a solid and long-standing reputation in Seattle and it would be hard to compete against them. But Mariah knew Lillian's recipes were superior and that eventually they would succeed.

Slipping her flats back on, she rose from her desk. After checking herself in the mirror that she'd installed in the office to ensure she would always be respectable before greeting the public, she headed out of the room.

When she made it to the storefront area, only a handful of customers were munching on their baked goods at the small countertop and bank of tables. Most were probably enjoying the free Wi-Fi Lillian's offered.

Jackson gave her a wink as he dealt with a customer at the register. "He's over there." Her brother inclined his head toward the far side of the store.

Mariah noticed a man kneeling in front of the display there, but she couldn't tell who it was. But as she approached and he rose to his feet, there was no mistaking the visitor's identity. It was none other than Everett Myers.

Fortifying herself and letting a rush of air out her lungs, Mariah walked toward the counter. "Good morning," she said with a smile. "May I help you?"

He returned the smile. "Good morning, Mariah."

"Mr. Myers, what can I get for you this morning?" she asked, purposely using his last name as she turned around. She grasped two plastic gloves and opened the display case.

He looked down at the pastries and then back up at her, penetrating her with his dark gaze. "Everything looks good."

The way he was gazing at her with such undisguised lust, Mariah doubted he was taking about the pastries. "Might I suggest the cheese Danish? We just baked them fresh."

"That would be lovely, but only if you join me?"

"Join you?" Mariah squeaked. Her voice sounded small even to her. "I couldn't possibly. In case you haven't noticed, I'm working."

"Looks like your brother has everything under control. What could it hurt to take a break and keep me company?"

He made it sound so simple that she should join him, and since resisting seemed only to incite his interest, as she'd learned yesterday, she said, "All right, but I can only spare a few minutes."

Everett glanced down at his watch. "A few minutes is all I have. And I will take your suggestion of a Danish along with a bottled water."

"Coming right up." She took a deep breath and reminded herself that Everett was just a man. But why did he have to look so darn handsome in his charcoal-gray suit and crisp white dress shirt that perfectly fit his athletic physique? Mariah could only wonder what lay beneath the clothes as she reached for the pastry and placed it on a glass plate, which was Lillian's signature. Aunt Lillian believed in serving people as if they were at her home, and not have them eat off paper or plastic. When she'd grasped a bottled water from the refrigerated case behind her, Mariah took the plate and mug to the table he'd secured.

She couldn't help but notice the smug smile Everett gave her as she left the display area, or the way his eyes roamed over her entire frame, taking her in from root to tip. "Here you are." She placed the items in front of him.

He rose to his feet. "Please have a seat." He pulled out a chair for her before resuming his own.

"Thank you," Mariah said, "So what brings you by, Mr. Myers?"

"Please call me Everett. All my friends do."

Mariah's brow rose a fraction. "And are we friends?"

"I certainly hope so," he answered, "If you hadn't noticed, I've been trying to remedy that."

Mariah couldn't resist a smile. "Yes, I have, and I appreciate the grand gesture of your stopping by, Mr.— Everett," she finally said. "But you needn't bother or try so hard. As I told you yesterday, I'm not interested in dating anyone right now."

"Does that mean you might be later?"

Mariah inwardly chuckled. Of course he would pick up on her word choice. "Later might be a long time coming."

"I can wait."

She placed both elbows on the table and steepled her fingers together as she watched him. "Am I a challenge to you, Everett?"

He didn't answer, because he'd chosen that moment to take a forkful of the Danish, and groaned aloud, causing a place deep inside Mariah to answer, just as it had yesterday. Her breasts tightened in response. She, or rather her body, was not immune to the virility of this man. "This is divine. Did you make it?"

Mariah flushed. "Yes, how did you know?"

He looked deep into her eyes. "I don't know. I guess that, because it was made with such love, I knew it had to be you."

Mariah swallowed hard and licked her lips. Everett's eyes followed her every movement and it made her uneasy that he was watching her so intently. "Um, I'm not sure what I'm supposed to say to that."

Everett took another forkful of pastry. "You don't have to say anything, since it's I who should be thanking you for the delicious start to my day. If you don't mind my asking, how did you get into baking?"

"I started baking in my tween years when I went to visit my aunt Lillian."

"Lillian Reynolds Drayson?"

"Yes, how did you—" Mariah stopped herself. Everett struck her as the type of man who never left anything to chance. If he wanted to know more about Aunt Lillian, he'd probably done his research. "Anyway, I used to visit her in Chicago during the summers and I would join her at the bakery. I learned the basics of how to bake at a young age. Once I grew older and was married, I had a lot of extra time on my hands and I began dabbling and trying new recipes."

"Your husband left you alone?" Everett sat back in his chair.

"It wasn't like that."

"No?" He quirked a brow as if he didn't quite believe her, but then shrugged. "If you were mine, you would only know one position and that's lying on your back."

Mariah flushed immediately at Everett's provocative statement. She'd never been so attracted to and aroused by another man before.

He gave her a mischievous grin. "Did I say something to offend your delicate sensibilities?"

"No, I'm just not used to men speaking to me like..." Mariah was at a loss for words.

"So openly about what they want?" he inquired. "I know what I want, and when I want something in life, I go for it with gusto, no holds barred. You get my drift?"

His eyes never left her face and Mariah was under no false illusion about what he meant. When Everett desired something or some*one*, he was fully committed. He was in. Mariah wondered what it would have been like if Richard had been like that in their marriage. Maybe if he'd been all in, their relationship wouldn't have ended and she wouldn't be divorced at twenty-six.

"Mariah?" Everett cocked his head to one side to peer at her questioningly. "Did I lose you?"

She blinked several times, bringing him and their conversation back into focus. "No, you didn't, but I really do have to get back to work."

"You're doing it again," he said.

"What's that?"

"Running away," he responded. "But lucky you, I like to chase." He rose from his seat, pulled several bills from his wallet and laid them on the table. He stepped toward her and Mariah was frozen, unsure of what to do. Was he going to make a move? Was he going to kiss her?

Instead, he just softly caressed her cheek with the palm of his hand, which was warm and tender, and said, "I'll see you soon."

And he was gone. Leaving Mariah to wonder and secretly hope when that might be.

* * *

Outside the bakery, Everett stared into the window at Mariah as she walked back toward the kitchen. What on earth had possessed him to come here just a day after she'd turned down a date with him? Although he'd dreamed of a certain beautiful honey blonde in his dreams, he certainly hadn't woken up this morning with the intention of acting on any of his desires. But somehow, as he'd exited the penthouse garage on his way to Myers Hotel, his car had taken him in a different direction, directly to Lillian's Bakery.

When he arrived, he'd thought about getting something to go, but on the other hand, he couldn't resist the pull he'd felt yesterday with Mariah. He'd wanted more. So he'd asked her brother to find her. And when she'd come out to the storefront, she'd looked just as sexy and scrumptious as he remembered. Sure, she was wearing a less than flattering apron that covered all her God-given assets. That was why he'd asked her to come around from the display—so he could take another real good look at her. Perhaps he'd hyped her up in his dreams to be more than she was, and reality would be like a cold splash of water in his face. But he hadn't been wrong.

Instead, when she'd come from behind the counter wearing low-rise jeans that sat seductively over her hips and a crop top that gave him just a hint of stomach and skin, Everett had been eager to know what secrets lay hidden beneath them. It hadn't helped that her full, round breasts were pressing against the thin top she wore, showing him that she might be a bit chilled.

Jeez. He glanced down at his watch and realized he'd better get to the hotel so he could make the morning's meeting, rather than stew over a baker who, if she had her way, could take him or leave him. Everett quickly drove the short distance to the hotel.

As he did, he realized he hadn't expected the full force of Mariah's sexiness to hit him with such magnitude as it had that morning, but he'd felt it deep in his groin. He'd had a hard-on happening when she hadn't so much as touched him. Matter-of-fact, she'd tried her best to keep him at bay throughout their interlude. That is, until he'd stuck his foot in his mouth and revealed exactly where she'd be if she were his woman. She'd be on her back in his bed and he'd ravish her all night long until she begged him to come inside her.

When had he gotten so horny? It hadn't been that long since he'd been with a woman, had it? Everett pondered the thought as he rode the elevator up to the administrative offices of Myers Hotels. Walking through the lobby had been a blur. As the doors opened, he blinked to get himself back in the game and on his morning routine.

The meeting was already under way when he arrived, and Everett merely stood back against the door, listening as the hotel's general manager went over the day's events.

When he was done, he glanced up and saw Everett. "Mr. Myers, is there anything you'd like to add?"

Everett shook his head. "Not at all, you go ahead. I'll just listen in."

Thankfully, the hotel pretty much ran itself, with Everett stepping in only periodically, when a major decision needed to be made. Hiring the best and brightest in the hospitality industry and paying them a fair wage had ensured that Myers Hotels were respected in the industry and one of the more sought after places of employment in the Seattle hotel market.

He slipped out before the meeting concluded and headed to his office. His executive assistant, Mildred, was waiting for him with his messages. There were the usual suspects, along with a message from EJ's school.

Everett immediately thanked Mildred for the update and closed the door to his office. Being a father came first, before business. It had been that way with his own dad and Everett was ensuring he did the same. Although Stephen Myers was a serious and austere man to some, he had always made sure that Everett and his mother were his top priority. Even when his father had been building the Myers Hotels into a well-respected luxury chain, he'd made certain he had time for his family. If ever Everett had a problem, his father had always been there to help him solve it. It was because of him that Everett was the man he was today. And it's why he'd wanted to emulate him by marrying his first love. He'd thought he and Sara would be together forever, until fate struck.

Everett picked up the receiver and dialed the principal of EJ's school, who'd left the message for him.

"Mr. Myers, thank you so much for the quick response," the woman said.

"When it comes my son, nothing is more important," Everett replied. "What's going on?"

"Well, EJ was having a hard time today, so I brought him to my office."

"Why?" Everett sat upright in his chair. "Is something wrong? Is my son okay?" Ever since Sara's death, he had become somewhat paranoid and hypervigilant about EJ's safety, but how could he not? EJ was all he had left.

"He's fine, he's fine. Physically, that is."

Everett understood her meaning. "And emotionally?"

"I learned there were some students picking on him…" She paused. "Because his mother is gone."

"I see." Everett's voice was clipped.

"I've disciplined them accordingly," the principal continued, "but EJ was clearly upset, as he has every right to be, and I just thought that—"

"I'll be there in twenty," Everett said, and hung up the phone. He grabbed his keys and sunglasses as he headed for the doorway.

"Is everything okay, Mr. Myers?" Mildred asked in obvious concern, since he'd only just arrived.

"It's EJ." And with those words, he was out the door.

He made it to the school in fifteen minutes, parking his car in the tow-away zone. No one would dare tow his vehicle, given the thousands he'd donated to this private school.

The look on his face must have said it all, because the receptionist rose as he walked straight past the front counter and toward the principal's office. He knocked twice and didn't wait for a response before entering.

"Mr. Myers!" The principal jumped up from her desk.

"I'm here to pick up my son."

He glanced across the room and saw EJ sitting at a table, while the principal looked up, startled, from her computer.

"Of course, of course." She rushed toward him. "And I'm sorry to have to bother you," she said, closing the door behind him so they could speak in private. "Just given the time of year, with Mother's Day coming in May, I thought it prudent you come."

"Thank you for calling me."

"You're most certainly welcome." She touched his arm. "And I can assure you that we don't tolerate bullying of any kind. The children have been reprimanded and their parents were contacted."

"I appreciate that," Everett said. "EJ, grab your things," he told his son over her shoulder, since he was several inches taller. He bent down to whisper in the principal's ear in a lethal tone, "Let's ensure this doesn't happen again."

The woman nodded.

Once they were outside the school, Everett stopped and turned to his son. "How you doing, buddy?"

EJ just he kept walking toward the car. Everett understood the cue that he didn't want to talk here, so he unlocked the Cadillac Escalade and EJ jumped into the passenger seat.

Everett came around to the driver's side. He turned on the engine, but thought better of it and said, "Do you want to talk about it now?"

"Can't we just go?"

"Not when something's on your mind," Everett responded. "You know you can talk to me about anything and I will always sympathize and be here to listen."

EJ turned to face the window and said nothing.

Everett sighed as he put the Escalade in gear. "All right. Well, when you want to talk about it, I'm here for you, okay?"

EJ didn't answer; he just nodded his head.

Chapter 4

Everett wasn't surprised when EJ claimed he was sick the following morning. Everett suspected it was a ruse, and normally would have made him go to school and face his bullies, because that's what a father taught his son. But in this instance, Everett couldn't make the boy do so, not when he knew this hurt went deeper because it was over the loss of his mother. He went to work instead, leaving EJ with Margaret, who'd keep any eye on him until Everett returned later that afternoon. He would make it an early day, so he could spend some time with his son.

But first he had a strong desire for another one of Lillian's pastries, or so he told himself as he walked toward the bakery. He opened the front door with a flourish and a bell signaled his arrival.

Everett was happy to find Mariah at the front counter instead of Jackson. "Good morning," he said, strolling toward her.

She sighed in apparent exasperation at seeing him for the second day in a row. "Everett."

"You're looking lovely today," he said, admiring the way her glorious honey-blond hair hung in soft waves to her shoulders. She'd clearly done something different with the style, but he didn't care. It just made her look all the more attractive to him. He'd love to rake his hands through it as he brought her mouth closer to his.

He liked everything about Mariah, from the color of her eyes, which reminded him of sandalwood, to her delicate round little nose, to the sinful curve of her alluring lips. Lips that he would love to kiss, tease and suck into his mouth.

"Everett?" Mariah was saying his name again and he had to stop staring at her as if she were a fresh piece of meat.

"Yes?"

"I asked you what you would like," she said, looking at him strangely.

"If I said you, would that be too much?"

She grinned at his come-on. "Are you always this much of a flirt?"

"Only with you."

"I'm flattered, really," she said, as the chime of the doorbell indicated another customer had just entered the bakery, "but as I told you before—"

"You're not interested," he stated, cutting her off.

She pointed her index finger at him. "See, you really are as smart as the internet says."

"Have you been looking me up?" Everett was intrigued as the familiar air of electricity he felt on the prior occasions with Mariah sizzled between them. There was no mistaking it. She was not as immune to his charms as she was leading him to believe.

Mariah flushed and he could see he was right.

"There's a line forming," she said, as yet another customer came through the bakery door. "What can I get you?"

"If you're not on the menu, then I guess I'll have to settle for one of those," Everett responded, pointing to the assortment of quiches they'd prepared as a breakfast selection. "And another of those scones from yesterday." He would bring a treat home to EJ in the hopes that it would cheer him up.

Mariah smiled. "Excellent choice." She opened the display case to procure his items. Once she'd rung them up, she said, "Have a great day and see you soon."

His brow rose a fraction. "Would you like to? See me, that is?"

"I always like paying customers."

He laughed as he made his way out the door. Mariah might be telling him to go away, but he suspected she was starting to enjoy seeing him come around just as much as he was enjoying seeing her each day. And if he had his way, it wouldn't be long before the walls she had erected around her would come tumbling down.

Mariah was grateful when she saw the back of Everett's head as he left the bakery. Today made the third time she'd seen him in as many days. She'd told him in no uncertain terms that she wasn't interested in dating him, but he kept coming back. The man was relentless and she wasn't sure how long she could keep turning him down, when it would just make more sense to go out with him and put him out of his misery. Maybe then he would see that they weren't a match and she was completely out of his league.

Everett was handsome and, according to everything she'd read online, wealthy as sin. Despite herself, she'd been unable to contain her curiosity about the man after he'd visited the bakery twice, and she'd tried to absorb as much information as possible on the man. She'd learned via an internet search about the accidental death of his wife, Sara. But the details were vague because Everett had secluded himself, keeping out of the news, pretty much right after the accident.

According to sources, he was currently single and had been that way since becoming widowed. So what could he possibly see in a newly divorced baker from an upper-middle-class family? For some reason Mariah presented a challenge to him, but perhaps as soon as he won he'd stop his pursuit of her.

"Was that Myers again?" Jackson inquired, coming up behind her and heading to the second register. He turned to the next customer in line. "Can I help you?" he asked.

"It was," Mariah said, as she smiled and handed her customer some change.

"Wow! Someone's sprung on you," Jackson said, after he'd fished out several pastries and boxed them up for his customer. "Here you go. Have a nice day."

Several minutes later, the storefront was empty and it was just the two of them, so Mariah turned to glare at her brother. "It's not that serious."

"Apparently it is for him," Jackson retorted. "He's been here three days straight."

"You can't count the opening, because he just met me," Mariah responded, reaching for a cloth underneath the register to wipe down the counter.

"I sure as hell can. The man was enthralled with you. Trust me, I know when a guy is interested."

Mariah laughed. "I guess it would take one to know one." She bumped his hip and continued wiping the displays.

"So what are you going to do about it?" He folded his arms across his chest.

"Nothing. Eventually, he'll tire of the rejections and move on."

"Ha!" Jackson laughed as he headed back to the kitchen. "You don't know men at all."

Mariah thought about her brother's words later that evening in her apartment, when she was cuddled with a bowl of popcorn, watching a romantic comedy. Jackson had been right that she didn't know men at all. Her experience with the opposite sex was limited to her college career before she'd met Rich, and there hadn't been much to speak of. She'd always been into her studies, leaving very little time for dating.

Now she had a rich, successful businessman like Everett Myers interested in her and all she could do was run. Mariah wasn't proud of it. She'd always prided herself on being a person who persevered even when things got difficult, as she had with her inability to conceive. She'd been the one who'd dug in the trenches, refusing to give up on her marriage even though she suspected Rich had checked out. Mariah had thought that she could win him back somehow and that in time he'd see that she'd done all of it for them, but he hadn't.

Mariah considered it one of her greatest failures. It was why she was reluctant to go down that path again so soon with Everett, even though she found him stunningly gorgeous. Every time he came into the bakery, Mariah caught herself holding her breath, and when he touched her, her entire body came alive. It made her feel things she hadn't felt in a long time, such as desire and passion. Whenever he was near, her skin became prickly and the place between her legs became heated. She wanted to push the feelings away, but Everett wouldn't let up. And did she really want him to? Of one thing she was sure—Everett could quench all her desires.

If he continued his quest of stopping by the bakery, Mariah wasn't sure just how long she could hold out before she finally gave in.

Later that afternoon, Everett returned to his penthouse and found EJ sitting at the breakfast counter eating one of the pastries he'd brought from Lillian's yesterday, while Margaret was at the stove, no doubt starting supper. Everett chuckled inwardly. Clearly, the boy wasn't that sick if he could enjoy the delicious concoction.

"Looks like someone's feeling better," Everett said, placing his briefcase on the counter.

EJ smiled and looked up, his face smeared with chocolate. Everett reached for a paper towel and threw it at him. "Wipe your face," he said with a laugh. "You have chocolate all over it."

"This is good, Dad," EJ replied, after wiping his mouth. "Where'd you get it?" After dinner last night, they'd been too full for dessert.

"Lillian's. And I brought another." He held up the box from that morning.

EJ reached for it. "I'll take it."

"Not before dinner, you won't."

"I was telling him the same thing, Mr. Myers, but he insisted on eating that one." Margaret gestured to the empty saucer in front of EJ.

"You'd better listen to Miss Margaret," Everett chided, pointing his finger in EJ's direction. "Don't you give her no sass."

EJ frowned. "I wasn't."

Everett loosened his tie and undid the top button of his shirt as he headed for the refrigerator. He took a bottle of beer out and quickly dispensed with the top before taking a generous swig.

"Why don't you come talk to me?" he suggested as he walked to the living room. "While Margaret finishes up dinner."

He heard an audible sigh, but EJ slipped off the bar stool where he'd been sitting and joined Everett as he settled on the couch. "So are you finally ready to talk to me about what happened yesterday?"

EJ shook his head., "No, but I guess you're going to make me?"

"Something like that."

EJ sunk deeper into the sofa cushions and was quiet for several long moments before he finally spoke. "There were some kids razzing me because I don't have a mother."

Everett frowned and sat upright. He hated hearing EJ talk like that. "You had a mother, EJ. Her name was Sara. She's not here with us now, but she loved you very much." It was important to Everett that EJ remembered her and knew that he'd been loved and was a product of that love.

"I know that, Dad, but I still don't like hearing about it. Have kids bring it up like I'm some sort of freak or something."

"You're not a freak." Everett patted EJ's thigh. "You're just different. And you have to be okay with that. You still have me, or am I chopped liver or something?" It was one of things he worried about—that somehow he wouldn't be enough for his son. Lord knows, he'd tried to be a father and a mother all rolled into one, but it was hard sometimes.

EJ gave him a reluctant half smile. "No, but it's…it's just not the same."

Everett wasted no time pulling his son into a firm hug and holding him close to his chest. "I know that," he said, leaning back to look at him. "And I know that I can't be your mom, but I promise you I will do my best to be both a mother and father to you. Whatever you need, I'm here." He gazed into EJ's dark eyes, which were cloudy with unshed tears, then tugged him back into his arms. "I'm always here."

"Love you, Daddy," EJ whispered into his chest.

Those three words were all that Everett would ever need.

Mariah stared at her reflection in the mirror in the bathroom of her two-bedroom apartment. She looked pretty darn good if she did say so herself. She was wearing her favorite pair of skinny jeans, a floral tunic and a long dangling necklace. She'd applied a trace of mineral foundation, mascara, and the finishing touch was lipstick. She typically never went to such trouble dressing each morning, since she spent the first few hours of her day in the kitchen. But the thought that Everett might show up again today had her making a special effort. Her stomach was in knots with eager anticipation of his arrival.

She must have been noticeably antsy because later that morning Jackson commented as much. "What's got you so jumpy?" he asked. "Every time the doorbell chimes, I can see you perk up. Are you waiting for someone?" One of his eyebrows rose with amusement. He knew the answer.

"No."

"Liar." He laughed as he continued with the fondant cake he was working on for an upcoming wedding. Jackson had become quite the cake aficionado and they'd already received a few orders.

"Am not."

"You're wearing makeup. And you're dressed up today." He eyed her attire and face before returning to his task.

Mariah glanced down at her outfit. She'd gone for casual chic, so as not to look as if she was *trying* to attract a certain person's attention or advances.

"C'mon, sis, I know you, and you can't get anything by me."

Mariah rolled her eyes and sauntered out of the kitchen. "Whatever." There was no denying that Jackson was right, but that wasn't what irked her. It was Everett. He was late. He usually came around 9:00 a.m. and it was after ten, which meant she'd gone through all this trouble for nothing.

She shouldn't be surprised that he'd finally taken the hint. She had given him the brush-off three times and he must have figured three strikes and he was out. She'd blown it.

The doorbell chimed and Mariah didn't bother looking up this time, so was surprised when she finally did and found his dark brown eyes looking at her.

"Everett." She swallowed the lump that suddenly formed by having the businessman yet again in her crosshairs.

"Hey." He smiled, showing off his sparkling white teeth.

"Hi." Mariah didn't know why she couldn't think of anything but a one-syllable word, and her heart was hammering in her chest.

"Surprised to see me?"

"Actually, no, I'm not," she replied, finding her voice. "You've been persistent, so I doubted today would be any different."

"Is that why you dressed up for me today?" Everett asked, raking every inch of her figure with his magnetic gaze.

Mariah started to say no, but knew it would be a bold-faced lie, so she led with the truth. "What if I did?"

Everett's eyes darkened and his expression shifted from flirtatious to something different, something she didn't recognize but knew to be dangerous. "Come from behind the counter and I'll show you."

Mariah wasn't sure she wanted to leave the safety that the counter provided. Everett looked as if he was ready to pounce and she wasn't certain she could or *would* fight him off.

"Mariah." He said her name again and it sounded silky and seductive coming from his lips.

She instinctively obeyed, ignoring the warning signals going off in her brain to beware. When she rounded the corner of the counter, Everett captured her hand and brought her forward until she was inches from his face, from his lips. Sensuously full lips that she had a hard time not focusing on.

"I'm glad you've come around to seeing things my way," he said, as his large hands skimmed over her forearms.

"Did I have much choice?"

He chuckled. "No, I didn't plan on giving up. But I have to admit that I didn't come here solely to see you."

"No?" She tried not to appear offended by the comment.

"Don't look so crestfallen," he said, caressing her chin with the pad of his thumb. "I have a business offer for you."

Why did he have to keep touching her? It was scrambling her brain and she couldn't think straight. "B-business? What business would you and I have?"

"That's what I would like to discuss with you, over lunch if you're free."

Mariah glanced behind her toward the kitchen. "I don't know. I haven't left the bakery since we opened."

"Can't your brother manage things in your absence for an hour or so?"

She blinked rapidly. "I—I suppose."

"Good." Everett obviously considered the topic closed. "Grab your purse."

"I didn't say I would go." She stood rooted to the spot.

He cocked a brow. "Are we really going to act like you weren't waiting for my arrival? If so, we can go back to your administrative offices, where we'd have some privacy, and see if that holds true."

The thought made Mariah warm all over, and nervous at the prospect of being alone with such a virile man, so she took the former option. "Uh—that won't be necessary. Let me just let Jack know, and I'll get my purse."

Several minutes later, she was sliding into Everett's Escalade as he buckled himself into the driver's seat. "I figured we could go to the Myers Hotel. There's a great restaurant and we can get in and out within the hour."

Mariah smiled. "Okay, thank you." She appreciated his thoughtfulness. But that didn't mean she wasn't nervous as hell being in the car alone with the man. A man she had secretly wished for, but still was uneasy being around. She couldn't explain the effect Everett had on her, but she felt entirely out of sorts. Her heart was thumping loudly in her chest and her pulse was beating erratically. So she tried to focus on something else. "So what kind of business offer did you want to discuss?"

"There will be time for that later," Everett said, looking over at her. "I'd rather know if this will be a one-time event, or will I see you again?"

"That's debatable."

"Then I'll just have to try my best to convince you."

They made it to the Myers Hotel in less than half an hour, and as he'd promised, the maître d' sat them immediately in a private corner booth.

"Thank you, Jacques." Everett said.

"You're most welcome, sir. Enjoy your lunch."

Mariah noticed the way the man showed Everett such deference. "Is it always like that everywhere you go?"

He shrugged. "Not always."

They perused their menus and in no time a waitress materialized to take their drink and lunch orders.

"What's it like to grow up with all this?" Mariah asked, motioning to the opulent decor of the restaurant on the fortieth floor, the windows of which overlooked the bay.

"It wasn't like this always."

"No?"

"No," he stated emphatically. "My father started this company from nothing. He only had the one hotel, which he and my mother put all their savings into. Luckily, with the right investments and partnerships, he was able to make it grow into a chain."

"Which you've taken a step further with your Myers Coffee Roasters importing business and coffeehouses in downtown Seattle."

Everett smiled. "So you really have done your research."

"It always best to know one's opponent."

"I hope that's not how you see me," he said softly, searching her face. "As an opponent."

"How would you like me to see you? As a potential love interest?"

"In time, yes," he responded, his gaze unwavering. "But as I told you, I'm a patient man. I can wait. That which cometh easily, can be easily lost."

Mariah nodded. "So why have you never opened coffeehouses nationwide?"

Everett sat back and stared at Mariah as the waitress returned with their drinks. He noticed how she'd deftly changed the subject to a more acceptable topic. Clearly, his interest in her made her uncomfortable, but at least she wasn't completely retreating as she'd done several days ago. She was slowly giving him an inch and he would take it and then some, but slowly, ever so slowly. His instincts told him that Mariah had been hurt before, which was why she was so cautious. He would have to take his time with her. Woo her.

"I didn't want another large chain," Everett said, finally answering her. "I wanted Myers Coffee Roasters to be high-end, unique, something the consumer couldn't get in any corner coffeehouse in Seattle. Haven't you noticed that the more exclusive something is, the more it's wanted?"

"You have a point there." She sipped on her ice water.

"But there is room for change, which is one of the reasons I wanted to bring you to lunch, among other things."

"Go on."

"I'd like Lillian's of Seattle to carry Myers Coffee Roasters. Both of our brands have a reputation for being the finest around, so I think it's a natural combination. What could be better than coffee with cake? What do you think?"

"Think? I think it's an excellent idea!" Mariah grinned unabashedly.

Everett was thrilled to hear the excitement in her voice at his pitch. He'd been thinking about it ever since he'd heard Lillian's was coming to Seattle. He'd never been a fan of Sweetness Bakery even though they had approached him about offering his coffee in their locations. Everett hadn't been interested in partnering with a bakery until now. Until Mariah.

"That's great!" He smiled broadly. "I was hoping you'd see that a partnership between us would be a good idea." And he wasn't talking just about business. Everett had known from the moment he'd seen Mariah that they would have more than a business relationship. There would be a personal one, too.

"I'll have to talk this over with my brothers first,"

Mariah replied. "But I don't see Chase or Jack vetoing an obviously great idea."

"Excellent! Then let's put business on the back burner and enjoy our lunch, which is just coming out now." The waitress returned with the salads.

When he dropped Mariah off less than an hour later, Everett couldn't resist watching her backside after he opened the bakery door for her. She was one fine looking woman and he was finally making headway. He just hoped that in time she would let down her guard so he could take their relationship to the next level. His gut told him that Mariah Drayson was a woman worth knowing, in every sense of the word.

Chapter 5

"Everett Myers wants to go into business with us?" Chase sat back on the couch in the bakery's office and absorbed the information that Mariah had just laid on him and Jackson after the store closed later that evening. She had been eager to spill the beans when she'd returned from lunch with Everett, but she'd kept Jackson in suspense throughout the day until she could fill them both in at the same time.

"Yep." Mariah beamed from ear to ear.

"I just knew that your good looks would come in handy one day." Jackson patted her back from the couch beside her.

"Jack!" She punched him in the shoulder.

"What?" He laughed. "You've got that man by the—" He'd been about to use a less than flattering word, but the look his older brother gave him halted him. "That man is falling for you so hard that he's willing to do anything to spend time with you, and that only works in our favor. We have to capitalize on it."

"I agree with Jack that the timing is great," Chase said more delicately. "Everett's offer gives us even more endorsement as the best bakery in town because his brand is high-end, with a solid reputation."

"We have to take it a step further," Jackson said, rising to his feet and pacing the floor. "We shouldn't just sell Myers Coffee Roasters, we should serve the java in the store."

"That's brilliant!" Chase jumped to his feet.

"Our initial concept included a café," Jackson continued. "With Myers's help, we can create a small café in the corner of the shop and serve coffee along with Lillian's pastries."

"And with a smart advertising campaign, we'd get all of the Myers coffee patrons coming into the bakery and build up our customer base," Chase added. "That's where you come in, sis." He pointed to her. "This is right up your alley."

"I'm getting excited, guys." Jackson rubbed his hands together in glee.

"So am I," Mariah said. "This could be the boost we need to set us apart from Sweetness Bakery."

"We'll bury them," Jackson stated. "And Everett Myers will get to spend more time with you in the process. It's a win-win for everybody."

Mariah snorted. "You just couldn't resist that dig, could ya, Jack?"

"Me?" He patted his chest as if he were innocent.

"Yes, you."

"C'mon, don't be mad." He pulled her to her feet, "Because before long we'll be in the black and success will be sweet."

"Yes, it will be."

Mariah was so excited at the prospect that she decided to call Everett and tell him the good news. He'd given her his business card with his private number already written on the back. It was as if he'd been waiting for just the right time to give it to her, even though she hadn't been compelled to give him hers. "Call me anytime," he'd said when he'd dropped her off after lunch, so she was going to do just that.

It was nearly 9:00 p.m. when she got to her apartment for the call. She hoped it wasn't too late, but she certainly wasn't about to phone him in front of her brothers. Jackson was already teasing her relentlessly about Everett's interest in her and she'd never live it down. She wanted to speak with him in the privacy of her own home.

"Hello?" His voice, when he answered, sounded breathless and in Mariah's opinion oh so sexy.

"Uh, hi. It's—it's Mariah," she said, stumbling over her words. "I hope I didn't catch you at a bad time?"

"No, you didn't. I was in the other room and heard the phone ringing. I have to say, though, I'm surprised to hear from you at this hour."

Mariah was surprised to be calling him, too. She could have easily waited until tomorrow and phoned him at the office, but for some reason she'd wanted to hear his voice before she went to bed. Perhaps so she could have another one of those erotic dreams she'd had since she'd met the man?

"Well, I was calling to tell you the good news. My brothers agreed that they'd like to go into business with you."

"That's great news, Mariah. I'm glad to hear it, though this could have waited until tomorrow."

"Are you upset that I called?" Her voice was shakier than she would have liked as she fell backward on her bed and nearly started hyperventilating. Had she miscalculated? Did he have someone else there with him? Was that why it was too late to call?

"Of course not," Everett answered smoothly. "I'm glad you did because it gives me hope."

"Hope for what?"

"That you might be as into me as I'm into you."

Mariah was quiet. Everett had a way of doing that to her, of being so blunt that she couldn't think of a pithy comeback. "Well, uh, we should get together tomorrow at the bakery perhaps and go over the details."

"I'm tied up during the day. How about dinner at 7:00 p.m. on Friday evening?"

If she looked up the word *relentless* in the dictionary, she would find a picture of Everett Myers. "I..." She wanted to turn him down, but didn't want to appear ungrateful for the incredible opportunity that had just landed in their lap, or jeopardize a potential business deal. And he damn well knew it. She had no choice but to capitulate. "Dinner is fine."

"Where shall I pick you up?"

Of course he wanted to pick her up, because in his mind this was a date, not a business dinner. She rattled off her address.

"I can't wait to see you, Mariah.," And just as she was hanging up she heard him whisper, "Dream of me."

Mariah hit the end button. Dream of him? Hell, she probably wouldn't be able to get him or the sound of his husky voice out of her mind. Tonight was one of those moments when she wished she kept a stress reducer in her nightstand drawer. Perhaps then she could relieve the ache between her thighs.

Everett smiled from the other end of the line after he'd hung up with Mariah, and lay back on the pillows of his king-size bed. He'd finally worn her down. She was finally starting to think of him outside of work. In her bed, perhaps? Was that where she was right now? He wondered what she was wearing. Was it one of those skimpy things women often wore to bed these days that they called pajamas? And was she thinking about him and what he would like to do to her? Did she know how much he would love to find out what secrets lay beneath the form-fitting clothes she wore? How much he wanted to taste her, and not just her mouth.

Everett took a deep breath to steady himself. He needed to get a grip because it would be a while before he unearthed all Mariah's secrets. But the best things in life were worth waiting for. He knew that the moment he had one taste of her, it would never be enough.

On Friday night, Everett excitedly rubbed his hands in eager anticipation of the romantic evening he had planned. Mariah had no idea what he had in store for her when he showed up at her apartment.

He was leaning in the entryway when she opened the door with a swish, and Everett nearly lost his footing. Mariah was spellbinding. She wore a beautiful concoction of a dress that was strapless and showed the swell of her breasts before swirling down to reveal the sway of her curvy hips.

He righted himself. "Good evening."

"So formal," Mariah said, closing the door behind her.

She must have realized how rude she was because she said, "Forgive me. I guess I should have invited you in?"

Everett shook his head. "I only want an invitation when it's freely given and you want me there." When she invited him into her apartment, it was his hope that it would be an invitation to her bed and not just her space.

Mariah flushed visibly.

Everett shifted his arm and produced a bouquet of red roses he'd been holding behind his back. "For the lady."

She recovered and gave him a weak smile. "You shouldn't have, but thank you." She stepped away long enough to put the bouquet in a vase before returning to the foyer.

He offered her his arm. "Ready to go?"

Mariah was shocked when they got to the curb and found a stretch limousine waiting for them. She turned to Everett. "A limo?"

"I wanted to be able to drink and enjoy your company this evening. This was my compromise."

She nodded and accepted the hand he lent to help her. The inside was plush, with leather seats, a flat-screen television and a wet bar. Mariah supposed this was how the wealthy lived, but the only time she'd been in a limo had been to go to her high school prom.

Once Everett joined her, the limo seemed smaller inside. He filled up the entire space with his strong masculinity. He looked especially fine tonight in the black suit jacket and white silk shirt he wore. The matching trousers encasing his hard muscular thighs caused a shiver of awareness to course through Mariah. Her breasts tingled and she could feel her nipples pucker, tight and sensitive in the clingy fabric of her dress.

She watched as Everett leaned over the wet bar, producing a bottle of champagne, and two flutes that he handed to her. He popped the cork effortlessly and poured them each a glass. Afterward, he placed the bottle back in the ice bucket.

He seemed very comfortable in this environment and easily lifted his glass to say, "A toast."

"To the start of a great business relationship."

She suspected he'd wanted to say something else, but deferred to her and said, "Cheers."

She clinked her flute against his and took a sip of the champagne. It was fragrant and delicious. She couldn't resist a small moan.

"You like?"

She shook her head. "This is a great vintage."

"This is a celebration, right? So nothing but the best." He held her captive with the intensity of his gaze. Mariah had no choice but to stare back into his piercing dark eyes.

"Yes, it is." She saw his eyes roam over her face, lingering at her lips and she knew he wanted to kiss her, but he didn't. He reined in his passion and took another sip of his champagne. Mariah couldn't help but be a little disappointed, because if he'd gone for it, she wouldn't have stopped him.

"Were your brothers surprised by my offer to carry Myers coffee at the bakery?"

Mariah shook her head. "No. In fact, they took it a step further."

"How so?"

"Well…" She paused for effect. "We'd like to not only sell Myers Coffee Roasters, but have a café on-site so customers can purchase a hot cup of coffee, too. What do you think?"

His full lips curved into a genuine smile. "I think that's a wonderful idea," Everett said, "But I'd have to be involved in every stage of the planning if there's going to be a Myers Coffee Roasters café inside the bakery, albeit on a smaller scale."

"Of course," Mariah responded. "I wouldn't expect anything less. It is your brand, after all."

"You know what this means, right?"

She suspected she knew what he was angling for, but played dumb. "No, what does it mean?"

"It means, as part owner of Lillian's of Seattle, you and I will see an awful lot of each other as we get this venture off the ground. How do you feel about that?"

"I'm excited," she said, and watched as his eyes grew large. "For the bakery," she added, and noticed his smile lessen. "This is a huge coup for us."

He frowned. "Is that all that you see?"

She could tell that he wasn't happy with her response, and didn't know how to dig herself out of putting her foot in her mouth.

When she remained silent, he said, "Just so we're clear, the only Drayson I'm interested in working with is you. So if this project is going to be successful, I need to know you're on board with that. Are you?"

Chapter 6

Everett stared back at Mariah. He hoped his meaning was clear—that he wasn't backing down from trying to win her over and he would use any means necessary to spend time with her. A condition of this arrangement would be that he would work with Mariah and only Mariah.

She seemed to be mulling over his words for several long, agonizing moments, making Everett wonder if he'd pushed her too far, until she said, "Yes, I'm on board with that."

She didn't see his inward sigh of relief because outwardly he was all cool. He had to be for this to work. "Good." The limo came to a stop. "Looks like we're here."

Everett exited first and helped Mariah out. She was pleasantly surprised to see they were in front of the Space Needle.

"I thought we'd dine someplace special. C'mon." He took her hand and led her toward the entrance.

After they'd passed through the store and made their way to the elevators, Everett could see that Mariah was looking around and wondering where they were going. She probably thought they were dining at the SkyCity restaurant with its 360 degree panoramic view of Seattle. And he could have done that, but it would be expected. Instead, he'd rented a private room on the SkyLine level, where they could have dinner in private while being waited on hand and foot.

He intended to show Mariah that he could be thoughtful and romantic. Maybe then she'd see just how enamored he was with her. Hell, just being in the limo had been divine. Her warmth had surrounded him, enveloped him, and he'd wanted more.

When she'd moaned after tasting the champagne, his reaction had been instant and visceral. He wanted to take her in his arms and kiss her delectable mouth until she made the same pleasurable sounds with him, underneath him and because of him.

The attendant on the elevator stated, "You're here, Mr. Myers. Enjoy your evening."

The door swished open and they stepped out. Mariah looked at him questioningly. "Follow me," he said leading her to the Puget Sound room, where a maître d' was waiting for them.

"Good evening, sir," the man said. "Everything is set up as you desired."

Everett offered him his hand and slid him a hundred dollar tip. "Thank you."

The maître d' opened the double doors. "No, thank you. Enjoy."

The room was decorated just as he'd requested. Soft, muted lighting and candles were everywhere, along with a table for two in the center and a grand piano in the corner for later, when he intended to dance the night away in her arms.

He turned to Mariah. "What do you think?"

Mariah was awestruck at the effort Everett had gone through to arrange a private room for them, complete with a piano!

"Everett, this—this is amazing," she commented as she walked toward the windows. She could see the Olympic Mountains, downtown Seattle and the marina from here. No one had ever done anything like this for her, certainly not Richard. They'd been young and poor when they'd first started dating, and even later, after they'd graduated and started their respective careers, he couldn't have afforded to do anything this lavish. But Everett could and he had. She was truly touched.

She spun around to face him. "You didn't have to do all this."

He smiled at her. "I know that, but I *wanted* to. Now c'mon, sit. The chef has prepared a delicious meal for us."

While they ate their starters of crab claws and second course of baby spinach salad, and shared a bottle of wine, Mariah learned more about Everett and his family.

"So you're an only child?" she asked. "You're missing out." She smiled. "Chase, Jack and I have always been thick as thieves for as long as I can remember. You can imagine that, being the only girl, there were times I've had to tell them to back down if someone was giving me a hard time. You know how it is."

Everett laughed. "I can imagine how protective they must have been over you, their little sister. And your parents— how's your relationship with them?"

Mariah reached for her glass of wine. "For the most part, it's good."

He picked up on what she wasn't saying. "But not lately?"

She nodded. "They weren't happy that my brothers and I decided to go into the bakery business. They think it's beneath us. They'd much prefer if we stuck in our respective corners or joined Dad's real estate business. Chase is an accountant, Jack is an entrepreneur and in my previous life I was an advertising executive."

Everett quirked a brow. "Advertising? What happened? Why'd you leave?"

"It wasn't the right fit." Mariah was evasive, because she didn't really want to expound more on the topic. It could lead to other questions, such as the breakup of her marriage, but she knew she couldn't avoid the topic entirely this evening.

"I can understand," Everett replied. "Sometimes it takes time to find the right path."

"My blog certainly helped with showing me the way."

"You have a blog?"

She nodded. "It's called A Sista Who Bakes. I kinda used my Chicago cousins' idea of their Brothers Who Bake blog to form my own. I started it when baking was just a hobby, especially after my divorce."

"Why did you divorce? If you don't mind my asking." Everett dipped a claw into the warm butter sauce. Mariah watched him suck the succulent sweet meat from the shell and felt her inner muscles tighten in response.

She took a sip of her wine. She'd known when she'd agreed to this date that eventually they'd have to talk about their past relationships. "We got married young, right out of college, and over time..." she paused "...we drifted apart. So the blog was more cathartic than anything. You know, a way to escape."

"I can understand. Sara and I were both young when

we met, but we'd known each other for years before our relationship became romantic."

"Sounds wise." Mariah reached for a crab claw at the same time as Everett and the electricity just from that close encounter caused a lurch of excitement to surge through her. The very air around them was electrified and seemed to hum.

She tried to disengage it with her next comment. "So when Aunt Lillian mentioned opening another bakery in Seattle, after my divorce, the pieces fit into place. And it offered me a change of scene from Chicago."

"Your aunt is a pretty amazing woman," Everett commented. "I read about how she started the first bakery in the early sixties. It couldn't have been easy in Chicago."

"No, it wasn't. I guess it's why I admire her so much," Mariah said. "And want to make her proud."

"You will."

Mariah stared at Everett. He said it with such conviction that even she believed it. "I will with your help. Having a Myers Coffee Roasters café at the bakery, even on a small scale, is a huge bonus."

"Aw, it's not all that."

"Of course it is. Starbucks isn't the only game in town and you've got quite the following. And if I'm honest, I prefer yours."

"Really?"

"Don't sound so surprised. It has the right balance of flavor."

"It's what I was going for."

Everett continued to expound on how he got started in the coffee importing business when their entrées arrived. She'd ordered the herb-crusted halibut, while he'd opted for the wild king salmon.

Mariah sighed in contentment. "You weren't lying when

you said the chef had prepared a mouth-watering dinner for us. This is scrumptious." She took another forkful of halibut.

"I'm glad you're enjoying it."

"I'm not just enjoying the food," Mariah admitted. "I'm enjoying your company." She hadn't thought it was possible to feel this way again after Rich. Their breakup had been devastating to her self-esteem as a woman. Everett, however, was quickly boosting it in a big way.

He grinned, showing a flash of white teeth. "So am I."

Mariah's heart swelled in her chest. He didn't need to touch her to have her completely mesmerized. All he had to do was pin her with his razor-sharp gaze and she melted. She could easily be putty in his hands if she wasn't careful with her heart.

Everett stared at Mariah. He'd been watching her all night and he couldn't get enough of her. They'd just finished a decadent dessert of bananas Foster, which they'd both devoured. Mariah ate with passionate relish. She wasn't one of those women who picked at her meal. She wasn't afraid to be completely herself. There weren't any airs about her. What you saw was what you got. And it was refreshing.

He gave the maître d' a nod that it was time for the pianist to come in. "How about a dance?" Everett said, rising to his feet.

"There's no music."

"I'm sure we could make our own," he replied. At Mariah's surprised look, he inclined his head toward the man who was sitting down at the piano.

"I would love to." She rose to her feet just as the pianist began singing Nat King Cole's "Unforgettable."

The lights from the city and candlelight illuminated the

room, bathing Mariah in a soft glow. Everett held out his hand for her to join him on the dance floor.

He felt as if he'd waited a lifetime to finally have a legitimate reason to touch Mariah. He slid his arm around her slender waist, bringing her soft body into contact with his hard one. To her credit, Mariah tried to keep a respectable distance between the two of them, but Everett was having none of it. He wanted to *feel* her and he wasn't going to let her hesitancy get in the way.

At first, she was a little stiff when his other hand grasped hers, but eventually she gave in and moved her body closer to his. He dipped his head and placed it against the side of her face. Not only could he smell the fragrant sweetness of her perfume teasing his nostrils, but he could feel the heat emanating from her.

And from him. He was scorching hot for her. He could feel the rising bulge in his pants and couldn't resist crushing her body firmly to his. He thought Mariah would push him away as she felt the evidence of his arousal, but she didn't. He heard her breathing hitch and become labored. Was she feeling as turned on as he was?

Without thinking, he leaned forward and kissed her forehead. Then he lowered his head so he could trail hot kisses down the side of her face as he inched closer to her lips. He hadn't meant to do it and thought she might pull away, but she didn't. Instead, she looked up at him through sooty, mascara-covered lashes and he had the answer to his question. Desire gleamed in her eyes, just as he knew it did in his.

He bent down and brushed his lips softly over hers.

Mariah had known Everett was going to kiss her when she'd looked at him. His pupils had dilated and he'd stepped even closer to her, allowing her to feel the hard, unyielding pressure of his arousal against her middle. She was power-less to resist the pull, and her arms involuntarily moved up and over Everett's shoulders as he laid hungry siege to her lips. When he deepened the kiss, raking his tongue across her bottom lip, her lips parted of their own volition. The touch of his tongue on hers sent a jolt of electricity spark-ing inside her. Her entire body awakened at the contact and she knew that he wanted her.

Right here.

Right now.

His hands moved caressingly down the length of her spine and rested on her hips. She suspected he was going to cup her bottom, but given that they had an audience, thought better of it. That's what jolted her out of the kiss, and she wrenched her mouth from his. She tried unsuc-cessfully to pull out of his arms. His hold on her was too tight. "Everett…"

"Hmm…?"

"There are people here," she whispered into his ear.

"I'm aware of that. Why else do you think I haven't ravished you on the spot?"

She glanced up at him and saw the devilry in his eyes. He was teasing her. "Perhaps we should…"

"Stop?" he asked, his gaze hooded. "That's a negative. If I promise to be good, will you let me hold you?"

The sexual potency Everett had just wreaked on her body told Mariah it wasn't a good idea, but it felt so good to be in a man's arms again. And not just any man's, but Everett's. She couldn't say no even if she tried to. "Okay."

They continued dancing to several songs, until Everett took a step backward. "Thank you."

She nodded. Had he known what that had cost her? To not retreat and run at the first sign that their relationship had taken a sudden shift in direction?

"How about we go to the observation deck to finish off the evening?" Everett offered.

"I'd like that."

Several minutes later, they were looking out over the city of Seattle, standing hand in hand. They were both silent as they took in the lights and the stars overhead. Mariah could still feel the current of sizzling chemistry passing back and forth between them. It was so palpable that her heart was hammering in her chest. Was it taking as much restraint on Everett's part as it was on hers for them not to kiss again?

But he kept his word and didn't kiss her. Instead, after a short time on the observation deck, he took her to the limo and they drove back to her apartment.

Mariah appreciated that Everett was respecting her wishes and doing the honorable thing, but had to admit she wouldn't have minded if he'd been a bit of a bad boy and stolen another kiss.

When they reached her place, he kept the limo idling as he walked her inside and up the stairs to her second-floor apartment. "Thank you for a lovely evening," she said in her doorway.

"I aim to please," he said with a bow.

She laughed. He truly was a remarkable man, and maybe in another life things might be different, but she doubted there would ever be more than this moment. She couldn't let it. She couldn't afford to get close and let another man in, only to have it not work out after he realized she wasn't a whole woman.

"We'll talk soon about the café..." She left the sentence hanging and turned toward the door.

That's when Everett surprised her and reached for her once more. And this time they didn't have an audience. He backed her up against the door, cupped her bottom and pulled her firmly and snugly against the pulsing length of his rock-hard erection. Mariah gasped and Everett used her shock to insert his tongue deep inside her mouth. Then one of his hands came upward to cup her breasts over the softness of the chiffon material. He brushed his thumb over her nipple and it hardened on the spot. Everett groaned and shifted the hardness of his shaft even closer into her core.

Mariah knew her panties were damp with moisture as he fully explored every inch of her mouth before tangling her tongue with his. His tongue continued to stroke hers over and over with such achingly slow flicks that she thought she'd die on the spot from so much pleasure. She was no expert in the lovemaking department, but she reciprocated his movements and hoped he was enjoying the kiss as much as she.

When he lifted his head, his eyes were dark with desire. "I wish I could say I was sorry about that, but I just had to have another taste of you. I'll see you tomorrow."

Seconds later, he was gone, leaving Mariah breathing hard and desperate for more.

Everett wasn't sure how he made it back to the limousine, given the painfully hard erection he was now sporting. If he hadn't left, he would have taken the keys from Mariah's hand and backed her up into her apartment, invitation or not. Then he would show her exactly how much he desired her, and vice versa.

He wasn't sure of much, but he was certain Mariah had wanted him to kiss her again. He'd felt her yearning, her craving to have his tongue in her mouth in the limo, and he'd had to oblige. Now all he had to do was figure out how he was going to pull back. Tonight, he'd shown Mariah his romantic and passionate side, but he also wanted her to see his restraint and that he could wait until she was ready to invite him into her bed.

During the evening, he'd sensed that she didn't have much experience in the dating department. Not that he'd had tons himself, but he'd sensed her nervousness even though she'd tried to mask it with conversation. Despite her nerves, she'd responded to him with abandoned enthusiasm, which made him even more of an admirer. He couldn't wait to see where their relationship would go next.

Chapter 7

"Well, look who the cat dragged in," Jackson said, when Mariah arrived late to the bakery on Saturday morning.

"Not today, Jack," Mariah cautioned. She'd slept fitfully the night before, all because of one man. Everett. How dare he get her so turned on and then just leave? Not that she'd ever be one for casual sex—heck, her ex-husband was her first and only lover—but she certainly didn't like being left high and dry!

Last night, Everett had kissed her senseless and turned on every dormant hormone in her body, so much so that she'd dreamed of him and awoke with an ache between her legs that only one thing could satisfy.

"What's got you in a huff?" Jackson asked.

"Nothing!" She grabbed her apron and tied it around her neck and waist, then began clanging pots and bowls as she prepared her station.

"Doesn't look like nothing to me," her brother responded. "It's not like you to be late or ill-tempered. That's my department."

"Well, you don't have the lock on being a jerk," she said, finally offering him a smile.

"Ah, now there's the Mariah I know." He continued kneading the dough he was working on. "I'd think you'd be on cloud nine since you convinced your admirer to invest in our bakery."

Mariah thought about Everett and then her mind wandered to his lips and how his bottom lip was fuller than the top. She remembered how she'd sucked on it last night with fervor. "I am happy."

"Coulda fooled me. What did lover boy say about our café idea? Was he on board?"

Mariah nodded. "He loved it, but insisted that he would be heavily involved with the concept from start to finish."

"Sounds reasonable. His name is on it."

She turned her back to grab some flour out of the pantry and added, "He wants to work exclusively with me on the project."

She didn't hear Jackson sneak up on her until he spun her around. "Are you sure you're not in over your head on this?"

Mariah pulled away from her brother. "Of course not. I can handle this expansion and Everett."

Jackson held up his hands. "All right, as long as you're sure, because Myers isn't interested in just the café."

Mariah tried grabbing the large bag of flour, but Jack took it out of her hands and carried it over to her station.

"Thank you, and I'm aware of Everett's intentions."

"It's Everett now?" Surprise laced her brother's voice.

"Yes. We went to dinner last night and—"

Jackson held up his hands. "Wait a second, you and

Myers went to dinner and you didn't lead with that? Is that what has you in a mood today? Did something happen last night? Did he do something untoward? If so, I can go over to his office and knock his block off."

Mariah suppressed a soft gurgle of laughter. "As much as I appreciate this brotherly affection, it's not necessary. I'm capable of taking care of myself. Furthermore, nothing happened that I didn't want to happen."

Jackson's eyes grew large like saucers. "So, something did happen?"

"I don't intend on discussing my love life with my brother, so drop it, okay?"

"Now he's part of your love life? Oh, Lord!" Jackson threw his hands up in the air again. "All I can say is be careful, since I don't want anything to get in the way of this project. It's too important for Lillian's."

"And it won't. I've got it covered."

"All right."

It sounded to Mariah as if Jackson didn't believe her, but she didn't care. She would deal with Everett in her own way. First by keeping their relationship on a more businesslike footing while the café was in process. Jackson was right about that. She couldn't afford for anything to jeopardize this opportunity, not even her interest in the man behind it.

Everett woke up with a smile on his face. He had finally sampled sweet Mariah and the taste had stayed with him all weekend. So much so that when he'd turned over he'd fully expected her to be lying beside him on the king-size bed. She hadn't been, but now Everett knew with certainty that he and Mariah would become lovers.

For days she'd tried to act as if she was unaffected by

him, but Friday night she'd given in to her own desires. And when he'd kissed her, she'd kissed him back. And it wasn't a demure kiss, but one full of fire and passion and a hunger like the one that had been building inside him from the moment they'd met.

When he'd cradled her in his arms in front of her apartment and his shaft had cocooned itself in her softness, he'd felt as if he was home. It had taken every bit of self-restraint for him to refrain from acting on his deepest desires, but he had to. Despite how responsive she was, Everett knew he had to tread lightly. If he came on too strong again, she'd retreat, and he didn't want that. It's why he'd decided not to visit today, but give her time to absorb everything that had happened between them.

Keeping his distance while working with Mariah on the Myers Coffee Roasters café was going to be extremely difficult, but he had to. He would visit the bakery every day as he'd done before, or whenever he could. He wanted Mariah to become comfortable with having him as a part of her life, so the transition from business partners to lovers would feel seamless.

"Penny for your thoughts?" His mother was standing in the doorway of his office on Monday morning.

"Mom, this is a pleasant surprise," Everett said, rising to his feet. "What are you doing here?"

"I was in the neighborhood for a charity meeting and figured I'd stop by and check in on you. How are you? And how's my darling grandbaby?"

Everett glanced at his mother. Gwen Myers was still stunning at fifty-eight. Her smooth café-au-lait skin showed no signs of aging and was expertly made up to go along with the Dior suit she wore with matching pumps.

"I'm doing great and EJ, well, he's had a bit of a tough

week at school, and especially at this time of year. But he'll pull through."

She sat down on the sofa along one wall. "What's going on?"

Everett sat beside her and filled her in on the bullying at school and EJ's response to not having a mother.

Gwen touched her chest in horror. "Oh, that poor baby. Everett, what can I do?"

"I'm sure a visit from Grandma would help tremendously and give him a bit of the mother figure he so desperately craves. Other than that, I'm not sure what else would help."

"I so wished you would have remarried after Sara." When she saw the stricken look on his face, his mother quickly added, "More so for EJ than for you, my boy." She patted his thigh. "Then he would have a mom."

"He has one."

"You know what I meant."

"I'm sorry, Mom." Everett rose from the couch, walked over to the window and stared at Elliott Bay. "I've always wondered that myself. Did I do him a disservice by shunning all those women? But the thing is—" he turned to face her "—I never really felt like any of them were genuine, but now…" His voice trailed off as he thought of Mariah Drayson.

His mother was perceptive and asked, "And now what?"

"Excuse me?" He turned around.

"I asked now what, but you looked a million miles away. Like you were thinking of something, or should I say some*one*?"

Everett tried to smother a smile, but his mother rose from the sofa and reached for both his hands. "Have you met someone?"

He nodded.

"You have?" Her voice rose slightly. "Oh, Everett, I'm so happy for you. Who is she? When can I meet her? What does EJ think of her?"

"Mom, slow down," Everett said, releasing her hands. "We haven't gotten that far yet. We only just met, but there's something about her that's different from the women I've met since Sara. She's special."

"Don't leave me in suspense. What's her name?"

"Her name is Mariah Drayson."

"Of the Seattle Draysons?" his mother inquired. "I've heard of them. Nadia Drayson sits on one of my charities and she's having a ball at the Myers Hotel later this summer, while your father has had some real estate business dealings with Graham Drayson."

"Yes, the same Draysons," Everett responded. "Mariah recently opened a bakery called Lillian's of Seattle."

His mother obviously didn't recognize the name, just stared at him blankly. "Lillian's is a popular bakery on Chicago's Magnificent Mile and they won a television competition a few years ago."

"That's excellent, darling. At least she comes from a family of good standing. Having a store on the Magnificent Mile is very exclusive."

"Mom, you realize you sound very snobby."

She looked chagrined. "I only want the best for my son."

Everett wrapped his arm around her shoulders and pulled her toward him in a hug. "I know, and I love you, too. But if I truly liked her, I wouldn't care where she came from, only how good her heart is."

"You can't be so naive, darling. You have to think about EJ with whoever you date, and whether she would be a good mother."

"EJ is never far from my mind," he said, even though he had to admit he hadn't been thinking of his son last night when he'd had Mariah backed up against the door of her apartment. "I will always put his interests and well-being above my own."

"Oh, I know you will. And you think this woman, this Mariah, could be a possibility?"

"It's too early to say, but something tells me the answer is yes."

Just before closing time on Monday, Mariah wiped down the counters. It had been a rather slow day and not seeing Everett all weekend or today had only added to her disappointment. She knew it was silly, but she'd started to look forward to his daily visits, count on them. She knew it was wrong, especially when she intended to halt any ideas of a blossoming romance that might get into his head after her scandalous behavior Friday night.

She'd had no intention of getting *that* close to him. All she could do was chalk it up to the romance of the evening. Everett had pulled out all the stops with the private dinner at the Space Needle, the champagne and the pianist. What woman wouldn't get caught up in the moment? It didn't help that he was nerve-sizzlingly attractive and that whenever he was around, her brain short-circuited and she lost herself.

His kisses had rocked her to her core, making her weak at the knees and fisting handfuls of his suit jacket in an effort to keep from falling. The strong chin, chiseled cheekbones, sexy dark eyes and irresistible smile combined with a hard, muscled and toned body had made Mariah want to throw propriety to the wind and ask him inside her apartment. If she'd done that, she was sure that Everett would have given her one helluva mind-blowing climax. He'd almost made her orgasm just from a kiss.

If she was honest, Richard had never made her feel that

way. They'd been young kids in love and figuring out each other's bodies. And yes, they'd grown together, eventually discovering what pleased each other. But none of their experiences had come close to what Everett had made her feel from his kisses and caresses. She could only imagine that she would probably faint from the passion and intensity of Everett full throttle. As intense as he was, she was glad he'd had the common sense to end things Friday night.

Had he regretted his actions? Was that why he hadn't visited the bakery since? Or were her kisses so abhorrent that it made him want to run in the opposite direction? She didn't have much to compare him to, but she'd given him as much of herself as she was capable of under the circumstances.

She wished she had someone to confide in. Most of her friends back in Chicago were married couples, and she didn't think they would understand what it was like to be newly single. She hadn't been back in Seattle long enough to make any new friends, and most of her crowd from high school had dispersed to other parts of the country.

And as far as her family went, she most certainly couldn't talk to her brothers about her love life, even though Jack always wanted to be in her business. Her mother had never been much into girl talk. But there was always Belinda in Chicago.

Mariah shook her head. Why was she second-guessing herself, anyway? Hadn't she said that she and Everett should keep things professional? The next time she saw him, she would act as if the date hadn't happened.

Just as she was about to close the bakery for the day, Everett showed up with preliminary sketches from his interior designer, along with the name of the general contractor he wanted to use to carve out the café space.

"Wait, wait," Mariah said. "Take a breath."

He'd walked in full of fire and zest for the project and sat down at a table with the sketches. There hadn't been his usual hello and flirtatious greeting; he'd gotten right down to business. Had he forgotten her kisses that quickly?

She surely hadn't, and it didn't help that he looked handsome as usual. He was wearing trousers and a button-down shirt instead of his usual suit.

He grinned abashedly. "I'm sorry—I'm so excited about the project that I couldn't resist taking the first step and coming up with a layout. I hope you don't mind?"

Mariah shook her head. "Of course not. You know more about the coffee business and what would be required." She looked over the drawings. "How did you get a copy of our layout?"

He shrugged. "Your permit is part of the public record and I have a few friends in the department."

Mariah bristled. It must be nice to have friends in high places. "It would also have been nice if you'd asked."

"Of course, I'm sorry. I'm sure you'd like to look this over with your brothers and get back to me. As I told you, I want to be involved in all facets of this project."

She couldn't forget. "And you still want me to run lead?"

He stared at her piercingly. "Yes, I still want you."

Mariah swallowed audibly. There it was again—that innuendo in his words. Add the way he was looking at her, as if she was the cherry on top of a hot fudge sundae, and it told her that perhaps he wasn't all about business, either, and that there was still a part of him that desired her. If she was honest, it soothed her female ego after his no-show all weekend and his right-to-business tactics now. "That's good to hear."

His full lips curved into a smile. "Great, because I'd like to bring some contractors by tomorrow so we can start getting this priced out."

"You sure don't waste any time, do you?"

"Why should I? I'm certain you're as eager as I am to get this project off the ground, especially for a start-up business."

"Well, yes, but we're not in dire straits. We've only been open a week." Mariah bristled again. She didn't appreciate Everett acting as if they were a lost cause and he was doing them a favor. Lillian's of Seattle would make it with him or without him. She would see to it, because she wouldn't let it fail.

Heck, just this morning she'd been working on a new creation. She wasn't sure of the name yet, but once she'd perfected it, Mariah just knew it would sell like hotcakes.

"I'm sorry," Everett said. "I didn't mean to insinuate otherwise. I'm here to help."

"Of course, and I'm sorry if I'm a little sensitive on the topic." She offered him a weak smile.

"Did something happen?" he inquired.

"No, not exactly, but my brothers and I have been summoned home for a family powwow dinner tonight. I'm sure it'll be just another attempt by our parents to convince us we made a poor decision by opening the bakery."

"Don't let their negativity get you down," Everett said. "Use it to fuel your passion and your determination to succeed. Show them *they* made the mistake by not supporting your dreams."

Mariah stared at him incredulously. She couldn't believe how impassioned his speech was, and he barely knew her.

"Don't look so surprised. I didn't get where I am without ambition and the drive to succeed."

"No, I don't suppose you did." And she'd had it herself once, before her marriage had gone to hell in a handbasket.

"So, it's all right if I bring some contractors by in the morning?"

Mariah nodded. "Absolutely. I'm sure this layout will work just fine, but I'll run it past my brothers."

Everett rose to his feet, towering over her. "You do that. In the meantime, I have to get going." He reached for his briefcase and started toward the door.

"Oh, okay." Mariah hated to admit she was enjoying his company and didn't want to see him go.

He must have heard something in her voice, because he said, "How about a kiss for the road?"

Chapter 8

"Baby girl." Her father planted a kiss on her cheek as Mariah entered the foyer of her childhood home later that evening. Although Everett hadn't gotten the kiss for the road, she had been happy to see him, and now it was family time.

"It's good to see you, Daddy." Mariah gave him a quick squeeze around his shoulders. She'd always been a daddy's girl and treasured the special bond that existed between the two of them. "You're looking well."

Even at fifty-nine, her father was a handsome man with his smooth, honey-toned skin. From his dark, close-cropped hair to his bushy eyebrows and ever present mustache, Graham Drayson was debonair. He was a suit-and-tie kind of guy, but tonight he wore trousers and a pullover sweater.

"C'mon, everyone's in the back."

"Including Mom?"

"Oh, don't be like that." He knew that at times Mariah's relationship with her mother was like oil and water.

But her father had loved her mother from the moment he'd met her, and it had been that way ever since. When Mariah had told him her marriage to Richard was over, he'd had a hard time understanding and accepting it. For her father, marriage was a life-long commitment. She respected that about him, along with the fact that he was a self-made man who'd done well for himself as a savvy real estate agent, consequently being able to give her and her brothers an upper-middle-class background.

Just look at what he'd done with their home. The stunning Queen Anne Victorian overlooked the water in one of Seattle's most exclusive neighborhoods. It had stained glass windows, a turret and sprawling landscaped grounds that her mother kept meticulously manicured. Nadia Drayson had initially hated the house, telling her father he was a fool for purchasing the ramshackle place, but Graham had seen the potential and called it "a diamond in the rough," then had lovingly restored it himself. It may have taken years, but her mother had finally come to adore the house, and it was her father's pride and joy.

"I'll try," Mariah finally said, as he led her by the arm into the family room, where Chase, Jackson and her mother were already seated around the large, sixty-inch flat-screen television. Her brothers were drinking beers, while her mom held a glass of red wine.

"Hey, sis." Jackson rose to greet her. "What's that you got there in your arms?"

Mariah glanced down. She'd forgotten that she'd brought the blueprints Everett had dropped off earlier, so she could get Chase and Jack's opinion. "These are the drawings I mentioned to you earlier."

Chase must have been eavesdropping because he said,

"Oh, yeah, let me see." He was jumping off the couch when her mother sidestepped him and came toward Mariah with her arms outstretched.

Mariah suffered through the obligatory kisses on either cheek. "Mom, how are you?"

Nadia pulled away and studied Mariah from head to toe. "I'm well, but I'm not sure I can say the same for you. What are you wearing? What's happened to you since you've been back in Seattle? When you were in Chicago you were always so elegantly dressed."

And here it goes, Mariah thought. The criticism, the put-downs. Could she ever do anything right in this woman's eyes?

Probably not. At fifty-seven years old, her mother was extremely polished and an impeccable dresser. She wouldn't be caught dead in Mariah's outfit of a simple shirt dress, which she'd belted at the waist and teamed with riding boots. Her mother had straight black hair and refused to allow herself to go gray, by monthly salon visits. Nadia Drayson lived the easy life, having long since stopped helping her husband build his real estate business, and shifting her focus to charity work instead.

"I'm sorry, Mom, but now that I'm a baker I don't see the point in wearing sheath dresses and Louboutin shoes."

Her mother gasped. "Oh, the horror. You can't speak ill of Louboutins."

Mariah couldn't suppress the gurgle of laughter that escaped her lips, and apparently neither could her brothers, who were standing nearby and probably waiting for World War III to erupt between them, which usually happened when they were within six feet of each other. But tonight was different. Mariah wasn't going to let her mother ruffle her feathers.

She held up the blueprints and glanced at her brothers.

"I thought we could look these over before dinner. That's if it's not ready yet?" She stared at her mother questioningly.

Nadia waved her hand, "Oh, that's fine, but don't take too long. I like my duck moist."

Mariah chuckled as she, Chase and Jackson walked down the hall to their father's study.

"So, let's see them," Chase said, pulling the prints from under her arm.

He unrolled the large drawings and spread them out over the table adjacent to her father's massive oak desk. She'd always loved that desk and sitting on his lap as she'd watch him work.

Chase studied the plans for several long minutes, going around the table to view them from all angles. "These are great."

"I know. That's what I thought" Mariah understood the basics about reading the drawings because she'd been involved in the bakery's design. Everett's designer had come up with an efficient use of the small space, while not taking away anything from the bakery.

"I agree," Jackson said, looking over her shoulder, "The plans even show some shop drawings of the displays that would house the Myers Coffee Roasters product. He thought of everything."

"He did say he wanted to be involved with every facet of the project," Mariah reminded them.

Chase looked up from the drawings and pushed his wire-rimmed glasses back into place on his nose. "How do you feel about that? I mean, you are the reason he's doing all this."

"Am not." Mariah knew it was a childish response as soon as she uttered it, but she couldn't help herself sometimes. Being around her older brothers made her revert to being a kid.

Jackson stared at her with those light brown eyes of his as if he couldn't believe she was actually lying to their faces.

"It may have been part of the reason," Mariah amended, "that Everett decided to partner with us, but it's good business. He wouldn't be doing this otherwise. I highly doubt he's doing this to lose money."

"Perhaps, but he could be doing it to get a piece of—"

Mariah pointed her finger at him. "Don't you dare, Jackson Drayson!" she warned.

Jackson flushed and had the decency to look embarrassed at what he'd been about to say to his younger sister. "Sorry, kid," He pulled her into the crook of his arm. "You know I wouldn't let some guy play you. I've got your back."

Mariah stared up at him. "I know." But she couldn't resist jabbing him in the ribs for the barb.

"Ouch!" Jackson feigned being hurt even though Mariah knew her punch had hit the brick wall that was his abdomen. Jackson believed in staying fit and toned. It was why the women flocked to him—his body and that good-looking face.

"So, now that we're all on board," Chase said, getting back down to business, "you'll let Everett know we approve, and get some pricing on this? We'll need three competitive bids, as we'll be responsible for half the costs."

"Why should we pay? When he came to us?" Jackson asked.

"Because we want a stake in the profit," Chase responded. "Mariah, do you want to discuss a percentage with Myers or shall I? I'll only ask for what's fair."

"No need. I already have a number in mind."

Chase stepped backward. "So, it's like that?"

Mariah smirked. "Don't underestimate me."

* * *

Mariah wished dinner could have gone as smoothly as her business conversation with her brothers had. They'd made it through salad and her mother's famous pretzel bread and were on the entrée course of orange duck when Nadia Drayson decided she wanted to revisit why her children had insisted on opening a bakery against her and their father's wishes.

Mariah suspected it was her mother's wishes and her dad had just gone along. As the old saying went, "happy wife, happy life." Mariah couldn't fault him for that, but wasn't about to listen to this same old love song again. What was done was done and their mom was just going to have to accept their decision.

"I don't understand why you did it," Nadia said. "Didn't we give you all the very best in life? The very best education? The world was your oyster. But instead you choose to open up a bakery and do manual labor?" She shook her head in despair. "I just don't understand."

"And you don't have to," Mariah snapped.

"Easy now," Graham admonished.

Mariah glanced up and saw her father's reproachful look. He didn't appreciate the way she'd spoken to her mother.

She forced herself to say, "I'm sorry, Mom, but you have to understand. This is a great opportunity for us to build something on our own. Aunt Lillian has given us the tools with her great recipes, and with some of our new ones, I know we'll do great."

"But it's a fickle business," her mother pressed. "Right now everyone is into health fads and gluten-free—it's poor timing. You should return to what you went to school for, advertising. It was your passion until…until—"

Everyone around the table stopped breathing at what they knew was coming.

"Until what?" Mariah asked through clenched teeth.

Her mother glanced up and faced her head-on. "Until your infertility. You were perfectly happy with your career and then you got obsessed with baby making at the exclusion of everything."

"So you're saying that the divorce was all *my* fault?"

"Nadia," her father interjected, "you need to—"

But her mother interrupted him. "Well, yes," she answered unapologetically before taking a sip of wine. "Haven't I always told you to put your man first, like I do your father?" She glanced across the table at her adoring husband. "Perhaps if you'd focused more on your marriage, you might still be together today."

Mariah was stunned by her mother's words. "Is that what you all think, too?" She glanced at Chase, who held his head down, and Jackson, who rolled his eyes upward, while her father looked appropriately chagrined.

When no one answered, she threw her napkin on her plate and rose to her feet. "Excuse me, I think I'll have my dinner elsewhere." She spun on her heel and fled from the room.

She heard the pleas of her father, "Wait! Mariah, wait!" Tears blinded her eyes. She just had to get out of there.

Once she made it to her car, Mariah let out a long, tortured sigh. She glanced up at the house. Her own family thought she'd been cuckoo for Cocoa Puffs by putting all her energy into trying to have a baby. They just didn't get why it was so important to her. The need and desire to have someone who would love her unconditionally was so strong, Mariah thought she would die when she'd learned she might not ever conceive. It seemed like a cruel twist of fate. But that was her lot in life and she was going to have to accept it, no matter how much it hurt.

Everett was exhausted and Friday hadn't come quick enough for him. He'd just gotten back from an unplanned trip to Vegas to check on one of the Myers Hotels. They'd had an unexpected hiccup with construction at the new location, so he'd had to leave EJ with his parents and fly there to straighten out the mess. He hadn't intended on staying three days, but he'd had to deal with some city officials to ensure the project got off the ground.

He was happy to be home in Seattle. EJ was so excited to see him last night that he'd stayed up well past his usual bedtime to be with him. Everett had been just as excited to see him and planned to spend some quality father-son time this weekend.

Everett also wasn't too happy with the fact that he'd gone three whole days without seeing the gorgeous honey blonde. Right when he was starting to make headway and Mariah was getting used to his visits, he'd had to leave unexpectedly. He just hoped he hadn't lost ground.

Which was why he was surprised when his receptionist informed him that Mariah Drayson had arrived and wished to see him. Everett sat up straight and straightened his silk tie. This was an unexpected surprise, but one that pleased him immensely. "Show her in."

Several moments later, Mariah strode into his office carrying what looked to be the blueprints he'd given her several days ago. "Good morning." She offered him a smile. "I hope I didn't catch you at a bad time."

He rose from his chair and walked toward her to greet her. "Not at all. It's good to see you, albeit a surprise."

She looked scrumptious in a suit with a laced up detail along the side of the jacket and pencil skirt, along with some sexy black pumps. He'd love to unlace every inch of that skirt so he could run his hands over the generous amount of leg she revealed. Had she worn this sexy outfit just for him? If so, he wholeheartedly approved.

Her hair was loosely curled around her face and her eyes were bright. "I'm sure. Usually it's you coming to me," she replied. "But I thought it appropriate that I come to you this time, since the offer and design you've presented to us is pretty irresistible."

"Pretty irresistible?" He flashed a grin. "Is that all? I was hoping for fantastic, magnificent and any other adjective you can think of."

Mariah laughed. "It's all of those things, with one caveat." She took a seat on the chair facing his desk.

"What's that?" he said, leaning his backside against the desk to face her.

"We want 40 percent."

"That's a large sum," Everett said, eyeing her warily. He shouldn't be surprised that she'd done her homework; Mariah struck him as a savvy businesswoman.

"Yes, but we're prepared to pay half the costs of the renovation."

"Considering you're a start-up in Seattle, I would think you'd need to keep your capital in reserve."

"True, but this investment is worth the risk."

"Well said, but I'm not giving you 40 percent."

She cocked a brow, obviously surprised at his firm tone.

Perhaps she thought she could sweet-talk him into it? And perhaps she could; it would depend on what the lady was willing to give him in return.

"Would you settle for thirty?"

"Hmm…" He rubbed his chin thoughtfully. "How about twenty-five?"

She smiled. "You drive a hard bargain, but I'm sold.

We have a deal." She offered her hand for him to shake, but instead of doing so, he used it to pull her toward him into his arms.

Everett didn't know what came over him. He hadn't intended to act on his impulse, but he'd missed her. A week was too long and he just had to kiss her. He lowered his head and, to her stunned surprise, brushed his lips across hers. He moved deliberately and with expert precision, but slowly and gently until she softened and her body strained to be closer to him, while her lips became more pliant.

When she sighed, he dipped his tongue deep inside her mouth and tasted her with leisurely licks and flicks. He delved deeper, mating his tongue with hers, and she raised her arms to circle around his neck. He growled and cupped the back of her head so he could kiss her more thoroughly.

Eventually, he pulled away, leaving them both panting and breathless.

Mariah touched her lips. "Everett, w-what was that?"

"I was sealing our arrangement with a kiss."

"A handshake might have been more appropriate under the circumstances."

"But not nearly as much fun," he responded, his voice husky.

"I have to go." Mariah quickly exited the room, much to Everett's chagrin. He would have loved for her to stay and barter with him. Show him that she was just as affected as he was by that kiss, but she was still fighting the attraction between them. *That's okay*, he thought. Because in time she would see that it was inevitable for them to become more than business partners.

"C'mon, you can't still be mad at me," Jackson said later that morning when she finally made it to the bakery. She'd left a message for both her brothers that she'd had business the previous evening and both of them had better be present to open up in the morning.

Both Chase and Jackson had been stunned by her declaration and each had left her several text messages, but she hadn't responded. She was still furious with them for not standing up to their mother when she went on the attack on Monday night. Mariah had been giving them the silent treatment the last few days. They were supposed to speak up for her, protect her. Instead, they'd let their mother bully her, which was par for the course, but she'd expected more from them. Adding insult to injury was their failure to state they didn't think Mariah's infertility or single-minded obsession with getting pregnant was the cause of her divorce.

"Yeah, we're sorry." Chase came toward her as she walked into the kitchen and reached for her apron on the hook. "Really sorry. I should have stepped in and stopped Mom from bashing you, and I apologize that I didn't protect you, little sis."'

Mariah glanced up with unshed tears in her eyes and nodded. Chase grasped her in his arms, picked her up and squeezed her in a bear hug.

"I love you, kid," he said. "Always have, ever since I saw you in the hospital and you came out of the womb bald as an eagle."

Mariah couldn't resist a laugh as he lowered her to the floor. "I was not bald."

"Was too," Jackson said, coming over to the duo. "Chase and I wondered if you were a boy because you didn't have any hair, and Dad really wanted a girl to dote on."

"And he got you," Chase said, caressing her cheek.

Mariah sniffed. It had been hard staying mad at her brothers for this long. It just wasn't part of her makeup.

She was the forgive-and-forget type. "So, how have you guys fared without me and Nancy?"

The older woman had been out all week with the flu, so even Chase had had to pitch in, roll up his dress shirt sleeves and help out. He might not know much about baking, but he could mix ingredients, roll out dough and cut it with a cookie cutter. Jackson and Mariah would do all the heavy lifting.

"Where were you, anyway?" Jackson inquired.

Mariah smiled inwardly. First she'd done something for herself and slept in until 7:00 a.m., if you could call that sleeping in. Something she never did. Was it to teach the boys a lesson? Sure, but she had enjoyed the extra hours of shut-eye.

By eight, she'd made her way toward Everett's office. Given his initial exuberance, she'd been surprised when he'd backed off and granted her some space, a week's time to be exact, to agree to a partnership between them. His risk had paid off. She'd come to him. She'd taken a chance that he was an early riser and he was. Was he surprised by her visit to his office? Yes, but he'd quickly recovered and stolen a kiss. When he'd drawn her toward him, it had been as if he was pulling her into some sort of force field. The sheer strength and demand of his will forced her to comply, to allow herself to be kissed thoroughly. That's when everything around them ceased to exist and she could think only of Everett and his searing kisses. Kisses that drove her mad until she'd had no choice but to run.

"Earth to Mariah!"

"What?" she asked, annoyed. She didn't appreciate having her daydream of Everett's full soft lips on hers interrupted.

"I asked where you were," Jackson replied. "No need to get snippy."

Mariah turned to face him. "I had a meeting with Everett and let him know our demands."

"And?" Chase stopped kneading the dough he'd returned to.

"He agreed to 25 percent," Mariah stated.

"He did?" Chase and Jackson asked in unison.

Mariah nodded excitedly. "Sure did. There was some discussion back and forth, but eventually he came around to my way of thinking."

Jackson's eyes narrowed. "And exactly what did you have to do to get him to see things your way?"

Mariah rolled her eyes at her older brother. "Get your mind out of the gutter, Jack. Anyway, what does it matter? His lawyer will draft up the agreement and this café will be up and running in no time!"

Chase walked back toward her and extended his hand, which Mariah shook. "I have to hand it to you, sis. I wasn't sure you could pull this off, but you did. You're right about one thing."

"Me?" She placed her hand on her chest. "Right about something?" She feigned scorn.

"Yeah, you were right that we underestimate you," Chase responded. "But I won't make that mistake again."

Mariah grinned unabashedly. Everett had learned the same thing today when he'd thought she would give in, but she'd stood her ground and walked away with a fair percentage for the business. She'd won personally, too, because he had made it clear with that kiss that he wasn't backing down from developing their relationship. And if she was honest with herself, she was looking forward to him trying.

Chapter 9

"A café inside the bakery?" Lillian Drayson asked over the phone when Mariah, Chase and Jackson shared the news with her and the entire Chicago Drayson clan in a conference call the following Monday morning.

"Yes," Chase replied. "In addition to selling Myers Coffee Roasters, a well-known brand in Seattle, they'll be setting up a café inside the bakery, selling cappuccinos, lattes and more."

There was applause in the background and Mariah looked at her brothers and beamed with pride.

"I think it's an excellent idea." Mariah heard Belinda speaking and was happy for her cousin's support.

"And I second that," Shari interjected. Coming from the head of operations for Lillian's of Chicago, it was high praise indeed. "I wish I would have thought of it myself."

"Perhaps Mariah can convince Mr. Myers to consider expanding his interests," Jackson said, glancing over at

Mariah, who colored with embarrassment. She knew her brothers thought that she'd been the driving force behind Everett's decision to partner with them.

"And I would certainly entertain the idea," Shari responded. "As we all would."

Several minutes later, the conference call ended.

"That went great," Chase said.

"Yeah, those Chicago Draysons are seeing that they aren't the only smart ones," Jackson added.

"Why must you always be so negative toward them?" Mariah inquired.

"I agree with Mariah," Chase stated. "We need to make and define our own relationship with our Chicago relatives. We can't let some past beef or grudge with our grandparents over money, a situation we weren't even part of, affect our business. Can you agree to that much, Jack?"

"Fine."

"Trust me, starting off a new business isn't going to be easy and we need all the help we can get," Chase said.

Mariah knew the café would be the boost that the bakery needed to increase sales. The development of the Myers Coffee Roasters café was going much faster than she and her brothers thought. Once they'd given the green light, Everett had several general contractors in, quoting on the work. It was a revolving door at the bakery. He'd also had a contract drafted and signed within days.

Each time a contractor came, Everett was right there with him. He made a point of stopping in to speak to Mariah. Not just to introduce her to whoever was there, but to say hello, see how her day was going or grab a pastry and run. Everett Myers was starting to become a permanent fixture in Mariah's life and she was getting used to seeing him every day. When she didn't, she was in a sour mood.

Jackson commented on it late one night when they were cleaning up the kitchen.

"What are you talking about?" Mariah demanded, even though she knew exactly what he meant. The contractors were finalizing their bids, so there was no reason for Everett to stop by every day as he had been doing.

Jackson scoured her with a disbelieving look. "You know what I'm referring to," he countered. "Myers hasn't been here in a few days and you've been sulking around like someone stole your puppy."

She rolled her eyes at him. "Very funny. My life doesn't revolve around him. If you hadn't noticed, I've been quite busy perfecting a new recipe I've been working on."

Her brother raised an eyebrow. "Oh, yeah, you have been pretty secretive about it. What've you got cooking?"

Mariah shrugged. "I'm not sure. I don't have a name for it yet, but I'm close. And when I'm done, I think it'll put us on the map and have Sweetness Bakery quaking in their boots."

He stepped back. "You're that confident?"

Mariah nodded excitedly. She'd had the idea for a while and finally started working on the dessert at home during her spare time. Not that she had much of it, since the bakery took up most of her day. "I think I'm on to something, Jack."

"Well, don't keep me in suspense. When are you going to let me try it out?"

Mariah smiled devilishly. "Soon. Soon."

"We're here," Everett said, when he pulled his Escalade into a parking space outside Lillian's on Thursday morning. The hotel, the coffee importing business and a chaperoning trip for EJ's school had kept him away from the bakery for nearly a week, so he was excited to see the progress on construction.

He'd brought his top barista, Amber Bernard, with him from his flagship coffeehouse in Pike's Market today. Everett had chosen Amber from his current staff to come work at the bakery and wanted her to meet Mariah.

It also helped that Amber wasn't bad on the eyes, either. She was petite, only five feet two, but her large personality more than made up for what she lacked in height. He felt Amber's easy and lighthearted temperament would suit the bakery and help build the customer base, just as she'd done at the Pike's Market location.

She had long brunette curls, big brown eyes and an infectious smile, while her wardrobe was just as colorful as the lady herself. She favored bohemian type outfits— gauzy patterned shirts, floor-sweeping skirts and flat leather sandals—but as long as she could sell coffee, that was just fine with Everett.

"C'mon, Amber," He unbuckled his seat belt. "I want to show you where you'll be working."

"Sure thing, boss," she replied, and followed him inside.

Mariah was standing at the counter and her smile at seeing him vanished when she realized he wasn't alone, but had a woman with him. "W-who's this?"

Everett saw the flash of jealousy that sparked across Mariah's face when she spotted Amber, and he quite enjoyed it. It meant that she was starting to see him as hers and that secretly thrilled him. "Mariah, I'd like you to meet Amber Bernard, the barista who'll be on-site for Myers Coffee Roasters. Amber, this is Mariah Drayson, the owner of Lillian's of Seattle and the best baker in this town."

He watched the tension ease out of Mariah as she

warmly smiled at Amber and extended her hand. "Nice to meet you."

Instead of accepting the handshake, Amber leaned toward Mariah and gave her a hug. "Great meeting you, as well. I look forward to working with you."

Mariah was obviously surprised by the open display of affection, but returned Amber's hug. "As do I."

"I wanted Amber to come by to meet you," Everett continued, "as well as see where she'll be working."

Mariah turned to her. "Would you like a tour of the bakery?"

Amber smiled back at her. "Love one."

Everett watched the two women walk away without a backward glance at him. "I guess I'll entertain myself?"

Mariah waved a hand behind her and Everett couldn't resist a chuckle.

Without thinking, Mariah circled her arm through Amber's. There was a warm, friendly aura around the barista and Mariah had seen it, felt it as soon as she'd gotten over her momentary pang of jealousy at finding Everett with another woman.

When she'd exited the kitchen and seen him standing there in the storefront, her stomach had lurched and her heart had begun palpitating faster in her chest. She'd missed him, and her body was betraying her by telling her that he was more to her than just a business partner. Seeing him with another woman had felt like a gut punch, because perhaps he didn't feel the same way anymore? Mariah was happy to know that wasn't the case and wanted to welcome Amber to her new workplace.

"How long have you known Everett?" she asked as she led Amber to the back of the building where the offices were located. Unfortunately, Chase had gone to the bank, so she wasn't able to introduce him.

"A couple of years now," Amber replied. "Mr. Myers likes to get know all his employees and routinely drops in on all the coffeehouses."

"Really?" Mariah wouldn't have thought he had the time.

"Yep." Amber nodded. "He really cares about us. And the company offers great benefits. Health insurance and college education assistance."

"Oh, my." Mariah touched her chest. "I hadn't realized. That's very generous."

"That's Mr. Myers."

Mariah was silent as she absorbed the information. He was fast becoming someone she not only liked, but admired and respected for his work ethic.

Amber stared at her strangely for a couple minutes before inquiring, "Are you and Mr. Myers involved?"

Her question startled Mariah. "Why would you ask that?"

She shrugged. "Oh, I don't know…all the sexual tension coming off the both of you."

Mariah didn't have a comeback from that because Amber was right. "Is it that obvious?"

She chuckled. "To me? Yes. I'm pretty good at reading people's auras and you guys are off the charts."

"Well, nothing's happened."

"Not yet," Amber said with a smirk. "But it will."

"How can you be so sure?"

"Oh, I just know."

"Do you?" Mariah paused for several beats before asking, "Why haven't you pursued him yourself?"

"Me and Mr. Myers?" Amber let out a hearty laugh. "Oh, that would never work. I'm too much of a free spirit for Everett. He needs someone more grounded. Plus I admire him big-time and would never ruin that, but he's a great guy. You won't go wrong with him."

Mariah was surprised by Amber's honesty and thoughtful insight. She wasn't sure she was any match for Everett, either, with all her baggage, but the barista seemed certain that a relationship was in the cards for them. "Thank you." Mariah didn't have any friends in Seattle, but something told her that she'd just made one. "Thanks a lot."

She started walking down the hall. "C'mon, let me show you the kitchen."

"This is where all the magic happens?" Amber asked from the doorway.

"That's right," Mariah replied. "I'd like to introduce you to my brother Jackson. Jack…" She motioned him forward.

"Who's this?" he asked, surveying Amber from head to toe.

Mariah rolled her eyes at him. She hoped her brother wasn't about to come on to her. "Jack, this is Amber, our new barista for the café."

His mouth formed an O. "Great to meet you." He wiped his hand on his apron and offered it to her.

She shook it with fervor. Amber didn't seem to care about Jack's dust-splattered apron. "Nice to meet you."

"I've got to check on my focaccia," Jackson said as he began walking backward. "Look forward to working with you." He rushed toward the convection ovens.

When the tour was over, Mariah led Amber back to the front. "That's about it."

As the barista surveyed the baked goods in the display cases, Mariah leaned close to Everett, who'd been waiting for them. "If I could have a word?"

"Sure."

They left Amber in the café area and Mariah led Everett toward the administrative office. Fortunately for her it was empty, because Chase still hadn't returned from his errands.

"As you can see, everything is going smoothly," she said. "We have construction under control, so your visits to the bakery won't be needed and we can limit our association."

Everett frowned and it was clear she'd offended him. She hadn't meant to, but the café was off the ground, so he didn't really need to stop by every day unless—

"Our association is far from over," Everett responded. "In fact, I'd say it's about to heat up."

"Oh, yeah?"

Before she could protest, Everett's arm encircled her waist and he pulled her to him and claimed her lips. It was a surprisingly gentle kiss considering he was angry with her, and Mariah knew she should take a step back, but she didn't, couldn't. All she could do was stand there and let him take over in a kiss so utterly thorough and commanding that her entire being became inflamed. He took his time feasting on her and when he sought out her tongue, she didn't dare pull away. She readily gave it up to him, causing him to draw her closer, tighter into his embrace as he greedily sucked on it.

She hadn't realized just how much she'd hungered for another one of his kisses until now. When he slowly pulled away, Mariah was slightly dazed and barely registered what he said as she inhaled a deep breath and released it.

"Come out with me tomorrow night," Everett stated, rather than asked. "And this time it will be about you and me. Everett and Mariah. Not Myers Coffee Roasters and Lillian's of Seattle. Say yes."

She wanted to resist. "Oh, I don't know..." Her head was still cloudy from his drugging kisses.

He used her uncertainty to seal the deal. "You know you want to," he whispered. "If you need further convincing, I can supply it."

Mariah felt his steady gaze boring into her in silent expectation. She'd felt the heat behind that kiss and knew he had, as well. He wouldn't give up and perhaps she should stop fighting the inevitable. The attraction between them certainly hadn't lessened. "Okay," she finally agreed. "I'll go out with you."

He smiled broadly, clearly pleased that he'd gotten his way. "Good." He bent down to steal another kiss. "Until next time."

Chapter 10

"Big date?" EJ asked Everett from the edge of the bed on Friday night, as he sat in his father's bedroom watching him get ready for an evening with Mariah.

Everett spun around to face him as he patted his cheeks with aftershave. "Yeah, but how do you know?"

EJ shrugged. "I just can tell. You're really happy and smiling a whole lot. I just figured you must really like her."

"And how would you feel about that?" Everett inquired, hiking up his trousers so he could bend down and be at eye level with his son. This was the first time he'd been this excited about a woman since he'd been widowed. But he had to be sure it was right for his son, too.

"I dunno."

Everett couldn't read what his son was thinking. "Yes, you do."

"I want you to be happy. So I guess if she makes you grin like that—" EJ poked his index finger into one of Everett's dimples "—then she can't be half-bad."

"She's not," Everett responded with a smile as he rose to his feet. "And one day soon I'd like you to meet her."

"For real?"

Everett smiled. "For real." He suspected that Mariah Drayson just might become a permanent fixture in his life, so she would need to meet his other half, his son. Everett just hoped she wouldn't have a problem with him having a child. He'd never brought EJ up in their conversations because he'd tried to keep their talks either on business, or light and playful. But tonight was about just the two of them. He was going to have to open up about himself and his past if he ever expected them to go the distance as a couple. And tonight would tell him all he needed to know.

Mariah was ready for her second date with Everett. She'd selected an asymmetrical, snakeskin-print, charmeuse maxi dress with gladiator sandals. She turned around so she could see a side view of her reflection in her bathroom mirror. The paneling spiraled into the shirred, flowing back and showed just enough curves, while the tank style revealed the slight swell of her breasts without being indecent. All in all, she was set for the evening.

Everett had told her to dress "comfortable yet casual" and she thought she'd pulled it off. She hadn't had anything she wanted to wear and had made a quick stop at Nordstrom to find something suitable.

When the doorbell rang, Everett was waiting for her dressed casually in dark trousers, a V-neck sweater and loafers.

He walked toward her as she reached for her shawl and purse. "You look lovely." His eyes raked every inch of her in the charmeuse dress.

"I'm glad you approve," Mariah said as she preceded him out of the building.

"Oh, I do."

Once outside, she noticed the fancy sports car sitting at the curb. "Nice ride," she commented. "You're driving tonight," she added, when he came around to the driver's side and climbed in.

He gave her a sideways glance as he turned on the engine. "I am. I wanted the night to be just the two of us."

Mariah glanced at all the gadgets and dials on the console. "This is quite impressive compared with your Escalade. How long have you had it?"

"Not long." He revved the motor. "I bought it for my thirtieth birthday. This is only my second time taking it out for a spin."

Mariah turned to face him. "If you want to impress me, Everett, you don't have to try so hard."

"I wasn't," he responded, and winked as he took off. "Trust me, if I were, you'd know it. But if I was, how would I be faring?"

She flashed a smile. "Very well indeed."

As they drove, they chatted about their respective days, before venturing on to the latest news topics. Conversation between them was always smooth. They had an easy camaraderie whenever they were together. Mariah didn't have to think of things to say to keep communication moving because Everett was knowledgeable on a variety of topics.

As they neared the Washington Ship Canal, Mariah began to wonder where they were going. The Ballard Locks would be an odd choice for a romantic date. She glanced down at her gladiator sandals. Even with a low heel, she wasn't prepared to stroll through the marina or climb any ladders to watch the salmon pass through the fresh- and saltwater locks.

Everett glanced over at her. "Wondering where we're going?"

"Quite frankly, yes," she admitted. "I'm not exactly dressed for a night at the marina."

He gave a low baritone chuckle and she felt her stomach leap in response. "Don't worry, I wouldn't dream of mussing you up, not since you went to all the trouble of looking good for me."

Mariah's breath hitched in her throat. She wanted to say she hadn't dressed up for him, but it would be a lie. She had and he'd noticed.

Everett stopped the car at the back entrance to the Carl English Botanical Gardens, adjacent to the Ballard Locks, and came around to open her door.

Mariah looked at the setting. "What are we doing here?"

He took her hand. "You'll see."

Everett's touch caused an electrical current to shoot right through her. And when she glanced in his direction, he winked at her. He'd felt it, too, that strange, inexplicable pull whenever they were together. It unnerved her.

An elderly man holding a picnic basket was waiting for them. "Good evening, Mr. Myers."

"Good evening, Joseph. I'd like to introduce you to Mariah Drayson."

"Good evening, madam," the older man said. "Please go inside and enjoy your evening."

Everett patted the man's arm. "Thank you." He took the picnic basket with his free hand, not letting go of Mariah's with the other. He led her through the garden grounds, and they stopped to admire the variety of plants from around the world, including flowering perennials, fan palms, oaks, Mexican pines and rhododendrons. The colors, fragrances and open air helped to awaken Mariah's senses and made her very aware of Everett and his own unique scent.

"Watch your step," he said as he led her off the trail and down a grassy slope.

The sun was setting, but Mariah could still see in front of her, and stopped suddenly, nearly catching Everett off guard. Farther down the hill a picnic area had been set up in front of a small stage with bright lights that illuminated the area. She'd heard about free concerts at the gardens but had never been to one. Except this time, there were no other people around except them.

She turned to Everett. "Did you do all of this?"

He grinned broadly. "I did. I know a few folks who help run the place and…" His voice trailed off.

Once again Everett was impressing her and reminding her that he would go to any lengths to romance her. "This is really special…" It was all she could manage to say as she continued walking down the slope of the romantic English-country setting with him.

When they made it to the blanket, Everett helped her to the ground before settling beside her with the picnic basket.

Mariah rubbed her hands together. "So what have you got in there?" she asked excitedly.

He laughed, "Oh, a little bit of this, a little bit of that."

"Well, let me see." She reached for the basket, but Everett slid it farther away. After growing up with two older brothers, Mariah was not to be outdone and rushed at him, tackling him to the blanket. In so doing, she ended up on top of his hard, lean body. Everett had an inherent masculine strength that oozed from his powerfully built frame and, heaven help her, she couldn't resist him.

They stared at each other for several seconds. Her throat felt tight and constricted and her insides burned hotter than an inferno. In the end, it was Mariah who gave in first and lowered her head. Her lips were hesitant, softly brushing his before becoming more insistent as they moved across his soft mouth. Everett took the bait and rose slightly as one of his hands came around the back of her head, bringing her closer to him so he could deepen the kiss.

It was a slow, languorous kiss and one that had Mariah warring with herself. She'd said that she would keep her distance from Everett, but the second he laid on the charm she was agreeing to a date. And now...now she was kissing him with a hunger and fervor that both surprised and incited her. So when his tongue licked the seam of her lips, demanding entry, she opened them. Greedily, taking his tongue and sucking on it while his hands roamed over her body to her buttocks and cupped her.

She wrapped her arms around his neck and her whole body fell atop him. That's when she felt the bulge in his pants. She'd done that. She'd turned him on with just one kiss. It secretly thrilled her that she could have such an instant effect on him, but why should she be surprised? He'd been doing the same thing to her from the moment they'd met.

"Ahem." A loud cough from above them caused them to pull away.

Everett was the first to recover from the passionate embrace and he spoke without removing his arms from around her waist. "Yes?"

"Sir, we'll be ready to begin in about fifteen minutes," Joseph said, a stone's throw away from them.

"Of course," Everett said smoothly. "Proceed."

Embarrassed at being caught, Mariah moved away and sat upright, straightening her clothes.

"Don't be embarrassed." He turned to her, stretching out on his side, and leaned his head on his elbow. "I enjoyed your spontaneity."

Mariah glanced at him through tremulous lashes. "You did?" She'd never been the aggressor during her marriage to Richard. He'd always been the one to initiate love-making and she'd thought that was normal.

Everett reached across the small space between them and lightly caressed her cheek with the palm of his hand. His eyes were dark and stormy with lust. The very same lust she'd felt moments ago and still felt. "Yes, immensely," he responded.

Everett watched Mariah as she swayed on the blanket to the smooth sounds of Brian McKnight, her favorite singer. She'd been stunned when he'd taken to the stage as they enjoyed a gourmet picnic dinner, and began singing "Cherish."

It had taken a lot of legwork on Everett's part, but he'd succeeded in securing the entertainer for a private concert for just the two of them. And the look on Mariah's face right now told him it had been worth every penny. Her eyes were alight with joy and Everett could see that not only was she enjoying herself, but she was starting to feel comfortable being around him. His slow and steady approach was working. It wasn't easy on his libido, though. Whenever he was around her, it was impossible not to want to take her to his bed and ravish her body all night. He recalled how his manhood had swelled in response to her spontaneous kiss. Even now he desired her, but he would rein it in until Mariah gave the word or a signal that she was ready to take their relationship to the next level.

For him, that meant introducing her to EJ, though he hadn't exactly shared that he had an eight-year-old son. Everett had assumed she would have figured it out when she'd researched him online, but then he realized she didn't know. Probably because he prided himself in keeping EJ's life private from the inquisitive eyes of the press. So he hadn't been forthcoming with the information. It was his job as a parent to protect EJ, and because he hadn't been sure where their relationship would lead, he'd kept the fact of EJ's existence to himself. But tonight gave Everett hope that Mariah could really be a contender as the next woman in his and EJ's life.

At that moment, she turned to him. "Everett, this is incredible," she said. "I can't thank you enough for this." She reached across the small space between them and took his hand and gave it a squeeze.

Everett felt a jolt of electricity run through him at her tender touch. "You're welcome."

When Brian McKnight began singing one of his popular love songs, "Love of My Life," Everett rose to his feet. "Would you like to dance?"

"Absolutely."

And that's how they continued the remainder of the evening—in each other's arms swaying to the smooth grooves. When he returned Mariah to her apartment nearly two hours later, he switched the car engine off and they sat for several long, excruciating moments. Did she not want the night to end, either?

He'd never considered himself a die-hard romantic, but the evening was made for lovers, with the music, the picnic with champagne, caviar and the stars overhead. But he wouldn't push, not until she was ready.

Mariah turned to face him. He couldn't see what she was thinking because it was too dark in the car's interior, but he could tell she was warring with herself. "Everett, I…"

"Yes?" He encouraged her to say whatever she was thinking, feeling.

She took her time, as if formulating her thoughts. "I don't think I've ever had such a great time like I did tonight. I didn't think you could top the Space Needle, but you did. This was truly the best date ever!"

Everett beamed with pride. "Thank you and you're welcome." He suspected there was something else on her mind and he waited for her to say more.

"Th-this isn't easy for me," Mariah stammered, wringing her hands. "You and me." She pointed to his chest and then hers.

"I know."

"You've been very patient and I'm sorry if I've given you mixed signals. I—I just wasn't sure I was ready to dive into another relationship after my divorce."

"And now?" he asked quietly.

"I can't deny the feelings I have toward you are growing, and I guess what I'm saying very ineffectually is that I'd like to pursue them and see where this goes. I won't fight you anymore."

If he could have jumped up and down, Everett would have. He knew how much that admission had cost her. So he treaded lightly and reached for her hands in the darkened space and clasped them. "Thank you for being honest with me and yourself." He smiled. "And this relationship can move as slow or as fast as you need it to, without any pressure from me."

"You mean that?"

He chuckled. If he was reading her correctly, she must have expected him to make a move on her so he could take her to bed tonight. And with any other woman, he might have, but not Mariah. She was special and a little bit delicate, so for now he would treat her like the princess she was. But when the time came for them to become lovers, he would unleash his desires. "Of course I do," he murmured. "Let me walk you inside."

They ended the evening at her doorstep, wrapped up in each other arms. And this time Mariah didn't resist his kisses. Instead she was a full participant, coaxing his lips apart with her tongue and diving inside to mate it with his. The kiss was like soldering heat that joined metals, and they fused together as one.

Everett erupted with desire and returned her ardor by covering her mouth with hungry kisses. Mariah gave herself freely up to the passion of his embrace, and when then finally separated, he caressed her cheek and said, "Good night, sweetheart."

As her apartment door closed, Everett realized that he was falling hard for the sexy baker. Which meant that now was the time. She had to pass one final test. It was time she met EJ.

Chapter 11

Mariah continued tinkering with the recipe for her new creation on Saturday morning at the bakery. She always tried to keep busy when her mind was preoccupied, and it was, thanks to her new relationship with Everett. She'd agreed to date him and see where it would lead. In the light of day, however, she was having cold feet.

What did she know about dating, anyway? Her experience was severely limited because she'd gotten married so young. And Everett, well, he was a grown man with a man's needs, and she had grave reservations about taking their relationship to the next level, in the bedroom.

She was sure a man of Everett's stature and reputation had been with many women since his wife's passing. Mariah had resisted the urge to find out more online, other than his business interests. She hadn't wanted to know how she compared to other women he saw, or his deceased wife, all of whom were probably more sophisticated than she.

She knew he'd been married and lost his wife, but reading any more about that loss would have been too personal and too intrusive. Mariah hadn't felt right reading about Everett's greatest tragedy.

So she'd decided to come to the bakery and perfect her creation once and for all. And she had. She'd also finally come up with a name for it, and consequently had woken up both her brothers to meet her at the bakery at 5:00 a.m. Jackson was used to being up so early, while Chase, a numbers man, didn't normally stop by the bakery until much later.

Needless to say, Chase came in bleary-eyed, wearing sweatpants and a T-shirt. "What's so urgent?" he inquired. "That you had to wake me from my peaceful sleep?"

Jackson shrugged. "I was already on my way, so it makes no difference to me. What you got, kid?" He was dressed for the day in dark denims and a fitted muscle shirt.

Mariah ignored both of them and held up her creation. "I have come up with the next great pastry." She lifted the covered platter. "I give you...the Draynut!" She removed the lid and presented her work with a flourish.

"What is it?" Chase asked, looking up at her. "It looks like a doughnut, but..." He stared at it as if it was a foreign object.

Mariah sighed wearily. "Just try it." She held out the platter, and reluctantly Chase and Jackson each withdrew a pastry and sampled it.

"Mmm..." was all Mariah heard from both of them after they'd taken their first bite.

"This is delicious, sis," Jackson responded, reaching for a second one. "What'd you put in it?"

She smiled wickedly. "I'll never tell. Matter-of-fact, I want to trademark this recipe and name immediately.

Chase, that's where I need your help. I want to ensure no one gets their hands on this and tries to replicate it. The secret ingredients need to be kept under lock and key."

Jackson seemed affronted, but kept eating his Draynut. "Even from me?"

"It's nothing personal," Mariah said. "But I think you can agree we have something great here, and for the moment I'd like to keep it close to the vest."

Chase reached for a paper towel from the nearby counter and wiped his mouth, because he'd already finished his sample. "I agree we don't want anyone else to get their hands on this, so you will need to give me the recipe for the trademark."

"When you have all the paperwork ready, let me know," Mariah said. "In the meantime, we should debut the Draynut at the grand opening of Myers Coffee Roasters café. I've already prepared a press release."

She held up the document she'd spent most of last night preparing, because she'd tossed and turned in bed after Everett had dropped her off, until finally giving up and coming to the bakery.

"Let me see that." Jackson read the one-pager. When he was done, he handed it to Chase. "That's really good, Mariah. You're doing some spectacular work, kid. Who knew you had it in you?"

Mariah smiled. She knew that Jackson's back-handed compliment was meant with love and affection. "Thanks, bro."

Chase turned to them both after he was done reading the press release. "Well done, Mariah, well done. What price point did you have in my mind for the Draynut?"

"I don't know. Maybe three dollars?"

"Too low," Jackson declared. "We need to go higher. This is a specialty item and the more expensive it is, the higher in demand it will become. Look at what happened with the Cronut phase in New York. Let's charge five dollars like they did."

Chase pointed his finger at his brother. "Jack has a point, Mariah. This—" he held up the platter of Draynuts "—is a gold mine and we want everyone to know that, like you said, it's the next best thing!"

Mariah smiled warmly. She was thrilled that her brothers were just as excited as she was by her new creation. "Let's do it!"

Later that evening, Mariah scooted out early from the bakery. They'd hired an intern. Kelsey Andrews was a cute blonde with short curly hair, a petite figure and gorgeous hazel eyes. She was working a few hours during their peak times and helping them at the cash register. It allowed Mariah a few hours off during the week to run errands, or in today's case, take a break.

She was meeting up with Amber at what looked to be an after-school center, she thought, as she drove up to the one-story building. The two women had hit it off after their first meeting, exchanged phone numbers and agreed to get together. Though Mariah had no idea that this was what Amber did in her spare time.

She was waiting outside by the curb as Mariah pulled up. "Thanks for the ride," Amber said as she got in. "My red Bug is giving me car trouble. I'd love to get rid of it, but I've had it for years.

"It's no problem," Mariah replied. "So, what do you do at the center?"

"I work with preteen girls as part of a group that fosters girl empowerment."

"That's wonderful."

"They're always looking for volunteers. You should

think about it. After a background check, you could qualify to help out these young girls. Just let me know if you're interested."

Mariah glanced at the school as she drove away. She wasn't sure she could be around small kids consistently, knowing she couldn't have one of her own. But then again, maybe it would be cathartic? Helping children might ease her own pain and loss.

"What's wrong?" Amber's warm brown eyes were staring at her.

She shrugged. "It's nothing."

"It's more than that," Amber replied. "There's a sadness in your eyes that wasn't there before I started talking about my work."

Mariah changed the subject. "How about a cocktail first?"

Once they'd arrived at a popular wine room, filled their wine cards with money and used them to help dispense the ounces of wine they wanted, they settled into two large, comfy leather chairs to chat and get to know each other.

Mariah learned Amber's family was originally from the South, but had migrated north. She was attending graduate school at the University of Washington and getting her masters of business degree.

"And in my spare time I'm an artist. Well, more like a jewelry maker, to be exact." Amber held out her wrists so Mariah could see the bracelets she wore, and then pointed to her ears and neck to showcase the matching earrings and necklace.

"Do you sleep?" Mariah asked, sipping her merlot. "Or maybe cure world hunger?" She laughed at her own joke.

And so did Amber. "I don't know." She shrugged. "I just like to keep busy. And as far as my jewelry—" she held up her wrists again and admired her adornments "—I've always loved making them and would love to sell them full-time."

"Then you should," Mariah said. "I for one would certainly buy them. I love the necklace you're wearing." She reached out to finger the different stones and beadwork on the chain dangling from Amber's slender neck.

Her new friend beamed and a smile spread across her lips. "Thank you. And I'll bring some of my pieces next time to the bakery so you can take a look."

"I would love that."

"But enough about me. Why don't you tell me what got you so down earlier?"

Mariah shrugged.

"C'mon. I know we're not best friends or anything, but I'd like to be an ear to listen." Amber slid her legs underneath her on the chair and faced Mariah.

Mariah mulled it over. What could it hurt to confide in Amber? It would be nice to have a sounding board, especially with Belinda so far away in Chicago. "All right, it's really quite simple. I can't have children," she blurted out. Sometimes it was better to rip off a Band-Aid rather than ease it off.

Amber was silent for a long moment. "And how does that make you feel?"

"Damaged. Diminished. Less than a woman. All of the above." Mariah took a gulp of her wine. She'd never been this blunt and honest with anyone before and shared her deepest thoughts, but something told her she could trust Amber.

Amber reached across the distance between them and squeezed her hand. "I know I can't tell you how to feel about it, but you're *still* an amazing woman and that hasn't changed. And whether or not you're physically able to birth a child, you can still be a mother. There are so many children in need out there who would be lucky to have a mom like you."

Mariah smiled at Amber with tears in her eyes. "Thank you, thank you. I think I needed to hear that. It's been hard having this hanging over my head. My infertility and my quest to get pregnant destroyed my marriage, and I fear it could do the same thing again."

"With Everett?"

She glanced at Amber. "How did you know?"

Amber laughed softly. "How could I not? The chemistry was coming off you two in droves when we met. I'd have to be blind not to see how into you he is. But I take it he doesn't know?"

Mariah nodded and drank more of her wine. "It's not exactly a topic of conversation you dive right into when you're getting to know someone, but if things progress between us…"

"You'll tell him," Amber said. "When you're ready. And when you do, I'll be there to support you."

"Thanks, Amber. I have to tell you that I really needed a friend here in Seattle and I'm really happy to have met you. I sure could have used you a year ago in Chicago," she said with a laugh.

"Well, I'm here now and feel free to lean on me."

"Oh, I will," Mariah stated emphatically. "I will. And you can do the same."

It was Sunday morning and Everett felt he deserved a treat for all his hard work, such as a pastry at Lillian's after he'd completed his usual weekend workout in his home gym. As he dressed in distressed jeans and a polo shirt, he knew the real reason he was going. He wanted to see Mariah.

Now that she'd agreed to date him, Everett didn't have

to make excuses to see her anymore. He could visit the bakery any time he wanted.

Except today was different. This time he was bringing EJ with him so he could finally introduce his son to the lady in his life. Everett had to admit that he was a little nervous at the prospect. He had no idea how EJ would respond to having another person, a woman, in his father's life. He might see her as an interloper in their relationship, and things could go badly.

On the other hand, EJ might like Mariah, which would please Everett immensely, because he so desperately wanted his son to like her as much as he did. There might not be a future if she wasn't receptive to his having a child. Everett knew it wasn't fair that he was springing EJ on her this way without any warning, but the right moment to tell her had never arisen.

Everett had spent the last four weeks trying to break through the wall and electrified fence Mariah had erected around her heart. Friday night had been the first time he'd felt comfortable enough to share his past, but the evening had been so romantic Everett hadn't had the heart to ruin it. Yesterday, after their date, he'd given some serious thought to whether or not Mariah was ready to meet EJ. He'd then decided it was time, and today was the day. Mariah might become angry with him due to his lack of forthrightness. So he'd kept EJ's existence to himself, but not anymore.

Today, Mariah would meet the most important person in Everett's life. He just prayed that EJ would become as important to her as he was to him.

EJ was waiting for him at the breakfast bar, already dressed for the day in jeans, a print T-shirt and sneakers. He looked like a mini version of Everett except he had a headful of curly hair, while Everett's hair was clipped short.

"Morning, Dad."

"Good morning, EJ," Everett said, on his way to his Keurig coffee maker. He inserted a K-cup and placed a mug underneath from the cupboard. The coffee percolated and was ready within minutes. "What are we doing today, Dad?" EJ asked.

"I thought we could stop by a bakery and grab a snack."

"We normally have a big breakfast on Saturday," EJ complained with a frown.

"I know," Everett said, sipping his coffee. "But I want us to try something different. Plus I want you to see the new location Daddy's been working on. You all right with that?"

"Sure," EJ said. "Guess so."

After he'd finished his coffee, Everett and EJ set off for Lillian's of Seattle. Traffic was light and they made it to the Denny Triangle section of downtown Seattle in no time. When he opened the door, the bakery was bustling with Sunday visitors getting a snack or picking up a birthday cake. While in line, he could hear patrons commenting about what was going on behind the temporary door they'd hung to keep the construction apart from the customers. He noticed Mariah was remaining mum at the register.

Everett had to admit that even with her honey-blond hair piled in a simple updo and very little makeup on, as usual, she still was the most beautiful woman in the room.

When the crowd began to dissipate, she finally looked up and noticed Everett and EJ in line. "Everett," she exclaimed, tucking her hair into place and smoothing her apron. "What are you doing here?"

He smiled as he placed his hands on EJ's shoulders

and walked him toward the counter. She was right to be surprised. He hardly ever came in on weekends since he spent most of them with his son. But today was different.

She smiled down at EJ. "And who do you have with you?"

"Mariah, I'd like you to meet my son."

Chapter 12

Mariah stared back at Everett, dumbfounded. Had she heard him correctly? Had he really said *his son*? She looked at Everett and then at the young boy at his side and had her answer. He looked exactly like Everett, just a miniature version. With wooden legs, she walked from behind the counter to greet him.

She bent down until she was the boy's height. "It's nice to meet you, EJ." She extended her hand. "Finally." She glanced up at Everett and could swear she saw him sweating bullets.

"Nice to meet you, too, Miss Mariah."

Mariah smiled into his endearing brown eyes and melted. He'd called her Miss Mariah. She'd never thought she'd hear a child say her name.

Mariah rose to her feet. "You hungry? We have some blueberry muffins that just came out of the oven."

EJ wrinkled his nose. "I don't like blueberries."

Mariah chuckled at his honesty. "How about chocolate chip? Will that do?"

A broad smile came across his small features as he nodded.

"C'mon." She held out her hand. "Follow me."

EJ started toward her and then glanced behind him at his father.

Everett nodded. "It's okay. Go ahead."

So EJ grasped her hand and walked with her toward the kitchen. Mariah couldn't resist a backward scouring look at Everett as they departed.

But once they made it to the kitchen, she was all smiles as she showed EJ around.

"Who do we have here?" Jackson asked as they approached the cooling table bearing a batch of chocolate chip muffins just out of the oven.

"This is EJ." Mariah lifted the boy onto a stool, then went in search of a plate.

"What's your full name, little fella?" Jackson inquired.

"EJ Myers."

"Is that short for Everett Myers Jr.?" Jackson glanced in Mariah's direction as she returned with a paper plate.

EJ nodded. "Yep, I'm named after my dad."

"And that's a very strong name indeed." Mariah reached for one of the muffins, placed it on the plate and slid it over to EJ.

"Thank you, Miss Mariah," he said, right before he grabbed the muffin and took a generous bite. Since it was still warm, the chocolate chips inside were a bit gooey and were now all over his face.

Mariah laughed as she walked to the paper towel rack hanging from the wall and ripped off a piece. "Here, wipe your face."

EJ accepted the paper towel but didn't use it. Instead, he bit into the muffin again.

"So," Jackson whispered, coming toward her. "You're just meeting EJ?"

Mariah didn't get a chance to answer before EJ did, with a mouthful of muffin. "Yep, my dad said it was time that I meet someone special because we might be spending a lot of time together."

Mariah's heart instantly warmed at EJ's continued honesty. It was so refreshing and revealing. How could she be mad at Everett when he'd told his son that she was someone special and he wanted them to get to know each other? It was clear to her that Everett saw potential in their relationship. Why else would he introduce her to his son? Otherwise, he would have continued to keep EJ's existence a secret, as he'd done for a month.

Of course, she was still upset with him on that front. Because although she understood his reasoning, he still should have told her he had a son. He hadn't introduced them because he hadn't known where their relationship would lead, but to blindside her? That wasn't cool and she intended to tell him so.

"Jack, can you watch EJ for a moment while I go speak with his father?"

"Absolutely," her brother said with a smile. He knew what Everett had in store.

"Be right back." Mariah squeezed EJ's shoulder before she exited the room. "You'll be in good hands with my brother."

"Okay." EJ was oblivious to her as he continued devouring the muffin.

Mariah passed by Kelsey, who was tending to the front of the house, and found Everett behind the wooden partition, in the café. There was no construction during the weekend, so it was just the two of them. As excited as she was at the prospect of Myers Coffee Roasters café opening and the debut of Lillian's of Seattle's Draynut, it was time Mr. Myers got a talking to.

The look on her face must have been a dead giveaway to her mood because Everett instantly stepped back when she entered the small area. He offered her a weak smile.

"Why didn't you tell me about EJ?" She wasted no time getting to the point.

"I know you're upset—"

"Darn right, I'm upset," Mariah said, folding her arms across her chest. "A child? A *child*? How could you keep something as important as your child to yourself?"

Everett sighed. "It's precisely for that reason that I did." Mariah snorted, but he continued. "When I first started visiting, you were adamant that you weren't interested in getting to know me."

"That doesn't make it right."

"I know that and I agree, but you have to understand my point of view as a parent. The parent of a child who has already experienced more loss than any child should, the loss of his mother. I didn't want to bring someone into his life who wasn't going to be sticking around. It wouldn't be fair. I made the choice and I stand behind it, but I will agree that I should have at least told you about EJ's existence. I guess I figured when you'd looked me up online that websites would have mentioned him."

She shook her head. "There's nothing about EJ online. You've done a good job of shielding him from the press, given the circumstances, and that should be commended."

"Thank you. So I take it you don't know much about Sara, his mother?"

Mariah shrugged. "I didn't read up on your deceased wife or the accident. It felt kind of morbid, as well as deeply personal. I didn't think I had the right. I guess I figured you'd tell me when you were ready."

Everett was introspective for several long moments, making Mariah wonder if she shouldn't have mentioned his wife. Were the memories still too painful even after five years? When he finally spoke his voice was soft. "Thank you for your sensitivity. I'd like to talk to you about it one day. But for now, it's just important that you and EJ get to know each other. He's never really had a female presence in his life other than my mother and Margaret, our housekeeper."

Mariah couldn't stay mad at Everett, not when he'd done it to protect his son. She walked over to him, pulled him close and hugged him for several long moments. Shifting slightly, she held his face with both hands and stared deep into his dark eyes. "Thank you for thinking me worthy of meeting EJ. I'm honored."

And without thinking, she kissed him square on the lips, not caring where they were or who might walk in and see them making out. His mouth moved over hers, devouring its softness, and she parted her lips so he could deepen the kiss. Mariah felt spirals of ecstasy radiating through her entire body and knew they'd turned a corner.

"Ahem, ahem." A knock on the wooden door showed Jackson at the entry with EJ at his knees. "Someone was looking for you. Said he's still hungry after the chocolate chip muffin."

Mariah and Everett separated, but he kept his arm wrapped around her waist. "How about some lunch?" he inquired, glancing sideways at her.

Mariah looked down at her watch. She was tempted, but it was just past eleven and she really should stay and work. "It's a bit early—"

"Don't worry, sis," Jackson said from the door. "Kelsey and I can handle the bakery until you get back."

Her face split into a grin. "All right." She slid from Everett's embrace and untied her apron. "What do you say, EJ?" She walked toward him. "Can I come, too?"

EJ looked at his father pleadingly.

"Of course she can come," Everett said. "C'mon." And together, the three of them left the bakery.

They ended up at a restaurant known for its breakfast and brunch offerings. Mariah settled into a booth with EJ and his son. As she sat across from them, she was a bit disconcerted. Everett having a son was an unexpected wrinkle in her agreement to date him. Although not unwelcome, it was certainly a game changer.

"So what would you like to eat?" Mariah asked EJ. It amazed her at how much he looked like Everett. He shared his nose and deep-set eyes.

"Pancakes!"

"Pancakes sound great," Mariah exclaimed. "And I make the best. Someday I'll have to fix you some." She glanced at Everett and he smiled, telling her it was indeed a possibility.

"You do? So does Daddy," EJ said. "Did you learn from him?"

Mariah chuckled. "No, from my mother."

"Oh." EJ frowned as if she'd just said something distasteful.

Mariah glanced up at Everett, her eyes filling with concern.

"I'll teach you how to make them," Everett said softly. "And now Miss Mariah can help, too? If she's interested?"

Mariah saw that Everett was worried after EJ's response to her mother comment. Did he expect her to run away because he had a child? She'd been hurt that he hadn't felt he could tell her about EJ from the beginning, but she understood his reasoning and would try to put it behind them.

"Absolutely," she said with a smile. "And perhaps we'll have some bacon and eggs with our pancakes. What do you say, EJ?" When the young boy nodded fervently, she looked at his father. "And what about you, Everett?" She hoped her ease with EJ would alleviate his fears.

"Um…I need some protein after my workout this morning."

Mariah eyed him while he looked at his menu. His personal training would explain his excellent physique. There was no flab on the man, nothing but a lean body. She'd felt his masculine strength every time they'd kissed and it caused sexual tension to prickle inside her.

"Mariah, the waitress was asking you for your order." Everett interrupted her thoughts. "I already placed mine, of steak and eggs."

She glanced up and saw the waitress standing at their booth with a notepad. After rattling off her order, Mariah returned her focus to EJ. "So what are you guys doing today?"

"Clothes shopping," Everett answered. "This boy is growing like a weed. I can't keep him in clothes. I think he's going through a growth spurt."

EJ frowned. "I hate shopping."

"So do I," she said.

EJ seemed surprised. "You do? I thought all girls liked shopping."

Mariah chuckled. "Most do, but I'm with you. It's rather boring. The best part is when it's over."

EJ laughed at her joke and Mariah glanced up to find Everett watching her closely. She hoped he knew that meeting EJ wasn't a deal breaker, so she said, "I'm so happy to finally meet you, EJ. Maybe we can hang out sometime?"

His son offered her a grin. "I'd like that."

Mariah's heart melted on the spot for yet another Myers man.

When she returned from lunch with Everett and EJ, Mariah was contemplative as she walked into the kitchen.

"Well, how did it go?" Jackson inquired. "Don't leave me in suspense."

Mariah grinned. "It went great. Because we were early, we missed the lunch rush."

"I couldn't care less about that. I want to know how you fared with EJ."

Mariah stared up at the ceiling and her mind drifted off to another time. A time when she'd wanted kids so badly she'd have done anything to have one. Tried anything. And she had. She'd quit her job. She'd eaten better. All in her effort to become a mother. And now, when she hadn't been looking for it, it may just have landed in her lap. "It was wonderful."

"You sound surprised," Jackson said. "You've always been good with children, Mariah. Even when we were teenagers, you had a way with them. You'd babysit and they'd actually listen to you. It was like you were the child whisperer or something."

Mariah couldn't suppress her laughter. "The child whisperer?"

"It's true. I bet you charmed the pants off Everett's son."

She hazarded a glance in her brother's direction. "I think I did, but I guess I'll find out, if Everett never calls me again."

Jackson chuckled drily. "Like that would ever happen.

You've had that man sprung from the moment he laid eyes on you."

Mariah blushed. It had been the same for her. She'd thought Everett was attractive at the grand opening, but she'd been too afraid to allow herself to feel anything. Yet she had in time and it was more than she ever could have imagined. Now if their relationship continued to flourish, she had the possibility of a family.

"So, what did you think of Miss Mariah?" Everett asked EJ on the ride home after their brunch as they drove to the mall.

"I like her," EJ replied.

"You do?" To say he was happy was an understatement.

"Yeah, she's really nice and I love her muffins," EJ said, taking off the light jacket he'd been wearing. "Is that why you always bring back pastries to the house?"

"Partially," he responded. "Now that I'm going to have a café there, Dad's going to have to visit often. How do you feel about that?"

"Will we still get a chance to see Miss Amber?"

Everett smiled, remembering how well EJ and the barista had hit it off. "Actually, you will," he responded. "Amber's going to be working at the bakery with Miss Mariah."

"Awesome!" EJ said, and glanced out the window.

Everett stared at him for several seconds before returning his attention to the road. EJ was taking the fact that he was starting to date again really well. He'd always said that he wasn't dating because of EJ, but his son was just fine. Had Everett been the one too scared to take a risk and meet someone new? Or maybe it had just taken the right woman to open up his heart to the prospect?

That woman was Mariah Drayson. And knowing that

she and EJ connected made Everett realize that he was ready to take their relationship to the next level. Every time they were together he'd been reining in his passion and desire for Mariah. Waiting for EJ's blessing? Perhaps. But now that that hurdle was past them, Everett didn't see any reason to hold back any longer.

He wanted to *be* with Mariah in every sense of the word. He wanted to wrap her in his arms, have her legs twine around his waist and lose himself in her sweet heat. To that end, he would arrange a romantic getaway, one that would make it very clear to Mariah exactly what was in store.

"Yes, that sounds lovely. Can't wait," Mariah said, ending the call as she leaned back at her desk in the back of the bakery several days later.

"Is everything all right?" Amber inquired from the doorway. She'd stopped by to see if Mariah had time for lunch because she had a few hours between class and when she was due at the after-school center.

Mariah blinked several times. The conversation she'd just shared with Everett had butterflies jumping around in her stomach. "Yes, yes, I'm fine."

"You don't look like it," Amber replied. "I'll go grab you a glass of water."

"No, no." Mariah didn't want her nosy brothers checking up on her. She rose from the executive chair and pulled Amber inside her office before closing the door. Chase and Jackson were both too intuitive and could always pick up when something or someone was bothering her. She'd never been able to keep things a secret from them, but in this instance she must, because it was about her personal life and she didn't want or need their interference.

"What's going on?" Amber looked at her warily.

Mariah sighed. "I need some advice."

"What kind of advice?"

"About me and Everett."

Amber smiled. "Who else?" she she said with a laugh. "What's going on?"

"Well, he's asked me to join him for a trip to Bainbridge Island.

"That sounds wonderful," Amber gushed. "They have the greatest shops and nifty arts and crafts stores. When I go there…" She paused when she saw Mariah's face. "Sorry, I guess you were talking about you. Go ahead."

"I love the island, too, but he made sure to mention it would be an *overnight* trip," Mariah whispered, as if her brothers had their ears pressed to the door and could hear every word.

"And is this your first *overnight trip*?" Amber asked, her voice rising slightly.

Mariah nodded.

"Oh, my." Amber's cheeks became stained with red.

"I don't mean ever," Mariah responded, "but I don't have a lot of experience in that department."

"Who's to say he does?"

"Have you looked at him?" Mariah inquired with a raised brow. "Haven't you noticed the way women look at him when he walks into a room?"

Amber shrugged. "Probably not, because he's always been my boss. But anyway, I'm sure it's like riding a bike. It'll all come back to you."

Mariah began pacing the floor. "I'm sure it will, but…"

"But nothing. I'm certain that Everett, being the sort of take-charge man that he is, will teach you all you need to know. Don't worry. Just enjoy the moment and let nature take its course."

Mariah smiled. "Thank you, Amber."

"Anytime."

After she'd left, Mariah tried to remember Amber's advice. Everett was a singularly focused, determined man, and clearly he was hoping they would become intimate during this getaway. A brief shiver went up Mariah's spine. It wasn't as if she didn't want him, hadn't wanted him. She'd just been too afraid to make any sort of moves other than a kiss. But Everett had plans now. This time, she wouldn't resist him, and they'd finally become lovers.

Chapter 13

Mariah allowed the wind to ripple through her wavy hair as she and Everett stood on the ferry to Bainbridge Island on Saturday morning. They'd parked the car and walked over to the deck railing so they could take in the scenery. It was only a thirty-five minute ride to the island, but from the boat she could see the snowcapped Olympic Mountains, Seattle's skyline and a view of Mount Rainier. Everett had dropped EJ off with his parents so they could have the day to themselves.

"Isn't it wonderful?" Everett asked, coming behind her and placing his hands on the rail, effectively blocking her inside his embrace.

"Oh, yes," Mariah said. She could feel the heat emanating from the wool jacket he wore and it surrounded her like a warm blanket. Or perhaps it was the smell of his masculine cologne that wafted to her nose? Either way, she was very aware of the man, the trip and all that it represented.

He hadn't said anything when he'd picked up her small suitcase and placed it in the trunk next to his an hour ago, but it was clear they both knew what this night meant.

Mariah, however, was a bundle of nerves and shivered from the cool wind whipping across the bay.

"I thought we could take in a winery," Everett said, when she finally turned around to face him and he wrapped his strong arms around her. "Or the distillery. Whatever you want, this day is yours."

"It's ours," Mariah said, standing on her tippy toes to brush her lips across his.

Everett didn't react at first and Mariah thought that he didn't like a public display of affection. But then those massive hands of his grabbed both sides of her face and he deepened the kiss. Without thinking, she opened her mouth and his tongue slid inside, circling with hers in a deliciously slow mating ritual as they each tasted the other.

When they separated, they took in ragged, deep breaths to fill their lungs with the oxygen they'd just been deprived of after trying to swallow each other whole. Everett was right about one thing. It was time.

Bainbridge Island was a local favorite on the weekends, so the streets of the quaint downtown area were bustling with people walking, talking, or moseying through the shops, eateries and coffee spots. After parking in a public garage, Mariah and Everett walked hand in hand through the town, browsing.

It had been months since Mariah had a day off and she felt guilty leaving Chase and Jackson when the bakery was still so new, but she needed this. Not just for physical reasons, even though she'd been working sixty-hour weeks, but for emotional reasons, too. Whenever she was around Everett she thought she might combust, and she needed a release.

The failure of her marriage had been a blow to her self-esteem. Afterward, she'd felt ugly and unlovable, not to mention heavy from the extra couple pounds she'd gained from stress eating after the divorce. Thanks to those long hours on her feet at the bakery, she'd lost all the weight she'd put on postdivorce, and then some.

Now, when she saw herself through Everett's eyes, she felt sexy. It was heady stuff. They should sell it in the nearest Walgreens or CVS Pharmacy.

Eventually, she and Everett stopped at one of the wineries for a tasting and tried several different wines, from cabernet sauvignon to chardonnay to pinot noir to malbec, all the while laughing and talking. Mariah was learning more and more about what made Everett tick and he discovered that although she had a lot of love from her father, it wasn't the case with her mother.

"Are you sad about that?" Everett inquired.

Mariah shrugged. "Would I like to have one of those TV sitcom relationships with my mother and go to her with my problems? Yes, but that's never been the basis of our relationship. It's always been my dad."

Everett grinned. "A true daddy's girl."

She grinned. "And proud of it."

After lazily drifting through the shops and stores, Mariah and Everett eventually drove to the quaint inn he had chosen. Right away she was struck by the unique architectural details throughout, such as its thatched roof and crown molding. The room the innkeeper led them to was bright and sunny thanks to large bay windows and French doors leading out to a beautiful deck with a view of the water, but it was also elegantly decorated in warm yellow and blues. It housed a large brick fireplace, a cozy sitting area with wicker furniture, and a massive four-poster bed that would easily fit the two of them.

"I hope you enjoy your stay," the woman said as she left.

Once the door closed, Mariah was nervous as to what to do next. She'd never stayed with a man in a hotel room, other than her husband.

But Everett made her feel at ease. "How about we get ready for dinner?" he said, placing her small suitcase on the bed. "If you like, you can use the shower first."

"Thank you, I'd like that."

When she emerged twenty minutes later in one of the fluffy white bathrobes waiting in the master bath, Mariah found the room empty. Everett was standing on the deck watching the sunset.

He didn't hear her as she approached, allowing her the chance to study him closely. He was a fine looking man. His muscled body in the loose-fitting jeans and polo shirt told her he was at ease in whatever he wore. Mariah was attracted to his confidence and wished she had more herself.

She'd taken an extra amount of time in the bath, ensuring she'd showered, shaved and shined enough to entice a man like Everett. She'd moisturized her skin with a fragrant Bath and Body Works lotion and spritzed perfume all over her.

He must have sensed her presence, and turned around. He didn't speak at first, just surveyed her from where he stood.

Barefoot and free of makeup, wearing a plush robe that was likely covering her naked body, Mariah paused in the doorway. Everett groaned inwardly. He heard the voice in his head that warned him to take things slow and make the night romantic by sweeping her off her feet. He blatantly ignored his own edict and instead decided to go for what he wanted more than anything, which was to take her to bed.

Slowly, he walked toward her, closing the French doors behind him, but never taking his eyes off hers. Mariah retreated and edged farther into the room, away from him. Everett couldn't quite make out the emotion reflected in those brown depths, but he intended to find out now.

He backed Mariah up until her legs were pressed against the king-size bed and there was no space between them. No place for her to run. One of his hands came up to caress her and he palmed her face with his hand. "You are so beautiful." She looked downward when he said it, but he lifted her chin. "I mean it. You are. And I'm going to show you just how much."

He reached between them and, grasping the belt of her robe, tugged it free until it fell open. Mariah's gasp at his audacity was audible, but she didn't say a word.

He took that as his cue and, using both hands, slid the robe from her body. It fell to the floor, baring all of her to his admiring gaze.

Everett's eyes roamed, taking in everything—the full swell of her breasts, her flat stomach, the curve of her hips and the triangular patch of curls that awaited him. But it was her up-tilting breasts that he wanted to sample. He'd been aching to touch, to taste, to pleasure them with his hands, his mouth and his tongue. He groaned. He could no longer help himself and lowered his head to take one in his mouth, while his arm curved around Mariah's waist so he could caress her bare bottom.

He took the nipple fully into his heated mouth and suckled, gently at first and then with long greedy pulls. His free hand moved to cup and tease the other breast with his fingers. He wanted everything all at the same time and Mariah didn't deny him.

"Everett," she moaned weakly when he switched to the second breast, claiming it with his lips, teeth and tongue. Over and over, he teased the sensitive bud, laving it with his tongue. He could see he was driving her mad with passion because she was moving against him, pressing to get closer to him.

He wanted to be just as close and swiftly lifted her into his arms and laid her on the bed. Before joining her, he disposed of his shoes, shirt and jeans, until he was standing only in his briefs. Everett knew he had to slow down the pace, otherwise, he'd have her legs in the air and be plunging inside her without making the moment last. He reminded himself to stay in control, until Mariah opened her arms to him, welcoming him into the bed. That's when Everett knew that keeping control would be a hard battle to win.

Mariah couldn't believe how Everett made her feel just by caressing and sucking her breasts. She was on fire from his kisses and caresses. The juncture between her thighs was already starting to ache unbearably. She'd never felt this kind of passion before. Never wanted to be taken, possessed, as she did by Everett in this moment.

As Everett undressed, removing each layer of clothing, Mariah's passion and desire for him grew. His broad shoulders were bare now, showing her the muscled chest she'd felt each time he'd held her when he'd hugged her goodbye. The rest of him was even better. His abdomen was taut and well-defined, his legs long and muscular, and the bulge in the black briefs he wore quite impressive.

Mariah swallowed. She sorely hoped he wouldn't be upset by her lack of experience. Her ex-husband hadn't been one to try more than a few basic positions and Mariah had deferred to him in that department. But now she was eager to please Everett and be a good lover.

And when he joined her on the bed and she felt the weight of his body, nothing else mattered except the two of them in this moment. He slid his arms underneath her, pulling her closer, and then kissed her softly, gently, reverently, and Mariah melted in his embrace.

While his lips traveled over hers, his hands moved lightly, slowly down her body, as if he was trying to memorize every inch and contour. Mariah sighed as she felt his hand on the curve of her back, her derriere, the soft flesh between her thighs and *there*. Everett was stroking her in the place that ached for his touch.

His tongue made love to her mouth, eagerly joining with hers on a wondrous journey of exploration and discovery. Meanwhile, the tips of his fingers danced between the curls as they opened her up like a bud. They caressed and probed her moist entrance before he smoothly slid his finger inside.

"Everett!" she cried, when a second finger joined the first. He circled her sensitive nub with his fingers and she arched against him, wanting more.

He gave her more by deepening his kiss while his fingers went farther, deeper, filling her completely. Mariah arched against him, her muscled walls clasping around him like a vise, but Everett didn't stop. He continued to thrust his fingers inside her. Harder, faster.

Pleasure coursed through Mariah and she could feel her body begin to quake, could hear a loud roaring in her ears just as her orgasm tore through her and she saw stars. She cried out at the release. But before she could recover, Everett left her mouth. She wanted more of his feverish kisses, but instead he placed his mouth where his fingers had been.

He cupped her from behind and brought her even closer, and then his tongue darted inside her.

"Ohmigod!" Mariah swore as she arched off the bed, but Everett grasped both her wrists firmly and had his way with her, tasting every inch of her until a second orgasm hit her and she screamed again.

She was so disoriented, she didn't realize Everett had once more switched positions and was lightly brushing damp tendrils of hair away from her face. "Are you okay?" he asked, looking down at her.

Mariah nodded, but was unable to speak. The kaleidoscope of emotions he'd unleashed was like nothing she'd ever encountered before, and they hadn't yet fully consummated their relationship. She wasn't sure just how much more pleasure she could take. "I... That was incredible," she finally gasped.

"I enjoyed tasting you," Everett said, licking his lips. "I've been craving you for a long time, Mariah."

She smiled weakly. "Have you?"

"Oh, yes." He grinned wickedly. "Which is why I'm giving you time to regain some strength."

"Oh, really? Why is that?"

Everett chuckled. "Oh, baby, that was only the appetizer. We have the main event, dessert, and then there's always seconds."

She titled her head and looked up at him through glazed eyes. "There's more?"

"Oh, much more," Everett murmured, reaching for her. He kissed her openmouthed, absorbing her gasp of surprise, which allowed his tongue to dive inside and explore every inch of her mouth. Sexual hunger emanated from him as he claimed her and made her his.

The feel of Mariah electrified every fiber in Everett's being. He'd been waiting for weeks and, deep down, maybe longer for a woman who could make him feel alive again.

And he had. He'd found that woman in Mariah and he couldn't wait to bury himself inside her. And she was ready for him. He'd ensured that she was wet and primed. And now, reaching for a foil packet from his pants pocket, he protected them both. Once he was sheathed, a fierce rush of sexual need enveloped him, and as if she sensed what he needed, she parted her legs for him and he settled himself between her thighs.

He kissed her wildly, passionately, as he drove his shaft inside her. Mariah groaned as he inched deeper and deeper, filling her completely. Then he began moving slowly, rhythmically. He wanted her to feel each and every stroke, wanted her to know how much he craved her, desired her. And that he was starting to fall in love with her.

Love? His mind wanted to rest on the thought, but the lower half of his body wanted release. He had no choice but to go with it. Back and forth. In and out. Slow and easy, then deeper and deeper.

Mariah's moans became louder as he rocked into her, joining their bodies as one. Her arms circled his neck, pulling his mouth down on hers. There was nothing gentle or tentative about her kiss, either. All the pent-up frustration from weeks of holding back was unleashed and their tongues dueled, wanting mastery. And when Mariah wrapped her legs around his waist, pulling him deeper and deeper inside her tight core, he began pumping harder and faster.

"Yes, oh, yes," she cried, as her release came, simultaneously shattering his control, and his entire body detonated into a million pieces.

Chapter 14

A wet tongue.

Warm hands working their way up and down his pulsing shaft.

Arousal.

Everett felt his body come to life and was momentarily disoriented as sleep began to leave his eyes. He glanced down and saw Mariah, naked on her knees on the bed, with her breasts bobbing forward. He wanted to reach for them, squeeze them and taste them, as he'd done last night.

But instead he was held captive. She was firmly holding him between her hands. He watched as she licked her lips to moisten them, just before taking his rock-hard erection between those full, deliciously sinful lips of hers.

"Sweet Jesus…!" His hips lifted off the bed.

She teased him, taking him deep into the heat of her mouth before releasing him so she could lick, suck, taste him, as he'd done to her last night. Hell, twice this morning. He hadn't been able to get enough of her taste, her smell. Mariah's unique scent was so hot that he might explode right then and there just thinking about that honeyed interior.

And now she was sucking him off as if her life depended on it. It was too much.

"Baby, baby," Everett said, trying to rise from the bed, "you have to stop now."

Mariah shook her head as her eyes connected with his. "Not until I make you come and taste you." She pushed his chest with such force that he fell back against the pillows and finally gave up the control he was so desperately trying to hold on to.

Instead, he just enjoyed her ministrations. The soft feel of her lips on his shaft, the light flicks of her tongue on its length. When she bobbed down again and took him completely into her mouth, Everett grasped her head and ground into her. Mariah took all of him, milking him until he could feel the tension inside his body steadily building and eventually reaching the peak.

"Mariah!" he groaned, just as he shuddered violently and climaxed.

Mariah took him and all his juices. When she was finished and his trembling began to subside; she looked up at him, licked her lips and smiled. "Now we're even."

Sunshine was beaming in from the deck when Mariah finally awoke a few hours later. For a moment, she had no idea what day or time it was. Thanks to the throbbing in her center, all she remembered was making love to Everett all night and most of the morning, until they'd fallen asleep again.

She smiled naughtily when she thought of the way she'd woken him before sunrise, with his manhood in her mouth.

Mariah had no idea what had come over her. She'd always wanted to do it, but it hadn't been her ex's favorite. He'd never been willing to lose control and give up his power by coming in her mouth.

Everett had. He'd trusted her with the most intimate part of himself, and because of it their love-making last night had been incredibly pleasurable and the most thrilling she'd ever had.

The door to their suite opened and Everett walked in carrying a cardboard tray with foam cups of coffee, and a paper bag. "Good morning, or should I say good afternoon?"

Mariah sat up, allowing the sheet to fall from her bare breasts, and reached for a cup. "Good afternoon and thank you."

"You're welcome." Everett sat beside her on the duvet cover and lightly caressed her cheek. "I enjoyed last night immensely."

"So did I." She took a sip of coffee. It wasn't Myers Coffee Roasters, but it would do in a pinch and covered her nervousness. She'd never woken up next to a man other than her ex-husband and was unsure of the proper etiquette. Was there one after they'd just spent all night making love and discovering each other's bodies?

Everett's expression turned serious and contemplative. "I hope you know that I didn't quite intend on coming on so strong. I'd planned to take you out and—"

Mariah placed her index finger over his mouth. "Don't apologize for being spontaneous. We were both living in the moment, which is clearly not something either of us do in our everyday life. Last night, this morning, couldn't have been more perfect."

That brought a wide grin to his gorgeous face, "About this morning..." He rubbed his chin thoughtfully, as if remembering how brazen she'd been in taking his shaft in her palms and making him come inside her mouth. It had felt not only erotic, but empowering, knowing that she could please Everett. "I didn't expect to wake up…"

"With you in my mouth?" she offered devilishly.

For once Everett was the one blushing, and his smile broadened. "Yeah."

"You're always the one giving," Mariah responded. "This morning was for you, about you."

"Has anyone ever told you you're incredible?"

"Not lately."

Everett plucked the coffee cup out of her hand and placed it on the nightstand. "Well, then, allow me to enlighten you." He slid the covers away and lowered her to the pillow.

By early evening, they were back in Seattle after a short ride on the ferry from Bainbridge Island. They were on their way to Everett's parents's place to pick up EJ. Everett hadn't turned toward her apartment, but was heading to his folks' home.

"I'm not properly dressed to meet your parents, Everett." She squirmed beside him in the passenger seat.

"Hogwash, you look spectacular." He eyed her in the tight white jeans, green turtleneck, scarf, denim jacket and riding boots.

"I'm severely underdressed to meet your family."

He patted her thigh. "You'll be fine. They'll love you." *As I do,* he almost added, but refrained. He couldn't give too much of his feelings away before Mariah was ready to hear them.

They pulled up to a wrought-iron black fence with a keypad. After he punched in several digits, the gate opened.

"This is where you grew up?"

He could hear the amazement in Mariah's voice. "Not entirely," Everett answered, even though he'd spent most of his teens here. "It's about ten thousand square feet, with five bedrooms and six and a half baths."

She gave him a curious look, but said nothing as he drove up the long, tree-lined path before pulling into the circular driveway of the large brick house set on more than an acre of land. Four pillars in front made it look like a plantation right out of the South.

"We're here," he said, turning off the engine and disembarking.

He was at Mariah's door in a flash and was glad he was, because the front door opened almost immediately. EJ came out and flew into his arms, shouting, "Dad, Dad!" followed closely by his parents.

Everett bent down and scooped him up. "How's my boy?"

"I'm good," EJ said, wrapping his small arms around Everett's neck and giving him a hug. "I missed you." Then he looked behind him. "Did you bring me something?"

Everett glanced behind him as Mariah exited the vehicle. "You know I always do. Babe," he called out to her, "can you get EJ's gift from the backseat?"

"Babe?" his mother said incredulously from the doorway.

Mariah gave him a hesitant smile. "Of course." She opened the back door and produced a puzzle she'd discovered on the island. "What do you think of this, EJ?" She held out the box as Everett placed the boy back on his feet.

"Thanks!" EJ bent down to start opening it.

"You can do that inside," Everett scolded.

"All right." EJ picked up the box and rushed inside, curious to see what they'd brought him. Everett had told her EJ enjoyed puzzles and she hoped he like the gift.

Everett walked over to Mariah and placed his arm around her waist. He could feel her trembling, and he wished she wouldn't worry, because his parents were pussycats. "Mom, Dad, I'd like you to meet Mariah Drayson, my girlfriend."

Mariah glanced up at him in surprise, but didn't correct him.

"It's a pleasure to meet you, Mariah," Stephen Myers said, smiling at her.

"Please come inside," Gwen added. "There's a chill."

They ended up in the European-style living room, where Everett's father had already started a fire. Mariah noted the plastered beam ceilings, limestone floors and high-end light fixtures, while EJ disappeared into the room his grandparents had set up for him for overnight stays.

"Brandy, son?" Stephen inquired, walking to the wet bar in the corner.

"Love one," Everett responded, as he sat on the plush suede sofa.

"I was just having a glass of Bordeaux, if you'd like one, Mariah," his mother offered.

"I'll have the same," Mariah replied, joining Everett on the sofa. Gwen wasted no time pouring a goblet and handing it to her, then sat on the chaise.

"How did you two meet?" Everett's father asked from the bar.

Everett turned to smile at her. "At Mariah's bakery."

"Oh, so you're the young lady my son told me about," his mother commented.

Mariah seemed surprised and turned to him. "You've been talking about me?"

Gwen laughed. "Yes, nothing but good things. So how was your trip?"

"It was wonderful," Everett reached for Mariah's hand. It was cold and a bit clammy, and he wished she would relax. His parents didn't bite. Especially with him by her side. "Bainbridge Island is a hidden treasure."

"Oh, didn't we visit there once, darling?" His mother glanced up at his father, who was returning with two brandies in hand.

Everett accepted one and sipped generously.

"We did," Stephen responded, sitting beside his wife on the chaise. "It's a great spot for lovers."

She coughed dramatically, as she'd just taken a sip of her wine.

"C'mon, Gwen, we're all adults here." His father laughed. "Don't act so surprised. Plus, it's high time the boy brought a woman home after nearly five years of celibacy. It's a breath of fresh air after losing Sara."

Everett rolled his eyes upward as he felt Mariah stiffen beside him on the sofa. He wished his father hadn't brought up his deceased wife. "Well," he said, then finished the rest of his brandy in one gulp, "I think we should grab EJ and head on home." He prodded Mariah to rise from the sofa and she placed her wine goblet on the table beside his glass.

"Everett, that's fine brandy you have there. It was meant to be sipped," his father reprimanded, sitting upright.

And boy, did he know it. Everett could feel the sting of the burning liquid going down like molten fire in his belly. "Sorry, Dad. We have to get EJ home and ready for school tomorrow."

"Oh." His mother frowned. "We'd hoped you'd stay awhile. We'd like to get to know Mariah."

"And you will," Everett said, speaking for Mariah, who'd suddenly gone as quiet as a mouse. He placed his hand on the small of her back. "I promise. We'll arrange for a dinner real soon."

"It was lovely to have met you," his father said, grasping both Mariah's hands.

"You both as well." She finally spoke as Everett led her to the foyer.

"I'm going to get EJ," he said to her. "I'll be right back, okay?" He hadn't liked the turn the conversation had taken and was eager to get back on the road with EJ and Mariah, and away from painful memories.

Mariah watched Everett climb the winding staircase to the second floor. She'd sensed his unease in the living room and his need for a quick getaway.

"I hope we didn't upset you, dear," his mother said from behind her, "when my husband mentioned Everett's wife, Sara."

"Deceased wife," Stephen corrected, from her side.

Mariah spun around. She hadn't heard them enter the foyer.

"No, no, of course not." She feigned a smile even though her stomach was knotting. It wasn't that she was jealous of Everett's dead wife. How could she be when she knew nothing about her? That's the part of him that Everett kept to himself. He hadn't confided in her even after she'd learned they'd shared a child. Did he not think he could talk to her about Sara?

"It's just that Sara was a big part of this family," his mother continued. "Had been for years, and losing her so suddenly, so tra—" her voice broke slightly "—tragically was a big blow to us and to Everett. He was so devastated—"

"Mother…"

The commanding tone coming from behind them

caused them all to turn around. The scowl on Everett's face as he held EJ to his side was unmistakable.

"I'm sorry, Everett," his mother murmured, clearly embarrassed at having been caught discussing a forbidden topic.

Everett's lips pursed together. "It's fine." He turned to his father. "Thanks for watching EJ for me."

"It was no trouble at all." Stephen Myers lowered himself to EJ's height. "We enjoy having our grandson around. Makes us feel young, right, Gwen?" He looked up at his wife, who had unshed tears in her eyes, but she merely nodded in response.

EJ gave his grandfather a hug. "Bye, Grandpa."

"Mariah?" Everett looked in her direction.

Mariah touched his mother's shoulder. "I'll see you again, sometime soon?"

"I would like that," Gwen whispered.

Mariah followed Everett and EJ out into the night. The air was chilly, but that was nothing compared to Everett's somber mood on the ride to her apartment. He was quiet, leaving EJ to chatter nonstop about the days he'd spent with his grandparents. Mariah couldn't understand why Everett was so upset that his mother had shared that part of him with her. They were dating, after all. Gwen probably assumed they'd spoken of Sara. Perhaps if he'd been more open and forthright, Mariah wouldn't be so desperate for the tiniest scrap of information about her from his parents.

Instead of turning off the engine when they reached her apartment, Everett kept it running as he pulled her suitcase out of the trunk and walked her up the stairs. "You don't have to see me to my door." She glanced behind him at EJ. "It's not good to leave your son in the car by himself with the engine running."

Everett nodded. "I'll see you tomorrow?" He asked it

more as a question instead of making a statement. How could he wonder, when they were so much more than business partners now? He brushed a kiss across her forehead.

"Of course," Mariah responded. She watched him turn to leave and couldn't understand what had just happened. They'd shared one of the sexiest, most romantic nights of her life and she couldn't let it end on a sour note.

Mariah dropped her suitcase and ran after Everett, catching him at the curb. She didn't care that EJ was sitting in the car, staring at them. When she reached Everett and he spun around to face her, she circled her arms around his neck and kissed him hard.

She kissed him passionately, using her mouth, her teeth and her tongue, and pressing her body into his groin to remind him of the mind-blowing sex they'd shared. She pulled away slightly to stare into his dark brown eyes and saw the man she'd been with yesterday. And kissed him again. He responded and pulled her even tighter to him.

Several moments later she could feel his erection pressing firmly against her core. Everett was the first to retreat and step backward. "W-what was that?"

Mariah let out a deep, ragged breath. She was just as affected by the kiss as he was. "A reminder of how good we are. We'll talk tomorrow." She blew a kiss at him and spun on her heel and walked away.

Chapter 15

Mariah had never felt so good. After she'd given Everett a kiss that rocked both their worlds, she'd thought she'd have spent the night worrying about why he was finding it so hard to talk to her about his past. Instead, she'd fallen into a deep sleep, probably because she hadn't gotten much sleep the previous evening after they'd made love all night.

She awoke on Monday morning in much better spirits than she'd gone to bed, excited about the day ahead because construction was starting on the café. They'd finally settled on a contractor and Everett had submitted the final drawings for a permit.

Thanks to Everett's connections, the approval process would be fast-tracked. The contractor had received the okay for an early start so they could begin work, and now Mariah was sure she'd see Everett just about every day throughout the project. He'd indicated he would be very hands-on.

So when he walked in later that morning in trousers and a button-down shirt, Mariah's heart began hammering loudly in her chest. She hadn't thought she'd still feel this giddy around him, but she did, just as she had the first time they'd met. Except this time they weren't strangers. They were lovers.

She watched as he donned a hard hat the foreman had given him. He smiled at her from across the room, causing her to tingle all over. She was so *aware* of him. How could she not be after the intimacies they'd shared on the island? She wondered if her brothers could tell. Chase and Jackson were both huddled in the storefront, whispering about something, while she openly ogled Everett while she acted as if she was stocking the display cases. Instead she was watching his every move.

Once he'd finished with the superintendent, Everett walked straight toward her and, right in front of her brothers, pulled her into his arms and kissed her. She heard the hoots and hollers of Chase and Jackson from behind them, but all she could feel was the thud of her own heart and the warmth of Everett's strong arms around her.

When they separated, Mariah smiled up at him. She wiped some of her lipstick off his lips. "Good morning."

He smiled back. "Good morning."

"As much as I know you lovebirds would like another day off, this is a place of business," Chase teased from behind her.

Everett let her go, much to her consternation. "We'll continue this later," he murmured in her ear. "How about dinner at my place with EJ?"

"At your place? Sure."

They set a time and soon he was waving to her brothers and exiting the bakery.

Jackson winked at her as Everett departed. Mariah

couldn't resist blushing, clearly confirming what he already knew: their relationship had blossomed.

Later than night, Mariah drove over to Everett's. Because it was a school night it had made sense for her to go there, so she brought dinner with her since Margaret had called out ill earlier that day. Everett lived in an upscale part of Seattle in one of the high-rises. She had to be buzzed in by security downstairs, then entered an elevator that climbed to the penthouse floor.

"Chinese food!" EJ yelled, and took the bags from her when she arrived. "Thank you, Miss Mariah," he said over his shoulder as he disappeared in what she assumed was the direction of the kitchen.

Mariah stepped inside and glanced around the elegantly decorated apartment. It was strange that this was her first time over. That's when she realized that Everett had been doing all the giving, all the chasing, and this was the first time she'd made the effort to truly get to know him. No wonder he didn't want to share more about his past with her.

"Can I take your coat?" he asked from her side.

Mariah turned around and allowed him to help her out of the denim jacket she wore over a maxi skirt, tank and crocheted sweater. She'd gone home after the bakery and changed before picking up dinner on the way.

"So, welcome," Everett said, as she walked farther into the living room and took in the modern decor, abstract art, flat-screen television and stunning glass dining table with parson chairs.

She turned to face him. "You didn't decorate this place, did you?"

He stared at her for several long moments before he finally answered, "No, I didn't."

Mariah nodded in understanding and quietly walked

toward the French doors to the terrace. She opened them and stepped out to the railing, staring at the dark sky and stars overhead. She didn't know why it hurt that Everett was still in the same apartment he'd shared with his wife, but it did.

She turned when she heard footsteps and accepted the glass of red wine that Everett held out for her as he joined her. She took a sip and swirled it around in her mouth so she could have time to formulate her thoughts, and turned back to face the city lights. "This is good."

"It's a good vintage," Everett said from her side.

"So, how long have you lived here?" Mariah asked. She was ready to hear more about Sara if Everett was ready to share it.

Everett shrugged. "I don't know. Nine years or so."

He felt fidgety and restless, as he had ever since his mother had brought up Sara's death in front of Mariah the night before, making him relive the aftermath of the accident. It was as if he'd time-traveled back to that awful place five years ago when his whole world had turned on its axis and he'd become a widow and a single father all in one breath.

He knew Mariah's leading question meant that she wanted him to open up about his past, about Sara, and he would. It just wasn't easy going back down the dark road, but last night Mariah had shown him that no matter how bad it was, she wasn't running. In fact, she'd run after him when he'd begun to retreat inside himself, and kissed him until he'd remembered that he was in the present. A present that included Mariah, a woman he was falling in love with.

Mariah sipped her wine.

Everett turned to her and leaned his back against the

stone frame of the balcony. "What's on your mind, Mariah? You have something you want to ask me. Questions. Ask them and I'll try my best to answer them honestly."

Mariah noticed that his voice was thick and unsteady. "All right." She faced him. "Are you still in love with Sara?"

His dark eyes never left hers for an instant and he didn't hesitate when he said, "No."

She felt reassured and nodded. "But you don't like to talk about her? About the past?"

His gaze bored into hers. "No, I don't, but I know that when you're in a relationship, sharing your past and what's shaped you is important. I'm willing to do that for you. If you're willing to do the same."

Mariah blinked and focused on his enigmatic face. He was challenging her. If she expected him to reveal all, it would be a give and take. He wasn't going to bare his heart unless she, too, was ready to talk. "All right!"

EJ stepped into the terrace doorway. "Are we going to eat now? I'm starved."

Everett turned to his son. "Of course. Let's go." He held out his hand to Mariah and she took it.

Later, after they'd finished dinner and watched a television show together and put EJ to bed, Mariah started to follow Everett into his bedroom, but stopped short at the door. She had felt more at ease in the living room, especially with a young, impressionable child in the house, but Everett had been afraid that EJ might overhear them talking and didn't want him to get hurt, so she'd acquiesced.

She stood in the doorway for several moments. When he saw that she hadn't moved, Everett came toward her and said, "It's not the same bed. I had it changed." He pulled her into the bedroom.

"Oh, okay." She hated that he understood part of her unease and insecurity. He began removing his shirt and un-buckling his pants. So she did the same, easing her sweater and tank over her head and sliding her maxi skirt down her legs. When she spun around in her bra and panties, she found Everett's hungry gaze on her. "C-can I have a T-shirt?"

He blinked several times and asked, "What was that?"

"A T-shirt?"

"Oh, yeah, I'll get one for you." He stepped toward an-other door that Mariah could see led to a large walk-in closet. He returned a few seconds later with a T-shirt in hand and held it out to her.

He didn't turn away as she undressed, and instead watched her unlatch her bra and place it next to her clothes, which she'd folded across a nearby chair, before slipping the T-shirt over her head. "I like you in my shirt," he mur-mured, throwing the covers back so they could get in.

"And I like wearing it."

He grinned as he pushed the pillows up against the headboard, turned on the lamp on the nightstand and slid into bed. Once he was settled, he held his arms out to her and Mariah slipped under the warm covers and into his embrace. They sat there in silence for what seemed like an eternity before Everett spoke. She was in no rush. She wanted him to talk when he felt ready, and she would lis-ten and be patient, the same way he'd treated her from the beginning.

"Sara and I grew up together," he began. "Our fami-lies had known each other for years, but we just saw one another as friends. Until we were older. And one night, after we both had broken up with our respective partners, we were sharing our woes over a bottle of wine and one thing led to another. Sara was worried that it would hurt our friendship, but it didn't, it only added to it. And so, after a year of courtship, we married. A year later, she was pregnant with EJ and we were over the moon."

Everett let out a long sigh and Mariah curled her arms tighter around him, letting him know that it was okay. She was there for him.

"The day EJ was born was one of the single greatest moments of my life." Everett's voice was shaky. "I loved our son and Sara was so happy. We thought we had an entire lifetime ahead of us with our boy, but three years later, she was taken in a blink of an eye." He snapped his fingers.

Mariah slid her hand into his. "What happened?"

"A drunk driver ran a red light and h-hit her head-on. Sh-she was still alive in the hospital and I raced to get to her."

Mariah sat up and looked at Everett's ravaged face. "And did you make it in time?"

He nodded as tears slid down his sculpted cheeks. "Long enough for her to tell me to take care of our son, to give him all the love sh-she wouldn't be able to. I—"

Mariah gulped hard and shook her head as tears welled in her own eyes at seeing her man in so much pain. "You don't have to tell me any more." She couldn't bear to watch him to relive the worst moment of his life.

"I have to," Everett murmured, "because you—you have to know what else she told me."

"What did she say?" Mariah wiped away his tears with the palm of her hand, and then her own.

"She told me not to be afraid to love again and that she was giving me her blessing. Can you believe that?" He cried openly, weeping aloud. "Even when she lay there dying…Sara was thinking of me and telling me that she was giving me permission to love again."

"That was incredibly selfless," Mariah said. "Sounds like she was an amazing woman."

* * *

Everett swallowed hard and bit back more tears. He didn't like what Mariah had just said. "She was, but so are you, babe." He turned slightly so he was facing her and could look into her beautiful brown eyes. "I don't want you comparing yourself to Sara. Because there's no comparison. You're your own woman and I want you for you." He wanted to say more, but didn't, because when he said he loved her, he wanted her to believe it, and not think he was placating her.

"You mean that?" she asked.

"I do." He leaned forward and kissed her forehead, her eyelid, her nose, her cheek before finally brushing his lips across hers. "I do." He wanted Mariah to know he was genuine.

He reached under the covers for the edge of her T-shirt and lifted it over her head. Then he bent down and began kissing his way to her breasts. He looked up at her again and repeated, "I do." Then he took her nipple in his mouth and suckled, while he palmed her other breast, alternating between firm and gentle squeezes.

Mariah began moaning as he laved the turgid bud with the tip of his tongue, before taking it fully into his mouth and sucking hard. "Yes, Everett, like that." Her head fell back on the pillows.

Everett didn't stop there. He made his way from her breasts to plant tender kisses along her abdomen, stomach and the curve of her hips. He scooted farther down the bed and when he reached the waistband of her bikini panties, grasped hold and slid them down her legs. Mariah lifted her feet so he could toss them aside. And that's when he took over, spreading her legs wide, so his eyes could laser focus on the patch of curls between her thighs.

"Look at me, Mariah."

She opened her eyes and stared at him.

"I want you for you," he said, and then darted his tongue inside her moist heat. He took his sweet time going for the prize. Teasing her until she whimpered in protest. He lifted his head. "And I want you to come for me. Come for me."

"Yes, for you," she cried.

Like a missile heading toward its target, his tongue went straight to her clitoris and when he reached the nub, his tongue ran over it with gentle sweeps at first. And then he sucked, causing Mariah to cry out as her thighs began to quiver uncontrollably. Everett felt the power of her orgasm hit her, but he didn't stop, just kept sucking until she fell backward on the bed. Only then did he raise his head, remove his boxers and glide atop her body. But instead of stopping their lovemaking, he lifted her legs over his shoulders and slid inside her wet heat. He felt as if he was home when Mariah welcomed him, her body stretching so he could fill her completely.

Everett grasped both sides of her face and plunged his tongue inside her mouth while his erection thrust deep inside her. He could see she was loving the angle because she undulated against him, and Everett was lost in the sweet sensation of being inside her, having her muscled walls contracting all around him. It didn't take long for him to come with a roar, his own release triggering another contraction from Mariah as ripple after ripple of pure pleasure soared through them.

"Everett," Mariah said a while later, after they'd both recovered from the mind-blowing sex. "It's never been this way for me before."

"You mean our lovemaking?" he asked, peering at her, where she was lying on his chest.

She nodded. "In my marriage, it wasn't this enjoyable."

"You have no idea what this is doing for my ego," he said, smiling down at her.

"It was just routine," Mariah admitted, glancing up from under hooded lashes. "But with you, it's intense and passionate and I can't count how many orgasms I've had while we've been together." Since he'd been so open and honest, Mariah wanted to share more with him, be more open herself.

"I'm glad you shared that with me."

She wished she could reveal more, such as her struggles with getting pregnant during her marriage. Or that one of the reasons sex had become so routine and boring was because of her infertility issues. But her relationship with Everett was still so new, so young. She didn't want to introduce this kind of drama, at least not yet. She just wanted to be with him and enjoy the moment. But in the back of her mind, Mariah knew it was just a matter of time time before her past came back to haunt her.

Chapter 16

"Belinda, it's so good to hear from you," Mariah said several nights later, while she munched on some popcorn at her apartment. She was on her own tonight because Everett had a parent-teacher meeting for EJ. They'd been spending almost every night together since their return from Bainbridge Island.

Mariah hadn't minded, because she needed some time to assess everything that had happened between them in the last week. She and Everett had gone from two people attracted to each other to lovers all in the span of a month. She hadn't moved this fast in her prior relationship with her ex-husband. They'd taken things much slower, but look where they'd ended up! The extra time had meant nothing because they'd still broken up.

While her relationship with Everett was progressing quickly, the chemistry between them was palpable and all-consuming. They'd moved well beyond the physical when he'd opened up to her about losing his wife. Mariah had watched him struggle with his emotions, and though he'd been open and upfront with her, she hadn't done the same and she felt guilty. She'd wanted to tell him all, but was scared of how he might react.

"Well, I figured I had to check on you," Belinda responded from the other end of the line, "because you've been MIA for weeks. Last I heard, you were opening a Myers Coffee Roasters in the bakery. So imagine my surprise when I hear from Grandma that you've created a new pastry sensation and didn't even share it with me."

Mariah sighed. "I'm so sorry, Belinda, it's just been crazy around here. Everything is happening so fast."

"Is that because of a certain owner of Myers Coffee Roasters? I know he was coming on pretty strong."

Mariah chuckled. "You know it is." She smiled, thinking of her man.

"So dish," Belinda exclaimed. "Catch me up on everything I've missed."

Mariah filled her in on how well the construction of the Myers Coffee Roasters' on-site café at the bakery was going. She told her cousin how Everett made his presence known not just for the café, but because of his personal interest in Mariah.

"So eventually I gave in and agreed to a date," Mariah continued, "because he wasn't going to give up."

"He's a smart man," Belinda replied. "You just needed to be courted."

Mariah laughed. "Something like that. And our relationship has blossomed from there and…" She paused for several beats. "Last weekend, we went away together."

Belinda giggled like a schoolgirl. "Oh, and how was that?"

"Scary, exciting, thrilling," Mariah answered. "It was

more than I could have ever imagined. And between us girls, better than any sex Rich and I ever had."

"Well then!" Mariah heard Belinda snap her fingers. "So what's next?"

Mariah hunched her shoulders as if her cousin could see her. "I don't know. Everything is going great. I've met his parents and and his son, and he's opened up to me about his deceased wife, but…"

"But what?"

"He doesn't know."

"That you might not be able to have kids?" Belinda offered.

"Yes," Mariah said, as a solitary tear trickled down her face. She wiped it away with the back of her hand. "What if he wants more kids? What do I do then?"

"Have you guys talked about children?"

"No, but—"

Belinda interrupted her. "No buts. Don't look at the cart before the horse. If he hasn't said anything, there's no reason for you to get upset about a phantom baby."

Mariah tried taking a deep breath, but it didn't work. "You say that now, but Everett is a good man and a wonderful father. I can't see him not wanting to expand his family."

"When the time comes, you guys will talk about it calmly and rationally. You'll share with him your struggles, and if he's the man you think he is, the man I suspect you're falling for, he won't care."

"I hope you're right," Mariah said.

"I am," Belinda stated emphatically. "You'll see."

As she hung up with her cousin, Mariah certainly hoped she was right, because Belinda was correct about one thing. Mariah was starting to fall hard for Everett and it would break her heart if he turned his back on her. But wasn't it inevitable, when she was less than a woman?

Mariah stared at the café. They were three weeks into construction and already had framing and rough-ins for the ceiling, electrical and mechanical completed and had received their building inspections. Drywall was now being hung and taped so the seams wouldn't be visible.

It was really starting to come together and in a couple more weeks they would be open. Mariah moved away from the storefront. Mariah was heading toward the kitchen to bring out more pastries when to her surprise her father walked in.

"Daddy!" Mariah rushed toward him, enveloping him in a hug. "What are you doing here?"

"Well, I thought I'd see how business was coming along." He glanced at the plywood door covering the café's entrance. "What's going on here?"

"Remember, I told you about it a few weeks ago?" she said. "We're partnering with Myers Coffee Roasters and we'll have a café on-site. Isn't that great?"

"You got Everett Myers to contribute to this place?"

"Don't sound so shocked," Mariah replied with a frown. Was it entirely out of the realm of possibility that Everett could see potential in Lillian's?

"It's not that, baby girl. I just don't want you to fail and get in over your heads," her father said.

Mariah folded her arms across her chest. "So Mother's been whispering in your ear."

"Oh, now, don't go harping on your mother. She and I only want what's best for you, for all of you."

"I know, but we have it under control. How about I show you around?" She linked her arm through one of his.

When they entered the kitchen, Jackson was just as surprised as she was to see their father. "Pops!" He greeted him warmly with a handshake.

Graham looked around the kitchen with its gleaming ovens, stoves and mixing equipment. "It's quite an impressive operation you've got going on here."

"We try," Jackson said with a sly grin. "Would you like something?" He gestured toward the chocolate chip cookies that he'd just taken out of the oven and were cooling on the racks.

"Oh, I don't know." Their father rubbed his stomach. "You know your mother doesn't like me eating sweets."

"It can't hurt this once." Jackson reached over and grabbed a cookie. "Try one."

Sure enough, Graham Drayson couldn't resist a hot chocolate chip cookie and devoured it within seconds. When he was done, he wiped his mouth with the paper towel Mariah supplied him with. "So when does the café open?" He pointed toward the storefront.

"In a couple of weeks," Mariah responded. "I would love it if you could attend the grand opening."

He kissed her forehead. "Of course, sweetheart."

Mariah sighed inwardly. She didn't know why she thought he might come without her, as he'd done today. She offered a weak smile. "Great!"

"Jackson, come here." Their father motioned him forward and pulled them both into a semicircle.

"Can anyone get on this action?" Chase asked, leaning in the doorway. He must have heard all the ruckus from the office. He stood there sans glasses, watching them.

"C'mon, son." Their father pulled Chase over into their tight unit. "Although I may not always agree with your choices, I want you to know that I love all three of you and will always be here for you, no matter what. Believe that."

"We do," Mariah said. "But it's always good to hear."

* * *

Everett stopped by her apartment for dinner the following evening, since EJ was at a friend's for a sleepover. It was the first time Mariah had allowed Everett or any man other than her brothers into her home. Initially, it had been hard getting used to having her own place, because once she'd she left her parents she'd gone to college, and then moved in with Rich as his wife. So essentially she'd never truly been on her own before, and it had been disconcerting. When they'd divorced, it had been an adjustment coming home every night to an empty apartment. The loneliness had been a silent reproach about all that had gone wrong in her marriage.

But having Everett here in her place was such a natural progression of their relationship. She was grateful that he'd opened up to her about Sara, and Mariah wanted to do the same and be as transparent as he'd been.

As a thank-you, she'd decided to make him a home-cooked meal of beef Wellington with salad, and a chocolate soufflé that she'd mastered during her lonely afternoons in her marriage.

Ever the gentleman, Everett arrived holding a bottle of wine, as well as a bouquet of roses. He was dressed in denims and a black T-shirt. She wasn't used to seeing him so casual, but it looked damn good on him. As for the flowers, she put them in a vase and led him to the kitchen, where she was preparing dinner. She filled him in on her father's unexpected visit.

"So your dad stopped by the bakery, unannounced?"

"Yes, he did," Mariah replied, refocusing her energies on cutting vegetables for the salad. "I was surprised, considering he and Mother have been dead set against our business venture. But I think he was curious, and at least that's more than Mother's done."

Everett must have detected the note of hostility in her voice because he said, "You and your mom truly don't get along."

Mariah shrugged. "Wish I knew why. Because I have always tried to be the perfect daughter. I tried to be the epitome of grace and class. I never dressed like the other girls in school because image was everything to my mother. In the end, I failed."

"You're talking about your divorce?"

"I was a disgrace," Mariah said, remembering the horrible argument they'd had when she'd informed Nadia that her marriage was over. "There hasn't been a divorce in the Drayson family in years. What had I done to cause him to walk away, she'd demanded to know, because of course, it had to have been me." Mariah furiously cut the cucumbers on the chopping block. "The fault couldn't be with Rich. He could never be lacking as a husband."

Everett walked over to her, took the knife out of her hand and placed it on the counter. He grasped her by the shoulders, forcing her to look at him. "It wasn't your fault alone. There were two people in the marriage."

"I know. I just spent much of my life trying to make Mom happy and failing miserably." Mariah sniffed.

"Parents can be hard to please," Everett commented. "Which is why I stopped trying long ago. Now I think my parents and I have come to an understanding. They know I'll always listen to their advice, but may not heed it. The thing is, I'm happy with myself either way. In time, you'll get there, too, and be happy with who you are."

"It's hard to teach an old dog new tricks, right?" Mariah laughed bitterly. "C'mon, help me set the table."

An hour later, after they'd eaten the delicious dinner, they brought their soufflé ramekins to the sofa to watch television. Mariah was wrapped up in Everett's arms when he asked out of the blue, "You've alluded to your marriage quite a bit, but not really told me much about its demise."

Mariah had been dreading this moment, when Everett would want to know more. She would share with him as much as she was able to. "Rich and I met in college and our relationship was fun and carefree. He proposed right after we graduated and it seemed like the next logical step. But the thing is, we hadn't really talked about the future and what we really wanted out of life. Or what were deal breakers."

"Something happened?"

Mariah nodded, sorting through her mind what she could share without getting into the baby-making fiasco. "We were too young, not ready for real life and the struggles that come with it. And when things got tough, Rich got going."

"So you didn't want the divorce?"

Mariah looked at Everett and could see the question in his eyes. "I'm not still in love with him, if that's what you're asking. Our marriage was over long before we signed the divorce papers. It was just that, like my mother, I thought that marriage was for life. We made vows. So I was prepared to dig in the trenches and try to weather the tough times."

"But your ex didn't want to?"

She pointed her index finger. "Precisely. And as you've stated, it takes two. Ultimately, we wanted different things, and instead of growing together and becoming stronger after the tough times, we grew apart."

Mariah wanted to say more, but couldn't. She'd already shared one of her worst failures in life, but to tell him about their infertility problems, too? If she opened Pandora's box and let those old wounds out, she might never

get them back in and they'd pull her under. Pull their relationship under.

Mariah didn't want that. She wanted a clean slate with
Everett, without all the baggage of her past weighing them
down. But was she deluding herself? Could their relationship really survive without full disclosure?

"You okay?" Everett hugged her tighter.

"As long as I have you?" Mariah asked. "I am."

And she meant it. She'd tried hard not fall in love with
Everett Myers, but it was impossible not to. He was everything she'd been waiting her whole life to find: an honest,
caring, compassionate man who loved his family, was a
great father, a respected and fair businessman and a phi-
lanthropist all rolled into one. She couldn't be luckier to
have found him. And now that she had, she would fight
tooth and nail to keep her man.

Chapter 17

Everett didn't see Mariah much over the next two weeks
except for the odd time or two when they squeezed in a
night together. She was either too tired from the bakery or
he was too busy with work or EJ, but he eventually made
a quick visit to check on the progress of the café, to ensure they would be ready to open the following Monday.

She quickly grabbed his hand and opened the plywood door. Once inside, Everett was shocked by what he
saw. The café was darn near built. The walls were up and
painted, the millwork and countertop installed and the
Myers Coffee Roasters sign hung down from the rafters.

He'd kept up with Mariah via phone and knew they were
much further along than the schedule the contractor had
provided, because he'd been promised a bonus if he finished earlier than expected. Everett could see he intended
to claim that bonus.

Mariah gazed at him, her eyes large and welcoming.
"Well?" She swept her arm around. "What do you think?"

Everett glanced at his surroundings. "This is fantastic, Mariah," he said, grabbing her in his arms and spinning her. "I had no idea." He was truly speechless, which was rare for him.

She nodded. "I know, right? Your vision really came together."

"Yeah, but I had no idea we were this far along."

"They've been moving pretty quickly," Mariah said. "I think we'll be ready to open after final inspections, cleanup, and of course, you need to stock the café on your end with the supplies and equipment."

"I'm ready," Everett said, peering down into her warm eyes. "The equipment was ordered and is sitting in my warehouse, ready for delivery."

"That's great." Mariah beamed. "Do you think you could be ready to open next week? I can't wait for my customers to try the Draynut."

He knew she was excited not only for the café but to debut her new creation. "Absolutely, we'll be ready. And once the customers taste your Draynut and my coffee, we'll be a surefire hit."

"Sounds good to me. How about a kiss before you leave?"

He had no problem complying with that request. He bent to kiss her, long and slow, and the world righted around him at last. He couldn't let days go by without kissing her, feeling her soft curves against him. "I missed this," he murmured, "missed you." In a short span of time, Mariah had become a big part of his life. He'd thought it would scare him, feeling this way again after the way he'd lost Sara, but it didn't. He welcomed it because it meant he was finally moving on with his life.

"We'll see each other on Friday," Mariah reminded him.

"I know, but it's so far away." He pulled her closer so she could feel his arousal pulsating between them. It didn't take much when he was around Mariah to get him aroused. She had that effect on him.

"Keep it in your pants," she said with a chuckle. "I promise to work off all that frustration *on Friday.*"

Slowly, Everett released her. "Promises, promises. I hope you're ready to keep them."

She smiled wickedly at him as she licked her lips. "Oh, I am. You'll see."

Mariah was excited about her plans with Everett. Although it was a weekday, having Kelsey help Jackson and Nancy in the bakery, Mariah was able to take Friday off. It had worked out perfectly with EJ's schedule, because he was home from school for a teachers' prep day. Mariah would finally get the chance to spend more time getting to know him. Everett's son was the most important person in his life and she wanted EJ to like her. It seemed he did, if their first lunch and subsequent dinner at the penthouse was any indication. And today, they'd be spending the whole day together at the Northwest Trek Wildlife Park.

EJ had wanted to do something fun and Mariah had heard about the park, which allowed visitors to see animals up close and have a zip line excursion. Although she was scared to death of heights, she knew that an eight-year-old boy like EJ would love it. After she'd confirmed the zip-lining was for five-year-olds and up, Everett had been on board.

And now they were in his Escalade on their way to the wildlife park. EJ oohed and ahhed when he saw the foothills of Mount Rainier. He talked animatedly during the entire hour-long drive south of Seattle.

"Are you excited?" Mariah asked him after they'd disembarked from the vehicle. Everett pulled out the backpack she'd stocked with bottled water and light snacks.

"I'm totally stoked," EJ said, grinning from ear to ear. "I can't wait to zip-line."

"How do you feel about that?" Everett asked Mariah as he closed the trunk and slid the backpack on.

"Oh, I don't know," she answered honestly.

"Are you scared, Miss Mariah?" EJ inquired. "If I can do it, you can." And off he went, running toward the ticket booth.

Famous last words, thought Mariah.

After they'd received their tickets, they boarded a tram for a narrated fifty-minute drive thorough the park's 435-acre free-roaming area for the animals. They saw different kinds, from bison to moose to caribou herds.

"What's that over there?" EJ asked when they passed a large animal with antlers.

"That's an elk," Everett answered.

"And what's that?" EJ pointed to another animal with antlers that curved under. He was so curious he asked questions constantly.

"That's a bighorn sheep," the guide responded.

EJ snapped pictures with the camera Everett had loaned him. "This is awesome, Dad," he said, turning to his father and Mariah, who were sitting behind him on the tram.

"I'm glad you like it," Everett replied. "But this was Miss Mariah's idea." He gave her a wink.

"I aim to please," she said with a smile.

They continued touring the wooded exhibits to see the bear habitats, then stopped for lunch before heading to the wetlands to see river otters and beavers play in the water. Mariah was enjoying the experience more because she was seeing through a child's eyes, EJ's eyes, and it made it all the more exciting.

Eventually they made their way to the zip line complex. Mariah glanced around at the aerial course. "Looks pretty challenging," she commented. She was rooted to the spot and watching other climbers above her.

"Don't be a chicken," Everett said, tickling her side. "Let's do this." He pulled her toward the entrance.

The guides suited the three of them up in helmets, as well as safety gear around their thighs and waists. EJ was so excited he was talking a mile minute. Meanwhile Mariah's heart thumped loudly in her chest.

"Listen to me," Everett said, pulling her to a stop and grabbing both sides of her helmet. "You're going to be fine. You're not by yourself. I'm here with you and we're doing this together, okay?"

Tears formed in her eyes at Everett's kindness and all Mariah could do was nod. A bit later she kicked herself for being afraid, once she found how fun the discovery and aerial courses were. Most required them to be agile, balanced and mentally tough to get across the tightrope and swinging logs, but Mariah did it. EJ, on the other hand, was a little monkey and easily maneuvered over the climbing wall and obstacle course with grace and nimbleness, much like his father did.

"That was awesome!" the boy said as they made their way toward the exit after they'd finished the zip line adventure. They'd been at the park nearly the entire day. "We have to do that again. Can we, Dad?"

"Sure can," Everett said, laughing at his son.

"And you'll come, too, Miss Mariah?" EJ asked, turning around to face her.

Mariah's heart soared that EJ would want her to come with them. She glanced over at Everett when she said, "Absolutely."

* * *

On the drive ride back to Seattle, the car was quiet, because EJ had promptly fallen asleep after all the day's activities, while Mariah was introspective. Everett reached for her hand as the sun had set during the drive. "Everything all right?" he asked, hazarding a glance in her direction.

"Yeah, I'm good."

"You sure?" He wondered what was on her mind. He hoped EJ hadn't been too much to handle today. Everett was used to his hyperactive son, but this was the first time Mariah had spent the entire day with them and he hoped she wasn't spooked.

She turned and smiled at him. "Today was pretty incredible."

Everett's heart swelled in his chest and he let out a deep sigh. "It was, wasn't it?"

She nodded and he was surprised when he saw unshed tears in her eyes. "EJ's a wonderful little boy," she declared.

"Thank you." He reached across and stroked her cheek. "And you're wonderful, too. Not many women would be game to zip-line through the air like you did. You continue to surprise me, Mariah Drayson."

Once they reached his penthouse, Everett carried EJ inside, while Mariah followed with the backpack. She was removing the remnants in the kitchen when Everett came up behind her at the sink and wrapped his big strong arms around her waist. "EJ's knocked out."

"Oh, yeah."

"So it's just the two of us," he said, seconds before his mouth nuzzled her neck. That left his hands free to roam over her body. When he found her breasts, he molded them in his palms. He loved the feel of them, soft and pliant.

Mariah let out a low purr. "Mmm…"

"You like that?" he whispered, taking the tip of her ear in his mouth and sucking.

"Oh, yes." Her head fell back against his shoulder as he continued tonguing her ear. His hands moved to the waistband on her jeans and pulled her shirt free, before he slipped his fingers inside. He pushed past the waistband of her panties and slid his hand lower. When he reached those damp curls, he groaned and then delved his fingers inside her core.

"Ah…" Mariah let out a deep sigh as he began stroking her.

"I've been wanting to do this all day," Everett murmured as his tongue darted in and out of her ear, mimicking what his fingers were doing inside her womanhood. Mariah began to undulate her buttocks against the hardness in his jeans. "That's right, love. I want you to come for me," he told her.

"Wh-what if EJ wakes up?" Mariah whispered, glancing in the direction of the hallway. She wouldn't want him to walk in on them in flagrante, especially since he was still getting to know her.

"Don't worry about my son, he's a hard sleeper," Everett said as his fingers quickened and he began thrusting deeper inside her. "So you can come as loud as you want."

"I—I can't!"

"Yes, you can." He squeezed one of her nipples through her shirt and twirled it between his thumb and index finger. "Come for me now."

"I—"

Everett wasn't taking no for answer; he wanted her to let go. He grabbed hold of one of her thighs, lifting it to give him better access so he could surge deeper, farther.

"Now!" He groaned into her ear as he teased her clitoris with quick flutters of his thumb.

Mariah compiled and her entire body quaked around his fingers. Her head fell back against him as an orgasm overtook her. When the last of the trembles subsided, Everett removed his hands from her jeans and spun her around to face him. He grasped both sides of her face and kissed her deeply, then bent and lifted her off her feet. Mariah wrapped her legs around his waist as he carried her from the kitchen to his bedroom.

When they arrived, Everett kicked the door shut with his boot and headed straight for the bed. He lowered Mariah to the mattress, but didn't release her mouth. She surrendered to his kiss and the torrent of sensations that exploded inside her as he nipped and sucked.

Eventually, he left her lips so he could bury his face in her neck and lick his way from her collarbone to her ear. Then he rose on his knees so he could start stripping. She was as hungry as he was, judging by how their clothes went flying every which way until they were both naked on the bed. He flipped her over onto her stomach and his firm, erect penis found its way to her wet passage.

He thrust inside her in one fluid movement and then began moving. He wanted her so badly and didn't understand why the need to possess her was so strong, but it was as if they were the only two people on earth and all that existed was the two of them and this moment.

Mariah didn't shy away from the intensity of his lovemaking. In fact, she seemed to welcome it, especially when he put his hands under her and lifted her so her curvy derriere could meet his thrusts, while the other hand fingered her clitoris.

She moaned, telling him she was enjoying everything he was doing. "Yes, Everett, like that." Her cries split the air and she repeated his name when her orgasm tore through her. "Everett, Everett, Everett."

He didn't hear her, couldn't, because he was lost in sensation, grinding his hips into her backside until the heat between them hit a fever pitch. And before he knew it, nirvana struck and his body jerked as the full force of his climax hit him. "God, I love you," he groaned in her ear, holding Mariah close as he collapsed on top of her.

In the aftermath, as they both lay sated on his bed, Everett realized exactly what he'd just said. He'd admitted that he loved Mariah. Had she heard him, since she, too, had been in the midst of euphoria? Although he'd intended to keep his feelings inside, he'd meant those words. He was in love with Mariah. Could she feel the same way?

Chapter 18

Mariah was awake even though her eyes remained closed. How could she sleep after what Everett had just said? He'd told her he loved her. Had it been in the heat of the moment? This wouldn't be the first time it had happened. Friends had told her that men could say things during the heat of passion that they didn't intend to. Had Everett meant it? Or did he wish he could take it back?

She was feigning sleep now because she wasn't sure what to do. She so desperately wanted to say it back to him, but she needed to hear it again to be sure that he'd meant it and hadn't just been overcome with emotion.

Mariah felt Everett stroking her hair as she lay against his chest, her favorite position when they slept together. "Mariah, are you awake?"

"Hmm...?" She rubbed her eyes and then glanced at him.

His own eyes were fathomless and she couldn't read what he was thinking, what he was feeling, until he said quickly, "I meant what I said."

"What?"

"Don't play coy, Mariah. I know you heard me," he replied. His dark gaze bored into hers, challenging her to lie and say otherwise.

She scooted upward toward the pillow so she could face him at eye level. Her eyes fluttered closed and then she opened them to look back up at him. "Yes, I heard you."

Everett reached across the short distance between them and pulled her closer until they were a breath apart. "I love you, Mariah."

Her voice caught in her throat. He'd repeated it, so he must mean it. She was about to repeat the words when Everett continued speaking.

"I know it may seem fast, but I can see a life with you, Mariah. Me, you and EJ, and maybe adding a little brother or sister one day."

All the air in the room suddenly seemed to evaporate for Mariah. She'd been dreading this moment. The day when Everett would say something that would ruin all chances of there ever being a future between them. And it had come. Just as she'd predicted it would. Except there wasn't an easy way for her to extricate herself from the situation without maximum damage.

The man she loved, who'd just said that he loved her back, wanted children, more children *with her*, which she knew was impossible or damn near. She'd tried unsuccessfully for nearly three years to get pregnant with Rich's child and couldn't. It had destroyed their marriage. She couldn't do it again. She couldn't, wouldn't put herself or Everett through that kind of pain, heartbreak and continued disappointment, month after month, year after year. He deserved more. He deserved a woman who could give him babies, lots of babies. He didn't deserve someone who was damaged goods.

"I—I have to go," Mariah said abruptly, and threw the covers back. In the darkness, she searched for her clothes, which they'd discarded in a hurry during the heat of the moment.

"What?" The expression on Everett's face was both hurt and disbelieving.

They'd just made passionate love together as if their lives depended on it, and she was running away. She had no choice. She had to do it now. It was bad enough that she'd allowed their relationship to get this far. She should have known that happiness wasn't in the cards for her, but she'd so desperately needed this and desired him that she hadn't wanted to see they were headed for disaster.

Mariah couldn't speak, couldn't look at him as she found her panties and slipped them up her legs.

"Mariah!" Everett sat upright. "What are you doing?"

"I have to go," she said. "I have an early morning tomorrow and—"

"That's crap and you know it," he responded. "You're running away again. Are you running because I said I love you?" He rose from the bed in all his naked splendor and faced her. "You—you don't have to say it back, not until you're ready. It's just that I…" He paused, as if trying to find the right words. "I was just overcome in the moment."

Mariah didn't dare look up at him as she wrangled with her jeans. If she did, she might give in and he'd drag her back to bed and make love to her again and again, not knowing that there was only the slightest chance that she would ever carry his child. She just couldn't do that to him.

When she didn't speak, his voice turned cold, "Mariah, please say something. And for God's sake, look at me."

Gathering all her inner strength and courage, Mariah took a deep breath and glanced up at Everett. Pain and hurt were etched across his handsome face, a face she loved.

She hated that she was the cause of it and tears sprang to her eyes.

Everett softened immediately and he brushed them away with the pads of his thumbs. "Don't cry, baby. Just come back to bed and talk to me, okay? Whatever it is, we can work through it together."

Mariah shook her head. "I can't. I just can't." She wrenched away from him and, without a glance behind, ran out of the bedroom. She had to. It was for his sake as well as hers.

As she sat in the taxicab that the shocked doormen had so graciously procured for her at this late hour, Mariah pondered what had occurred. She was no good for Everett and he would only resent her in the end, as Rich had. She never wanted to see in Everett's eyes the same look Rich had given her. So if that meant she was destined to be alone, then that was her lot in life and she was just going to have accept it.

Everett stared into his coffee mug as he sat in his office at the Myers Hotel the next morning. He'd gone through the motions of getting dressed and having a big Saturday breakfast with EJ, but his heart wasn't in it. Everett had dropped his son off with his grandparents and made his way to the office, hoping that work would be a distraction. It wasn't. It had been hours and he'd finally hit a wall. He still couldn't believe that after they'd shared an idyllic day together with his son, made love as if they were last two humans on earth and he'd said he loved her, Mariah had walked out on him.

She hadn't given him a reason for her behavior. She'd just stormed out of his bedroom in the middle of the night, for Christ's sake. Everett ran his hand over his head. He couldn't understand it. Should he have waited to tell he loved her? Clearly. But her over-the-top reaction had stunned him. She'd completely shut him out, reverting to the Mariah of old, who had brick walls barricaded around her heart. If he was honest, he was not only hurt; he was angry. Was having his love that abhorrent that she'd had to rush out of his bed?

Everett just couldn't understand and started analyzing those last few moments. That's when it hit him. If he'd read her expression correctly, perhaps it wasn't the idea that he loved her that had freaked her out. She'd become silent when he'd mentioned wanting more kids and giving EJ a little brother or sister. Did her reaction mean that she didn't want kids?

Everett leaned back in his chair. How could that be? Mariah was so great with EJ and clearly adored his son. He could see her as a mother. Had he really been wrong about her? He shook his head.

Darn it! He wanted a big family. Had always wanted one even when he'd been with Sara, but it hadn't been in the cards. But Mariah? He was in love with her and knew she would be a good mother if she could overcome her fears. But what if she wouldn't? Didn't want to? Would he be willing to give up his dream of enlarging his family for Mariah? This whole time he'd been under the assumption that they were on the same page and that she'd be open to starting a family with him. But perhaps they weren't. Was this a deal breaker?

Or had she run away because he'd said he loved her and she wasn't ready yet?

He had to know for sure one way or the other.

Rising from his chair, Everett put on his suit jacket and headed toward the door. After everything they'd shared, he deserved answers from Mariah and he wasn't going to take no for answer until he had them. It shouldn't surprise her, because that had been his MO from the beginning.

Everett made it to Lillian's in half an hour. He swung open the door and searched the storefront for Mariah's honey-blond head.

"Hey, boss," Amber yelled from the café.

Everett glanced up and started toward her. She was stocking shelves with Myers Coffee Roasters. "Amber, have you seen Mariah?"

"Sorry, I haven't," Amber said. "Is there anything I can do?"

He shook his head and without another word to Amber left the café and stalked purposely toward the kitchen. Jackson was coming out with a large silver pan and stopped short when he saw him. "Everett, what's up?" he asked.

"I'm looking for Mariah."

Jackson frowned. "She's not here. Didn't she tell you?"

"Tell me what?" Everett asked impatiently. He needed to find Mariah and talk to her. He didn't have time for riddles.

"Mariah called Chase and me early this morning and told us she wouldn't be in today," Jackson replied. "Said she was going to Chicago for the weekend."

"Chicago!" Everett roared.

Jackson took a step backward. "Hey. Listen, man. Perhaps that temper is the reason my sister rushed off to Chicago in the middle of the night."

Everett dragged in a deep breath, trying to calm his frayed nerves. "I'm sorry for raising my voice, but that's not the reason Mariah left."

"What then?"

"That's between me and your sister," Everett responded. "Should she happen to call you, you can let her know I'm ready to listen when she's ready to talk."

Without another word, he strode from the bakery.

Once he reached his car, Everett slammed his fist on the steering wheel. When was Mariah going to get tired of running and instead fight for what they had? Turning on the ignition, he headed back toward the hotel.

"Not that I'm not excited to see you and all," Belinda said from the driver's side of her sports car as she glanced sideways at her cousin. "But an early morning phone call to come get you at the airport wasn't quite what I expected when I asked you to keep in touch."

Mariah sighed heavily. "Sorry for the short notice, cuz. I just needed to get away in a hurry." She'd called Belinda early that morning after she'd booked a spur-of-the-moment flight from Seattle to Chicago.

Belinda glanced at her again. "Is this about you and Everett?"

Mariah was silent and glanced out the window. She had come to Chicago for a sympathetic ear. Although she and Amber were forging a friendship, it was nice to confide in family.

"How about we talk over pastries at Lillian's?" Belinda inquired. "I bet we can find something there to cheer you up."

"Sounds good." But Mariah didn't look up from the window.

Once they made it to the Magnificent Mile and parked in the garage reserved for Lillian's, they walked the short distance on Michigan Avenue to the store.

When she entered, the familiarity of her surroundings brought a smile to Mariah's face, as did the smell of fresh baked goods. The bakery was similar in design to Lillian's of Seattle, but was bit more ornately decorated than their store due to its prime location on Chicago's most famous street.

"Mariah, is that you?" Shari Drayson said from behind the counter. "What the heck are you doing here?"

"She's here for a weekend retreat," Belinda replied, as Mariah surveyed their storefront displays for a breakfast treat.

"Give me a hug," Shari said, coming around the corner with her arms open wide.

Mariah turned from the display case and saw Shari's pregnant belly bump. Her hand flew to her mouth and she cried, "Omigod!" and rushed toward the back of the bakery.

Shari grabbed her pregnant stomach as she watched Mariah flee past her. She turned to her sister. "Was it something I said?"

Belinda shook her head. "No, it's not you. Let me go talk to her."

Mariah had found her way to the administrative offices in the back of the bakery and shut the door. She sat down in the conference room and cried. She cried for everything she'd never had and never would. Several minutes later, she heard a soft knock on the door. "Come in."

Belinda walked in and closed the door behind her. She headed toward Mariah and offered her a handkerchief. Mariah gratefully accepted and blew her nose. "Thank you."

Her cousin gave her a smile as she sat down beside her. "How you doing?"

Mariah shook her head. "I'm a mess. Shari must think I'm insane. Did you see how she clutched her stomach when I ran by? I must have scared the living daylights out of her."

Belinda chuckled. "More like startled her by your reaction."

"I'll apologize to her."

"You're just one raw nerve, Mariah, if seeing Shari's pregnancy can affect you this way. What's going on?"

Mariah nodded in agreement. "I know I am. And I can tell that I overreacted just now. I guess the timing of seeing Shari, after last night with Everett, was just too much."

"What happened?"

Mariah looked upward and blinked several times. "Everything."

"How about we get those pastries to go and talk at my place?" Belinda suggested.

Mariah gave a weak smile. "Sounds great."

Their talk didn't happen until later that evening, because as soon as they arrived at Belinda and Malik's condominium on Lake Shore Drive, Mariah begged off for a nap. When she awoke, it was dark out. She hadn't meant to sleep the day away, but the strain and exhaustion of the last twenty-four hours had caught up to her. She'd traveled to the wildlife park and back to Seattle after zip-lining, she and Everett had made incredible love, then she'd run back to her apartment.

She'd been unable to sleep and had gotten on her computer to make travel arrangements to Chicago. She'd needed to get away and think. Figure out what she was going to do next. She knew that running out of Everett's apartment had been wrong. She also knew she would have to face him soon, but in that moment she hadn't been able to. And knowing Everett, he wasn't going to accept her leaving him with no explanation and would hunt her down until they hashed things out.

She'd been right. As she looked down at her cell phone, which she'd silenced while she napped, she could see that she'd missed several calls and texts from Everett. The last one from him said Fight for us. She knew he was right. She'd done the exact opposite by running away to Chicago.

There'd been another from Jackson telling her that Everett had stopped by the bakery and left him with a message: He's ready to listen when you're ready to talk. She wasn't going to be able to stay away forever. They needed her at the bakery and the café was opening on Monday. But she was going to take this weekend for herself to figure some things out.

After a quick shower, Mariah slid into a velour jumpsuit and headed to the kitchen. She found Belinda standing over the stove, stirring contents in a pot, what looked like the makings of dinner.

"Smells good," Mariah commented.

"Thanks," she said. "It's just pasta primavera. I can manage that much. Isn't it funny that I'm a great baker, but a terrible cook?"

Mariah burst out laughing. "Cooking requires creativity and you've always struck me as being somewhat..." She couldn't find the right word without offending her cousin.

"Rigid?" Belinda offered.

Mariah laughed again. "A bit."

Belinda snorted. "You wouldn't be the first to think that way. Malik said the same thing once, but he's softened my edges. Finding someone who loves you as you are, with all your faults, is pretty spectacular."

Mariah nodded and sat down at the breakfast bar.

"How about a glass of wine?"

"Love one."

"Grab a glass." Belinda inclined her head toward the wine goblets hanging from the ceiling. "I already have a bottle open for the sauce."

Mariah reached for a glass and held it out so Belinda could fill her goblet. It was white wine, but she didn't care. She could use some relaxation and took a generous sip.

"So, you want to tell me what happened last night?"

Belinda asked as she put her own goblet to her mouth and sipped.

"Everett, EJ and I had a wonderful day yesterday," Mariah started. "And I could really see us together as a family."

"Is it a problem that he has a child already?" Belinda inquired, leaning against the counter by the stove so she could keep an eye on dinner. "Because I wouldn't have thought so."

Mariah shook her head. "Not at all. I love EJ. He's a great kid. Wonderful, actually. He calls me Miss Mariah. Can you believe that?"

"He sounds respectful."

Mariah nodded. "Then we came back to Everett's, and after EJ went to bed, we made love. And then—then he told me he loved me."

"Oh, Mariah, that's wonderful."

"I know. And I should have been happy. And I was. For all of a millisecond. Because then he said he could see us together as a family and that we could give EJ a little brother or sister."

Belinda nodded. "Now I understand."

"Do you?" Mariah asked, scooting off the bar stool with her wine goblet. She walked to the floor-to-ceiling window to look out over Lake Michigan. She was silent before turning around. "Everett loves me, but he wants more children I can't give him."

"You don't know that."

"Don't I?" Mariah cried, and she couldn't help it, but tears began biting at her eyes. "I tried for three years with Rich, and even with the fertility treatments, it would never take."

"You have to tell Everett."

"And have him stay with me out of pity?" Mariah asked. "I can't!" She shook her head. "I won't do that to him."

"So instead you would deny him, deny yourself, love?" her cousin asked. "That could be a very solitary life, Mariah."

"It's what I deserve. I'm broken."

Belinda put down her wine goblet and rushed toward her, grabbing her by the shoulders. "You are not broken, Mariah. You are an incredibly warm, kind, giving woman with a lot to offer Everett and his son, but you have to tell him the truth. Don't shut him out."

Mariah clutched Belinda's hands as her cousin held her shoulders.

"You have to tell him," Belinda repeated.

Her words echoed in Mariah's head later that night as she tried to sleep. She knew Belinda was right. That she had to put all her cards on the table. And then, only then, if Everett chose to walk away, would she be able to say she'd done everything in her power to fight for what they had.

Chapter 19

Everett stopped by Lillian's on Sunday for one final inspection before their grand opening tomorrow. He was also hoping that, what, Mariah was there? He hadn't heard so much as a peep out of her since she'd run of his apartment more than twenty-four hours ago. He'd left countless messages and texts and received no response.

Was it over between them? He didn't understand any of this and it was driving him crazy.

He was reviewing the inventory log when Amber stepped into the café, carrying a large box. "Hey, boss," she said with a smile.

"Here, let me help you with that." Everett took the box out of her hands and set it on the counter.

"Thanks." Amber brushed her hands on her jeans. "So what brings you by? I could handle overseeing the equipment deliveries."

"I know." He'd just needed something to do to keep his

mind off Mariah. He looked up and found Amber studying him. "What?"

"You just look down and not your usual self."

"Have a lot on my mind." He began emptying the contents of the box onto the counter.

"Mariah?"

He glanced up from his task. "You know about us?"

Amber nodded. "Mariah and I are friends."

He turned around. "So you've heard from her?" He felt the first glimmer of hope he had all weekend.

She shook her head. "No, I haven't, but don't give up on her."

"I don't know, Amber. Mariah's not exactly being forthcoming and talking to me," he responded, "so it's hard not to think that she doesn't want to be with me and my son."

Amber touched his arm. "It's not like that, Mr. Myers."

"Call me Everett."

"Everett. There's just more to the story than you know."

"So she's shared her feelings with you?" Mariah could share them with Amber, a virtual stranger, and not with him? Her man, her lover. It boggled Everett's mind.

"She'll be back," Amber said, avoiding answering his question. "And when she does, please let her talk and tell you everything, because it won't be easy for her to do that. It's a like a raw scab, if you know what I mean."

Everett nodded. He understood that kind of pain, because that's how he'd felt when he'd opened up to her about Sara and her accident. The only difference was he'd done it, and Mariah was still keeping secrets from him. A secret Amber knew, but couldn't share with him.

"Thanks, Amber. I appreciate the insight."

"Anytime."

Now all he had to do was wait for Mariah to get back. Would she show up for the official launch of Myers Coffee Roasters café tomorrow? She would have to. It was her family's business. And when she did, Everett would be waiting, because he wanted answers. No, he needed them. He needed to know if she loved him just as much as he loved her.

"I'm surprised you asked *me* to take you to the airport," Shari said, when she arrived at Belinda's condo late Sunday evening to pick up Mariah. Belinda and Malik had a previous engagement that they couldn't cancel on short notice and had left for the evening.

"I know," Mariah said, "and I'd like to explain. Can we sit for a moment before we head out?" She motioned toward the living room, which was immaculately decorated in all white. It might look stark and cold to some, but it was Belinda's style and suited her and Malik's life.

"Sure," Shari said, joining her on the sofa.

Mariah glanced at her cousin, who looked beautiful as ever in jeans and a pullover sweater. However, since Mariah had last seen her, Shari's pregnancy had blossomed from a small baby bump to a large rounded belly. "First off, I want to apologize for how I behaved when I arrived yesterday. I was in a bad place and I completely overreacted."

"I'm listening," Shari said. Her small hands rested on her growing abdomen and Mariah had to admit she was just a little bit envious, but that was her cross to bear.

"You may not know this, but during my five-year marriage I tried for nearly three years to get pregnant," Mariah began. "I tried everything, Shari." Her voice shook as she spoke. "Fertility treatments, homeopathic remedies… I even quit working because I thought the stress was keeping me from getting pregnant. Nothing worked. And yesterday, when I saw you with the one thing I wanted most in the world, I freaked out. And I'm sorry."

Shari slowly rose from the sofa and came to sit beside Mariah, grasping her hands. "I'm sorry for you, Mariah. I had no idea that you'd gone through all of that. You've always been so close to Belinda that I didn't want to intrude. I wish I could have been there to help you through this when you were here."

Mariah patted her hand. "I wouldn't have let you. I wouldn't have let anyone, which is probably one of the reasons my marriage failed. Anyway, I just wanted to tell you that I'm truly happy for you and Grant and wish you the best."

Shari nodded. "Thank you. It means a lot coming from you, because I know how much it has cost you." The two women rose and hugged. "So how about I get you to the airport?"

"Oh, absolutely," Mariah said. "I have a man back home waiting for me, who deserves so much more than I've given him."

Mariah arrived on a red-eye on Monday morning with barely enough time to rush home, shower and change before she was due at the bakery. She would have to see Everett this morning at the ribbon-cutting ceremony for the café opening. It was going to be difficult to smile and act as if nothing was wrong when a serious discussion lay ahead of them, but she had to. They would have a talk later and she would tell him everything.

Today was not only the café's grand opening, but the debut of her Draynut at Lillian's. Mariah couldn't believe they were charging a whopping five dollars for the pastry, but Chase had been adamant about the price point. She just hoped that their customers would be willing to splurge on it, as well as purchase a high-end cup of coffee at Myers Coffee Roasters.

In the *Seattle Times*, Everett was running an ad Mariah had created to promote the new café location at Lillian's. It was also on his company's website and Facebook pages. Jackson was doing the same on their end for Lillian's. He'd already uploaded images of the Draynut on Instagram and set up a Pinterest page with all their baked goods. Mariah wasn't much into social media herself, but was glad Jack was on top of it.

"Good morning," she said, breezing into the kitchen at 6:00 a.m.

"You realize what time it is." Jackson glared at her.

"Yes," Mariah said, wrapping the apron around her waist and tying it at her neck. "And I'm sorry I'm late, but it was a long weekend."

"I certainly hope you enjoyed your jaunt to Chicago, while the rest of us here—" he glanced at Nancy and Kelsey, who they'd recruited to help out during her impromptu disappearing act "—have been slaving away."

Mariah came up behind him and rubbed his back. "I'm sorry, Jack, but it really couldn't be helped. But I'm here now and ready to dig in. Where do you need me?"

"Making your infamous Draynuts, for starters." He sighed. "I didn't want to do anything wrong and mess them up."

She smiled at her brother, hearing for the first time a bit of uncertainty in his voice. Usually Jack was so self-assured. "You couldn't. You're a great baker, Jackson."

"Not as good you, but I'm not bad." He offered her a warm smile. He never could stay mad at her for long. "So, chop, chop, the clock is ticking."

They worked in harmony for a couple hours until the hands of the clock edged toward nine, when they would open the bakery's doors. They'd settled on a later opening to ensure Mariah had enough time to bake up the Draynuts nice and fresh, while Nancy and Kelsey continued the additional pastry batches in the kitchen. Amber had arrived an hour early to ensure the café was ready for the opening.

Everything was starting to come together.

Mariah and Jackson finally stepped away from the kitchen to change, then met up again in the storefront, watching the crowd grow outside the store. There was already a line wrapped around the corner. They were just discussing it when Chase came through from the back, dressed in his usual suit and tie. He wasn't alone.

"Look who I found hanging outside the back door," he said. Everett stood in the doorway behind him, wearing a charcoal suit.

Mariah's pulse skittered at an alarming rate and a lump formed in her throat as she gazed at him. Outwardly he looked the same, that vital man who had captivated her from the very first time she saw him. But his eyes... Looking at his eyes, Mariah could see that a light had gone out. Had she done that to him? She hadn't meant to, but she'd been struggling so hard with her own insecurities that she hadn't been able to voice them to him.

Did he think it was his fault? That he'd done something wrong?

It wasn't; it was her. She was damaged. And she needed to tell him that.

"There was a line out there," Everett was saying, cutting into her thoughts, "so I had to park in the back and come in the rear." His eyes never left Mariah's as he spoke. They were silently pleading with her for answers. Answers that couldn't come now, but would soon.

Soon she would tell him.

"Your ad and my leak must have done it," Jackson said. He'd leaked word of the Draynut on their social media sites yesterday, hoping to generate some buzz. Clearly, it had worked.

"I took the liberty of sending a few folks from my team to divide the crowd from the press. I thought we'd let the media in first so we could capture the grand opening," Everett said. "Hope that's all right?"

"That was quick thinking," Chase replied evenly. "Thanks, Myers."

"No problem."

Chase bumped Mariah's hip as he came toward her, startling her out of daydreaming about Everett. "Excited?"

She forced a smile. "Heck, yeah. I just hope the Draynut lives up to our high expectations."

"It will, it will, sis," Chase said. "You've created a winner."

"Thanks, Chase." She hazarded a glance at Everett, but he was already walking toward the café. Dear Lord! She hadn't even checked in on Amber. Mariah sighed heavily She really was failing on all fronts.

"Everything okay over here?" Everett asked Amber after he'd opened the front door and allowed members of the press in to set up. Several local newspeople had arrived for the ribbon cutting ceremony for Myers Coffee Roasters café and the Draynut's debut.

As much as he craved to talk to Mariah and find out exactly what was going on with her, he also wanted to ensure the opening went off without a hitch. He knew he didn't have to worry; Amber was not only an expert barista, but a seasoned manager able to oversee operations. However, Everett liked being hands-on.

It was why he'd limited his cafés to the Seattle market. Not only had he always wanted to be available, but he'd wanted to be able to stop in and check in on business whenever the mood struck him, just as his father had with the hotels. And look how well it had served him!

Nonetheless, Everett was here now and would roll up his sleeves and get dirty if needed. But apparently he didn't need to, because everything was in order. The displays were stocked with Myers Coffee Roaster beans, as well as ground coffee and carry mugs for purchase. The menu boards mounted on the wall proudly displayed their signature coffee selections.

"I have it all under control," Amber was saying.

"Of course you do." He eyed his bohemian barista, who was decked in the standard Myers Coffee Roasters black shirt over a flowing blue skirt, with some chunky jewelry on her wrists and around her neck. Her hair was signature Amber in tight curls that hung to her shoulders. "I have the best staff."

"Thanks, boss—Everett." Amber smiled brightly. "We'll make you proud."

"Well, then let's open this place," Everett said as he stepped back over the threshold into Lillian's bakery section. "We're a go here!" he yelled across the room. He avoided looking at Mariah, which was hard, considering she'd looked spectacular in a black-and-white pleated skirt and simple red keyhole top.

He'd nearly stumbled when he'd seen her standing beside her brother when he'd come in. He'd known she wouldn't miss the launch, but was business the only reason she'd come back?

Had she come back for him?

The clock chimed nine, signaling it was time to start, and Mariah watched Chase open the doors to let the general public in. Soon, customers were filing into their small establishment.

As she stood at the register, Mariah was surprised at just how many people had come out. They had a steady stream of customers, and she and Jackson were handling them easily until a reporter asked to interview her about her concept for the Draynut.

Chase came over to the register, allowing Mariah to join the newswoman, who was just finishing an interview with Everett.

The reporter, a fresh-faced Asian woman, turned to her and said, "Mr. Myers was just telling us that you two worked closely on the concept for the café."

Mariah glanced over at Everett through hooded lashes. Of course he would give her part of the credit, when he'd come up with the whole idea in the first place. But that's who Everett was—a kind and giving man.

"Yes, we did," Mariah said, smiling into the camera. "It's been a great partnership."

"And the Draynut?" the reporter asked. "Looks like it's a hit with the locals." The camera turned to pan the bakery, which still had a lineup an hour after opening. "How did you come up with the idea?"

Mariah answered all her questions, but her mind was still on Everett, who'd quietly left the interview area.

"I think we have it," the reporter finally said, interrupting her thoughts. "Thank you."

"No, thank *you*." Mariah shook her hand.

She was about to search for Everett when Jackson called out to her, "We need more Draynuts."

"I'm on it," Mariah replied, heading toward the kitchen. Her conversation would have to wait.

It was nearly two hours after opening that the line at the bakery slowed down and Mariah and her brothers had a chance to breathe. They left Kelsey in the storefront to deal with customers while they went to the kitchen.

Once away from the public, Jackson held out his palm. "High five! High five!" he yelled, slapping his siblings' hands "Was that not an incredible day or what?"

"I can't believe it, either!" Mariah clasped both hands to her cheeks. "We sold out of every Draynut and have orders for tomorrow."

"We did it!" Chase pumped his fist in excitement. "The Draynut is on the map and that was a great start." He leaned against the kitchen counter. "And very encouraging, but we have to think about how we can keep the momentum going."

"C'mon, Chase," Jackson said. "Can't we enjoy our success for a minute before we have to think about the bottom line?"

Mariah nodded. "I'm with Jack on this one. This was no easy feat, so let's just enjoy today and think about strategy tomorrow."

Chase shrugged. "If that's how you guys feel, then I'll defer to you both. But we can't rest on our laurels too long, because Sweetness Bakery is an institution just like Myers Coffee Roasters." He pointed toward the café, which still had a small line. "And we have our work cut out for us if we intend to overtake them."

"I agree with you," Mariah said. "But I have a few things I'm working on. I spent years perfecting the Draynut recipe. So all that time I was at home, and you all thought I had nothing but babies on the brain, I was working."

Jackson walked over and kissed her on the cheek. "We couldn't thank you enough, sis. And I'll be right here with you, trying to find the next best thing."

"Then let's celebrate," Chase said. He headed to the large commercial refrigerator and pulled out a bottle of champagne.

"When did you get that?" Mariah asked.

"Yesterday," he answered, "because I knew we had a winner on our hands. Get some cups," he said, as he popped the cork.

Jackson and Mariah rushed over with red plastic cups before the champagne could spill on the floor.

"Can we get in on this celebration or is it just for family?" Everett asked from the doorway, with Amber standing behind him.

Mariah warmed inwardly when she saw her man. "C'mon in," she said, laughing, "We couldn't have done this without you."

She handed her cup to Amber, then reached for more for herself, Everett and Nancy and Kelsey. When they all had champagne, Chase toasted, "To teamwork!"

"To teamwork!" they all shouted in unison.

Everett placed his cup in a nearby trash can. "Well, as much as I'd love to stay, I have to get to the office. But I just want to say great job to everyone. I'm looking forward to our collaboration here."

"So are we." Chase walked over to him and shook his hand.

Everett started toward the back door, where he was parked, but was stopped by a hand on his arm. He felt a spark of electricity. It was Mariah. He spun around to face her.

"Can we talk?" she asked. Her face was flushed from the craziness of the last few hours and there was an an almost imperceptible note of pleading in her face. A face he'd come to love, but which in the last couple days had caused him such heartache.

Everett shook his head. "Now isn't a good time. I have to get to work."

She eyed him suspiciously, as if she didn't believe him,

but said, "All right. Then later? I could come over to your place?"

He nodded. "That's fine."

He watched her shoulders visibly sag in relief, as if she'd thought he would say otherwise. He wouldn't do that to her or to him. They did have to talk, but without an audience and when they had plenty of time.

And now wasn't it.

"What time?" Mariah inquired.

"After 7:00 p.m."

"I'll be there."

Everett nodded and headed toward the door. It was so hard to walk away from Mariah, when all he really wanted to do was pull her in his arms and kiss her until the ache went away. But he couldn't, not until she was honest and bared her heart to him, as he'd done. Until she did, there was no hope for a future together.

Chapter 20

Mariah was nervous as she made her way to Everett's. Earlier, when she'd tried to speak to him, his implacable expression had been unnerving. She had no idea what his mood would be. It had been nearly seventy-two hours since she'd walked out of his bedroom in the middle of the night after he'd told her he loved her. She'd wanted to tell him she loved him just as much, but she'd been too scared. And now, she risked losing him because of her fear of getting hurt again. She just prayed it wasn't too late.

After a quick stop home to shower and change into a velour jumpsuit, she made it to his penthouse exactly at 7:00 p.m., as he'd requested. Her legs felt wooden as she approached his door.

Everett opened it wearing drawstring sweats and a dark T-shirt. "Hey." He gave her a tentative smile. "Come on in."

Mariah stepped inside and felt as if she was walking on eggshells, unsure of what to do next. Everett certainly wasn't making it any easier, because he didn't greet her with a kiss.

The apartment was quiet save for some jazz music playing softly in the background. "Where's EJ?" she inquired as she followed Everett into the kitchen.

"With my parents," he responded, pulling two wine goblets out of the cabinets. "I thought it best that we have some privacy. Wouldn't you agree?"

She nodded as a lump formed in her throat.

"Wine?" he asked, holding up a bottle that had already been uncorked.

"Yes," she managed to squeak. She supposed some liquid courage wouldn't hurt.

He poured each of them a glass of wine and handed her one before heading toward the living room. She followed him to the sofa. He sat far away from her on one side, so she took his cue and settled opposite him. He leaned back against the cushions and crossed one leg over the other.

Mariah turned to face him and found he was studying her quietly, waiting for her to speak.

She cleared her throat and then took a sip of the delicious vintage before placing her goblet on the cocktail table in front of them. She clasped her hands nervously together in her lap. Apparently, he wasn't going to make this any easier for her, so she was going to have to speak.

"I'm sorry about the other night," Mariah began. "I shouldn't have run out and left you like that."

He sipped his wine. "No, you shouldn't have. You left me without an explanation, leaving me to wonder what it all meant. So tell me, Mariah, what does it mean?"

She swallowed. "It means I'm scared."

"Why?" He sat up and placed his goblet next to hers. "Have I done something wrong?"

She shook her head. "No. No, you didn't. You did everything right. Just as you've always done. You've been patient with me, kind, giving, loving…" Her voice trailed off.

"Then why? Why would you leave me?"

Mariah heard the accusatory tone in Everett's voice and knew that she'd hurt him terribly. She gulped and hot tears began spilling down her cheeks. She shook her head. "I was scared. Scared that you would leave me once you found out."

"Find out what?" Everett asked. "Jesus, Mariah! Don't you know that there's nothing you could ever say that would change my feelings for you? I want to marry you," he blurted out. "I want you to be EJ's mom and my wife."

"What?" Had he really just said he wanted to marry her?

He smiled softly. "You heard me. I said I want to marry you. And I think you want to marry me, too, but there's something holding you back. What is it? You have to talk to me, baby."

Mariah wished she could say yes to his marriage proposal with no reservations, but she had to tell him her predicament. "I can't, because you have to know that I…" She flushed with embarrassment and her cheeks burned at having to tell Everett the secret she'd held on to that had been her shame for years. Gulping, she gazed at him in despair. "I may not be able to have children."

"What?" Everett left his spot and immediately scooted closer to her on the couch. His large hands grasped hers. "What do you mean?"

"I could be infertile."

A deep frown etched Everett's forehead. "How do you know? Have you been tested?"

Mariah nodded. "I've been poked and prodded every which way but Sunday." She attempted a laugh, but instead it turned into a sob, and that's when Everett's arms encircled her, pulling her close. He gently rocked her back and forth as she buried her burning face in his shoulder and wept.

When she began to calm, she lifted her head to meet his searching eyes, "My quest to get pregnant broke up my first marriage. I quit my job so I could try fertility treatments and homeopathic remedies, but nothing worked. I tried for three years to conceive. The stress and strain was too much for our young marriage and he began to resent me, until eventually we drifted apart. I don't want that to happen to you and me. If it did, I—I wouldn't survive."

"So instead you ran?" Everett asked, searching her face. Hearing Mariah's confession was a surprise, of course, yet it explained so much. Her reluctance to date him so soon after her divorce, and why she'd run the other night when he'd told her he loved her and had brought up having more children.

Mariah nodded. "I was scared, and then you told me you loved me and it was all just too much."

"Listen, baby..." He reached for her hand. "I am so sorry for all the pain you endured, trying to have a child. I don't care if you can't have kids." He paused and then corrected himself, "Well, that's not exactly true. I do want more kids. But I won't put you through that again. That would be your choice. If we're just meant to be a family of three, I'll be fine with that. Or maybe someday you might consider adopting?"

He couldn't lose Mariah. He loved her too much and he would do anything for her, because that's what you did when you truly loved someone. You made sacrifices and risks for those you loved.

* * *

Mariah stared back at Everett, dumbstruck. He would be willing to adopt? After her ex-husband, she'd thought that wouldn't be an option for most men, but then again, Everett wasn't your average man. He was better. And he was hers. "Do you really mean that? You'd be willing to have other children even if they weren't yours?"

"Of course I would."

"I—I'm floored," Mariah admitted. It was beyond anything she had ever expected. "I never thought you'd consider adoption. I know how proud you are of EJ, and so many men have a thing about passing on their heritage. Are you sure, Everett? There are so many women out there who could give you your own biological child. *Children*."

"There is no one out there who can give me what I want, because that's you. Besides which, we could hire a surrogate, perhaps, to carry our biological child. Whatever you want, sweetheart. We have options."

"And what about Sara?" Mariah knew it was silly to bring his deceased wife up at a time like this, but she had to get all her fears, all her issues, on the table and lay them bare.

He frowned. "What about her?"

"I just know how much you loved her, and you still live here…"

"That's true, but I firmly believe you can have more than one great love in a lifetime. Mariah, I love you," Everett continued. "I love you for you, not for what you can give me, or to help me get over my dead wife. I love *you*."

Everett loved her so much that he was willing to forgo having another child? He'd adopt or agree to surrogacy? This wonderful, incredible man loved her. And Mariah finally believed it. Her heart soared with joy and she clutched both sides of his face, finally saying what had been in her heart for weeks. "And I love you, too, Everett. I love you with all my heart."

"You do?" His voice rose with joy, as if he was surprised to hear her say so.

She nodded as tears slid down her face. "I do." She kissed his cheeks, one at a time, before coming to his mouth and brushing her lips across his. In seconds, Everett's arms was encircling her waist and pulling her forward as he deepened the kiss.

He dropped backward on the couch and she fell atop him happily as they hungrily kissed as if they were starved for the taste of each other. They wildly touched and caressed, and it didn't take long for clothes to start flying across the room and landing on the floor, they were both so desperate to get closer and join as one. Their bodies felt so good, so right, so made for each other.

Once they were naked, Everett reached down between them to make sure she was ready for him. Mariah's breasts turned to hardened points. She was so hot and wet for him, just as she always was whenever they were together. That didn't stop Everett from stroking her core. She tried clenching her thighs, to brace herself for what was to come, but he was having none of it and spread her legs apart to accommodate his searching fingers.

He stroked her damp, trembling sex with one finger and then two, thrusting deep inside her. Mariah felt every pulse-pounding increment of time as he teased her swollen flesh. She clutched at the fabric of the couch as he continued to kiss her passionately, before nuzzling his lips against her cheek, her neck. His breath gusted hard and hot against her ear. When she began to shudder beneath his fingers, Everett removed his hand and instead of settling himself between her thighs, leaned backward on the couch so Mariah could ride him.

She slid on top of his already throbbing manhood. "Everett," she moaned, as she impaled herself atop him. Slowly, he began rolling underneath her. Having him inside her, moving slowly, rhythmically, was so intense Mariah knew it was just a matter of time before another climax would hit, just as strong as the first.

"Jesus," Everett groaned beneath her, "I love you so much, Mariah."

"I love you, too," she cried as she undulated against him. Everett was stirring her into a frenzy and she could feel the pressure of another orgasm coming.

Everett continued to urge her on, clutching her bare bottom as he helped her slide up and down his hardened shaft. "Yes, like that, Mariah." His breathing was becoming ragged and the sounds he made caused excitement to ripple through her. "Like that, sweet angel."

He knew how to find her sexual peak and greedily give her every part of himself, and Mariah knew she would never tire of having him buried to the hilt inside her. She loved this man and would love him to her dying day. That he was willing to make adjustments for them to expand their family told her just how lucky she was to have Everett and EJ in her life.

When Everett flipped her over onto her back and began pounding into her quivering flesh, Mariah heard herself scream and Everett roar as both their bodies erupted. She clutched him to her breasts and whispered over and over, "Everett, Everett, Everett..."

Chapter 21

Early the next morning, Mariah and Everett rolled out of bed much earlier than she would have liked. Last night they'd finally made their way to his bedroom after they'd christened every inch of his penthouse, from the couch to the floor to the kitchen countertop to the terrace outside. There was no place he hadn't taken her, and Mariah had loved every minute of it, just as much as she loved the man himself.

They'd come up for air and showered early so they could head to Everett's parents' home to pick up EJ and take him to school that morning. Everett was excited to tell him the news.

"Are you sure he's going to be happy about this?" Mariah asked in the SUV. Although they had shared an amazing day at the wildlife park and spent some evenings together, she and Everett had fallen in love rather quickly, in barely two months, and she wasn't sure that was enough time for EJ to catch up with his feelings toward her.

"Yes, I'm sure," Everett responded, squeezing her hand. "EJ adores you."

Mariah sure hoped so.

When they arrived, his parents and EJ were sitting at the kitchen table. Based on the plates and cutlery, it looked as if they'd just finished breakfast. EJ was already dressed for school in chinos and a polo shirt.

"Hey, Mom, Dad," Everett said as he reached for Mariah's hand. "I have some news."

"Morning, son." His father nodded over his morning cup of coffee. "Mariah." He smiled warmly at her. "It's good to see you again."

"You as well," she replied. "Mrs. Myers." She smiled at his mother, who looked questioningly at the two of them, given the time of day.

"Dad!" EJ rushed toward him, nearly tackling him to the ground. He noticed that Everett didn't release Mariah's hand, and he glanced up at the two of them. "What's going on? Are you both here to take me to school?"

Everett gave Mariah a sideways glance and she nodded in approval. "We're here because I asked Mariah to marry me and she said yes."

"What?" Shock was evident on his mother's face. "Really? So soon?"

"Yes, really, Mom." A grin spread across Everett's face.

"Congratulations, son, that's great news." His father rose to offer his hand, which Everett enthusiastically pumped.

"Thanks, we're really happy," he said, and then bent to look down at his son. "But I'm hoping someone else is happy about our news."

Mariah watched the exchange between father and son. "How do you feel about it, EJ? About having Mariah as your mom?"

EJ's curly head looked up at Mariah, so she, too, crouched lower so she could face him. She knew what a big deal this was. It had been EJ and his father for the last five years, and this would be a big change, having her in his life, sharing his father's time. EJ's response would set the tone for their relationship and could potentially end their short engagement before it had begun.

"I know this is kind of sudden for you," Mariah said to EJ, "but I'm hoping that I can spend my life with you and your dad, if you'll let me. Because I love him…" She glanced at Everett, who had tears in his eyes. "And—and you." Her voice trembled, but she continued on because she had more to say. "I—I know you already had a mother and I wouldn't dream of replacing her, but I'm hoping that in time you'll let me in because I'd love to be your mom. If you want me."

EJ surprised her by rushing toward her and wrapping his small arms around her neck. "Omigod!" Her heart welled with love and tears streamed down her cheeks. That tiny action had touched her heart more than he would ever know, and she hugged him back with all her might.

Everett came toward them and wrapped his arms around the two of them. "I love you both, and we're a family now."

Mariah glanced up at him. "That's right. Forever and always."

* * * * *